BOUNCING
OFF
THE
MOON

Tor Books by David Gerrold

Jumping Off the Planet
Bouncing Off the Moon

BOUNCING
OFF
THE
MOON

DAVID
GERROLD

TOR®

A TOM DOHERTY ASSOCIATES BOOK
NEW YORK

BOUNCING OFF THE MOON

Copyright © 2001 by David Gerrold

This book is printed on acid-free paper.

A Tor Book
Published by Tom Doherty Associates, LLC
175 Fifth Avenue
New York, NY 10010

www.tor.com

Tor® is a registered trademark of Tom Doherty Associates, LLC.

Library of Congress Cataloging-in-Publication Data

Gerrold, David
    Bouncing off the moon / David Gerrold.—1st ed.
        p.   cm.
    "A Tom Doherty Associates book."
    ISBN 0-312-87841-9 (alk. paper)
    1. Artificial intelligence—Fiction. 2. Interplanetary voyages—Fiction.
3. Runaway teenagers—Fiction. 4. Teenage boys—Fiction. 5. Brothers—
Fiction. 6. Moon—Fiction. I. Title.
PS3557.E69 B6 2001
813'.54—dc21   00-048810

First Edition: April 2001

Printed in the United States of America

0 9 8 7 6 5 4 3 2 1

for Jim and Betty and Mae Beth Glass,
with love

BOUNCING

OFF

THE

MOON

BOARDING

THERE'S THIS THING THAT **D**AD used to say, when things didn't work out. He would say, "Well, it seemed like a good idea at the time." I never knew if he was serious or if he was doing that deadpan-sarcastic thing he did.

The thing is, it usually *wasn't* a good idea at the time.

Like going to the moon. That was *his* good idea, not mine. Not Doug's or Bobby's either. But like all of his good ideas, it worked out backwards. We got to go, and he had to stay behind, still holding his ticket and wondering what happened—the last time I looked back, he had *that* look on his face. And *that* hurt.

We made it to the elevator with less than six minutes to spare. They were just about to give away our cabin to a worried-looking family waiting on standby. The dad looked upset and the mom started crying when we showed up. They wanted our cabin on the outbound car so desperately that the dad started waving a fistful of plastic dollars at us, offering to buy our reservation—we could name any price we wanted.

Doug hesitated. I could tell he was tempted, so was I—poverty does that to you—but Mickey just pushed him forward and said, "We don't need their money." So we ducked into the transfer pod and the hatch slammed shut behind us with the finality of a coffin lid.

This time, we were going in through the passenger side, and I knew what to expect, so the shift in pseudogravity as the pod whirled up to speed didn't bother me as much as it had before. I'd nearly thrown up when we'd transferred from the car that brought us up the orbital elevator to Geostationary.

Dad's good idea *this* time had involved smuggling something—or pretending to smuggle something so the real smugglers would go un-noticed—and in return, he'd get four tickets up the Line, but the only thing he was smuggling was *us*. He told us we were going on vacation, and it would have been a great vacation, except it wasn't *really* a va-cation. The whole time, he was planning/hoping that we'd decide to go outbound with him to one of the colonies and not go back to Earth and Mom.

It would have worked if Mom hadn't found out. And if whatever it was that we were supposed to be smuggling hadn't been so important that some really powerful people were trying to track us, bribe us, threaten us, and have us detained by any means possible. It would have worked because after we thought about it, we *wanted* to go.

So we went. Without Dad.

Without Mom too. The guys in the black hats had shuttled her up. My cheek was still stinging from her last angry slap. It wasn't a great good-bye. And the hurt went a lot deeper than my cheek.

The hatch of the transfer pod opened and we were looking down a narrow corridor. "Come on, let's get to our cabin," Mickey said, giv-ing me a gentle nudge on the shoulder. "The outbound trip is only six and a half hours. I think we should all try to get some sleep while we can."

"I'm not tired!" announced Stinky—he was only Bobby when he wasn't Stinky. "And I'm not going to bed without a hug from Mommy!"

"He's contradicting himself again," I said.

Douglas—also known as Weird—gave me a look, one of the looks he'd learned from Mom. "Charles, if this is going to work, I *need your help*." He turned back to Stinky, trying to shush him with logic. "Mommy isn't here, remember?"

We were halfway between nowhere and nothingness, on a cable strung between Ecuador and Whirlaway. There weren't many floors left to drop out from under us—and in a few minutes, we'd be dropping even further away at several thousand klicks per hour. Douglas was right. We were on our own.

"Give him to me," I said. In the one-third pseudogravity of the cabin, Stinky was only cumbersome, not heavy. He was still crying, but he reached for me—maybe I should have been flattered, but it seemed like an ominous moment. Was I going to be the Stinky-wrangler now? Probably.

Douglas was already too much of an adult. He thought logic was sufficient. Well, so did I—but with Stinky, you have to use Stinky-logic, which isn't like adult logic at all. "Hey, kiddo," I said, maneuvering him into a hug. "I didn't get my hug either." He slid his arms around my neck in a near stranglehold. "Attaboy. We'll trade hugs. But no doggy-slurps—"

Even before I finished the sentence, Stinky was already licking my cheek—*slurp, slurp, slurp*—like an affectionate puppy. It was his favorite game, because I always said, "Yick, yick—bleccchhh! Dog germs!"

And that was all it took. Mommy was forgotten for the moment.

It was an old game—it went back to the time I'd been whining for a puppy, and Mom had said, "No, we can't afford a puppy—and besides, we've got the baby."

"Stinky isn't a puppy!" I answered back.

"*Yes, I am!*" Stinky had shouted at me. He didn't even know what a dog was then. "*Am too!*"

And then Weird had said, "Put him on a leash, take him for a walk, you'll never know the difference," and that was how the slurp game began. We didn't have a dog, we had Stinky. But I still would have preferred a dog. Most dogs drop dead by the time they're Stinky's age.

I tried to wipe my cheek, except the little monster had such a hammerlock on me that I couldn't break free. Time for the next move in the game: "No hickeys! No hickeys!" I shouted, and began tickling him unmercifully. He broke free in self-defense, shrieking in feigned panic. I grabbed him in a bear hug, ready to tickle him senseless, then remembered where we were and stopped before he peed in his pants. For a moment, we just stood where we were, him gasping for breath and me just holding on. Hugging.

I flopped backward onto the floor and pulled him down to my lap, curling him into my arms. "I miss Mommy too," I said, almost forgetting about my cheek. He wrapped his arms around me and hung on the way he'd done back in Arizona, in the big meteor crater.

Hard to believe that was only a week ago—Stinky had been acting up, as usual. He'd run away from us, down the path that led around and around, down to the bottom of the crater. He was playing "You can't catch me." Then he tripped and slid down the crater wall, and I'd thought we were going to lose him, but he only slid a little way down and then stopped. I was closest to him—I flattened myself on the ground and tried to get to him.

But when I looked down that steep wall, all the way to the bottom, I was paralyzed. But then Douglas grabbed me and Dad grabbed Douglas and I grabbed Stinky, and somehow we all pulled each other back up onto the narrow path and . . . for a moment, we hung there on the wall of forever, everyone holding on to each other—and Stinky had wrapped his arms around me like an octopus.

When it happened, I was angry—so angry, I couldn't even say how angry—but the whole thing also left me with a funny feeling about him. About what it would have been like to lose him. And now that he was grabbing on to me the same way again, I began to realize what the feeling was. It was the same thing I felt. A grab for safety.

The difference was that Stinky had someone to hang on to. So did Douglas, now—he had Mickey. I was the only one who didn't. Which was sort of the way I wanted it, at least I thought I did. Except maybe I didn't.

The enormity of what we'd done was just starting to sink in. Mom and Dad's custody hearing had ended up in an emergency court session in front of Judge Griffith. She thought she could resolve it by asking me what I wanted.

And I—in my infinite wisdom—had simply blurted out, "I want a divorce." I mean, if Mom and Dad could divorce each other when things got ugly, why couldn't I divorce the both of them? All I'd wanted to do was make them stop fighting over us kids so much—

But Judge Griffith had taken my angry words at face value. She gave Douglas his independence; that was okay, he was almost eighteen; and then she gave me a divorce from Mom and Dad—and she assigned custody of both me and Stinky to Douglas.

So yeah. At the time, it seemed like a good idea.

But now—here we were, alone in our cabin, and I was sitting on the floor, holding Bobby in a daddy-hug because I couldn't think of anything else to do. I guess Bobby thought that I could take care of him—but I wasn't even sure that I could take care of myself.

I was torn between the feeling of not wanting him all over me and knowing that I didn't have much of a choice in the matter. As little brothers go, he'd never been much fun. And whose fault was that anyway? I'd replayed this conversation in my head plenty enough times. Douglas had told me more than once that it was my fault Stinky was the way he was. He said I'd resented him from the day he was born.

But that wasn't true. I'd resented him long before that.

It was Stinky's fault Mom and Dad got divorced. He'd been an accident, and Mom got angry at Dad, and Dad got angry at Mom, and then he moved out or she threw him out, it didn't matter—but if Stinky hadn't come along, we'd still be a family. Or maybe not. But at least things would have been quieter.

After he was born, Mom was different. She didn't have time for me anymore. She didn't have time for anything. Everything was about Stinky, and I had to help take care of him too, instead of just getting to be a kid. So of course, I was angry at him.

And now, both Mom *and* Dad were gone, and the only person poor Stinky had to hang on to was me. I suppose, if I thought about it, I didn't really hate him. I just wished he'd never been born.

BREAKING AWAY

TWO WEEKS AGO, WE'D BEEN in West El Paso—just another tube-town for "flow-through" families. Which is a polite way of saying "poor people."

The way it worked, they laid down a bunch of tubes, three or four meters in diameter, sealed the ends, and let people move in. They called it no-fab housing.

The best that can be said about living in a tube is that it's almost as good as not having anyplace to live at all.

El Paso gets sandstorms, *big* ones, and when the wind blows it turns the tubes into giant organ pipes. Everything vibrates. You get *really* deep bass, well below the range of audibility, four cycles a second—you don't hear it, you *feel* it. Only you don't really know what you're feeling, you just get this queasy feeling.

Burying the tubes doesn't help. They bury themselves anyway, as the sand settles around them. Tube-towns sink into the ground sometimes as fast as a meter a year. The Earth just sucks them in. So they just keep adding more and more tubes on top. Our tube-town was already five layers deep.

You're supposed to get air and sunlight through these big vertical chimneys—more tubes—only that creates another problem. The wind sweeps down one chimney and up the other, making the whole house whistle. The harmonics are dreadful.

And there isn't a whole lot anybody can do about it either, except leave. The Tube Authority told us we could move out anytime. There were plenty families on the waiting list to move in.

So when Dad said, "Let's go to the moon," well—it really did seem like a good idea at the time, once we realized he was serious. I don't think Douglas and Bobby believed him any more than I did, at least not at first, but hell—if it would get us out of the tubes, even for a couple of weeks, we were all for it. "Sure, Dad. Let's go to the moon." I figured Barringer Meteor Crater was as far as we were ever going to get, especially after Stinky's little misadventure.

But Dad was more than serious. He was actually *determined*. He'd already made plans. He'd hired himself out as a courier and gotten tickets up the beanstalk for all four of us. All we had to do was secure a bid from a colony and we'd be outbound on the next brightliner to the stars. Just one little problem. . . .

I mean, *other* than Mom.

There was this big storm, Hurricane Charles—and no, I did not appreciate the honor of having a hurricane named after me—it had pretty much clobbered Terminus City at the bottom of the beanstalk, so all groundside traffic was shut down, no one knew for how long. So we couldn't go back, even if we wanted to—which we didn't—because while we were all fighting with each other in Judge Griffith's courtroom, the United Nations declared a Global Health Emergency.

That was the *other* reason why Dad wanted to get off the planet so badly. He'd figured it out, just from watching the news; it wasn't hard, but most people weren't paying attention to that stuff. By the time most people knew, the plagues were already out of control.

While we were boarding the first elevator up the beanstalk, the Centers for Disease Control was announcing—*admitting*—that yes, the numbers did suggest the possibility that maybe, yes, we could be seeing—but there's really no need for anyone to panic, if we all take proper precautions—the first stages of a full-blown pandemic—um, yes, on *three continents*, but all this speculation about a global population crash is dangerous and premature—

And about twenty seconds after that, the international stock market imploded. More than a hundred trillion dollars disappeared into the bit bucket. Evaporated instantly. So even if there wasn't any real danger, there wasn't any money anymore to deal with it. And that *was* a real danger. Because everything was shutting down. And if that wasn't enough bad news, a woman in southern Oregon said that giant worms had eaten her horse.

They used to call this kind of mess a polycrisis. And everybody just shrugged and went on with business. Only this one was more than just another cascade of disasters, it was an avalanche of global collapse. They were calling it a meltdown.

But we were nearly forty thousand kilometers away, and it was all just pictures on a screen. It couldn't touch us anymore. I didn't know how Douglas and Mickey felt about the news, but the Earth seemed so far away now it didn't matter anymore. Maybe that was the wrong way to feel, but that's what I felt anyway.

A departure bell chimed and our elevator dropped away from Geostationary. We were outward bound. Every second that passed, the Earth fell even farther behind us. *Above* us.

Everything from Geostationary is *down*—down to Earth or down to Farpoint—because Geostationary is at the gravitational center of the Line. It's where the effects of Earth's gravity on the Line are exactly balanced by the tension of Whirlaway rock at the other end. So whichever way you go, dirtside or starside, you're going *down*.

Our tickets were paid for all the way to Asimov Station on the moon, two and a half days away. All we had to do was enjoy the ride as best we could—

—and try not to think about the agents of whatever SuperNational it was who still believed that Dad had hidden something inside Stinky's programmable monkey and would probably try to intercept us to get it away from us, even though there was nothing in it except a couple of bars of extra memory, which were just a decoy anyway because someone else was smuggling the real McGuffin off the planet and out to wherever. I was hoping it was all the missing money, and that someone had made a mistake, and we really had it instead of whoever was supposed to—but Doug said it didn't work that way, the best anyone could be carrying would be the transfer codes, so never mind.

But . . . it was past midnight, and if anyone was really chasing us, they couldn't get to us until we got to the moon. And there was nothing we could do either until we got there. We'd been running for nearly twelve hours already, and we were all exhausted. So even though I could think of at least six arguments we should have been having, what we did instead was crawl into bed. Mickey and Douglas bounced themselves into one bed. Stinky and I flopped over backwards into the other, with the intention of sleeping most of the way out to Farpoint Station.

The trip up to Geostationary takes twenty-four hours. The trip *out* to Whirlaway takes only six and a half. This is partly because you travel faster on the outward side, but mostly because the outward side of the Line isn't as long. Instead, there's a huge ballast rock the size of Manhattan at the far end. It's called Whirlaway, and inside it is Farpoint Station.

But we wouldn't be going even that far. The thing about the Line is that it's not just an elevator, it's also a sling.

Tie a rock to a string, whirl it around your head. That's how the Line works. If you let go of the string, it flies off in whatever direction it was headed when you let go. A spaceship can fly off the end of the Line and get enough boost to go to the moon or Mars or anywhere else, using almost no fuel at all except for course corrections along the way. Jarles "Free Fall" Ferris, pilot of the first transport to leave Whirlaway for Mars, was supposed to have said, "Well, the old man was wrong. There *is* such a thing as a free launch."

But depending on where you're going, there are only certain times of the day when you can launch a ship from the Line. Otherwise you have to wait twenty-four hours, give or take a smidge for precession, for the next launch window.

Actually, you can launch from any point on the Line, depending on where you want to go. If you launch below the flyaway point—also called the gravitational horizon—you become a satellite of the Earth, because anything below flyaway doesn't have enough "delta vee" to escape Earth's gravity; the sling doesn't give you enough velocity to break free. But above the flyaway point, you get flung far enough and fast enough that you go up and over the lip of Earth's gravity well, and then you just keep on going. The farther out on the Line you get, the faster you leave.

For some places, like L4 and L5, you don't want a lot of speed, because then you have to spend a lot of fuel burning it off. Douglas knows all about this stuff. He says that trajectory is the biggest part of the problem. How fast will you be going when you get where you're going? If you're catching up to your destination, you won't need as much fuel to match its speed as if you're intercepting it head-on, because then you have to burn off speed in one direction and build it up in the other. So there are a lot of advantages to slow launches—especially for cargo, which mostly doesn't care, because if all you're doing is feeding a pipeline, nobody really cares how long the pipe is, as long as the flow is steady.

Douglas had tried to explain it all to Stinky, more than once, but Stinky never really got it. He kept asking what held up the rock and why didn't it fall back down on Ecuador? Finally, Douglas just gave up and told him that the Whirlaway rock was hanging down off the south pole and we were going down to it. I think it made his head hurt to say that; he has this thing about scientific accuracy, and that's part of what makes him Weird—with a capital W.

I hadn't paid any attention at all to Doug's lectures, but it sank in anyway, by osmosis. I didn't think it mattered because we were going all the way to the end, to Farpoint Station, because that would give us the most flyaway speed and get us to Luna faster than any other transit.

At least that's what we thought at the time.

 RUDE AWAKENINGS

SOMEBODY WAS SHAKING ME AWAKE. It was Douglas. "Come on, Chigger. We've gotta go. *Now.*"

"Huh? What?"

"Don't ask questions, we don't have time."

I sat up, rubbing the sleep from my eyes. "What time is it?"

Douglas pulled me to my feet and pushed me toward Mickey, who steered me toward—there was *someone else* in the cabin?—he was tall and skinny and gangly. I blinked awake. It was Alexei Krislov, the Lunar-Russian madman, the money-surfer who'd tried to help us elude the Black Hats on Geostationary. "Huh? How did you get here?" I blinked in confusion. He was wearing a dripping wetsuit. Was I still dreaming?

"Shh," he said, finger to his lips. "Later."

Douglas scooped up the still-sleeping Bobby and Mickey grabbed the rest of our meager luggage, hanging it off himself like saddlebags. When he reached for the monkey, it jabbered away from him and leapt into my arms. After that incident on One-Hour, where the monkey had led me on a wild breathless chase, I'd programmed it to home toward me whenever Bobby wasn't playing with it. I'd told it I was the Prime Authority.

Alexei opened the cabin door, peeked both ways—there was no one there—then led us aft toward the cargo section of the car. Actually, it was the bottom of the car, but the car was a cylinder rotating to generate pseudogravity, so the bottom was the aft. I was too groggy to pay much attention to what we were doing, I was still annoyed at being dragged out of bed. I looked at my watch. It was two-thirty in the morning. What the hell? We were still four hours away from Farpoint.

Alexei pushed us into the aft transfer pod, and we all grabbed handholds. Pseudogravity faded away as the transfer pod stopped spinning in sync with the passenger cabin. Now we were in free fall again. I know that lots of people think free fall is fun. I'm not one of them. It makes me queasy, and it's hard to control where you're moving.

Alexei opened the door on the other side and pushed us quickly into the cargo bay. I felt like one of those big balloons they use in the Thanksgiving Day parade. We floated and bounced through tight spaces filled with crates and tubes and tanks. The walls were all lined with orange webbing. Alexei led us through two or three more hatches, I lost count, and finally brought us to the last car in the train. It was cramped and cold and smelled funny. He jammed us into whatever spaces he could, then went back to seal the hatch; he did some stuff at the wall panel, and came swimming back to us, pushing blankets ahead of him. "Bundle warm. Is a little like Russian winter here, *da*?"

The blankets didn't look very warm; they were thin papery things, but Alexei showed us how to work them. They were big Mylar ponchos; you put your head through the hole, pulled the elastic hood up over your head, and then zipped up the sides, leaving just enough gap to stick your hands out if you needed to. We looked like we were all plastic-wrapped, but as soon as I turned the blanket on, it turned reflective and I started feeling a lot better. Pretty soon, I was all warm and toasty and ready to go back to sleep—only I wanted to go back to the bed we'd already paid for.

Mickey and Douglas were still sorting themselves out, finding corners to anchor our bags, and stuff like that. Douglas was bundling up Stinky, who still hadn't awakened. That's one good thing about low-gee. You sleep better.

I looked to Mickey. "What's going on?"

Alexei bounced over. "Is Luna you want to go, yes? Krislov will get you there. I promise. The elevators are not safe. Not for you. So I come to get you, *da*. I swim the whole way." He slapped his belly, indicating the wetsuit. He started to peel off the harness, which held his scuba gear. "I take free ride in the ballast tank. Nobody knows I am here. My people book for cabins to Luna. We all get bumped for Mister Fatwallets. No problem. We still go home." Grinning proudly, he tucked his Self-Contained Universal Breathing Apparatus into the orange webbing on the wall.

Mickey finished what he was doing and floated down—or was it up?—to drift next to Douglas. He angled himself into the same general orientation and looked across at Alexei. "All of you? You're *all* leaving? All the Loonies?"

Alexei looked grim. "As fast as we can, *gospodin.* Is very bad, all over. Worse than you imagine. Worse than you *can* imagine. But no problem." He reached over and squeezed Mickey's shoulder. "Alexei will take care of you. What you told me was very useful, *da.* I looked, I saw. I made calls. I have clients who worry. I solve their problems. I move their money from here to there, I make money moving it. I move a lot of money now, I make a lot. What you told me, Mickey—I am very rich now. I was rich before, but now I am very very rich. Believe it. Before they shut down money wires, you have no idea how much dollars and euros this clever Lunatic has dry-cleaned. And with money wires shut down now, Alexei cannot send the money on, so Alexei takes care of it. A very great deal of it. I cannot count all the zeroes. And I keep the interest too. But shutting down the flow of money will not keep it on Earth, no. Money is like water. It goes where it wants to. And if there is not a way, it makes a way." He tapped his chest. "I am the way. I find the way. I deliver in person, if necessary. Do you know how much money I am worth because of you? Never mind, you cannot afford to ask."

Krislov grinned. "I tell you this, you are worth almost as much. Remember? I make promise to you? I keep that promise. I flow the money through dummy companies. I cannot hold all companies in my name, so I put some of them in your names. All your names—even the monkey. You are all technically very very rich. At any moment, there could be billions of techno-dollars flowing through your accounts, around and around and around—we keep the money going, they can't find it. They shut the wires down, the money is supposed to stop. But it doesn't. It leaks. Every beam of light is a leak."

I interrupted with a yawn. "Yeah, but—*why did you have to wake us up?*"

"Because, while I am floating in ballast, I am still on phone. I am coordinating, yes? *No.* The wires are shut down, remember? But I listen to Line chatter. Why? Because I am nosy, *da?* Yes, I am—but also because in my business, it is a good idea to listen. So I listen to Line chatter. And I hear. What do I hear?" He opened his palms in a free-fall shrug. "I hear about paladins. Do you know what paladins are, Charles?"

I shook my head.

"Bounty hunters. Freelance marshals. They specialize in extradition. They track you down, they catch you, they bring you back where you don't want to go. This is why I ride in ballast. I always make my own travel plans. Is much safer, because suddenly—I can't imagine why, can you?—people at Geostationary want to talk to Alexei. About business? Probably, but maybe I don't want to talk about business. Certainly not *my* business. So after I deliver you to passenger cabin, I go to cargo bay. As soon as car is on its way, I think we are all safe, but I am wrong. I listen to Line chatter, what do I hear? I hear about paladins at Farpoint waiting for cars to arrive. Maybe they are looking for me? I am disappointed. Only a little. Mostly they are looking for dingalings. Four dingalings and a monkey. Award money is substantial. You are very valuable to somebody, Douglas and Charles and little stinking one. And Mickey too.

"So, I float in tank, I think—I think I cannot let them catch Dingillians. Why? Because some of my companies are in your names and until I can get where I can rearrange the money-flow, I do not want you in that pipeline. Also because I owe you. So, I think—and *da*, I can do it. I come and get you. I wake Mickey and Douglas. They grab you and Stinky. We all come back here. We bundle up warm."

"But—so what?" I asked. "If we're not in our cabin, they'll search the rest of the cars. They'll still catch us."

"I don't think so," Alexei laughed. Something went *thump* just outside the cargo bay. "Because we are getting off here."

FALLING

THEN SOMETHING ELSE WENT CLANK and *thunk* and finally *bumpf*. Alexei held up a hand for silence, as if he were counting off something in his head. "Wait—*da!*" He gestured excitedly. "Feel that?"

"No—what?" It sort of felt like we were moving sideways. It was hard to tell in microgravity.

"We are off of track. Swinging around into launch bay."

"Launch bay—?"

"Not to worry, little frightened one. Is not the first time a Lunatic has done this. Is first time that *Alexei Krislov* has done this, yes—but is because this is first time I have need to."

"Do what—?" I demanded. Even Douglas looked worried.

Something outside the car made a noise that sounded like *un-clank*—and then everything was abruptly silent. All the background noises of the Line and the elevator car were gone. The effect was *terrifying*. I'd never heard so much silence in my life before.

"We are on our way to moon," Alexei said. "We cheat the bounty marshals. We ride with cargo. In four hours, elevator arrives at Whirlaway. Marshals show warrants, they go to cabin, they open door—but Dingillian family is nowhere, *da? Da.*"

A horrible cold feeling was creeping up my spine. "Where are we?" I demanded. "What did you do?"

"We have jumped off Line. We go to moon. We ride with cargo."

"We're off the Line—?"

"*Da.*"

The cold feeling turned into a churning one. "*Douglas*—!" I wailed.

The emptiness outside the walls pressed in on me like a nightmare. I couldn't escape. It was even worse because there were no windows! It was down in all directions—we were falling into the dark!

I started flailing in panic—"*I don't want to do this! We've gotta go back. Make him take us back! I can't do this, Douglas! We've gotta go back—*"

Douglas grabbed me, held me tight in the same kind of bear hug that I always used on Stinky. He pushed me up against something, a tank or a tube, and anchored himself on the webbing to hold us both steady. "Chigger—don't go crazy on me!"

"I can't do this, Douglas. I can't!" I started blubbering. "I'm scared! There's nothing to hold on to out here!"

"Hold on to me—just hold on. I'm right here." He held me tight in one arm, his face close to mine. He touched my face with his free hand. "Look at me, Charles. I'm just as scared as you. But we're not going to die. Nothing bad is going to happen to us. I've got you right here. And you've got me. We've got air, we've got water. We'll be three days getting there—"

"*No, Doug, please—*" I started to come apart. "I can't do this, not for three days. There's gotta be a way to get back—"

"Charles, you know better than that. *There isn't any way back.* The pod has been flung off the Line. We're going to the moon. There's no way to stop it. There's no way to turn it around."

"I can't, I can't—I can't do this!"

"Yes, you can. Listen to me. Look at me. We're very comfortable here. It's just a few days. We have air, we have water, we have food, we'll keep warm. You've got your music. It'll be just like Armstrong and Borman and Collins. We can pretend we're in an Apollo capsule. Like pioneers."

"An Apollo capsule? Like Lovell and—and—? Whatever their names were?"

"Swigert and Haise." That was Douglas. Even in the middle of a crisis, he had to be accurate. "We can do this, Charles. We have to. We're all we have. And Stinky needs you to be brave for him. I can't do it. He listens to you, not me."

In my head I knew he was right, but that didn't stop me from being so scared I couldn't speak. My helplessness just came bubbling out. Douglas held on to me and let me sob like a baby into his shoulder. I was so afraid. It was *everything*. Mom and her slap. Dad and his lies. Douglas and Mickey. Stinky. Not knowing where we were going. Everything out of control. It had been bad enough being stuck on a high-tension line, caught between everyone and everything—now my worst fear of all had just come true. We were helplessly falling forever. We were a million klicks from nowhere and getting farther away every second.

So I held on to Douglas and cried, because he was all there was to hang on to—even though he was falling just as fast and just as far as I was.

But you can only cry for so long . . . and then after that, it's boring. Even worse, it's silly. . . .

I sniffed and wiped my nose unashamedly on Doug's shoulder.

He backed off a bit so he could look me in the eye. "Are you all right?"

"No," I admitted.

"Can you hold it together?"

"I don't know."

"Because I don't want to have to sedate you."

"Like Stinky?"

"Yeah," he admitted. "And I hated doing it."

I didn't answer. I could see the logic of it. Who needs an hysterical eight-year-old? Especially if you've already got a crazy thirteen-year-old?

He asked again, even more serious this time. "Chigger—can you hold it together?"

"I'll try." I was thinking about the tranquilizer. It might not be such a bad idea after all. But if I was going to die, I wanted to be awake for it. And wasn't that a stupid thought? Wouldn't it be better to be asleep, so you wouldn't know when it happened?

"Listen—" His voice got very quiet, very serious. "All we have is each other."

"Yeah, I know."

For a moment, we just studied each other. He was wondering if I could be trusted—and I was wondering the same thing. I needed him to be strong for me, and he needed me to be strong for Bobby. I didn't know if I could do it. I'd spent so many years shutting them out I didn't know how to let them back in. I didn't know what to say. And even if I did, I didn't have any words—

Finally, I blurted, "I don't have anything to hang on to."

"Nobody does," he said. "Ever." Like that was supposed to reassure me. The funny thing was, it sort of did.

I let go of him. "I think I'll be okay now."

"You're sure?"

I was starting to feel embarrassed. "Yeah," I said, and pushed past him back to the others. Mickey and Alexei looked at me with concerned eyes. "I'm fine," I said. "I just have this—fear of cramped spaces. And heights. And falling. And the dark. . . ."

"Wow," said Alexei. "Is triple whammy. Not a good combination for space travel, *da*?"

Mickey gave him a shut-up-stupid look, then reached over and put his hand on my shoulder, ostensibly to steady me, but he was slow in taking his hand away, and I knew he meant it as moral support too. Douglas settled in next to him, and the two exchanged grown-up glances; Mickey's had a question mark, Douglas's had a reassuring period.

Mickey's look to Alexei hadn't worked. Alexei kept talking. "I don't understand this fear," he said. "Where I grow up, you fall slow, you have time to turn yourself so you land on your feet. You bounce, you don't hurt yourself. So why be afraid?"

Douglas said bluntly, "Try it in Earth gravity sometime."

"Earth?" He made a face, shook his head. "I do not think anyone will go to Earth for a long time. I certainly will not. I have Luna muscles, Luna bones. I have no desire to be toothpick-man on planet of crazy dirtsiders. You haven't heard latest news, have you? Ecuador has nationalized the Line. Armed troops have seized Terminus."

Mickey didn't look as surprised as I thought he would. "How'd they get access?"

"According to Line chatter, hurricane relief teams came in to use Terminus as a base. Troops came in with teams, to help prevent looting—but then they started arresting Line personnel. The situation is still . . . how you say, very fluid? Traffic is running again, but most cars up are carrying troops. They have already seized One-Hour. Maybe there will be fighting at Geostationary. The U.N. is in uproar, of course—"

Mickey looked worried and upset. His mom was still at Geostationary.

Alexei was still talking. "We are lucky to get away. Who knows what will happen next?" He gestured dramatically. "But one thing I am sure, Luna will finally prove what I have been saying all along— Luna doesn't need Earth anymore. We are self-sufficient. We will be new center of human consciousness. Not Earth."

Douglas and Mickey exchanged another glance. This time, Douglas had the question mark. Mickey answered, "Yes, Alexei is militant in his Lunacy."

Alexei didn't bristle; he wore his madness like a badge. "The laugh is on you, *Mikhail*. If not for my paranoid Lunacy"—he tapped his head with his fingertips—"you would be in custody very shortly. In another four hours. At the end of the line, how you say, literally. And whose custody would you be in? Up for the highest bidder, I think. And if we are all at war, who knows? Bad accidents happen in war. No, my Lunacy is saving your life. Again. No, no, you can thank me later. The money I have made today is all the gratitude I need."

FLATING

ALEXEI SETTLED US AT THE far end of the pod, in the little bit of space between the cargo containers and the hull. He tucked us and our gear into the orange webbing on the aft bulkhead, spacing us around so that our mutual center of gravity was congruent to the central axis of the pod.

If we wanted to go anywhere in the pod, we'd have to squeeze around pipes and cables and supporting rods—and big green glops of hardened foam that looked like industrial-strength boogers. But there was no place to go anyway, so we just stayed where we were, wrapped in our plastic blankets and looking at the ominous round wall of cargo containers in front of us. It was like being a bug at the bottom of a piston.

The crates were all big wedge-shaped things, four to a circle, each anchored firmly in place by plastic clamps and foam boogers. Mickey explained that the thick foam pads were how the cargo engineers kept the containers from breaking loose and rattling around in transit. I didn't see how the crates would have much chance to rattle or break loose; we would be in free fall the whole way, wouldn't we? But there was a lot I didn't understand.

"The accommodations aren't pretty," Mickey admitted, "but we won't be uncomfortable. Cargo pods are designed for supercargo. Sometimes Line engineers have to ride with supplies, so there's mandated life support for at least five people at a time."

Alexei grinned. "Is very convenient, no?" He showed us the arrangements. "See those blue tanks all around? They hold water. Many liters. Microdiaphragm pumps move it around for balance. Water is very convenient that way. Green tanks have oxygen. Brown cabinets hold food—well, MREs."

"MREs?"

"Meals Ready to Eat. Three lies in as many words, no? Be sure to drink much water. MREs make lumps like concrete in bowel. With no gravity, lumps get even harder. Very much pain. Learn the hard way, yes? Very hard. That is the problem. Too hard even to work out with pencil. Not to worry—if you don't like MRE, you are not hungry enough. Starvation is not as painful, but takes too much longer."

He pointed toward the other end of the pod—I thought of it as the front, because that was where we'd entered. "Use that end for bathroom. Use plastic bags, like this? See. Put waste in yellow containers with biohazard symbol. Be very careful. Is possible to make very bad stink in here. Very unpleasant. See those little fans everywhere to keep air moving? They don't make stink go away; only spread it around equally. Don't worry, I teach you how to be careful. Any questions?"

Mickey and Douglas seemed to be okay with the arrangements, and I figured I'd learn as we went along—and we'd all take turns trying to explain it to Stinky when he woke up. Maybe we could keep him from wetting or soiling himself for three days.

But there was something else that was bothering me.

"Um—"

"What?" That was Douglas.

"You agreed to this?"

"Mickey and I did, yes."

Mickey said, "We didn't have a lot of time to talk about it, Charles. We had fifteen minutes to decide before the capsule was launched."

"You took Alexei's word for it that there were marshals waiting for us—?"

"Alexei might be a lunatic, but he's an honest one." Mickey held up a headset. "You want to hear the playback? You want to listen to the Line chatter?"

I did, but that wasn't the question. "But the marshals will figure it out, won't they? When the elevator arrives at Farpoint and we're not in the cabin, they'll just phone ahead to Luna. There are marshals on Luna, aren't there? They'll just catch us in the cargo pod."

Alexei nodded. "Very good, Charles. But Luna is not Line. Very much not. On Line, you are always known. Always under camera eye. Not on moon. I will get you down safely, and you will see. Things disappear very easily. Luna is beautiful that way. You will love moon. Especially fresh food. Is big promise. I am hungry already, thinking of salad. Sweet corn, ripe tomatoes, fresh peas . . ."

Maybe it was me, maybe it was the lack of sleep, but everything was happening just too fast here.

"Excuse me—? Did I miss something? This is a cargo pod, isn't it? They know where we're going to land, don't they?"

"No," said Alexei. "They know where we're *supposed* to land."

I didn't like the sound of that. Even before I asked the next question, I knew the answer was only going to make things worse.

Alexei said, "Now you want to know *where* we will land, don't you?"

"Uh—okay, where?"

Alexei grinned through his scraggly beard. "We will come down where they can't go. Not easily. Very bad area. The maps are not accurate. Not the official ones. From there we go to land of tall mountains and deep ice mines. Is very beautiful. A little dangerous. But not too much—not to worry. You will like. By the time they get to cargo pod, we will all be somewhere else."

"But they can track us, can't they? As soon as they figure out we're in one of the cargo pods, they'll—"

Alexei's PITA* beeped; he glanced at his wrist. "Ah, there it is now. Time for first orbital correction. Everybody brace yourselves. Hang on to the webbing. This won't be too bad." Mickey reached over and grabbed the still-sleeping Stinky.

"Is just a little one—" Alexei started to say, but he was abruptly interrupted by a deep-throated rumble that rattled the whole cabin like an El Paso windstorm. It was loud and bumpy, and we were all shoved sideways up against the hull so hard it was almost impossible to breathe. It felt like we were hanging upside down in a cement mixer. I wanted to scream—but didn't have the air for it. And just when I was making up my mind that I was going to scream anyway, it stopped, and that spooky eternal silence closed in again.

"Is that it?" Douglas asked.

"Oh, no," said Alexei. "We have maybe fourteen or fifteen more.

*Personal Information Telecommunications Assistant.

All the way out." He looked back over to me. "What was question again, Charles? That they will track us? Yes, they will. That is the point of the course changes."

"Fourteen or fifteen more? All like *that*—?"

"It's done with solid-fuel chips, Chigger," Douglas started to explain. "They burn unevenly and that rattles everything—"

"*I know how they burn!*" I almost said a whole bunch of other stuff too, except I was too busy concentrating on my next breath. "And why so many course corrections anyway? Can't they aim this thing—?" I looked to Alexei.

"Not course corrections. Course *changes*. Is very precisely aimed," Alexei said, "and we are making serious alteration in trajectory. Is not unheard of. Sometimes cargo gets preempted from one location to another."

"But they're still tracking us, aren't they?" Douglas asked. "Chigger's right. This thing broadcasts a locater signal—they'll know where we are as soon as they figure it out, won't they?"

"Eventually, yes, they'll figure it out. The key word is *eventually*. So our job is to make eventually later than sooner." Alexei continued proudly. "First, this is not only pod to launch. Do you remember five others? All of those pods have been preempted too. Some rich new Luna company bought them in transit—I cannot imagine who, can you? All the pods have been retargeted for different places. Whoever tracks pods thinking we are in one of them will have to send marshals to six different landing sites, all of them difficult, except two."

"Oh," Douglas said. "And—?"

"And?" Alexei looked puzzled.

"You said *first*, as if there was a second."

"Oh. Yes, well *second* is much more subtle. This is why we have fourteen course changes on each pod. So that no one who is tracking can predict final orbit and landing site until we are already on track. All those changes—we will look like we can land anywhere on Luna. The last burn will not happen until we are on final approach, and that will bounce us off the screens for many long minutes. Whoever tracks will have to spend long minutes projecting—guessing probable touchdown sites. Your lunatic Russian friend is very clever, yes?"

"Yes, very clever," agreed Mickey. He'd been very quiet up to this moment. Now his tone of voice had gone all strange, and he asked, "Just where *are* you bringing us down?"

Alexei grinned. "This is cleverest part. I show you. We started out in Earth equatorial plane, yes? Each of our course changes pushes us more and more up. We go toward north pole of moon—they think we are aiming for North Heinlein, approach pattern is perfect for that—but no, as we come into Lunar orbit, we go three times around and make extra burns. Last change puts us in crazy-mouse orbit. You know crazy-mouse orbit? Near polar, but not quite; elliptical with lots of wibble-wobble. Great fun. We can come down anywhere we want from crazy-mouse, but no one knows where until last minute. Other pods do same thing too, we make them all crazy."

"But what do *we* do?" Mickey asked.

"We will be in crazy-mouse just long enough for people tracking us to say, 'Oh, shit.' We loop *over* top of moon, come down around farside, aim for ground, brake very suddenly, and bounce down in southern hemisphere."

"*Bounce* down . . . ?" I asked.

"Yes, is very easy. Great fun. You will laugh much. Like rollering coaster." And then he looked honestly puzzled. "Do you not know how these things work?"

I looked to Douglas, accusingly. He had that constipated weasel expression—the one that said *no, I didn't tell you the worst of it.*

CHANGES

PULLED MYSELF OUT OF the pocket of the orange webbing that Alexei had stuffed me into. I grabbed Douglas by the leg and pulled him down away from Mickey and Alexei, so I could talk to him privately. If I'd been scared before, now I was beyond scared. There wasn't a word for it. I couldn't believe I was still rational. I should have been gibbering.

Douglas's first words were, "I didn't know myself, Chigger, I didn't have time to ask. I'm sorry—but we still would have had to come this way. Think about it."

"I have been!" I lowered my voice so he wouldn't hear the sob in my throat. I was terrified. "This is *real* stupid, Douglas."

"Yeah, I know—but we *didn't* have any choice."

"We could get *killed*."

"I don't think so. Mickey isn't stupid. And Alexei—"

"Alexei's a lunatic who doesn't have enough sense to be afraid of gravity. Why didn't we just stay on the elevator and deal with the marshals at Farpoint? We didn't do anything wrong. They can't arrest us."

Douglas shook his head. "Chigger, you've already seen how these people work. They throw lawyers at you. And they keep throwing lawyers until one of them finds something that sticks. And even if they can't find anything, they still keep you stuck in the courtroom. Either way, you're stopped, which is all they want to do anyway—stop us long enough to get their hands on the monkey."

"So why don't we just give it to them? We didn't make the deal to smuggle it. Dad did. We don't even know who's supposed to collect it on the other end. Or where the other end is. And besides, there isn't anything in it anyway—just a couple of bars of industrial memory, filled with decoy code."

"We don't know that. We don't know what's in it. Maybe it's the real stuff. Maybe they lied to Dad too—"

"Who?"

"Whoever. I don't know. But you heard what Dad said to fat *Señor* Doctor Hidalgo. We don't sell what doesn't belong to us. Maybe he suspected something."

"Oh, great. So that means if there really is something in the monkey, then we could be arrested for smuggling it—?"

"Yeah. Probably." Douglas looked at me gravely. "I just didn't think we should take any more chances."

"You panicked, didn't you?"

He didn't answer immediately. I was right. And I wished I wasn't. I'd always believed that Douglas was infallible.

He held up a hand. "Let's not have this argument. Please, Chigger?" He said it just like Dad. "We're on our way now. We can't go back. Whatever else, this *is* our ride."

He was right about that much, despite the way he said it, so I shut up. For a moment anyway. But this still wasn't settled. I turned back to him. "Okay, but you gotta promise me something."

"What?"

"That you won't do this anymore—make decisions without asking me. That's what Mom and Dad used to do. And we always hated it. Remember what you said before? You said 'if this is going to work, I need your help.' We're in this together, aren't we?"

Douglas put his arms around me and pulled me close. "You're right, Chigger. I'm sorry. I wasn't thinking. I mean, I wasn't thinking about that."

"No, you were thinking—but you were thinking about the logic stuff, not the people stuff, because that's the way you are." And then I realized, "I'm not too good at it either, am I?"

He ran his hand over the top of my bald head. It was an eerie feeling. I still wasn't used to it—even though we'd all shaved ourselves smooth two days ago. Everyone who lives in space does, for cleanliness reasons. Douglas sighed sadly. "Yeah, I guess social skills was another of those lessons that got dropped out in the divorce." He kissed me— something he'd never done before, at least I couldn't remember ever being kissed by my big brother. He said, "Okay, Chig. I promise. No more family decisions unless everyone in the family is part of them. Even Stinky."

"Pinky promise?"

"Pinky promise." We hooked little fingers and shook on it.

There was one more thing I had to ask. "Douglas?"

"Yeah?"

"Are you and Mickey . . . you know? Gonna get married?"

"I don't know. We haven't really talked about it yet. Does it bother you?"

"I just want to know. Will he be part of our family too? Is he going to help make decisions?"

"Um, Chig . . . He *is* part of it. We have to include him."

"But we just met him two days ago."

"Three."

"Whatever. It's just—how can you make that kind of a decision so *quickly*? It's not *logical*."

"Oh, look who's talking about logic now."

"You know what I mean," I said.

"Yeah, I do. And yeah, you're right. It's not logical. But . . . I've never had anybody love me before. Not like this. And I don't want to lose it. It's very confusing. Maybe it'll happen to you someday. And then you'll understand."

I couldn't imagine it. So I didn't say anything. I didn't even make a face.

Douglas ran his hand over the top of my head again. He took a deep breath. "There *is* a decision that we do have to make very soon, Chig. All of us. What colony are we going to head out to? We'd better start thinking about that now. Because that *will* be a one-way trip."

CARGO

IF I'D THOUGHT THE TRIP up the elevator was boring, the cargo pod was even worse. At least the elevator had all the cable channels, ha-ha. We could have had some video reception if we'd linked to either an Earth or a Lunar station—but if we started downloading, then our presence on this pod would be obvious to anyone with access to the tracking software. And the whole point of this trick was that they wouldn't know *which* pod we were in.

Alexei spent an hour explaining to us how the pods were built and how they worked. That was sort of interesting for a while—but it wasn't really his purpose to entertain us. He said it was essential to our survival that we understood what kind of vehicle we were in.

"Is only a cargo pod, *not* a real spaceship," he said. "Is idea to have efficient and cheap way to send supplies and equipment to Luna or Mars or asteroid belt or anywhere else. You put stuff in box, you give box a push—you fling it off Line, *da*? Eventually, it arrives. Cost for fuel is negligible. You are already out of gravity well, so you only need fuel for course corrections along the way and a little bit more for braking at destination. Is very convenient, if you are not in hurry."

Then he showed us how the pods were built. "You see all these polycarbonate rods lining the shell? That is the skeleton of the pod. Very light, very strong. You put framework together like Tinker Toy, you clamp cargo wedges into frame, then you attach outer bulkheads all around. Polycarbonate shells—all prefab, all the same. Stamped from injection molds. Because they make only one trip, reusability is no concern—you think, *da? Nyet.* The shells are product too. Open up pod, take out cargo, close up pod, turn it into house. Very *good* house."

Alexei pounded on the bulkhead with his fist. "This is why you find windows and plumbing and wiring in walls—not just because World Space Agency mandates every pod must have basic life support, but because every pod shipped will expand living space at destination. Very clever, yes? We have transport, we have life support, we have new home." He pounded a crate. "Is tradition on Luna, at least one of these crates always contains furnishings, yes. We live in most expensive shipping boxes in solar system. Very nice, *da?*"

I shrugged. Maybe Alexei thought this was exciting, but I didn't. We'd grown up in a tube-town—which is really just a polite way of saying we lived in a giant sewer. No kidding. Any tube that failed the structural integrity tests for piping sewage was still considered strong enough for housing. They all came out of the same factory. So I didn't see that a used shipping box was all that much of an improvement, especially not one with 450,000 kilometers on it.

On the other hand, if you had to live in a used shipping box, you could do a lot worse than a Lunar cargo pod. Alexei showed us how the hull of the pod was made out of six simple pieces: four identical curved hull sections, each describing a 90-degree arc, and two identical circular end pieces. Each piece was designed to fit into every other piece, and each panel had its own hatch and window.

Also, each hull unit had two survival cabinets, one at each end. Each cabinet contained the minimum basic life-support supplies necessary for one person for three days; so the pod had eight total. Alexei showed us how each of the survival cabinets held food, water for drinking and ballast, oxygen-recyclers, self-heating blanket-ponchos, first-aid kits, plastic toilet bags, and personal survival bubbles because you can't pack space suits in enough different sizes. And please read the instructions before opening anything.

Mickey explained that the pods were essentially the spacegoing version of an Antarctic explorer's travel-hut. A onetime pod doesn't need the same kind of precision machinery as a reusable vehicle, and it's unnecessary to build a whole lander for the delivery of cargo, so the steering and braking systems were the cheapest brute-force method possible.

"Is the engines that are most clever," Alexei said, glancing at his wrist. "*Nyet*—not to worry. We are fine for another ninety minutes. Time enough for lesson. I explain fuel rods. Is really quite simple. How do you fire rocket in space? No oxygen in vacuum, *da*? So you put oxygen in fuel mix. Make whole thing one solid tube of fuel. Ignite at one end, it burns until fuel is gone. Is very efficient booster system. But one big problem with solid-fuel booster. Timing. Once burn starts, you cannot turn it off. So is not good for precision burns, *da*? *Nyet*, we find a way. Is much simpler than you think—we use Palmer tubes. Invented by engineer with too much time on hands. Name of John Palmer. Playing with his poker chips at Las Vegas. Very famous story, I share with you.

"Dr. John Palmer, famous engineer, sits at roulette table, thinks of mathematics of chaos and order. How good luck, bad luck both run in streaks. How random numbers cluster up. Thinks about composition of solid-fuel boosters. Meanwhile, he stacks chips, red and black, red and black, red and black. Then he runs out of blacks, so he stacks two red, one black, two red, one black. Suddenly light goes on in head. He pushes everything onto double zero and gets up from table. Wins eleventy-thousand plastic-dollars anyway—almost forgets to collect winnings, he is so excited.

"He rushes back to laboratory and invents Palmer tube. I explain. He slices solid-fuel rod of metallized hydrogen into little flat poker chips. Very thin. In between, he puts little polycarbonate separators, even thinner. Separating disks are made of several layers, perforated and corrugated and shaped to be strong on one side but weak on the other; crisscrossed with grooves so that weak side looks like business side of nail file. Strong side looks like mirror. Very clever, *da*?

"Then Palmer gets even more clever idea. When he makes separator chips, he paints circumference with liquid conductor. When he makes rod, he glues *insulated* wires down each side. He makes whole thing in polyceramic tube, holds fuel rod like gun barrel.

"Works like this. Turn on current, juice goes down wires, *da*? All the way to end of tube, to bare ends of wires—last separator in line has shiny side out, grooved side in. Conductive ring around separator chip completes circuit, ignites fuel chip in front of it. Creates ring-shaped ignition. Most efficient explosion. Fuel slice vaporizes, separator vaporizes—*bing*! Next separating disk in line is shiny side out, strong enough to protect next fuel slice—remember, separator only weak on grooved side, not shiny side; so when force of explosion hits shiny side, next separator works like back wall of combustion chamber for just that moment. *Da?* So you get one little poof of thrust. Only one.

"But explosion also heats ignition wires, melts insulation off— enough so that bare wires now touch next separator disk. If there is still current, that disk completes circuit and ignites fuel slice behind it—and whole process happens again. Fuel slice explodes and vaporizes separator disk that ignites it, but does not ignite *next* disk again. And just like before, next separator is back wall of combustion chamber and you get next little poof of thrust. And process starts again. Wires melt a little more, and if there is still current, next disk goes *bing* too. Everything happens very fast—*bing, bing, bing, bing, bing, bing, bing, bing*—like so.

"As long as current flows through wire, disks blow off the end of the tube, one after other. Is like packing whole bunch of bullets in same barrel, but no bullets, only charges. When you burn enough fuel, you turn off current. Explosions stop. Thrust stops. Is beautiful clever, *da? Da?*

"But firing tubes like this—*bing, bing, bing, bing, bing*—makes very unpleasant pulsing effect. Not a fun ride. Like sitting on machine gun. Not a problem. You bundle tubes together. Tubes not work in sync, all the little *bing-bings* average out. Instead of machine-gun feeling, you get corrugated road. More tubes, more average, more smooth— but smooth not needed for cargo, packages don't complain, so is still rough ride, but tolerable, *da?* Never mind. We get there. Palmer bundles guarantee delivery. Is simple brute-force brilliant. If one tube in bundle fails, no problem; others make up difference. Thrust monitor in bundle manages everything. You need this much thrust? Fire tubes until. *Da!*

"Here is more brilliance. Palmer tubes can be any size. As thin as paper clip, as thick as elephant leg—we have elephant on Luna, you know, baby female; you must come to our zoo, see baby elephant bounce—much funny. Anyway, Palmer tubes and Palmer bundles can be made all sizes. Use different size bundles of tubes for all different purposes. Heavy lifting, braking, steering, attitude adjustment, lots of useful boost. Launch to orbit from Luna or Mars. Very efficient. Bring asteroids home for mining. Deliver cargo pods anywhere. Fling them off Line, steer them to destination, brake to match orbit.

"This is why Palmer tube is so brilliant. Volume manufacture makes space travel cheap. Palmer tubes as easy to make as pencils.

Put in red goop here, blue goop there, black goop over there, run the
machine, stack the firing tubes here. Bundle together, plug in timing
caps and thrust monitor. *Da?* Very cheap. You can put three sets of
boosters and a thrust monitor on a pod for less than a thousand plastic-
dollars. And whatever part of tubes are left over at destination can be
used for other things.

"You know story of Crazyman Tucker? He lived in old cargo pod.
Very nice pod too. Much fancy. He collected unburned ends of tubes
for years, he finally bundle them into big cluster, launch his pod into
Lunar orbit. Another cluster of tubes sends him off to rendezvous with
Whirlaway rock. He almost makes it too. What some people won't do
to avoid export taxes, *da?* But rescue costs more than taxes. So he lose
entire fortune anyway. He should have used Palmer tubes for more
mining. Get more rich. But he say, 'What good is money on Luna? Nothing to do but throw rocks at tin cans. And you have to bring your own
rocks.' Is very forbidding planet. But you will like, I promise. I teach
you to fly at Heinlein Dome. You will have so much fun, you will never
want to leave."

At that, Douglas spoke up. "Thank you, Alexei. but we're going out
to a colony."

"I know that, *gospodin*," said Alexei. "But if you don't get a bid,
you are welcome on Luna. I promise."

"We have an insured contract for a colony placement," said
Mickey. "And with all the money you say we've earned, we should be
able to buy our way onto the next outbound ship."

Alexei grinned. "I will miss you, *Mikhail*. And if you change mind
and decide not to go, I will enjoy not missing you even more." His PITA
beeped then. "Oops—here we go. Everybody hold on tight, please."

CHOICES

MICKEY KNEW A LOT ABOUT the colonies; working as an elevator attendant, he'd met a lot of outbound colonists. And Alexei knew most of the starship crews; he knew all the best gossip about the different worlds.

"You stay away from both Rand and Hubbard," Alexei warned. "Not very happy worlds. Not at all. The sociometrics don't work. Not like promised. The Randies had to turn themselves into a cult. The Hubbers had to invoke totalitarian control—or was it the other way around?" He scratched his head. "No matter. I tell you how bad it is— the brightliner crews won't go dirtside anymore."

"I heard they weren't allowed to," said Mickey. "It's prohibited now. So they can't report back."

"That too," agreed Alexei. "The smart thing is, stay away from colonies founded on political or religious ideology."

Douglas nodded. "I'd already figured that out." He turned his clipboard around so we could all see it. Half the names on it were already crossed out.

We'd taken time to sleep and eat and give ourselves deodorant sponge baths before we got too smelly. I helped wash Stinky when he finally woke up, and even he smelled tolerable when we were done.

I told Stinky that we were in the cargo pod, but apparently it didn't sink in, because midway through the breakfast, he started complaining. "How come we don't have a real bathroom? How come we can't go to the restaurant to eat? When are we gonna get there? I thought you said we'd be there when we woke up. How come we don't have any real beds?"

Oops.

So Douglas and I told him that we were hiding in the baggage compartment, because we were playing hide-and-seek, so Howard-The-Lawyer wouldn't find us. That he understood immediately. And it was a lot easier than trying to explain Whirlaway to him.

We endured two more course changes—Stinky thought they were fun—and then we finally settled down for a family meeting about where we were going.

Very quickly, we decided that if any one of us had a strong objection to a specific world, we'd take it off the list. Mickey immediately vetoed Promised Land, New Canaan, and Allah. "They're all orthodox," he explained. "You can immigrate only if you convert."

Douglas was already checking them off the list. "The sociometrics for religious colonies aren't good anyway. Long-term instability, almost always leading to schisms, holy wars, revolutions, and pogroms."

"So let's just eliminate all of the ones with sociometric liabilities," I said.

"They all have sociometric liabilities," said Mickey. "We have to consider them each on their own merits and then decide what set of problems we're willing to take on."

Douglas agreed. "You want to do this alphabetically?"

"Um, wait a minute—please?" They both looked at me. "Maybe we should make a list of things that we want. That way we'll have something to measure each planet against. Then we can give each colony a score, and that way we can—what's the word?—prioritize them."

Mickey and Douglas exchanged glances, nodded. "Sounds like a plan."

Douglas said, "You start, Chig. What do you want?"

The picture in my head was Mexico. The Baja coast. Our one short day at the beach. A bright blue sky over a wide emerald sea. Yellow sand and tall green forests. And wind—breezes that smelled good. Real flowers.

But first things first. "Normal gravity," I said.

"That's good thinking," said Mickey. "Most people don't think about gravity enough. Most people can handle a ten or fifteen percent boost. It's like gaining five or ten kilos. But it's extra stress on the heart, on the feet, on the bones; there's a higher risk of injury; and you age faster, you sag more. Also, your life expectancy is reduced."

Douglas made a note. "Gravity, that's important. We'll give that one a lot of weight." And then he added, "Not just gravity, we have to think about the whole planet. What kind of star does it circle? What color is the light? How long is the year? How severe are the seasons? What's the atmosphere like, what kind of weather does it have? How long are the days? Is the air breathable? Or will it be someday? What kind of terraforming is possible?"

And as he said that, all my visions of a tropical beach disappeared. We weren't going to Hawaii. We were going to Mars. Barren red rock, stretching off in all directions. Clusters of domes hiding beneath angling solar panels. Antennas sprouting like needles. Storage tanks huddling against the ground to withstand the enormous winds and dust storms. Agriculture domes. Tubes snaking from one place to the other because the atmosphere was too thin to breathe. Long ugly days. Cold dark nights.

Tube-town again.

Only this time, uglier than ever. Because there wouldn't be any-place *else* to go.

I knew what kind of planet we had jumped off. I was just beginning to realize what we might have to jump onto. . . .

Douglas must have seen the look on my face. He asked, "Chigger?"

"I want a colony that has an *outdoors*," I said. "Breathable air. I want to go outside."

"Mmm," said Mickey, frowning. "That does limit our options."

"I don't care," I said. "I don't want to live in a tube anymore."

"Nobody does. But sometimes that's all there is."

"I don't care. That's what I want."

"Would you accept a world that had garden domes? I hear some of them can be very nice."

Alexei spoke up then. "We have garden domes on Luna. Very pretty. We put a dome over a crater and fill it with air. We bring in manure and water, seeds and insects, pretty soon we have garden. Well, not pretty soon. Sometimes it takes twenty years to get garden dome going. But for much people, garden dome is all the outdoors they need."

I shook my head. "Maybe that's okay for Loonies. It's not okay for me. I want a real sky."

Douglas made a note on his clipboard. "Outdoors. Very important."

Mickey didn't look happy about that, but he didn't argue it either. He said, "There are a couple of other things we need to consider. Where we can live, what kind of work we'll have to do, what kinds of laws there are—y'know, every colony has its own idea of the way things should be. What you can believe, where you can live, *who can marry who* . . . . Stuff like that."

Douglas looked up. "I hadn't thought about that."

"Well, we have to." He added, "There are some places that won't let us keep custody of Bobby. You'd better put that at the top of your list. In fact, we'd better limit ourselves to places that recognize 'full faith and credit' of other places' laws. Otherwise, Judge Griffith's custody rulings could be set aside by anyone who chooses to file a 'writ of common interest.' "

Douglas frowned, but wrote. He stopped, looked across at Mickey. "You're trying to make a point, aren't you?"

"Uh-huh."

"Go on."

"I think we should limit ourselves to signatories to the Covenant of Rights."

Douglas didn't say anything to that. I could tell he was thinking it over. He didn't like the idea, I knew that much, but he could see the point.

It wasn't that we disagreed with the U.N. Covenant of Rights. Not in principle, at least. But back home, there were a lot of people who said the Covenant was a recipe for anarchy or totalitarianism—or both at the same time. So we had never ratified it.

The Covenant recognized the basic rights of all people—that every human being was entitled to equal access to opportunity and equal protection under the law. That all people were entitled to freedom of belief, freedom of expression, freedom of spirit. That all people were entitled to access to food and water and air, access to education, access to justice. And most important, that all people were entitled to equal representation in their government. And that no government had the right, authority, or power to restrict or infringe or deny those freedoms. And so on. It was pretty dangerous stuff.

Some of the folks back in tube-town said that the only way all those freedoms could be guaranteed equally would be to establish a totalitarian dictatorship. Then no one would have any freedom, but we would

all be equal. Other people said that if we signed the Covenant, it would mean we'd have to repeal half our laws, and our civilization would break down. They said that men and women would have to share the same toilets and that rich people would have to sleep under bridges with poor people and everybody would have to share all their property so nobody had more than anybody else. And besides, only the One-Worlders wanted us to sign it because that would be another step toward ceding our independence to the U.N. And once there was a world government in place, the rest of the world would loot our economy. And so on.

But the way it looked now, it didn't really matter after all. The last news we'd heard, *nobody* had an economy anymore.

Douglas said, "I know you mean well, Mickey, but I'm not comfortable with the Covenant of Rights. It sounds like collectivism."

Mickey looked at him expectantly. So did Alexei.

"I mean, you can't just let people have rights without controls. You get a breakdown of society. You get corruption and immorality and fraud. The system breaks down, a little bit at a time. You get multigeneration welfare families, and parasites feeding at the public trough. You get teener-gangs and disaffected subcultures and dysfunctionals of all kinds. You get riots and crime and . . . and immorality. All kinds of degeneracy. You have to have some limits on what people can do; otherwise, it all erodes away and eventually falls apart." He gestured vaguely behind himself. "I mean, all you have to do is look at what's happening back there on Earth."

Mickey replied, "I could just as easily argue the opposite side of it, Doug—that the meltdown is a result of too many oppressive controls."

"I don't think so—"

"Well, then let me put it to you another way. Do you want a place where you and I can stay together? Only a Covenant world will guarantee that. None of the others. If they haven't signed the Covenant, there's no evidence that they're committed to anyone's rights."

Douglas sighed in exasperation. "Y'know, back in Texas, that kind of talk would be subversive."

There was a long uncomfortable silence at that. Mickey and Alexei exchanged a glance, waiting.

Douglas looked from one to the other. I could see he was struggling

with it, trying to wrap his head around a whole new idea. Finally, he said, "Things *really* are different out here, aren't they?"

"Yeah," said Mickey. "They are."

Douglas sighed. He hated losing arguments. "All right." He scribbled something on his clipboard. "Mickey wants a Covenant world. Very important."

MONKEYS

THERE **WAS A LOT MORE** than that too. I never realized there was so much stuff to consider.

Like language, f'rinstance. What if the perfect colony was one where no one spoke Spanglish? We'd have to spend six months just learning to speak French or some other weird tongue, before we could begin to function like real people.

And skin color. We didn't think of ourselves as racist, or anything like that, but we all wanted to go to a place where we looked pretty much like everybody else, because we wanted to fit in.

And food. That one was *real* important—especially after eating a few of those damn MREs. On some worlds, they grew their protein in big vats of slime. On others, they farmed insects. By comparison, even pickled mongoose sounded appetizing.

Both Douglas and Mickey had a lot of information in their clipboards about all the different colony worlds, so we spent a lot of time talking about each one and scoring it on all the different things that were important to us. We crossed off some colonies immediately, with almost no discussion at all. Others, we talked about for an hour or more. I hadn't realized there were so many different *kinds* of colony worlds.

Other than that, we napped and crapped—and got slapped into the aft bulkhead every time there was a course change. I can't say I ever got used to them; they were all uncomfortable; but at least I got smart enough to take a lot of deep breaths whenever Alexei's PITA beeped.

Every so often, we'd climb around to one side or the other, to peek out one of the little windows, hoping to catch sight of either the Earth or the moon. We never did get a real good look at the moon; we were angled wrong, coming around behind the dark side, trying to catch up to it; but once we got a spectacular view of the crescent Earth. It was the size of a basketball held at arm's length—and it looked so big and so small, both at the same time, it was scary. And it was so bright it made my eyes water. It gave me a funny feeling inside to know that we would never go back.

We'd never see Mom or Dad again either. And that felt strange too. Because I didn't feel anything for them, just gray inside. Like I didn't know what to feel. Maybe I'd feel it later. I just didn't know. I wondered if Douglas felt the same way—or if he was still so confused about his feelings for Mickey that he didn't have room for any other kind of feelings.

But with so much other stuff happening, I didn't get a chance to talk to him about it. I also had to take care of Stinky.

Stinky thought free fall was fun. He wanted to go bouncing and careening around the cargo pod, except there really wasn't much room for that, except for the little bit of open space at each end. I'd started thinking of our nest at the aft end as the top. The bottom was the space we used as the bathroom, although a couple of times, Mickey and Douglas went up there when they wanted some privacy.

Alexei busied himself with eavesdropping on the various news channels. I could see his fingers twitching when he did. He said he wanted to get on the phone and start calling. He could make a lot of money with just a few phone calls—but any unusual traffic from this pod would certainly alert whoever was watching that this was the occupied one, so he resisted the temptation. He said he was part of a web of money-surfers who took care of each other's business when any one of them was in transit or had to go underground for a while. That way, the money was never where anyone might be looking for it. Just the same, he worried about the opportunities passing by.

So it was left for me to entertain Stinky whenever he got bored, which was almost constantly. Fortunately, we had the monkey to play with, so the two of us started teaching it things and making up games. The monkey was pretty smart—smarter than I would have guessed for a kid's toy. *Smart enough not to draw to an inside straight.* Smart enough to play an aggressive game of chess. Even smart enough to hold its nose whenever Stinky farted.

I shouldn't have been surprised by its ability to play chess or poker. It was, after all, a toy—and even Douglas could write a chess or a poker program, the logic wasn't that hard to chart. Simulating intelligence is so easy, even Stinky can do it.

But every so often, I caught the monkey studying me thoughtfully—or maybe it was just my imagination. Maybe that was part of the way it had learned to interact with its human hosts. But it made me wonder. What if the monkey really was watching us? Recording everything? What if the monkey was some kind of a spy? Maybe the monkey's job was to travel with us and monitor . . . that was the part I couldn't figure out. That was where I ran out of paranoia.

"I wish you could talk to me," I said to it. "I wish I could just order you to explain yourself. That would make everything so much simpler."

The monkey just cocked its head and looked at me curiously, as if waiting for me to give the order. Yeah, right.

Some people thought robots were fun. I didn't. I thought most of them were a damn nuisance. Because they did exactly what they were told. They didn't do what you *meant*, they did what you said. Which was kind of funny if you were a kid, but it was frustrating too. I never had the patience for it, but Stinky did. And so did Douglas. They had the logic genes. I guess they got that from Mom. I got the music, and not much else, from Dad. I didn't resent it, not really, but sometimes I wished I could understand things the way other people did. It would make life a lot easier. I wouldn't have to work so hard at everything.

It was halfway through the second waking period—I couldn't think of them as "days" when nothing really changed—when Stinky finally figured it out. *It.*

We had gone up to the front window to look at the moon, which was still a crescent, but starting to fill out enough that we could see the sharp edges of craters all along the terminator line. When we got bored with that, we started making up songs about bouncing elephants, and then we decided to teach the monkey how to dance, which is hard enough in gravity, but in free fall it's impossible—so it was silly enough to start Stinky giggling, which is sort of good most of the time, because once he starts giggling he just keeps on going; but it isn't always a good idea because sometimes he giggles so hard he pees in his pants.

But this time, he and the monkey started imitating each other, and it was hard to tell which of them was funnier—and which of them was more amused by the other. They really did look a lot like twins.

—Until in the middle of everything Stinky asked *the* question. The one I'd been hoping he wouldn't. "Chigger, who's going to meet us on the moon? Mommy or Daddy?"

I knew that he wasn't simply asking who was going to meet us. He was asking if we would ever see them again. And I honestly didn't know what to say to him. For one of the first times in my life, I felt sorry for the little monster because there just wasn't any way to soften this blow. And . . . even though I didn't like thinking this thought, maybe it *had* been a mistake for Douglas and me to insist on keeping him with us. Maybe he would have been better with Mom. Or even Dad.

Except—I knew he wouldn't have been. And I knew if I'd had to choose at his age, I'd have chosen to leave instead of stay, even if I didn't understand all the reasons why. Or maybe I wouldn't have chosen to leave, maybe I'd have been too scared to, but I wouldn't have been better off staying. But Stinky didn't know that—because he wasn't thirteen or eighteen, and he didn't know any better. All he knew was that his Mommy and Daddy weren't here. And he missed them.

And he was looking to me to give him an answer.

So I told him the truth. *As best as I could.*

Which means, I weaseled like an adult.

"I don't know, kiddo. Remember, Dad promised us a trip to the moon, and this is our vacation. And Judge Griffith said he could go too. So I'm sure he's going to try to meet us when we get where we're going—he just doesn't know that we're taking the long way around."

"And what about Mom?"

I thought about fat *Señor* Doctor Hidalgo, who had flown Mom and her friend up on an expensive shuttle flight for the emergency custody hearing. Would he shuttle her to the moon and try to head us off there? If he thought he could get his hands on the monkey, he would. It seemed to me he was trying to get off the Earth anyway. So whatever game he was playing, bringing Mom along might be part of it.

"I think she might get to the moon too, I didn't have a chance to ask her before we left. We had to leave in a hurry, remember?"

He shook his head. I didn't expect him to remember anything. Mickey had drugged his ice cream and that had kept him pretty drowsy for half a day.

But whatever else he was, Stinky wasn't stupid. "We're not going to see them anymore, are we? We're going on the brightliner by ourselves."

"Well, Mickey will be with us—I think. Do you like Mickey?"

"Douglas likes him." Which was his way of saying no. Because if he really liked Mickey, he would have said so. Maybe he resented Mickey for the same reasons I did. Or maybe he was just jealous that Douglas was spending so much time with him. Or maybe he just didn't like Mickey for no reason at all.

"Do you miss Mom?" I asked.

"Uh-huh, don't you?"

"Um . . . I don't miss the yelling."

That must have been answer enough, because he changed the subject. "I'm hungry. Do we have anything to eat besides those awful *emmaries?*"

"Not till we get to the moon, kiddo. Sorry."

"Okay. I'll wait."

FINAL APPROACH

AFTER SEVEN OR EIGHT MORE course changes, each one more painful than the last, we finally got a good look at the bright side of the moon. Well, part of it anyway, as we came around the northern edge of the terminator. We still had three more burns to put us into a near-polar orbit, what Alexei called the crazy-mouse orbit, so that meant we'd actually orbit the moon a couple of times—down the front and up the back—before finally heading in.

The second time we came around the bright side, it filled the window, but it was hard to tell how close we were; Douglas said that's because the moon has a fractal surface; there's so many craters of so many different sizes that a close view looks a lot like a high view, and vice versa.

But the landscape below us was moving slowly, so I took that as an indication that we were still fairly high—and when I pressed my face close to the window, I could see the horizon, and it was still curved. So that meant we were at least a hundred klicks high, if I had done the math right. Probably not. Math was not my best subject.

The dark side of the moon was hard to see clearly; there was some light reflected from the crescent Earth, but not enough, so everything looked all gloomy gray. And the bright side, when we crossed the terminator again, was almost too bright to look at directly. Douglas said that the Lunar surface reflects more light back at you when you look at it head-on, and that's why a full moon is noticeably brighter than a half-moon, it's something to do with refraction and the way the Lunar dust scatters light.

Alexei joined us at the window. He took one glance and grunted. "We are coming in very fast. Good."

I took another look. He was right. The ground below us was moving noticeably faster.

"We are looping over top of moon in a few seconds. Look for north pole; there it is—" He pointed toward the horizon. "See those lights near terminator edge? That is north station. Biggest ice mine on Luna. Be sure to wave at the Rock Father."

"The Rock Father?" Stinky asked. "Who's he?"

"You don't know the Rock Father? Shame on you. Is Lunar legend. Lost Russian spaceman, freezes every Lunar night, wakes up every Lunar day. Is immortal. Lives at Lunar North Pole, like Father Christmas, except he has no reindeer, no elves. Rock Father is everyone's Crazy Uncle Loonie. Plays pranks on ice miners. Steals supplies. Rearranges markers. Hides in shadows where no one can see. One time Rock Father even puts up black featureless monolith in Clavius crater. Proportions one by four by nine. Standing on edge. No footprints anywhere around. Make American explorers much crazy. Rock Father laugh forever."

"But why is he called the Rock Father?" That was me.

"Because he is father of all Loonies. The Rock Father answers all prayers. Mostly, the answer is no. But sometimes not. Rock Father is there once in every life. He answers most important prayer—he knows, even if you don't."

"Do we have to make a wish?" Stinky asked.

"Prayers are not wishes," Alexei said. "But most terries don't know the difference. This is why Rock Father hardly ever listens to terries."

He glanced out the window again. "Hokay, enough." He began herding us back to the other end of the pod. "Is now time for everyone to strap in and get ready for landing. I am afraid landing will be rougher than expected. We are coming in faster than I planned. Not too much faster, but enough. This will be more crunch-down than bounce-down. We will rattle a little, but if we precaution properly, we will all be safe—" His PITA beeped, and he shouted, "Whoops—hang on!"

This course change was the longest and roughest one yet. Every-thing rattled and roared and shook. The monkey slipped out of my grasp and was thrown somewhere down below. I was pinned flat against the top of one of the cargo crates. I didn't see where anyone else was, but when it finally stopped Stinky was crying and Douglas was holding him tight. Mickey had a nosebleed, and even Alexei looked a little shaken; he was a skinny undermuscled Loonie; he probably hurt worse than any of us. But I didn't feel too much sympathy for him, because this had been his idea from the beginning. And he'd suckered the rest of us into joining him.

The monkey came climbing up from below—I was thinking of it as below now—and wrapped itself around me. Absentmindedly, I pat-ted its head. When even the robots get scared, you know you're having a rough time.

"We are fine, we are fine," Alexei assured us, a little too quickly. "Mickey, help me please. We must make sure cabin is ready for bounce-down. I will inflate interior balloons manually. I start at bottom and work my way up. You will please secure dingalings in web? Space everybody carefully."

I didn't like the sound of that. I was still worrying about the words *crunch-down*. And Alexei didn't sound all that confident himself.

Mickey started strapping in Stinky. There were elastic belts set into the bulkhead at various places. He pulled several of them across Stinky's chest to form an X-harness with a latch at the center.

"See this button?" Mickey explained. "That's the emergency safety release. Don't press it until after we're down and *after* we stop bounc-ing and rolling. It might take a few minutes. There'll be an all-clear bell. If you don't hear it, don't press the button. Do you understand, Bobby? You wait until we come and get you. Promise?"

"I promise," Stinky said. He said it *that* way, and I already knew how that promise was going to get kept—with him getting loose and bouncing all over the pod as soon as he felt like it. No, Mickey didn't know who he was talking to.

I pulled myself over and faced the devil child squarely. "Listen to me. This is a *real* promise, Bobby—not a pretend one. Not one where you say you promise and then do what you want anyway. If you don't keep this promise, you could get hurt. *Real badly*. You don't want to get hurt, do you?"

"Nuh-uh."

"Then you absolutely must not under any circumstances whatever, no matter what you think, no matter what happens, press that button—not until Mickey comes and tells you it's okay to press it. Okay?"

"Okay," he said.

"Promise?"

"Promise."

"Pinky promise?"

"Pinky promise." We hooked pinkies and shook.

I turned to Mickey. "Is there some way to disable that button or put it where he can't reach it?"

Mickey shook his head. "That would defeat the purpose of the emergency release—"

"He's not going to keep his promise," I said.

"*Will too!*" Stinky shouted at me.

"Will not," I snapped right back.

"*Liar! You big liar! I'll show you!*"

"I'll bet you a million dollars—"

"I'll bet you *a hundred million zillion dollars!*"

"Okay, it's a bet. If you push that button without permission, you owe me a hundred million zillion dollars and your monkey."

"*Not my monkey!* Douglas!"

"Then don't push the button," I said. "Not ever. Not unless Mickey says you can."

Douglas moved between us then. He pushed me back away from Stinky. "Chigger," he whispered. "Was that necessary?"

I whispered right back. "You want him to stay in the harness, no matter what? We're talking about Stinky. Logic and promises won't do it. He'll only do it if he can spite someone."

Douglas got it. "Y'know, he's a lot like you."

"Yeah, I know—that's how I know he'll push the button. *Because I would.*"

Douglas didn't want to argue. There wasn't time anyway. He pulled himself back toward Mickey and whispered something in his ear. Mickey nodded.

Douglas came back to me. "Come on, Charles. It's time to buckle you in. We'll put you in this harness, close to Bobby." He pulled me into position and began pulling straps down, the same way Mickey had strapped in Stinky. "I'll be on the other side. Mickey will be up there, and Alexei will be down there. That should balance the weight fairly evenly."

He struggled with the latches for a bit—he couldn't get the X-harness centered on my chest—until Mickey came over to help. He loosened two of the belts, pushed me sideways, then tightened them again. He leaned in and whispered to me, "You're very convincing, you know that? Douglas thinks we should tranquilize Bobby again. It's safer. It'll make things harder on the ground, someone will have to carry him. But if you really think he can't be trusted—"

I thought about all the times someone had told him not to do something—and how quickly he'd done *exactly* what he'd been forbidden to do. Like running down into the Barringer Meteor Crater. Like calling Mom from One-Hour station after Dad had told him not to. He did this stuff deliberately—as if to prove that no one could control him. *No one.*

Mickey saw it in my face. "I really hate to do it to a little kid like that . . ."

"He's *not* a little kid," I said. "His middle name is Caligula."

Mickey sighed. "All right. Do you want a sedative too? This could get pretty rough."

I considered it. I thought about all the burns we'd already been through. It was very tempting. But . . . I shook my head. "I'd better not."

"You sure?"

"No. Yes. You said it's going to be hard enough to carry Stinky. Who's going to carry me?"

"Good point." He finished securing me in the webbing. "I was hoping you would say that, but Douglas asked me to make the offer. That's pretty courageous of you, Charles. Here, put this O-mask over your face."

"Oxygen—?"

"Just a precaution, to make sure you have an air supply after we blow the inflatables. Whoops—you have company." He was talking about the monkey, it was just climbing its way back up to me—pulling itself hand over hand through the webbing. I was glad I'd programmed it to home in on me. I would never have been able to find it otherwise, not in the mess of this cluttered cargo pod.

"I'll strap it in with you," Mickey said, tucking it into the webbing and pulling a safety belt around to secure it. To the monkey, he said,

"Don't push this button, unless Chigger tells you. Do you understand?"

The monkey made a face at him—crossing its eyes and curling both its lips back. Neither of us had any idea what the expression meant.

Alexei came back then and helped Mickey strap in Douglas. We must have been running out of time, they both were pretty urgent in their movements. When they finished, Alexei double-checked Stinky, then went to his own landing station and webbed in as quickly as he could. "Are you secured, Mikhail?" he called.

"I'm good," said Mickey.

"Hokay!" hollered the mad Russian lunatic. "Get ready for bubbles—" He snapped a code word to his PITA, and a second later, the inflatables began filling the cargo pod—hundreds of self-inflating balloons. They came bubbling up from the other end of the cargo pod, filling every available space so tightly it would have been impossible to move, even if we weren't webbed in. The bubbles pressed up against my face like someone holding a pillow over my nose. I was grateful for the O-mask. The packing bubbles would have suffocated me.

It made me uneasy to be so completely immobilized. All I could see was bubbles—the bluish light of the pod was fractured like a hall of mirrors; it was like looking into shattered winter. And it was cold in the pod too. We'd had to turn off our blankets for the bounce-down.

"Stand by!" hollered Alexei. His voice came muffled through the bubbles. "We begin braking now. It will be rough—"

BOUNCE-DOWN

I THINK I PASSED OUT. I wasn't sure. One moment I was trying to scream and the next moment everything was eerily silent. "What's happening now?" I called. I don't think anybody heard me.

But a moment later, Alexei's voice came muffled through the cabin. "We burn off speed. We have come around very fast. Must burn off more speed. Twice more speed. Aim at surface, dive to landing site, then brake hard for last kilometer down. Is very nasty maneuver, but only way to get to safe house. Very safe house."

I couldn't believe he was conscious. Of all of us, Alexei seemed the weakest. He was tall and gangly and skinny—he didn't have the muscles for Earth gravity, and I'd assumed he didn't have the endurance either. Living so long in lesser gravity, his bones should have softened, his heart should have shrunk.

It made me wonder if he had been working out in the high-gee levels at Geostationary. Despite all his disclaimers, he must have been; he was handling the heavy gees better than any of us. Maybe he'd been preparing for this kind of escape for a long time. Just how much illegal stuff was he involved in anyway?

"What next?" I shouted.

Alexei had explained the operation to all of us, more than once, but I still wanted to hear him confirm the successful completion of each phase of it.

"More braking—"

"I'm already broken," Douglas gasped.

I was glad that Stinky was tranquilized. I don't think I could have stood it if he were screaming and crying and I couldn't get to him. That business at the meteor crater had been bad enough—I still had nightmares. Even so, I thought I could hear him whimpering in his sleep. The poor little kid, I almost felt sorry for him—everything he was going through. It had to be worse on him than any of the rest of us.

Alexei's PITA beeped. I started gasping for as much breath as I could before the rockets kicked in—

—this time I did pass out. I woke up to the sound of Alexei's PITA beeping again. I was beginning to hate the sound of that thing. I had just enough time to say, "Oh, sh—" and then the rockets fired again.

I didn't remember waking up after the next one. I was just awake and cussing, spewing every dreadful word that I'd ever gotten my mouth washed out for using. The third time I repeated myself, I stopped to take a breath.

"Is impressive. For a thirteen-year-old."

I ignored him. "Is anyone else alive?" I called.

"Yo," said Mickey.

"I'd ask if you're all right," called Douglas, "but nobody who's seriously hurt cusses that enthusiastically."

"What about Bobby?"

"He's not making any noises," called Mickey.

"He is fine," said Alexei. "I am certain."

"Can you see him?"

"Please not to worry. Little stinking one is fine."

"*Don't call him Stinky!*" I said. And wondered where that came from. There was a sound from Douglas. Laughter? Probably. But only family members had the right to call him Stinky. No one else. And only when he really deserved it.

"We will be down soon," Alexei said. "You will see for yourself, everyone is fine."

"Where are we now?"

"We have broken orbit. We have fired twice to dive in toward bounce target. Only one more burn—the last one. We brake hard to burn off speed. And then we bounce."

"You hope—" But I said it under my breath. I was saving most of my air for breathing.

Alexei heard it anyway. "You will like Luna, Charles. I promise. No bad weather. No weather at all—"

And then his damn PITA went off again.

This was the worst one of all—at least the worst one that I was conscious for. The noise was unbearable. Even if I could have stuffed my fingers into my ears, it wouldn't have done any good, the whole pod was roaring and shaking and rattling. *Whose good idea was this anyway?*

And this time, I had a very clear idea of the direction of *down*. It was directly in front of me. All the packing bubbles were pushing up against us—we were hanging from the top of the cargo pod, while several hundred tons of widgets and whatnots trembled ominously only three meters away. Those crates were *aching* to break free of the violent deceleration and smash upward into our faces. Just how strong were those foam dollops anyway?

And finally when I was convinced that the incredible noise would never end, *it did.*

We were in free fall again.

But only for a few seconds.

Something went *bang* on the outside of the cargo pod. A whole bunch of things went *bang.* The "Lunar parachutes." The external inflatables. Alexei had explained this too. We were landing on balloons. A whole cluster of them. Very strong, very flexible. From the outside, the cargo pod would look like a plastic raspberry.

Depending on our angle and speed, and the kind of terrain we were landing on, we could bounce for five or ten klicks. Alexei said that usually, you try to undershoot the target and bounce the rest of the way to your final destination. He said that some pods had bounced over fifteen kilometers from their initial touch-down points, but that those kinds of bounce-downs were carefully planned. The pods had come in very fast, and at a very shallow angle—and they were aimed down a long slope or something like that.

But we wouldn't have that kind of ride, for which I was very grateful. The target zone had a lot of rough terrain, and Alexei wanted to minimize our bouncing—so as soon as it was safe, the pod was programmed to deflate the balloons and let us just crunch in. I wondered what Alexei's definition of *safe* was. I hoped that Armstrong was telling the truth when he said, "It's soft and powdery. I can kick it with my foot."

And then we hit—*bumped*—something. The impact came from the side, and it was hard enough to knock the breath out of me with an audible *Oof!* I heard Alexei say something that sounded like "*Gohvno!*" I got the sense that *gohvno* was something I didn't want to step in.

And then we were in free fall again—or maybe not. But we were still airborne—except there isn't any air on Luna, and we weren't being borne by anything—we were just up.

And then down. We bounced again—this time from the other side and even harder than before. The whole pod went *crunch!*

And then we were up again—floating for a long agonizing moment—until *crunchbang!* We bounced again. I couldn't believe the balloons were working. This hurt!

Floated and bounced, bounced, bounced—and then abruptly crunched to a stop—was that it? Were we down? We were hanging sideways and upside down in the webbing—

I fumbled for the release. It was hard to move; we were still pinned by the packing bubbles. They smelled of canned air.

"Don't anyone move—" shouted Alexei. "We're not done yet."

We waited in silence for a moment.

Nothing happened.

"Douglas?"

No answer.

"Mickey?"

I called louder.

"Ymf," said Mickey.

"What's happening?"

"Wait," said Alexei.

The cargo pod *lurched.* Sideways. "Is the balloons. Rearranging selves. Everybody wait."

"Douglas? *Douglas—?*" Where was *Douglas?* I had this sudden nightmare knowledge that he had died in the crash. Then I would be really *alone.*

"Is not to worry. Nobody is dead," said Alexei. "Everybody wait! Pod must settle itself!" The pod continued to shudder and jerk and bump. Slowly, it began to hump itself upright. The pod was pumping air from balloon to balloon, pushing itself up with plastic muscles.

"Everybody stay still," said Alexei. Like we had a choice.

I was still worried about Douglas. "Mickey? Can you see Douglas? Is he all right?"

After a moment, Mickey called back. "He's fine. He's groaning."

The pressure on my chest began to ease. The packing bubbles

were starting to wilt, slowly deflating. I guessed they were timed or something.

Finally, the cargo pod groaned and settled itself. "Please to wait—" cautioned Alexei. It bumped and lurched one more time, then sagged into an exhausted upright position. We were hanging from the webbing at the top. The only good news was the Lunar gravity. One-sixth Earth normal. It felt . . . strange and easy at the same time.

As soon as he decided it was safe—and not soon enough for me— Alexei unbuckled himself and began climbing around the webbing like a human spider. He unbuckled Mickey first. Mickey's face was covered with blood. He held a soggy red handkerchief over his nose. He must have had a nosebleed all the way down.

"I go find first-aid kit," said Alexei. "You take care of dingalings." He dropped down between two of the crates, and we heard the packing bubbles squeak and squeal and pop as he pushed his way through. It was a funny noise. It sounded like someone with water in his boots, squelching through a sewer. The canned air smell got stronger.

Mickey lowered himself to a crate, standing knee deep in squooshy balloons. He picked his way over to stand beneath me. Still holding his head back, still holding the hanky over his nose, he called up to me. "Can you free yourself, Charles?"

"I think so."

"You'll have to help me with Douglas. We'll lower him to the top of the crates. All right?"

"All right." I fumbled around with the latch for a moment—it wasn't hard to unbuckle, but my hands were shaking so badly from the landing that I couldn't coordinate. Finally, I managed to free myself—

I was never very good at gymnastics, but in Lunar gravity, everything was so surprisingly easy that I wished we could have had gym class on the moon, it was a lot more fun. I hung from the webbing without any effort at all. I did the math in my head; I weighed nine kilos.

Mickey pointed and I went hand over hand to Douglas. He looked pale, but he was breathing steadily into his O-mask. I wondered if he'd passed out during braking or if he'd bumped himself unconscious during landing, a concussion would be very bad news, but we wouldn't know until we got him out of the webbing.

Mickey stood just below me, still holding his hanky to his nose. He gave me careful instructions, step by step, how to lower Douglas without dropping him. Even though falling three meters in Lunar gravity is no worse than falling half a meter on Earth, we still didn't want to take any chances. People had broken noses, arms, legs, and hips by underestimating Lunar gravity—especially after prolonged free fall. And we were all very shaky from the bounce-down.

"Lower him feet first, Charles. Grab him under his arms and hold him till I get his legs. I know it's awkward, but he should be light enough that you can handle him. All right, ready?" Mickey started to take his handkerchief away from his nose, but it was still bleeding too badly.

"Maybe we should wait until Alexei gets back. Let him do it."

"I can manage. We'll do it quickly. Wait a minute." He wiped at his nose for a second, then looked up. "Okay, ready?"

"Ready." I unbuckled Douglas with one hand, then reached and grabbed him before he could fall out of the webbing. He started to slip out of my grasp, but I caught him by the collar and held on. That was enough. Mickey grabbed his legs and lowered him.

Still hanging from the webbing, I scrambled over to check on Stinky. He was sleeping like a baby, and almost as cute. "Leave him there for now," called Mickey. "Let's take care of Douglas first."

I let go of the webbing and dropped down to the top of the crates. I dropped impossibly slow. It was *amazing*. We really were on the moon! I hit a little harder than I expected, and I bounced almost all the way back up, laughing with delight. Mickey gave me a nasty look. "There'll be time enough for that later." He put his hand back to his nose.

Alexei came climbing back then and yanked me out of the air. "Learn to walk before you fly," he said. He popped open the first-aid kit and began pawing through it. "Here, this will stop nosebleed very fast." He held up a tiny spray bottle, and Mickey tilted his head back.

While they did that, I went rummaging in the kit for old-fashioned smelling salts. I found a little flat packet of ammonia, cracked its spine, and held it under Douglas's nose—he didn't react. I waved it under his nose again—*come on, Douglas!* I was ready to jam it up his nostril when he suddenly flinched and said, "Stop it, Charles!" He made a terrible face and pushed me away with both hands.

He sat up, still wrinkling his nose in disgust as he looked around. He blinked in surprise. "What happened to you, Mickey?"

"Ahhh," said Alexei, turning around. "The dead have come back to life. Welcome to Luna! My home sweet home!"

STEPPING OUT

MICKEY FINALLY GAVE UP and put cotton up each nostril and a clip on his nose to pin his nostrils together. He'd just have to breathe through his mouth for a while.

The funny thing was, he'd been trained in all kinds of safety procedures on the Line, so he was practically a space doctor. Alexei was equally well trained, so you'd have thought between the two of them they could have figured something out—but apparently the low air pressure in the pod, combined with the lighter gravity and everything else, made this particular nosebleed slow to heal. But we couldn't sit around waiting for Mickey to stop dripping. Alexei was certain about that. We'd lose the advantage of our landing.

The two of them pulled a variety of instruments out of the first-aid kit and began checking everyone out. Ears, eyes, nose, blood pressure, blood gas, adrenaline, blood-sugar levels, I didn't know what else. Except for a lot of residual jitters, we all checked out normal. As normal as possible under these conditions.

Finally, Douglas and Alexei bounced up to the webbing and brought Stinky down, and Mickey checked him out too. He was fine, but he'd be asleep for several hours longer. I whistled a few notes from Beethoven's Seventh Symphony—what I called the Johnny-One-Note theme; it wouldn't sound like a melody to anyone who didn't recognize the theme, just some vague tuneless whistling—but it was a clear signal to the monkey. It came bouncing down to join us. It squatted next to Stinky and pretended to take his pulse. Or maybe it wasn't pretending—I remembered reading in the instructions that it was supposed to be a pretty good baby monitor. It would howl for help if a baby stopped breathing or had a temperature or something like that. But if it was seriously checking Stinky, then it wasn't finding anything wrong with him. It sat back on its haunches and waited patiently.

For a damn stupid toy, it sure had a terrific repertoire. And it was smart enough to know when to stay out of the way. Maybe it listened to stress levels in human voices. Or maybe it just sniffed for fear. Douglas might know. Maybe I'd remember to ask him later.

"All right," said Alexei, looking at his PITA. "We have not a lot of time. We must get moving quickly. Is everybody ready for nice walk? Everybody go to bathroom, whether you have to go or not. I mean it. You are constipated from free fall. Once you start bouncing on the moon, everything shakes down. Is not fun bouncing with pants full of poop." He practically stood over each of us to make sure we complied.

Once that business was taken care of, he started snapping out orders in Russian to his PITA. It projected a map of the local terrain on the bulkhead. "We are lucky childrens. We have not got too far to go. Here, see? *Da?* We go here to Prospector's Station. We change clothes, we look like ice miners. We catch train, we go to Gagarin City. Much good food. You like borscht? With cabbage and lamb, one bowl is whole meal. I am hungry already. Come, climb down now to bottom of cabin. Bring everything useful. We will not be coming back. Grab food and water, all you can carry. Mickey, bring first-aid kit too. Waste not, want not." He disappeared between the crates again, but his voice came floating up, issuing a long string of orders. The packing bubbles began squelching again.

"Can you take Bobby down?" Douglas asked Mickey. Mickey nodded. I looked to Douglas, concerned. He wouldn't have asked that unless he still felt pretty bad.

"Are you all right?" I asked.

"I'll be fine. I just need a little time."

I whistled for the monkey—"*Who's Afraid of the Big Bad Wolf?*"— and it jumped onto my shoulders for a piggyback ride. I followed Mickey and Douglas down through the crates and webbing, down through the big foam plugs and the still-deflating bubbles. This sure wasn't space travel the way we saw it on TV.

When we got to the bottom of the pod, the footing was uneasy and squishy because of all the collapsed packing bubbles. I tried to peek out the windows, but there was nothing to see—only the sides of the landing balloons, plastered hard against the glass.

Alexei was pulling orange webbing off the walls. "Everybody carries his own luggage here. No robots, no porters. Luckily, we have portable pockets." He turned around, lengths of netting drifting from his hands. "Who is to carry littlest dingaling?"

"I will," said Douglas.

Mickey looked to him. "Are you sure you can handle it?"

Douglas wasn't all that certain about it, but he nodded anyway. "I'd better carry him. When he wakes up, he'll feel safer with me."

"Good point."

Alexei was rigging harnesses out of the webbing—apparently it had been designed for this purpose too. Douglas took off his blanket-poncho, and Alexei began hanging webbing on him. Mickey made sure that Stinky's blanket was turned on again, and as soon as Alexei was done, he secured Stinky in the improvised harness on Douglas's back. Then they started packing oxygen bottles, rebreathers, food, and water, into the webbing on his front. Also some medical supplies. Probably more sedatives. Finally, Mickey pulled a pair of goggles down onto Douglas's head and fitted them carefully over his eyes; then he helped Douglas put his poncho back on so it covered everything. With Stinky on his back, he looked like a fat shiny beetle.

That done, Alexei and Mickey began sorting everything else into equal packages of supplies. Everyone had to carry his own air, food, and water. I picked up one of the packs to test the weight and was astonished (again) by how light it felt.

"You are still thinking Earth gravity," said Alexei. "But you will get used to Luna very quickly. Take off your blanket now."

Mickey secured one pack on my back and another on my front. The one on my front had two oxygen bottles and a rebreather. He put goggles on me just like Douglas's—they completely covered my eyes and were held on by a thick elastic band; the elastic had padded cups that closed over my ears like expensive headphones. Finally, Mickey pulled the blanket-poncho back over my head, fastened it, and turned it on—I hadn't even realized how cold I was getting. I thought all my shivering was still from the shock of landing. The monkey bounced onto my shoulders and settled itself happily. I barely noticed its weight.

Alexei and Mickey outfitted themselves with even more stuff. Alexei was wearing his scuba suit again; it covered his whole body like a giant rubber glove, but he looked odd without fins on his feet. He had a lot of other gear too, a lot of closed equipment that I couldn't tell what it was for, and even a couple of suitcaselike boxes that he wouldn't let anyone else carry.

"Isn't that heavy—?" I started to ask, then shut up.

Alexei grinned. "You learn fast." He popped open a bright red panel and began pulling out flat packages the size and shape of seat cushions. "Everybody gets his own personal bubble. Read safety instructions, dingalings. No smoking. No shoes with cleats. No handball. Use plastic bags for peeing and pooping. Same as in pod. Put all trash in proper receptacles. If you fart, is your problem, not mine."

The bubble had a flexible circular opening just big enough to fit around a full-grown person. Mickey helped me into mine; it was like climbing into a giant condom. I even wondered aloud what would fit into a condom this big. Without missing a beat, Mickey replied, "You know what that makes you . . . ?"

Once inside the bubble, everything looked blurred through the transparent material. The bubble was made out of three separate layers of Mylar, each one "sturdy enough to support life under conditions of normal usage"—although I wasn't sure what "normal usage" actually meant in these circumstances. Each layer had its own zipper, and they could be opened in series from either inside or out.

Alexei showed us how the bubbles were designed so that they could be linked together, so two people could pass things back and forth if they had to, but it was a tricky operation, and he hoped we wouldn't have to. He also showed us how to use the glove-extensions that were designed into the walls of the bubble—that was in case you needed to handle something outside.

As soon as everybody was bubbled up, Alexei stepped over to one of the sidewalls of the cargo pod. He put his hands through the plastic gloves—"Always use gloves!" he shouted. "Don't try to push buttons through wall of bubble. Very stupid. You know what we call people who do? Statistics. Okay, I open airlock now." He started pressing buttons on the circular cover of the closest hatch.

I watched with interest. Alexei hadn't explained this part. I knew there was no airlock *inside* this cabin, and there was certainly no airlock on the *outside*. The only thing on the other side of that bulkhead was hard Lunar vacuum.

The hatch cover popped open and slid sideways on its tracks, re-vealing—the inside of a matching hatch cover on the other side of the bulkhead. "Okay, get ready for more beautiful clever—" Alexei unclip-ped a panel on the wall and pulled out two white circular rings, just the right size to fit into the hatch; they held layers of mylar folded over and over into a fat bulge—the whole looked like a plastic tunnel, all collapsed. On each side, there were three zippers, kind of like our bub-ble suits. Alexei opened one set of zippers, but not the other.

He slipped the rings into the space between the two hatches, then began fitting the ring on our side into a deep groove. The edge of the ring was as thick as a tube of toothpaste, but not quite as squishy; Alexei worked his way around the circle, pushing it firmly into place.

When he had the ring fitted all the way around the hatch-groove, he reached up above the hatch with one hand and below the hatch with the other, and pulled two matching levers sideways—the edges of the hatch-groove tightened firmly on the ring. Then he went around the circle again—three times, pressing the edge hard and making sure that the grip was firm all the way around.

Finally satisfied, he slid the hatch cover back into place and sealed it. "We wait now, for ninety seconds. We wait for seal to harden and test itself. Thirty seconds should be enough, but on Luna we do every-thing three times safely. Remember, universe does not give first warn-ings or second chances." We waited in silence. Finally, Alexei looked at his PITA. "Okay, ready?—eighty-eight, eighty-nine, ninety!"

He turned to a panel next to the hatch and unclipped its safety cover. He unlocked a second safety cover within and pressed the top button. It lit up, and said, "Armed." He pressed the next button, and it flashed, "Opening." We heard and felt the outer door of the hatch pop-ping open and sliding sideways.

Alexei peered through a peephole in the hatch itself, then began turning a small valve next to it. We heard the hissing of air. "I am filling airlock now," he said. "We let air from cabin inflate outside bal-loon. Very simple. We use cabin air. Waste not, want not. You will no-tice pressure change, maybe. As we increase space for air, we get lower pressure throughout total environment. Are you noticing? I can feel it. But Loonies are more sensitive than terries. We grow up that way."

I watched, but I couldn't tell that anything was happening. After a bit, the plastic bubbles we wore seemed a little puffier, but not very much. And then my ears popped.

The hissing continued slowly. From time to time, Alexei peered through the peephole again, checking to make sure the airlock was inflating properly. I wondered how he could see clearly through the plastic bubble he wore, but apparently he wasn't having any trouble. Our bubbles puffed a little more, but mostly they still hung on us like big plastic wrappers.

After a bit, Alexei grunted in satisfaction and popped the hatch again. He slipped his goggles into place and slid the door sideways against the inner hull. Bright Lunar sunlight came filtering in through the opening. On the other side was a plastic tube opening into the airlock, a big plastic bubble. I peered through the hatch in curiosity, to see how it all worked. There were three zippers in the tube so it could be triple-sealed, the same ones Alexei had unzipped before inflating it. Clever.

"Make sure your goggles are on tight," advised Mickey. "It's going to get very bright." He reached over and tapped one of my earcups through the plastic. "And don't take these off or you won't be able to hear anything. This is also your communicator."

"I'm not stupid—" I started to say.

"Sorry, Charles. I didn't mean to suggest you were. It's part of the safety briefing. Required by law and all that. Can you hear me through your headphones? Are you ready?"

I nodded.

"Good. All right, I'll go first, then Douglas and Bobby, then you, Charles. Alexei will be last. Charles, Douglas—you want to be very careful coming through the hatch; it's all plastic on the other side—I'll help you through. If you feel any resistance, stop. Don't try to push or force your way through. You don't want to risk tearing the Mylar. It's strong, but there have been stupid accidents. Oh, and before you do anything else, put your gloves on and make sure you can do this—" Mickey held up his hands and wriggled his fingers. "Until you're inflated, you want to keep your hands available."

He watched carefully to make sure that Douglas and I followed suit. I found the closest set of gloves in my bubble, unzipped the covering patch, and shoved my hands through.

The hatch was only a meter and a half wide. Mickey would have had to bend down to step through it, but instead he scrooched low and dived straight through. He slapped the ground with his hands and bounced gracefully upright, turning around to face us and spreading his arms like an acrobat who'd just completed a difficult trick and was expecting applause. He grinned through the hatch at us.

"I can do that." I started to step forward—but Alexei grabbed me by the plastic and pulled me back. "Douglas next," he said.

The hatch was almost too small for Douglas—he had four oxygen bottles and two rebreathers strapped to his chest; air for him and Stinky both; and he had Stinky on his back.

But it turned out to be a lot easier than I expected. Alexei told Douglas to hold himself straight, then he picked him up, turned him horizontal, and passed him carefully through the hatch like a stick of wood. Together, he and Stinky and all their supplies must have weighed less than fifteen kilograms. All that Alexei had to do was lift, turn, and push. Douglas went right through. Mickey grabbed Douglas on the other side and turned him upright. Through the hatch, I saw the two of them exchange a quick hug.

Then it was my turn. I lowered my goggles into place, stepped forward—the body condom made moving a little sluggish, even in low gee—but I was determined to dive through the same way I'd seen Mickey dive. But before I could, Alexei grabbed me, turned me sideways, and threw me through the hatch like a torpedo.

Four hands grabbed me on the other side, both Mickey and Douglas at the same time. They stood me up like a cardboard statue.

I looked around in amazement. We were inside a big round bubble, almost the size of the cargo pod.Maybe bigger. It was hard to estimate the volume of a giant balloon from the inside. An inflatable airlock! Beautiful clever! Just like Alexei said.

The bubble had two portals. The one I'd come through was a tube that led back to the cargo pod. On the opposite side of the airlock, the other portal was still zipped tight. Even as I turned to look back, Alexei was already diving in. He bounced upright, just as Mickey had. Behind him, the pod was a big lumpy shape, a dark cylinder with plump landing balloons sticking out all over it.

Beyond the blank wall of the bubble, everything was blurred—of course. I was looking through the plastic bubble I wore *and* the wall of the airlock at the same time. Even so, I could make out the raw shapes of things, both dark and bright.

Above, the sky was pure black. Impossibly black. To one side, there was a glare so intense I couldn't even turn in that direction—my eyes watered just from the sideways brightness. But to the other side, there was a shining silver land with an impossibly close horizon!

I stood and gaped. Uneven rolling surface, broken rocks, jagged lumpy outcrops. A rising wall of mountains off to one side. And every-where—stark silence! *We really were on the moon!*

Wow!

Whatever else happened, I didn't care. Dad had kept his promise, even if he wasn't here, and I was suddenly filled with a rush of hot feelings. I wanted to thank him. He should have been here. He de-served to be here. And for a moment, I wished he *were* here—I wished I had someone to share this with.

Wow was insufficient.

This was . . . *the moon!*

Did Luna affect everyone this way?

And then I started laughing. I suddenly knew why Alexei was so crazy. I understood what it meant to be a *Lunatic*.

WUNDERSTORM

WE MUST HURRY." ALEXEI'S VOICE was loud in my ears. It sounded like he was directly behind me; the sound in my earphones was processed to come from the same direction as the broadcast signal, the only audio cues possible on the moon. I turned around to see him sealing the inner hatch of the cargo pod. That was it, the door was shut, we weren't going back. He bounced himself across the bubble to the opposite side—to the other airlock portal.

As he began opening the first zipper, he asked, "Who goes first? Mickey, do you want honor? Or you, Charles? Do you want to be first dingaling on moon?"

"Huh? Me?" I looked around. Maybe he meant some other Charles . . . ?

Douglas said, "Go ahead, Chigger. If you want."

"Uh—" I was about to say no, I wanted Mickey to go first, but I didn't want to look afraid either. "Okay," I gulped. Before I could change my mind, Alexei pulled me to the outer portal; it was identical to the one we'd just come through, only still folded up tight.

"Is close fit," he said. "I walk you through it, one step at a time. No fear, *da*?"

"*Da*."

"Good. Now we open one zipper, one zipper only—like so, *da*? Nothing more. Not yet." Very carefully, very slowly, he unsealed the first section of the tube. As the first air puffed into it, it inflated outward. "You step into tube now, Charles. No fear, okay?"

"Okay." I stepped carefully forward. It was hard to walk while wrapped in a personal bubble—I had to bounce more than walk, but maybe I could do this, with a little practice.

Alexei pushed me into the tube. I almost filled it. "Hokay, ready? I zip you up now. Watch how I do this. I pat out as much air as possible. Waste not, want not. You want tube tight around you please." He locked the zipper into place and I was sealed in the tube.

"Now turn around and face next zipper, Charles. Unzip it just like I show you. Just like that, *da*. Very good."

The next section of the tube puffed out like the previous one. I stepped into it and began pulling it close to me. As I zipped up the section behind me, I tried hard to keep the plastic close and push as much air as possible back into the tube. "Very good, Charles!" Alexei's voice came mostly through the earphones now.

As soon as the second zipper was locked in place, I turned around to the third and last one. This was *it*. One more step and I'd be alone on the Lunar surface. For a moment, I hesitated. . . .

"Go ahead, Chigger. You can do it." That was Douglas. I was glad he said that.

"Is good now, little dingaling. Open last zipper."

I swallowed hard. The seal was just in front of my face. All I had to do was grab it, unclick it from its safety catch, and pull it down. But it was more difficult than I thought. Sitting on my head, the monkey suddenly hugged me close. Did it understand? It patted the top of my head three times. Just like Douglas sometimes did.

Well, if even the monkey believed in me . . .

I pulled the zipper down—

—and my bubble puffed out around me. I was in a two-meter balloon. My ears popped at the sudden change in pressure. The tube spit me out like a watermelon seed, and I bounced across the Lunar surface, screaming in shock—then laughing in hysterical relief. It *was* funny.

"Don't go bouncing!" Alexei and Mickey both screamed at once. "Stay where you are. Wait for us."

"I'm not doing it on purpose!" I shouted back. I turned around to look at them. I was farther away than I thought. Ten meters, at least. I could see how small the cargo pod was—and the inflatable airlock too.

That was a scary moment—not because I worried that we were in any danger, but because for the first time I was *separated* from everything else. I was *alone* on the moon.

I still had my hands in the gloves of the bubble suit. I went down on one knee and reached out to *touch* the ground. Armstrong had been right—it *was* soft and powdery! Strong tears of emotion started welling up in my eyes. *Luna!*

The monkey patted me on the head again, three more times. Just like Douglas. So it wasn't an accident.

I stood up and looked around, being careful not to face the glare from the northeastern horizon, where the sun was just creeping over the edge of a rill. It would be creeping over that rill for a long time. Sunrise on the moon was fourteen times longer than sunrise on the Earth.

More to the north, there was something large and bright *and blue* in the black sky. The *Earth.*

How beautiful it was.

Half of it was cloaked in shadow, the other half was gleaming with day. Beneath the streaks of white cloud, I could make out the eastern shoreline of Africa. That big lumpy shape was Madagascar, wasn't it? I thought about all the horrors we'd left behind; they must be raging across the planet even now. But it looked so peaceful from here—how could anything on that soft blue world be horrible? It looked so fragile. For a moment, I regretted leaving. If I'd spoken one word differently, we could have all been home by now—

Home in a cramped tube. With Mom yelling at us. And the wind whistling overhead. And the whole house vibrating like an organ pipe.

No. I wouldn't have traded this moment for anything.

The moon.

I wished I could have said something more meaningful, but it all just came out as a single syllable—*wow.*

I'd seen people talk about this on television—that sense of awe that you feel whenever you arrive on a new world. Ferris, the most famous astronaut of all, said it best. "It doesn't matter how many previous landings you've made. Every landing is different, and every time, you're filled with a flood of so many different emotions at once, so powerful and so profound, that the only word that comes close to describing it is *wunderstorm.*"

Once he came to our school and he talked about the first landing

on Mars. He compared it to looking at a landscape by van Gogh—
Wheatfield with Crows. The first time you look at it, what you see is
startling, and then it's even more startling, and then as you start to
look at it closely, you realize just how startling it really is. The light is
different—not wrong, *different.* And after a bit of puzzling, you begin
to realize that this is an uncompromising vision; it isn't going to meet
you halfway. You have to go all the way there or not at all. You have
to surrender to it, because you can't change it. And then, only when
you accept it on its own terms, can you see how beautiful it really is.

I could understand that. It's kind of like the music of Stravinsky
or Coltrane or Hendrix. The first time you hear it, it doesn't make
sense. You have to learn how to listen to it. Eventually, you have to
accept it for what it is, not for what you think it should be.

And now I could see that the moon is like that too. It is what it is.
Everything is different than what you're used to. Not wrong, *different.*
The sky, the light, the horizon, even the shapes of rocks. Even the way
the ground rolls away is different. *Everything.* Uncompromising.
Scary. Harsh. Hostile. Beautiful.

Wunderstorm . . .

"Luna to Charles, Luna to Charles. Come in, Charles. . . . ?"

"Huh?" I turned around. The unreality of everything was getting
more intense, not less. Mickey was already out of the inflatable airlock;
he was standing in his own two-meter bubble, helping Douglas through
the exit tube. Stinky was a big inert bulge on Douglas's back. Douglas
unzipped the third zipper and puffed out into the Lunar vacuum like a
big piece of popcorn. He didn't go bouncing across the ground like I
did—Mickey caught him head-on, and they bounced back only a meter.

Alexei was the last one out of the balloon. He puffed up, but he
didn't bounce at all. Obviously, he'd had a lot of experience. He hop-
skipped around to where the airlock was still connected to the cargo
pod and began zipping shut the seals of the connection tube.

"What's Alexei doing?" I asked.

"I am disconnecting airlock," he called.

"But why? What if we have to get back in the pod?"

"We are not coming back to pod. It won't be here anyway. But if
we did need to reenter, is another airlock package here by outside
hatch." He slapped the hull of the pod.

Alexei pushed the bubble up against the cargo hull to force as
much air into the main part of the inflatable as he could, collapsing and

sealing each section of the tube in turn. When the tube was folded back into itself and all three connections were secure, he turned to the hatch of the cargo pod. He reached up and down at the same time and grabbed two levers matching the ones on the inside of the pod. He yanked them sideways and the slot in the hatch ring widened, releasing its grip on the circular ring of the airlock.

Then he worked the ring loose carefully. Once it was clear, he pushed it up against the wall of the inflatable, securing it with Velcro patches. The airlock sat alone on the barren Lunar soil, a big bulbous blob of air—like a single drop of water perched on a waxy leaf. We didn't have to worry about it blowing away, of course, but the ground wasn't very level, and if it started rolling downhill, it might start bouncing, and it could go quite a distance. It might even rip or puncture.

But Alexei turned around, grinning. "Who wants to hold leash? Charles? Is good job for you, *da*?"

"Huh?"

"We take airlock with us. You never know when you might need a roomful of air. Waste not, want not, *da*?"

I was beginning to hate that. I wanted to waste something, just for spite.

He bounded over to me in that peculiar Lunar hop-skip of his. He trailed a length of flat ribbon, which he slapped onto one of the Velcro pads on the outside of my bubble suit. "There. You will bring plastic house. Is everybody ready to go? Hokay, we practice Luna walk. Pay attention, dingalings. Bounce on balls of feet like this, *da*? Not too high. Cannot walk in bubble, have to hop-skip, have to bounce. Looks easy, *da*? Is not. Is tricky. Alternate feet—bounce on one, bounce on other— hop-skip. No, Charles—keep hands in gloves. Helps keep bubble upside up. See bottom side? Extra thick—heavy on bottom to keep bottom side down. Bounce on padding, less risk to rip or puncture. Hold bubble upright by keeping hands in front gloves and bounce, hop-skip—watch, now!"

He came bounding toward me. He looked like a silver beetle trapped inside a glass onion. But he made very good time, bouncing and skipping across the dark silvery dust.

"You will learn quickly. But try not to fall down. You don't want to dust your bubble."

"Why not?"

"Because then everybody will know you are clumsy dingaling. They will know you are just arrive here." He turned away to see how Douglas and Mickey were doing. "Yes, just like that," he called. They were bouncing slightly on the balls of their feet, testing their weight in the soft Lunar gravity. They moved in slow motion—almost like dancers. I thought of Tchaikovsky and the *"Waltz of the Flowers."* No, the other one—the *"Waltz of the Snowflakes."* Only these snowflakes were silvery and danced inside giant transparent Christmas tree ornaments. We must have looked very silly, but at the same time beautiful in a Lunar kind of way.

"All right, everybody ready? Let us go. Take small steps first. Get used to Lunatic-walking. Learn to walk before learning to bounce. Follow me. Holler if I go too fast." He pointed southward and went bounding off. Douglas followed, little steps first, then as he felt more comfortable, he began taking bigger hops. Mickey looked back to me. "Come on, Charles—"

I took one last look at the bright blue marble of the Earth. It was directly behind us. And then I followed. The inflatable airlock came bouncing after me like an oversize balloon.

A WALK IN THE DARK

WE DIDN'T GET VERY FAR—just to the top of the first hill. And it wasn't much of a hill. Alexei made us stop so he could check our rebreathers and our air supplies again. We were all fine, but if any of us had needed personal attention, he would have taken us into the inflatable so he could open our bubbles. Even if we didn't have the inflatable with us, he could have still joined any two bubbles together at their openings. But nobody needed immediate attention, and I was glad about that.

Once that was finished, Alexei turned and faced the distant cargo pod. From here it looked pitifully small in a very large landscape. Despite the nearness of the horizon, once you gained a little height, the moon could be a very large place.

As Alexei had told us, there were no footprints leading away from the pod—just occasional soft dimples in the Lunar dust where we'd bounced along. A skilled tracker would be able to follow the trail of depressions, but only if the dust was thick enough and the shadows were right.

"Might want to shield eyes," Alexei said, and did something to his PITA.

"Huh? Why?" That was Douglas.

"Watch." He pointed.

In the distance, the cargo pod shuddered. It jerked upright—then a flare of dazzling white appeared underneath it, and the cargo pod lifted away from the gray plain.

"What are you doing, Alexei?"

"I hide the evidence." The bright flame of the pod sputtered in the sky and went out. "It will come down again, thirty or forty klicks west of here. In darkest shadow, very rough terrain, very uneven. Hard to find, harder to get to. When trackers come looking for pod, maybe they will look in wrong place first, lose valuable time, *da*?"

I couldn't see the pod anymore. Either the skin of the bubble was too blurry, or the pod was too dark, or the sky was too black. Without the flame, it was gone.

I wondered if we'd feel the crash, or if it would bounce down again. Either way . . . we were truly *alone* on the moon now. I shuddered— and it wasn't just from the cold seeping up through my feet.

Mickey must have seen how scared I was. He took a half skip toward me, close enough to press his bubble against mine. He grabbed my hand and gave it a quick squeeze. Then he whispered, "Are you going to be okay, Charles?"

"Yes."

"You sure?"

"This isn't like the pod. We're on solid ground. I'll be fine."

"Do you want me to stay close to you, just in case?"

"Uh—if you want to."

"I'll do that."

"Okay."

"Thank you, Charles."

"You can call me Chigger."

Behind the goggles, under the silver poncho, it was hard to see what anyone was thinking, but Mickey's sudden bright smile was clear. "Thanks, kiddo."

"Hokay," said Alexei. "We go. Everybody, on the bounce—come, we must hurry—"

"How far is it?" I asked. "How long will it take to get there? Where are we going—?"

"Thirty klicks, give or take some. Six hours, maybe. We go catch train. No more talk. Use up oxygen. Follow me, this way—"

It wasn't that hard to hop-skip across the Lunar surface. It just took a little practice to find the right rhythm. After a bit, Douglas and I were just as good as Alexei and Mickey. The four of us bounced along like a bunch of Happy Flubbies from that god-awful kid show that Stinky used to like so much. For a while, Douglas and I were even shouting, *"Boinng! Boinnnnng! Ba-boing-boinnngg!"* with every bounce—at least, until Mickey started singing. "*It's a small world, after all . . .*" and Alexei threatened to puncture all of us.

But it was exhilarating great fun—it was kind of like skipping and kind of like hopping and kind of like flying, but mostly like nothing I'd ever done before. The feeling of speed and power and strength—it made me feel like Superman, like there was nothing I couldn't do. I started laughing and shrieking and giggling—so hard, I couldn't stop—

That's when Alexei called the first rest break, and the first thing he did was check my oxygen balance to see if I was getting too much or too little, or what. "You are too light-headed." He looked surprised to find that my rebreather settings were all fine, even allowing for the increased exertion of bouncing.

"I'm laughing because it's fun," I said. "You remember fun, don't you?"

"We have six hours to go, little dingaling." He frowned. "Will you still have laughter thirty klicks from now?"

"I bet I will," I promised. "You were right—I like Luna."

"Do not get overconfident!" he snapped at me. "Overconfidence kills. You will not make very pretty corpse—and I have no intention of dragging you across Luna for burial." Alexei was suddenly very unhappy and very grumpy. None of us had ever seen him this way before. Had he heard something on his radio?

He seemed to realize it himself; he turned back to me, and spoke in a gentler tone. "Just concentrate on being safe. Is too dangerous to have fun here. Hokay, break over. Pay attention—see tall rock to left, with head sticking up into sun? We head toward notch, just to right. We stay in shadow. Let's go—on the bounce."

After that, it wasn't as much fun. After the novelty wore off, it was just something to do. But there was a lot to see—and I wished we could just stop and look at stuff sometimes. Some of the rocks glittered, and I wanted to pick them up and take them with me, but we didn't have sample bags, and the first time I stopped, Alexei yelled at me again, so I didn't do that anymore.

To say that the scenery on the moon looks different is an understatement—kind of like saying the *Titanic* had a rough crossing. *Everything* on the moon is different. But it's the kinds of differences that are surprising. There's no wind or water erosion on the moon, so all the rocks look scruffier and the ground looks harder. It's hard to explain. You have to see it in person. Even pictures don't work.

Mostly we were in shadow. To the east, the sun was lurking just beneath the edge of a long broken rill. A couple of times we had to dart through streaks of sunlight, and once in a while, if we bounced too high, the sudden sideways glare felt like a hammer blast. A couple of times, Alexei said, "*Gohvno!*" and once he said, "*Chyort!*" which sounded even worse. I assumed it was in reaction to the intensity of the sunlight, but I didn't ask. It could have been anything. His dark mood was headed toward pure black.

Every fifteen minutes we stopped to rest for five, no matter where we were—unless it was in sunlight. I didn't ask why; it wasn't too hard to figure out. Our silvery ponchos could keep us warm against the cold Lunar night and they could reflect away some of the intermittent sunlight that hit us, but they couldn't cool us off in the direct glare of the sun.

Every time we stopped, Alexei checked my rebreather, and Mickey checked Douglas's. I protested that I could look at my own numbers, but both of them cut me off at the same time. Safety demanded that everyone check everyone else's settings.

By the time of our fourth rest break, it was pretty much routine. Mickey had taught Douglas and me how to read the rebreather displays, so now all four of us were checking each other at every stop. Alexei even showed us how to share our air in an emergency. The rebreathers had tubes that could connect directly through special valves on the front of the bubble suit. If someone needed air in a hurry, you could just plug right in. But you had to make sure the connection was secure or you could explosively evacuate your rebreather. "Useful only if you want to become a self-propelled object."

So far, our oxygen use was just about what Alexei had expected. We would have enough to get where we were going—if we didn't make any wrong turns, and if we didn't have to double back to go around something.

The problem was, the ground was getting rougher. We were approaching a place where two craters overlapped; the wall of one was broken by the wall of the other. The only way to get to where we were going would be to cross some very uneven terrain. But we had to do it. We had to get out of the crater we were in and onto the plain beyond.

Alexei finally admitted he was worried. But we already knew that. The more he studied the display on his PITA, the worse his language got. I asked Mickey if he knew what Alexei was saying, but all he would translate was, "Your mother was a hamster," which didn't make any sense at all.

Mickey stayed close to Douglas; I think he was worried about Stinky, but Douglas could reach back and squeeze Stinky's arm or his leg and report, "He's still warm. He's still breathing," and that was as good as we could hope for right now.

What we really hoped was that he wouldn't wake up until we got to where we were going. The train station, or whatever it was, Alexei had picked out.

For some reason, I wasn't scared anymore. I felt like I should have been, but I wasn't. We were off the Line, off the map, very far from anywhere safe, about as alone as we could be—and I felt fine.

I wondered if other people felt this same way on Luna—alone and free at the same time. The only sound was the sound of my breathing, and the distant noises of everyone else grunting across the ground playing through my earphones. The bitter cold of the ground tried to seep through the bottom of the bubble, but the poncho kept radiating, and the air in the bubble stayed just warm enough. The light from beyond the rill was bothersome, but my goggles adjusted themselves to block the worst of it. *I felt fine.*

I thought about that.

I should have been worried. I should have been scared. But I wasn't. Why not?

Because I was safe with Douglas? Maybe. That was part of it, I'm sure. But maybe it was more because there wasn't anyone else around to tell me what to do or where to go or who to be. It wasn't the silence *outside* that was so wonderful. It was the silence *inside*—the freedom from all those voices that weren't mine.

It was like when I used to go up in the hills away from the tube-town, so I could listen to my music. It wasn't just the music. It was the silence.

This was such a sudden realization, I stopped in mid-bounce. Wherever we finally ended up, it had to be a place where I could have silence every day. A place where I could listen to my own thoughts.

CLIMBING THE WALL

AT THE SIXTH REST STOP, Alexei made us all eat half an MRE—the red one marked *high-energy pack*. It was made with lots and lots of high-energy stuff—like hydrogen, kerosene, Palmer-chips, and plutonium. It tasted exactly like its list of ingredients, only not as good.

At the seventh rest stop, Alexei tied us all together with a nylon cord. There was a loop on the front and back of each bubble, and he secured the line through both loops. He put himself in the lead, me directly behind, then Douglas, then Mickey bringing up the rear. The inflatable airlock bounced along behind Mickey.

We were heading uphill now, and the slope was getting steeper and trickier. He didn't want anyone slipping and bouncing away. "If you roll downhill and get big puncture and lose all your air," he told me as he secured the cord, "I will be very unhappy. It will ruin my whole day. So I keep you close. We go slowly now. No more bouncing. Just tiny hop-steps. Very careful."

I took his warnings to heart and stayed close behind him. A couple times, I stopped to look back—to see how Douglas was doing—and each time, he yanked me forward. I got the feeling he didn't want me to see how much trouble Douglas was having, climbing up the hill with Stinky on his back. Stinky couldn't have weighed more than four kilos, five at the most. But even five kilos starts to get heavy after a couple of hours. And Douglas had to carry supplies for both of them. I didn't think he was used to this kind of sustained exertion. But he didn't have much choice in the matter. Alexei couldn't do it—obviously. And Mickey's strength was questionable because of all the time he spent *out* of Earth's gravity. And besides, Stinky was *our* responsibility, not *theirs*.

But even with the frequent rests, I could see that Douglas's endurance was wearing thin. And we hadn't even gone a third of the way yet.

Halfway up the slope, it stopped being a slope and became a wall. Even worse, it was a wall in *sunlight*.

"Oh, *chyort!*" I said. "Why didn't we go around?"

"This *is* around," said Alexei. "Is not so bad as it looks. If you are fast." He was fumbling with a tool he had hung *outside* his bubble. I hadn't paid much attention before, but he had several pieces of external equipment hanging off his back. The one he selected now looked like a miniature harpoon gun—because that's exactly what it was.

It had a windup spring, and it fired a dart with an unfolding plastic grapple. A long lightweight cord hung from the dart in a flimsy-looking roll. Alexei studied the wall above, then hesitated and turned back to the display on his PITA. He zoomed in on the Lunological map and grumbled at the numbers. I could see him turning them over in his head—and coming to the conclusion that we really didn't have a choice in the matter anyway, we'd come this far, we didn't have the air to go back down and try another way, so it really didn't matter after all, did it?

"Hokay," he announced. "Let's see if Alexei is as clever as he brags." He hefted the dart gun and turned on its laser sight. Because there was no atmosphere, there was no dust to highlight the beam, so he had to track the red target dot up the wall above us and dance it around his aiming point. He was aiming at a broken shelf in the shadow of a tall outcrop. Above it was the sunlit portion of the wall. The range finder said the shelf was only fifteen meters up, but it looked a lot farther.

"Is not too bad," Alexei decided. "We will do this in two steps. First stop is shelf. Map says it is wide enough for all of us, and we will still be safe in shadow. Second stop will be harder. Longer climb, all in sunlight." He began winding up the spring in the dart gun. "But this will work," he said slowly, "if everybody follows direction. So pay good attention. We use first climb for practice. Learn to climb. We go up to first shelf, all of us. We catch breath, then we go—*bing, bing, bing, bing*—up to top and over, back into shadow quickly. You will have to move fast, very fast. Is longer climb, so you must keep moving. No time to admire view unless you wear sunblock two million. Any question?"

We all shook our heads.

"Douglas?" That was Mickey. "Do you want me to take Bobby? We can transfer him here—"

"No. I'll take him over the top. The other side is downhill, isn't it, Alexei?"

"Yes, other side is downhill. We go back to Lunar plain. Downhill, uphill, but nothing like this. Nothing too serious."

Something about the way he said that last part. "Nothing too serious . . . ?"

"Nothing you can't handle, little dingaling. Get past this part first, please?" He turned back to the wall. It was harder to take a range sighting on the top of the ridge because it was blazing bright and the laser dot was invisible in the glare. Finally, Alexei gave up in disgust. "Never mind. I know how high from Lunar survey. I do this by ear."

He sighted carefully and fired the dart gun—the dart soared lazily up, unfolding its long grappling prongs as it went. It rose out of shadow and blazed in the hard light of the sun. The line followed it up in silence, uncurling and turning bright as it went. At the apex of its flight, the dart hung motionless in space for a long moment—then it began drifting back with a deliberate slow grace, arcing over and down—it disappeared out of view behind the glare of the wall above us. The line went looping after it, flying across space in lazy swirls.

Eventually, the line began to settle and fall back. After what seemed like forever, it finally went slack. Alexei waited until it was hanging like a bright yellow streak against the wall; he held up the display on the base of the dart gun so I could see. It showed a row of green ready signals. According to the readouts on the butt of the pistol, the grapple-dart had landed somewhere over the wall of rock and the grapples had securely deployed. We hadn't heard anything, of course, so we had to depend on the signal sent back through the line. Alexei punched a couple of buttons, and two more green signals appeared. "Grapple has tested itself," he announced. "It will hold us." He locked the safety and hung the gun on the back of his balloon.

"Hokay. Now pay attention. I teach dingalings to do this. Is not too hard—even a dingaling can learn. First, take hands out of gloves. Now put gloves away, please. You do not want them sticking out and catching on something. Here, I'll help. Now reach below and switch to other gloves—big red gloves under regular ones. Put your hands in—*da,* feel that? See how glove is molded around big castanet-claw? That's your grabber. Close glove, feel how it clicks shut? Make sure you feel click. That click means grabber has closed very tight around cord or tool or anything else you reach for—holds very very tight, so don't put anything tender inside. Especially not anything you are attached to."

"How do you unclick it?" Douglas asked.

"Is good question. Squeeze again, also press with thumb and middle finger—feel little click? That is grabber releasing grip. Very easy. Click, unclick. Grabber holds you up even if hands get tired. Pay attention to this, Charles dingaling. Make sure grabber goes click. If it doesn't go click, you have no grip. Very bad news. You don't want that. Do not try to hold cord without grip. You will risk slipping. If you slip, maybe you cut or rip glove. Very bad news if that happen. I have to write letter to manufacturer of bubble and ask for refund. So don't slip. Instead, make sure grabber goes click. Practice now. Click, unclick. See?"

He made me do it over and over again until he was sure I had it right. "Hokay, good. Now this is how you will pull self up, hand over hand. Slowly. Grab, click, pull—unclick other grabber, grab, click, pull—unclick first grabber, grab, click, pull. Understand? If no click, stop and try again. Don't unclick one until the other is clicked. Don't go to next step until you check that previous step is success."

"What if the clicker breaks?"

"I will write letter and get refund."

"I mean—what happens to me?"

"You will not have to worry about letter. I will."

"Oh, good. I hate writing letters."

"All right, watch me now. I will go first. To show you how it is done. Pay attention to feet. Watch what I do. Do you know how to rappel?"

"Rappel?"

"Down mountainside. Kick, slide, kick, slide—? You have seen pictures, *da?* We are going to rappel. But not down—*up.* You do not want to scrape bubble against rock, do you? *Nyet.* Hook feet in loops there. Pull knees up. Brace yourself against wall. Kick away from wall. Then pull self up. Lift knees again and brace self to come back. Hold self against wall, kick and pull. Brace, hold, kick and pull. Understand? Watch. I will go first. I will make it look easy. Then you will follow.

You will make it look clumsy. We will all laugh at you. But you will get to top without mishap, because you will be slow and careful. And we will all pat you on back, and say, 'good job, well-done, little dingaling.' And you will have great adventure to tell grandchildren about some-day. Unless you are like Mickey and Douglas. Then you will have to tell someone else's grandchildren. Not to worry, I will lend you some of mine. They will not believe that senile old Lunatic smuggled crazy terries across *Lunnaya zhopa*. Bottom of moon. Moon's rectum. Place where sun never shines. Truthfully, it *never* does. We will be there soon. The *priamaya kishka*. You will tell them you were crazy terrie. They will believe. Hokay? Watch now, here I go."

Was he serious? Or was he saying all that stuff to distract me? Either way, it worked. I was distracted.

Alexei pulled himself up the cliff wall in a series of three fast bounces. His movements were quick, but they were also deliberate and careful. He'd done this before and his experience showed. He stretched his right arm as high as he could, grabbed and clicked. He kicked away from the wall, pulled himself up as high as he could, grabbed and clicked. His feet came back to the wall and he braced himself. He looked down at me and grinned, unclicked his lower hand, reached up, grabbed, clicked, kicked away from the wall, and pulled.

Once more and he was at the top. He kicked away from the wall and pulled sharply at the same time—he floated over the edge of the shelf and disappeared from view for a moment. He popped back into view and waved down at us. "Hokay, dingaling! Your turn."

"It's Dingillian," I corrected.

"If you can get to top, I will learn new pronunciation. Until you get up, you are still dingaling."

Douglas moved up beside me. "You okay, Chigger?"

"Yeah, I can do it. Can you?"

He nodded. "I'm getting tired, but I can do it. Let's get this over with."

I closed my eyes and visualized the steps—what they would feel like. I took a deep breath. I reached up with my right hand. I grabbed. I squeezed. The glove went click. "Remember to kick!" Alexei shouted. I had almost forgotten. I kicked and pulled at the same time—I was a little heavier than I expected, but a lot lighter than I was used to. I bounced up and away from the wall. I reached as high as I could with my left hand, grabbed, and clicked. "Pull your knees up—" I had plenty of time to brace, everything was slow motion. My feet hit the wall. "Don't look down—" Too late. I was already looking.

I was higher than I thought. But I wasn't scared. I'd been this high when I did the rope climb in gym class. As long as I didn't look back to see the rest of the slope we'd climbed—

I took a breath, visualized what I had to do next. And did it. This time it was easier. Unclicked the right hand. Kicked away. Swung up. Grabbed. Clicked. Pulled up knees. Braced. Looked up. Alexei waved. He was closer than I expected.

"Is good. One more. *Da?*"

"*Da.*" Closed eyes. Took a breath. Opened eyes. Unclicked, kicked, swung, pulled, grabbed, clicked, braced. It was easier to do than describe.

Alexei was almost close enough to reach out and pull me up. "Kick and pull sharply up," he said. I did, and he grabbed my arm—both arms—and swung me over the top, setting me down firmly on a slab of Lunar rock. He reached over and slapped the top of my head. "Is good job, little dingaling. Not as clumsy as I expected."

The monkey patted my head too. I'd almost forgotten it was there.

"I thought you said you weren't going to call me dingaling anymore."

He pointed to the wall above us, where it turned into blazing sunlit rock. "I said when we get to *top!*"

TO THE TOP

DOUGLAS CAME UP THE WALL next. Despite the weight of Stinky on his back, he came up easily. At least, it looked easy to me. He was only a little bit out of breath when he bounced onto the shelf. Mickey came right after; he pulled the inflatable airlock up after himself.

We took a rest break then. We weren't catching our breath so much as cooling off. Alexei wanted us to turn off our heaters and radiate away some of our heat. I don't know how much good he thought that would do, I was already cold, and it scared me to think of the kind of heat we'd be experiencing in a few minutes. But he kept saying, "Not to worry. Is just an extra precaution. Bubbles are insulated both ways."

When we checked each other's air, Alexei advised each of us to release a few seconds of oxygen into our bubbles from the spare tanks we carried. "And put rebreather tube in mouth for climb up, please?" I was beginning to think this was far more dangerous than he was letting on.

To the east, the hills were outlined by an edge of light. Sunrise. We were just below the edge of their shadow. Just how bright was the full force of the sun in hard vacuum? We were about to find out—one good bounce upward and we'd know.

I reached up and touched the monkey on my head. "Why don't you swing down and climb into the harness on my back?" I said. To my surprise, it understood exactly what I wanted. It bounced down, climbed up under the poncho, and secured itself in the harness on my back, just like Stinky was secured on Douglas's back. "Thank you," I said to it. I bounced lightly on my feet, testing my balance.

"Hokay," said Alexei. "Anybody ready? I go now. Watch please?" He grabbed the cord. "Here I go—" He bounced up into the light. His bubble glittered with reflections. And then he was up and up and up and over the top and gone.

A second later his voice came loud in our ears. "I am fine, thank you for worrying." He added, "Is not as hard as it looks. Is nice view from up here. Charles dingaling, is your turn."

Douglas gave me a good luck slap on top of the head, and I clicked onto the rope. I closed my eyes, visualized, and leapt—

The sudden bright wash of light from the east felt like a hammer-blow. Even my goggles weren't enough to keep me from being dazzled. I felt like I'd opened a furnace door, just from the glare alone. The whole inside of the bubble sparkled with reflections that wouldn't quit.

—and grabbed the rope and clicked. Released, kicked, and pulled. Suddenly my goggles were blurry, with hot tears streaming from my eyes. From the light. Grabbed for the rope, missed—clicked anyway, and swung around out of control for a moment, turning first away from the sun, and then right back into the full force of it—I unclicked my empty hand, looked up for the rope, found it, grabbed, clicked, remembered to test, banged the wall, I'd forgotten to bring my knees up, bounced and hung for a moment, and said, "Oh, *chyort!*" The tears were real now. Tears of frustration.

"Keep coming!" cried Alexei from above. "Don't stop!" shouted Douglas and Mickey from below.

I swallowed hard, visualized—was it getting hot in here or was it my imagination? Had I scraped my bubble? Did I hear something hissing? Was I losing air?—visualized again and unclicked, kicked, and climbed. I fumbled again—but this time grabbed the cord anyway, clicked, and hung, braced myself against the wall. I couldn't see. The tears were a torrent. The light was awful. If I could just see—

"Only three more and you are here, dingaling! Keep coming!"

Visualized, unclicked, kicked, grabbed, clicked and pulled—okay, I could do this. Two more times. Took a breath, did it all again on the other side. Once more—except I couldn't see a thing. My goggles were wet, my eyes were flowing. I pulled my hand out of the lower glove and pushed my goggles up, tried to wipe my eyes with my wrist. That was a mistake. My goggles fell off my head and bounced away somewhere below me. I felt them hit the floor of the bubble. Even with my eyes closed, the light was an orange blast. I said some of those words that mom hated so much.

"What just happened?" Douglas demanded.

"He dropped his goggles," Alexei said. "Not to worry. Is easy enough, we do it with eyes closed. Come up, dingaling. You are almost here."

It *was* getting hot in here. It wasn't my imagination. The sweat was dripping from my armpits. If I could just see—I squinted up. The rope was a blurry line. Maybe if I could get the goggles. I pulled my knees up, bringing the floor of the bubble almost up within reach. I reached around, fumbling for the goggles. If I could just find the goggles—my hand scrabbled frantically.

"Charles!" That was Douglas. "Don't stop! Keep climbing!"

"I just want to grab my goggles. I can't see!"

"Forget stupid goggles! You are close enough to do without."

And then I swung around just a little bit and my view widened beyond the bubble to the scenery outside.

I was hanging on the inside wall of a Lunar crater. It was big, round, and deep. The pod had come down on the far side and we'd crossed the rubble-strewn floor, always keeping to the shadow until we'd finally climbed its steepening slopes—until we'd finally had to pull ourselves up the wall. From this perspective, it looked bigger and deeper than the Barringer Crater in Arizona, only it was painted in hard colors of black and silver and bright.

And I was hanging halfway up the inner wall.

In a bubble of air. Baking in the sun. Surrounded by vacuum and dark. And nothing below me and nothing above me, hanging only by a single arm. My arm was getting tired. And no one anywhere could save me.

I knew the distances weren't the same here on the moon. I knew the gravity wasn't the same. I knew my weight was lighter. But my eyes told me distance and my brain remembered Earth. And my stomach clenched.

"Please, little Dingillian. Put hand back in glove. Reach up. I will pull you, but you will have to kick away from wall. Hokay?"

For a moment, I forgot everything—even the light. I could hear myself thinking—*This is a really stupid way to die.* And then the other side of my brain argued—*No it isn't. This is really dramatic.*

And then I got annoyed, and said, "You're both wrong—"

"What's that, dingaling?"

I didn't answer. Somehow I got my hand back into the glove. I ignored the light and heat and unclicked. I kicked away from the wall, swung myself up, grabbed, and clicked, braced against the wall, unclicked, kicked, swung, grabbed, clicked, braced—"Now!"—and kicked straight down, bounced up—and Alexei grabbed my arm and pulled me over the top, pushing me into the shadow of a looming crag.

I flopped down cross-legged on the broken Lunar rocks and let the tears flood out of me. My eyes were dazzled so badly, I could hardly see.

"Is he all right? *Is he all right?*" That was Douglas.

"He is fine. He is just shaked and baked a little. Wait—" Alexei hovered over me, checking air and temperature and everything else he could think. He looked all over my bubble for leaks, but the pressure meter said it was fine.

"Can you sit here quietly, Charles? I bring your brother up?"

I managed to nod, and Alexei moved back into the light, and started calling instructions down to Douglas.

I wiped my eyes with my hands, again and again. Suddenly, someone was handing me an alcohol-wipe. The monkey. The package was already open, but my hand was shaking so bad I couldn't take it. So the monkey reached up and began gently washing my face. I had to laugh at the absurdity of it. When the monkey finished, it held up my missing goggles. It wiped them off carefully and dried them, then made a big show of inspecting them with a harsh monkey squint. Finally, it handed them over, and I managed to get them back on and my poncho adjusted.

"Okay, you," I said. "On my head again." The monkey did it in a single bounce.

I stood up and turned around. Alexei was just swinging Douglas over the edge, pushing him into the shadow next to me. He grabbed my arms. "Are you all right?" His tone was beyond concerned. It was scared.

I nodded. But I still felt jittery. He stood there, watching me, waiting for me to say something, but I was caught in another one of those terrible churning *wunderstorms*, realizing a thousand things at once. Not just the ordinary stuff about how dangerous adventures were—but the extraordinary stuff about how much I loved my brothers and how lost I'd feel without them—and how much it would hurt them if they lost me. I didn't want to hurt them anymore.

And there were a bunch of other thoughts in that *wunderstorm* too—about Mickey and Alexei and the monkey. But I couldn't say any of it right now. I couldn't say anything. It would all have to wait.

SUMMIT

AFTER **M**ICKEY **PULLED HIMSELF UP,** he and Alexei checked me over again. Then they checked Douglas. Then Douglas checked them. It was a little crowded in the shadow of the crag, but it was safe enough for the moment.

Alexei insisted that we each drink some water and take a few bites of high-energy pack. He wanted us rested before we started down the other side. There was probably a lot that we all wanted to say. I knew that Douglas was angry—he probably wanted to know why Alexei was putting us all in such danger and why Mickey had agreed to this. Mickey should have known better. I could almost hear the argument— it sounded a lot like Mom and Dad.

But Douglas was smart enough not to raise the subject here. We weren't exactly out of danger, and our first priority had to be getting to safety. And after we got to safety, then the argument wouldn't matter anymore, would it?

For a while we sat in silence. Mostly, I was waiting for my eyes to undazzle. All I could see were big purple splotches everywhere. Nobody said anything at all. We just listened to ourselves breathe. We were tired. This wasn't fun anymore. And even though none of us would say so, we were all scared. It was real now—we could die out here.

Alexei had deliberately chosen this landing site because it would be hard to get to. He had chosen this path across the broken Lunar surface because we would be hard to track. We were out of view of any of the Lunosynchronous satellites, and the ones in polar orbit were equally unlikely to spot us.

We were hidden in the shadows, we were masked by the rocks. And even our thermal signatures would be partially lost in the hash of heat and cold. So there wasn't much likelihood of someone finding us. We weren't going to be picked up unless . . .

Douglas was thinking the same thing. He looked to Mickey. He took a breath. "Mickey . . . ?"

"What?"

"I'm thinking that, uh . . . maybe we should call for help."

"Douglas? Are you all right?"

"This is awfully rough. On Charles. On Bobby." He hung his head. "On me too. I almost didn't make it up the wall either. We can't keep taking chances like this—" He looked up, looked across at him. "How do you feel?"

"I'll go along with whatever you decide." And then he added, "I think the safety of you and your brothers comes first."

Alexei was looking down the other side of the wall. He was looking at his PITA. He wasn't looking at us. He said, "I understand your fears. But you are doing all right. Hardest part is past us now. Is all downhill from here. If you choose to go on."

Douglas ignored him. "How long do you think it would take them to get to us?" he asked Mickey.

Mickey shrugged. "We're close enough to Gagarin Station. They could have a boat out here in three hours. But we'd have to climb down to someplace level."

"Yeah, I already figured that out."

"Did you think about the marshals?" Alexei asked.

"What about them? They were waiting for us at Farpoint. We're beyond that now. Aren't we?"

Alexei shrugged.

"Aren't we—?" Douglas repeated.

"Possibly. Possibly not. *Probably* not." He took a breath. "Most certainly, I think not. There are bounty marshals on Luna. It takes only a phone call from Farpoint to North Heinlein or Asimov or Armstrong or . . . Gagarin."

"Gagarin?"

Alexei shrugged. "Is possible." He took his hand out of his glove to scratch his chin. "Is certainly a logical place to start looking for me.

Maybe not you. That's why we drop pods everywhere. So they have no way to know which where to start. Remember, they don't know that I am with you. They might figure it out, because I am not at Geosynchronous anymore. But they have no way to know for sure. So Gagarin could look like red herring. Is inconvenient to get there from north. Only one train line. They would have to take transport. They might not do that on a wild-moose chase. Might check easier targets first. Whole point is to go where it is too inconvenient for marshals. That makes time to keep going, stay ahead of them."

I kept waiting for Douglas to turn to me, to ask me what I was thinking, but he stayed focused on Mickey.

And meanwhile, Alexei nattered on. "But let's play thought experiment game. Say we send signal. Everybody knows we're here. All over news instantly. No secrets on this rock. Rescue boat gets here in three hours. Maybe less, but don't cross fingers before they hatch. Fifteen, maybe thirty minutes to transfer us into boat and get up again. They are in no hurry. They will follow procedures. We take three hours back to Gagarin or wherever else they choose to take us. You figure it out. If Gagarin, that gives marshals six hours from time of distress call to intercept us. Anywhere else, even longer."

"Is six hours good or bad?" I asked.

"If marshals are serious about catching you, they can get to anywhere on Lunar surface within two hours. They have fast transport. Is not impossible. Depends on how many marshals, how desperate they are, how much confusion from big blue marble."

Douglas didn't say anything to that. Neither did Mickey.

"If you want to send distress call, Douglas, I will understand; but I promise, if marshals want you bad enough, then there will be marshals waiting for you. But if you send distress call, I will not wait with you. I will go on without you. We have broken many laws getting here. But they do not know for sure I am here, and I already have many alibis." He sighed. "This is part of why I put you into money-surfing web. So if something bad happens and you get caught, all the money used to purchase six pods will look like your own. My hands are washed. Lawyers will argue that purchase of all six pods and evasive trajectories was intent to escape legal warrants waiting at Farpoint. They will tie you up in paper." He made a face. "So, no, I do not advise calling for help. It could get very ugly for you."

That almost sounded like blackmail. Like fat *Señor* Doctor Hidalgo, who'd almost threatened us too. Even behind his goggles, even bundled in his poncho, I could see that Douglas didn't like what Alexei was saying.

He turned back to Mickey. "Say we go back down to the crater floor. How long would that take? Fifteen minutes? Thirty? We could all get into the inflatable and wait for them, couldn't we?"

"Is better to go forward," said Alexei. "Better landing site on this side." No one paid him any attention.

"Is that what you want to do?" Mickey asked Douglas.

"What I *want* . . . and what I have to do are two different things. I have to think about Bobby and Charles first."

"Um—?" I said.

Douglas shook his head, dismissing me. "No, Chigger. I have to make this decision for all of us."

"Well, that didn't take long."

He looked up sharply. "What didn't?"

"For you to break your promise."

"What promise? Oh—"

"Yeah. *That* promise." To Mickey, I said, "That he wouldn't make any more decisions for all of us without talking to me."

"Chigger." Douglas put on his patient grown-up voice. It was scary—because for a moment, he wasn't Douglas anymore. He was *someone else.* "I'm really scared here. You nearly got killed. And I nearly didn't make it up either. We're not trained for this. I'm sorry. This was a mistake. I'm sorry for getting you into this. We should stop here—"

"You sound just like Dad," I said angrily. *That was who he'd become.* "Remember when he told us he was leaving. How he wouldn't stop apologizing: 'What I want and what I have to do. We made a mistake. I'm sorry. I have to call it quits before it gets worse. Blah blah blah.' And remember how we all felt? We were so angry, because we wanted him to keep trying, just a little bit more—"

"This isn't the same."

"Yes, it is. It's quitting. Dad taught us how to be quitters. Real good."

"It's surviving."

"Yeah, Dad said that too."

"You have a better idea?"

"Yeah, I do. Let's keep going. We can quit anytime. We have to go down the mountain anyway. Let's go down and see how we feel when we get to the bottom."

Douglas looked to Mickey. Mickey shrugged. "He's right. We have to go down, no matter what. And we have enough air. We don't have to decide here. You want to think about it?"

Douglas looked at me. Even though his eyes were hidden by his dark goggles, I could see he was annoyed. He didn't like being backed into a corner. Not by me, not by Alexei, not by Mickey. But he was always logical, and that was his real strength. So finally, he nodded, and said softly, "All right, we'll wait."

Mickey put his hand on Douglas's bubble, as if to touch his shoulder. "Can you make it down? Or do you want me to take Bobby?"

Even though I couldn't see his expression, even though his body language was hidden by the poncho, I could see he was tired. I could hear it in his voice. "No, I'll take him. But when we get down, we need to rest—maybe even a nap?"

Mickey and Alexei exchanged a glance and nodded to each other.

"Turn heaters back on, please. Everyone take a little fresh air," Alexei said. "And we will start down the other side."

"Wait a minute—" I said. I could finally see clearly again. I stepped out into the sunlight, as close to the edge as I dared. I looked back down into the crater we'd just climbed out of. It was deeper than Barringer—and wider. But I wasn't afraid of it anymore. It was just scenery. It looked like a Bonestell.

I stepped back away from the edge, back into the shadow. "All right, I'm ready."

Alexei reached over and slapped my hands with his. "Good job, Charles Dingillian. We go now. *Da?*"

"*Da.*"

IN CONTROL

THE FUNNY THING, DOUGLAS WAS right. This was too dangerous for us. This was a mistake. It had been a mistake from the beginning. It was a whole cascade of mistakes—Mom's, Dad's, Mickey's, and all the lawyers and judges who'd stumbled into this with us.

But most of all, it was *our* mistake. And everything we were doing now was only making it worse. We were getting farther and farther away from help. Every step we took was only making it harder for someone to find us and rescue us.

And then there was that business with Alexei. The more I thought about what he'd said, the more it pissed me off. He'd threatened to abandon us. He'd gotten us into this and he wasn't going to help us get out—not unless we did it his way. And I didn't like that. And probably neither did Mickey and Douglas. But none of us were talking about it, so maybe that was even more evidence how serious this was.

Or maybe Alexei was right. He was a smuggler and a spy and Ghu knew what else. He knew this stuff. He knew the dangers. And, supposedly, he knew how to avoid them. Maybe it was just an overdose of *wunderstorm* and we were getting panicky.

And then we started down, and there wasn't a lot of time to worry.

The way down didn't look as easy as the way up. Alexei had brought us to a place where the rim walls of two overlapping craters intersected. Most of the slope below us was hidden by long sideways shadows. Even so, we could see that the way down to the floor of the second crater was a broken avalanche of ugly rock. It was a rubble-strewn slope, gashed by several nasty chasms.

I didn't see how we were going to negotiate it—maybe by jumping from boulder to boulder? But it turned out to be a lot easier than that.

Alexei retrieved the grapple-dart from where it had secured itself and wound up the cord carefully; then he reloaded the dart gun and sighted down into the rubble and beyond, marking the range to the distant silver plain. He muttered to himself in Russian and I got the feeling he was doing some complex calculations in his head.

Finally, he made a decision. He sighted down into the rubble, tracking the laser dot as far as he could toward some distant landmark. Then he aimed the pistol forty-five degrees upward, and fired. The grapple-dart flew up and away, trailing the cord after it in great un-curling loops. As before, it glittered in the sunlight, yellow against the black sky above.

The dart arced over and down into the gloom below, and as the line fell back into shadow with it, it began blinking out along its length. As before, we had to wait until the butt of the dart-pistol confirmed that the grapple-dart had secured itself.

Now Alexei looped the other end around a convenient boulder and began pulling it as tightly as he could. Periodically, he'd turn and look down into the gloomy crater below with his goggles set for light-enhancement. Then he'd grunt and resume tightening the cord. Mickey helped him. When they were done, we had a Lunar zip line.

"All right, *Mikhail*, do you want to go first? Or should I?"

"I think you'd better."

Alexei nodded agreement. "I think so too. All right, Dingillians—this part will be easy." From his equipment pack, he produced four little wheels with handles, he handed one to each of us. "Use your grabbers. Click right grabber here, reach up, put wheel on line, click left grabber here. Once you are clicked, you cannot fall off. So enjoy ride. Pick up feet, hold knees as high as you can, ride line all the way down to bottom. Is long way, *da*? So do not go too fast. Twist handles this way for braking, wheel will slow. Twist other way to release brake. Is good idea to control speed all the way down, especially for beginners. When you get near end, you will see ground getting closer. That is time to go very slow. Even slower than that. Slower than very slow. Do not scrape bubble suit. You will do fine. I promise. Is great fun and best way to go anywhere on moon. Any questions?"

I raised a hand.

"Yes, Charles?"

"Did you do this on purpose?"

"Do what?"

"Choose the bounce-down sight so far from where we have to go? I mean, couldn't you have brought us down a little closer?"

"I could have, yes. But I wanted the bad guys to look somewhere else. So we hike a little bit and they go to look in six places much farther away. By the time they don't find us, we will be past wherever else they think to look. If I did not think you could handle this, Charles, I would not have used this plan." He added thoughtfully, "I make this plan a long time ago, I am very proud of myself that it works so well. You should be proud too—that you are strong enough to keep up. We are almost on schedule. Wait for my signal. I will call you down as soon as it is safe. Hokay, any other questions? No? I see you all on the bottom." He swung his wheel over the line, clicked onto the handles, kicked off with his feet, and sailed away over the edge.

"*Waaaaaaaa-haaaaa! Hoooo-hooooooooo-hooooooooo eeeeeee-yyyy!*" He wailed all the way down—or at least as far down as he had the air to shriek. He floated down across the Lunar landscape like something out of a bizarre dream—a silver sprite in a shimmery ball.

And then there was silence. It stretched out for the longest time.

The three of us looked at each other.

"Why doesn't he say something?" I asked.

"Maybe he's concentrating on his landing," Douglas said.

"What if he fell off?"

"He can't fall off."

"What if the bottom of the line is in a jagged rock field and he got punctured before he could warn us? What if it's not safe to go down after him?"

"Charles, stop scaring yourself. Nobody else is going down until Alexei tells us it's safe."

"But if something happened to him—?"

"Nothing happened to him," said Douglas.

We both looked to Mickey.

Mickey was studying the PITA on his wrist. "His signal is clear. His readouts are green. He's alive. He's just not talking. At least, not to us. He might be calling ahead to someone else. Not to worry."

We waited in silence. I looked at the Earth for a while. It hadn't changed its position in the sky. And the terminator line didn't look all that different from before. Most of Africa was still waking up. *To another horrible day.* We'd only been traveling two hours. We still had a long way to go.

And then, the worst thing of all happened.

Stinky woke up.

And announced, "I gotta go to the bathroom. Where are we?"

Mickey and Douglas and I all groaned at the same time.

"Can you hold it?" said Douglas.

"No," said Stinky. "I gotta go *right now!*"

"Uh-oh—" I said. I knew that tone of voice.

And in that same instant, I had a chilling insight about Stinky— and why he was the way he was. I was only angry at Mom and Dad. But Stinky was angry at everyone. It was about *control.*

Everybody in the family had authority over him. Everybody older had power. He had none. There was only one thing he could say to bring everything else to a stop. There was only one thing he could do to seize control.

And every time he did, everything else came to an immediate stop. At that moment, his single declaration became the ultimate power in the family. Whenever things were totally out of control—there was Stinky demanding, "I gotta go *now.*" If nothing else, he could always be depended on to focus the dilemma on himself.

Without even thinking about it, I stepped over to Douglas. "Stinky! Can you hear me?"

"Yes. Where are you, Chigger?"

"I'm right here." I reached over and pressed against the back of Douglas's bubble, patting the bulge on his back that I assumed was Stinky. "Feel that?"

"Yes. I gotta go!"

"Listen to me. You've got to hold it. If you go now, you'll have to sit in it for six hours, for the rest of the day. And you won't be able to escape the stink. Is that what you want?"

"But I really really gotta go! I mean it!"

"Wait a minute—" That was Douglas. "Maybe I can work something out in here. Bobby, can you wait a minute—I've got a bathroom bag. You'll have to climb down from my back—"

"I'm all tied up, I can't get out. I gotta go."

Mickey said, "Can you turn around, Douglas? I'll invert the gloves and untie him. Or do you want to use the inflatable?"

"Bobby!" I said. "Which do you want to do first? Go to the bathroom or ride the roller coaster?"

"What roller coaster?"

"The one right here. The Lunar roller coaster."

"I can't see it. Douglas has his blanket over me."

"Do you want to go on the roller coaster?"

"Yes!"

"Can you hold it—?"

"Um . . ."

" 'Um' isn't good enough. Can you hold it?"

"I'll try—"

" 'I'll try' isn't good enough either. We have to know. Can you hold it for a few minutes more? Yes or no."

"Yes."

Mickey turned to me. "Charles, we can do it here. Douglas can take care of him in the bubble. Or they can go into the inflatable."

"Mickey, he went to the bathroom back in the pod, just before bounce-down. He doesn't have to go—not as badly as he says he does. He hasn't eaten anything in the last twenty-four hours, he doesn't like the MREs. And even if he had eaten, he'd be constipated anyway."

"And what if you're wrong?"

"I've spent the last eight years monitoring his bowel and his bladder. After you've cleaned him up a couple of times, you start paying attention to these things."

Mickey wasn't convinced. "He sounds awfully insistent to me."

"He does this *everywhere*," I explained. "At home, in the car, on trips. Nobody else can ever use the bathroom if he doesn't want them to. If he's not the center of attention, he's gotta go. He does it to escape spankings. He does it to get me in trouble. And he did it at Barringer Meteor Crater—you heard about that?—because somewhere he's figured out that announcing that you have to go to the bathroom is the reset button for reality. You notice, he hasn't said a word for the past two minutes? If something interesting is happening, he forgets he has to go."

Right on schedule, Stinky piped up. "I wanna go on the roller coaster!"

Mickey turned back to Douglas. "What do you want to do?"

"Chigger is right. Let's keep going."

"We haven't heard from Alexei—" Mickey fiddled with his phone. "Alexei—? Can you hear me. Respond please?" To me, he said, "It's a long way down. If he went slow—"

"He could still answer, couldn't he?" I bounced up and flipped my wheel over the cord, clicking my grabber onto the other handle with an ease that surprised me. I was getting used to this stuff.

Before I could kick free, Mickey blocked me. "Charles, wait—"

"Why? If something happened to him, we're on our own. Waiting up here is only going to use up oxygen. You have to stay with Douglas and Stinky. I can do this—"

"Mickey, he's right. Let him go. We have to get down from here."

Mickey sighed and stepped out of the way. I don't think he liked any of us right at that moment.

I didn't care. I kicked free.

GETTING DOWN

I **SAILED OFF THE ROCKS** and out into open space—above the crater wall, above the rubble-strewn slope, above the gaping chasms, toward the distant gray Lunar plain. Parts of it were so dark the shadows were tangible.

There wasn't as much sense of motion as I expected—and there wasn't as much falling feeling either. Even so, my heart lurched in my chest. Here I was again, hanging in open space—

I tried looking up. That didn't help. The cord was zipping by too fast. I looked down. That was even worse. I could see how fast the ground was coming up. The line was too steep. I twisted the handles as hard as I could.

The wheel slowed, the vibration in my hands and arms changed. But it didn't feel slow enough. "Oh, *chyort!*" I should have started sooner.

"Charles—?"

"I'm trying to slow down." The ground was coming up awfully fast. And I was feeling *really* stupid. I twisted the handles harder—but they were already at their limit; they clicked into a locked position. The wheel was stopped—but I was still going! The wheel skidded and bounced along the cord. Was this what happened to Alexei? Betrayed by the Lunar laws of physics? There wasn't enough weight on the wheel, there wasn't enough friction between the wheel and the line, they were both too polished—*and the line was too damn steep!* I was just going to keep sliding all the way down—until I slammed into a big unfriendly boulder.

It was a long way down. More than a klick, maybe two. How fast would I be going when I hit bottom? Fast enough to hurt? Fast enough to puncture the bubble suit? Twenty kph? Thirty? More? If only I had a couple of Palmer tubes—

That gave me an idea. I took my hands out of the connecting gloves and hurriedly connected the emergency rebreather tube to the valve of the bubble suit. It snapped immediately into place. This was going to be tricky. I pointed the valve and opened it in a series of short bursts.

I couldn't hear the outrush of air, but I could feel it. I came skidding to a stop on the line. My downward rush was halted. The line wasn't as steep here. The brakes held. I took my finger off the valve. I couldn't believe it—it worked! I'd traded a few minutes of air—maybe more—for a safe landing. A fair trade. I shoved my hands back into the gloves and looked down. I was hanging thirty meters above a yawning abyss. It was too dark to see how deep the bottom was.

"Chigger?" That was Douglas. "What was that screaming about?"

"What screaming?"

"You were screaming."

"No, I wasn't—was I really?"

"Yes, you were. What happened?"

"I was going too fast. The brakes didn't work. Well, they worked, but they didn't. Alexei screwed up, I think. Even if the wheel doesn't turn, you'll still go skidding down the line. But it's okay. I stopped myself. I used some of the air from my rebreather."

"How much?" That was Mickey.

"Not too much. Just a few squirts."

"Charles, I don't want to alarm you. But it's hard to tell how big a squirt is in vacuum. Don't panic. We've all got spare bottles. We're not going to run out of air. But that's not a real good idea."

"It was the only one I had, Mickey. Anyway, you and Douglas are going to have to do the same thing."

"No, we're not. I'm going to figure something else out. Where are you now?"

"Hanging maybe a hundred klicks over nothing in particular."

"How much farther do you have to go?"

I peered ahead. "The ground levels out soon. So does the line. It looks like maybe two or three hundred meters. It's hard to tell."

"You'll have to go very slow."

"I know that!"

"All right. Just keep talking."

My arms were starting to get tired. I reached up, grabbed the handles firmly, took a breath, and carefully began *un*twisting—not very much, just enough to unlock the brake and let the wheel start rolling. Only a little bit. I began moving forward. Very slowly. So far so good.

The thought occurred to me that I might have reacted out of panic. The line had a lot of sag in it. Of course the highest part would be the steepest. Lower down, the line would level off enough that the brakes would be more effective.

The more I thought about it, something felt wrong about this. Alexei had planned everything else so carefully; why did he screw this up? Lunar explorers used all kinds of tricks for getting up and down steep slopes. This couldn't have been the first time he'd done this. So why didn't he know better? Had he been careless? Or stupid? Or what?

The ground came gliding up to meet me. Everything was back to slow motion. It was like one of those flying dreams where you drift along like a cloud. I tightened my grip and came to a halt, suspended only a couple of meters above the Lunar dust. The line went on farther, but the ground dropped away again. Maybe this would be a good place to get off . . . ?

Two meters. I did the math in my head. One-sixth of two meters. It would be like jumping off a chair. I could do that. "All right," I said. "I've found a stopping place. It's not too far to the ground. I'm going to drop down here. Wait a minute." I looked up at the wheel and the handles and visualized what would happen when I released my grip. The wheel would pop off the line, dropping me down. I just had to be ready. "Here goes—"

My hand came free and I fell. The bubble bounced down onto the ground. I didn't fall over.

"I'm down."

"Good job, Chigger. All right, now move out from under the line. You don't want to get accidentally bumped. We're coming down now. Mickey and I are coming down together."

"Huh?"

"You'll see. Just keep out of the way."

I stared up the line and waited. Several very long moments later, three luminous bubbles appeared very high up. One very large one, and two smaller ones with silver figures inside. They were moving very slow—painfully slow.

"I can see you," I reported.

"We can see you too," Mickey called back. "We'll be down in a bit."

It took longer than a bit, but I could see them clearly, so I wasn't worried. When they finally did arrive, they hung lower on the line than I had. In fact, they were holding their knees up so they wouldn't scrape the ground. They brought themselves to a stop, hanging all together like the last three grapes on the stem. Douglas lowered his long gangly legs to the ground and unclipped himself and Mickey.

He showed me how they'd used some of the leash to the inflatable to tie their two wheels together to make a kind of pulley rig. With both wheels locked, the cord had to twist around first one wheel, then the other. It couldn't skid—at least not very well.

"We should have thought of this before," said Douglas. "All three of us could have come down at the same time. With your wheel rigged in, we would have had even better control. We did skid a bit at first, but not as hard as you did."

We were on a low hill. Mickey was already settling the inflatable on the level crest of it, opening up the first zipper of the entrance tube so Douglas could go in and take care of Stinky. As soon as Douglas was on his way in, Mickey came over to me and checked my air bottles.

"How bad?" I asked.

"Not as bad as it could have been. You used up half an hour of breathing. Maybe more. You'll just have to swap in one of your O-bottles earlier, that's all. Later on, we might have to equalize your air supply with mine or Douglas's. What you did was very smart, Chigger—and also very stupid. I hope you realize that. We don't have air to waste. Alexei didn't leave us much margin."

"I didn't have time to think, Mickey."

"I know you didn't. And I'm not bawling you out. We've just got to be more careful from here on. Okay?"

"More careful than what?" I asked.

Mickey looked exasperated. "I mean, we're going to have to think harder. Do you understand what I'm saying?"

"Do you understand what *I'm* saying? Is there anything I could have done different?"

He got it. Or maybe he didn't. "All right. Fine. Let's just drop it."

He turned back to the inflatable. "Doug, do you need my help?"

Douglas was already inside. There was a smaller silver beetle next to him—Stinky. I couldn't see what he was doing, but from his posture, it looked as if he was squatting over a toilet bag. "No, I think we've got everything under control."

Mickey turned to me. "Chigger, you stay here. I'm going to follow the line down to its end and look for Alexei."

"I'll go with," I said.

"I'd rather you didn't. It might not be very pretty—"

"I've seen dead bodies before," I lied. Well, in the movies anyway. "Besides, you might need help bringing back the extra oxygen bottles and all the other stuff that Alexei was carrying."

"All right," said Mickey. "But if you throw up inside your bubble, you'll have to live with it."

"I'll be fine," I said. I hoped I was right. I followed him, hop-skipping over the hill.

END OF THE LINE

WE FOLLOWED THE CORD FOR several hundred meters. The ground was uneven, and generally sloping downward, though here and there it rolled upward too. There were boulders everywhere, of all sizes—some as big as cars or houses, others even bigger; so we couldn't really see too far in any direction. But we weren't worried about losing our way. Not as long as we kept the line in sight. Mostly it was ten or twenty meters over our heads.

Mickey turned his transmitter all the way up and called for Alexei to respond, *please*. We waited and waited, but there was no answer.

Several times we paused to circle around some of the bigger boulders, just in case Alexei had come down behind one of them, or even on top of one. But if he had, we didn't see him. Mickey kept checking his homing device, but Alexei's beacon didn't register. Maybe he was out of range. That was possible. Or maybe it was no longer transmitting. That was possible too.

Then we came to a place that was very slow going. The boulders were too big and uneven and we had to watch our bounces carefully. When we got past that, we took a short rest, each of us taking a small drink of water. Mickey looked over at me. "Y'know—Chigger, you're a pretty good kid."

I didn't know how to respond to that, so I just grunted something that might have been thanks.

"At first, I thought you were a whiny pain in the ass—but you can take care of yourself. Better than I expected. I respect you for that."

And then he added, "I hope that maybe you're starting to respect me too."

"Yeah, I guess so," I said.

"Charles, you resent me. I see it on your face every time you look at Douglas and me together. And I don't blame you. Douglas and Bobby are all you've got left, and I must seem like an intruder to you."

I didn't know what to say to that either. After a bit, I mumbled half an agreement. "Well, yeah."

"So, let's agree to work together anyway, okay? Because we both care about Douglas. And Bobby."

"Um. Okay."

We slapped gloves, kind of like a handshake, only clumsy, and then we checked in with Douglas. He told us to be glad that odors cannot travel through the vacuum of space.

We pushed on.

After another fifteen minutes of bouncing and skipping through house-sized boulders, we came around a tall rocky prominence and stopped. We had finally reached the end of the line. Literally. The place where the grapple-dart had anchored itself.

Mickey bounced up to the top of a boulder, then bounced over to the next. He tilted himself forward to inspect the dart. "It looks fine," he said. "I'm going to see if I can loosen it and bring it with us. We might need it again."

"But Alexei had the pistol."

"Well, we'll just have to find him."

I was already circling the outcrop, looking for Alexei's body. I wanted to find it—and I didn't. I was morbidly curious—and I was terrified. If Alexei was dead, then where were we . . . ?

"All right, I've got the grapple-dart," said Mickey. "I'm coming back down." Two quick bounces and he was beside me again. Above us the line was falling slack. "Did you see *anything*?" Meaning, did you find *Alexei*?

"Uh-uh. It's like he popped off the line and flew away into space."

"Knowing Alexei, I could almost believe that." Mickey bounced up and grabbed the sagging cord above us. He pulled the free end over the rocks and began winding it up. "Even without the pistol, this might be useful. Waste not, want not, remember?" He handed me the line to hold, then circled the promontory, looking for anything I might have missed. He spiraled outward among the boulders, then came back to me. "Nope. He must have jumped off earlier. We could search for days and never find him." After a moment, he added, "And we don't have enough air for that."

We started back toward Douglas and Mickey resumed winding the cord. "You know," he started, thinking aloud. "There was a lot of horizontal slack at this end of the line. He might have had time to slow down, even stop." And then he added, *pointedly*, "You might have too."

"Yeah, but I didn't know that."

"No, you didn't."

We picked our way back slowly. We took turns gathering up the cord and winding it in loose coils. It looked unnaturally thin to me—but everything on Luna seemed spindly. If they made it only one-half as strong as it would need to be on Earth, it would still be three times stronger than necessary for Luna.

We spread out and searched from side to side, looking for any sign of Alexei. Even a track on the ground would have been welcome. We searched as carefully as we could—but we were in shadow, there were a lot of boulders, and it would have been easy to miss him in the dark.

Mickey stopped to study his PITA. He whispered something to it, studied the display. "All right," he said, with terrifying finality. "I'm going to call it. You know what that means?"

"You think he's dead."

"It means we can't waste any more oxygen looking for him. If he's dead, we can't help him. And if he's alive, we still can't help him—" He stopped and faced me. "Do you know the first law of Luna?"

"Uh—no," I admitted.

"It's very cold, it's very selfish. *Take care of your own well-being first. Otherwise, you have nothing for anyone else.*"

"That doesn't sound selfish to me. It sounds like good advice."

"It is. But a lot of dirtsiders don't like it. The equations are too cold for them. You know what that means?"

"Everybody does. Not enough air."

"That's right." He took a breath. "All right. Let's go back and talk to Douglas. It's time to make a decision."

Douglas and Bobby were sitting together inside the inflatable. Bobby was munching an MRE and sipping at a canteen. I checked the time. We'd have to take another bathroom break in an hour. If we waited until he went now, we might manage two hours, two and a half. Maybe.

Mickey and I stopped outside the inflatable. We checked each other's air supply. We were both fine. Mickey told Douglas what we had found—and what we hadn't found. He traced lines in the thin dust. "Here's where we started. Here's where we are now. Here's the closest two train lines. We could have gone to this one, to the east. It's only half the distance, in fact it's still closer, but there are some steep crater walls in the way. And we'd be in sunlight a lot of the time, dodging from shadow to shadow. Experienced Loonies wouldn't have had a problem with it, but it's too risky for beginners. So Alexei had us going the long way, but safer—heading for this other line here. This way, we stay mostly in shadow, and the biggest problem is that one little crater rim—yeah, *that* was a *little* one—and a little bit of sunlight, and making sure that we have enough air. He thought we could do it. So did I. I still do."

I couldn't tell what Douglas was thinking. Behind the blurry wall of the inflatable, he was an unreadable silver ghost.

"If we call for help," said Mickey, "we'll probably end up in the custody of bounty marshals. Alexei was my only real connection on Luna. I might be able to make some phone calls, but I can't think of anyone who'd get involved for us. For you. Unless—"

"Unless what?"

"Unless you know who paid your dad to carry the monkey. They'd certainly have an interest in reclaiming their property."

"No, they won't," said Douglas. "It's a decoy. Having us caught by bounty marshals serves them perfectly. It's a public distraction."

For an instant, the monkey tightened its grip on my head, reminding me it was there. For an instant, I wondered again if it was really a decoy. But something told me I didn't want to voice that thought aloud. "So what's our alternative?" I asked. "Without Alexei, can we still get to the train?"

"I think so. My maps are good. Not as good as Alexei's, but he showed me the way, and I think I can get us to Prospector's Station."

"And then what?"

"Then we keep going. We take cargo trains. We zigzag. We avoid interception points. We get to the catapult somehow. Or we sit here and call for help. But we have to decide in the next few minutes, because if we don't start moving soon, the window closes. We won't have enough air."

"How much air?"

"My guess is six hours if we're active, eight if we're resting. We can call for help anytime, Douglas. But if we're going to move, we have to move now."

"What about the closer train?"

Mickey pointed east—toward the harsh glare of the rising sun.

Douglas turned and looked. He didn't like what he saw. I could see that much in his posture. "And the farther one?"

Mickey pointed south, toward the darkness.

Douglas stared into the gloom. "You really think we can do it?"

"Alexei thought so. And he knew the risks better than any of us."

"All right," Douglas said. "Let's do it."

"You want me to take Bobby?"

"No, I promised him he'd stay with me. Let me get packed—"

A HUNCH

WE DIDN'T TALK ABOUT ALEXEI. Not too much. There wasn't much that either Douglas or I could say—and whatever Mickey was feeling about his friend, he wasn't saying anything to either of us. I got the feeling he was as much angry at Alexei as he was grieving.

After a little bit of discussion, we decided to go for thirty minutes at a time between rest breaks. It was mostly downhill, and we were getting our Luna legs now, and Mickey was worried about my air. He didn't say so, but he checked my readouts a lot. He wanted to get us to Prospector's Station quickly.

For a while, we were moving through boulders, and then just rocks, and finally, we were back on hard rock and thin dust again. That was easiest. We were heading toward a landmark that Alexei and Mickey had identified as our halfway point.

About fifty years ago, in the first days of serious Lunar exploration, the Colonization Authority put down thousands of surveying beacons all over the Lunar surface. These were nothing more than self-embedding spikes with reflectors on top. The reflectors were dimpled with hundreds of little right-angle corners so that any beam hitting them would be reflected straight back to its source.

The length of time it took for a beam to return told you how far away you were. By triangulating on several reflectors, you could calculate your position almost to the centimeter. The reflectors also made it possible to make highly accurate surveillance maps of the Lunar surface. The geography of Luna was actually better known than that of Earth—because two-third's of Earth's geography was underwater.

We were heading for one of those reflectors now. There was nothing else there, just the reflector. But three generations of Lunar explorers used the reflectors as opportunities to recalibrate their PITAs.

The reflectors were also good for data storage, sort of. Anyone could point a beam at a reflector from just about anywhere, as long as they had line of sight.

Suppose you're on Earth and you aim a beam at a Lunar reflector. Luna is 3.84E5 kilometers from Earth. The beam travels 384,000 kilometers one way, or 768,000 kilometers round-trip. That's 768,000,000 meters, 768,000,000,000 millimeters, 768,000,000,000,000 micrometers. 768,000,000,000,000,000 nanometers. Or . . . 7,680,000,000,000,000,000 angstroms. There are 10 angstroms in a nanometer.

A blue laser, emitting at 4700 angstroms produces one wavelength every 470 nanometers. One wavelength every .47 micrometers. One wavelength every .00047 millimeters. One wavelength every .00000047 meters. 4.7E-7 meters.

So if we divide 7,680 trillion angstroms by 4700, we get 1.634 trillion wavelengths between Earth and Luna. Round-trip. If I'd figured this right, if you used one wavelength per bit, you could put nearly 1.634 terabits on a round-trip beam. Or 204.25 gigabytes every three seconds. Not too bad. About 100 hours of music, recorded in hi-resolution mode.

That sounded a little low to me. But I was figuring it in my head, and it was possible I'd screwed up the numbers. And I was using a blue laser because that was the only angstrom number I could remember. If you used an X-ray laser, you could multiply that by 10,000, and that would be 2,042 terabytes every three seconds. Which represents a much bigger music collection—about a million hours in hi-res. More if you played all the repeats.

If you used 8 beams, each one a different wavelength, all synced together, you would send 8 times 2,042 terabytes—16⅓ petabytes round-tripping between Earth and Luna. Was that enough to hold the sum total of human knowledge? No, probably not. I'd heard somewhere that the human race had so many recording machines functioning, we were generating a couple thousand terabytes of information *per day*. So maybe the Lunar circuit was only big enough to hold a week's worth of global data. But if you threw out all the crap that wouldn't matter a week from now, 16⅓ petabyes was certainly enough storage to hold the most *important* information the human race needed.

But the moon is only visible a few hours per day. So your connection only works as long as the moon is in the sky. On the other hand, if you're broadcasting from L4 or L5, you've got a permanent line-of-sight connection with Luna—and the farther away from Luna you get, the more data you can have in transit. As fast as it returns, you retransmit it. Round and round it goes and no piece of data is ever more than a few seconds away.

There was a time—before I was born—when some folks thought that Lunar reflectors could be used to store the entire world's knowledge in a network of laser beams zipping around the solar system. But by the time the reflectors were in place, the cost of optical data cards was already in free fall, and it was obvious that using the reflectors for data storage was another one of those good ideas that was obsolete by the time the technology was ready. You could put 500 gigabytes in a credit card. You could put 500 terabytes in half a pack of playing cards. You could put it in your pocket. Or inside your robot monkey. . . .

Oh, hell. Memory wasn't about size anymore, it was about density. You could even put a few petabytes into a monkey if you packed them tight enough. Maybe even an exabyte or two. That should be enough to hold the sum total of human knowledge. Of course, *those* would be expensive. Petabyte bars were worth thousands. Exabytes were worth millions. . . .

Hm.

But if you only wanted to smuggle 2,042 terabytes of information from the Earth to the moon, you didn't need to hire a courier and a bunch of decoys. You could go out in the backyard, lash your xaser to your telescope, point your telescope at the target, feed a signal into the beam, and fire away for a few seconds. Cheap, easy, impossible to intercept.

Dad had bought two cards of used memory for the monkey—which would have seemed weird at the time, except Weird and I had been distracted by Stinky's near-headlong tumble into Barringer crater. Why would we need so much memory for a toy anyway? And what was in that memory? I hadn't had a chance to look at the cards closely, and I wasn't going to do it with anyone else around.

What was it that had to be transported that couldn't be transmitted? Money? Codes? Information? No. All that could be phoned in. So it had to be something that couldn't or wouldn't travel by beam.

There was only one thing I could think of . . . and it almost made sense. Maybe.

Quantum computing couldn't be beamed. I didn't understand all the details of quantum computing, but it used optical processing. The internal lasers of the processing unit were split into multiple beams and parallel processed. Interference invalidated the process. You couldn't measure the beams, you couldn't look to see where they were—the minute you did that, you changed the data.

You could beam the results of a quantum process, but if you transmitted the process itself, you created interference and invalidated the result. So all quantum computing was specifically linked to its hardware. You couldn't even guarantee that one quantum processor would exactly duplicate the results of another quantum processor. That had to do with chaos theory and fuzzy logic and the fact that quantum processors are affected by the time and place they're operating in. So quantum processors are best suited for weighted synaptic processing—*lethetic intelligence engines*.

A trained intelligence engine was worth at least a quarter trillion dollars. Maybe more. Depending on the training. And you couldn't just pipe the training from one engine into the next, because quantum doesn't pipe. Each engine had to be specifically trained.

According to Douglas, who was reporting what he read in *Scientific American*, they had finally gotten to the point where the intelligence engines could be trusted to train each other. I didn't understand the details. When Douglas started talking about forced coherency, congruent processing, and the fissioning of holographic personalities, my eyes glazed over. I finally had to tell him that if he was going to stay on our planet, he had to speak our language. What he did manage to get through to me was that there was a way of making two quantum processors marry each other so that their processing was temporarily synchronized—which meant that computers were finally moving from *simulated* sentience (which is what the monkey was) to *actual* sentience in a chip. Not that the average person would notice. Simulated sentience was good enough to fool most folks.

It didn't make sense that we might be carrying an actual IE unit in the monkey, those things were guarded like plutonium. Despite the fact that IE chips were always the McGuffin in every movie about high-tech robberies, it was impossible to steal one—because they guarded themselves. Anything interfering with their beams invalidated their processing—and every alarm in Saskatchewan would go off simultaneously.

No, it was my hunch that we might be carrying one of the quantum synchronizers—some kind of industrial smuggling or something. We didn't have to understand what it was. All we had to do was deliver it.

Only thing is—now that we had thoroughly screwed up Dad's travel plans . . . we had no idea where we were going or who we were supposed to deliver this thing to. Maybe the marshals trying to intercept us were working on behalf of the rightful owners. And maybe not. How would we know?

Anyway, it was only a hunch. Probably, it was something more mundane—like a bunch of codes—if it was anything at all. Dad said it was a decoy, but what if it wasn't. What if the smugglers thought it would be safer for the decoy to carry the McGuffin?

But even if the monkey had a quantum synchronizer or whatever inside, we'd have no way to tell just by looking at the outside of the card. And if there were some way to open it and look inside, that would be interference, and that would ruin it. So whatever it was, it was never going to be anything more than a hunch to me.

But . . . maybe I should think about this hunch for a bit.

Suppose we really were carrying something. It would have to be something *extremely* valuable, and the mule carrying it would have to be *extremely* stupid—I didn't like that part, but it made sense. A mule smart enough to know what he had would be smart enough to sell it to the highest bidder. The trick was to give it to someone who would be happy just to get a ticket offworld and who wouldn't fit the profile of a smuggler. Like a dad going to a colony with his kids. And the damn custody battle made it even better, not worse, because it was just the right kind of distraction. Smugglers didn't take their kids with them. Smugglers didn't have angry wives chasing them. And . . . if you had that kind of money to invest in that kind of mule, then you also had the kind of money to buy his way through customs or anywhere else.

Wasn't it convenient that Mickey was there? And his mom, the lawyer? And Judge Griffith too? And what about Alexei? Was he part of that plan too? No, he couldn't be. He didn't fit in—or did he? Who was on which side?

Or was I just being paranoid?

Could I even be sure about what Douglas said he knew? *No—don't go there, Chigger. That's* really *a shortcut to lunacy.*

Well, we were in the right place for it. That was for sure.

Along about then, Mickey stopped us and came back to check my oxygen. "I thought so," he said. "I should have made you change tanks at our last break."

"Huh?"

"You've been muttering in my ears for the last three kilometers."

"I'm fine. See?" I flipped the readout up so I could see it. It was flashing a pretty shade of red. "See?"

"Yes, I see—that's very nice. Does the word *hypoxia* mean anything to you?"

"She was Socrates' wife. I think."

"Wrong." Mickey was fumbling with the front of my bubble. For some reason I couldn't focus clearly.

"Hypoxia was queen of the Amazons," he said. "The Amazons lived in Scythia on the banks of the longest river in the world. They cut off their right breasts with scythes, so as not to interfere with their sword arms. Hercules killed Hypoxia at Troy for not checking her oxygen. Here, try to focus—" He clicked his air hose to the valve in the front of his bubble. Just like I had. An oxygen-jet.

"Are we stopping somewhere?"

"Yes, we're stopping right here." He pushed himself up close to me and hooked his bubble valve to mine. I couldn't see what he did next, but I started to hear a strange hissing sound. "I'm losing air, I think. I'm hissing."

"Take a deep breath, Chigger. Again. Again. Again. Keep on breathing. That's good. Can you see me now? Look at my hand. How many fingers can you see?"

I blinked. "All of them?"

"Close enough. Look at your readout again."

I looked. "It's flashing red." And then I started to get scared—

"Relax. You're breathing on my air now. Pay attention. We're going to change tanks on your rebreather. If you can't do it, I'll do it for you. Take your hands out of your gloves and I'll reverse them inward and—"

"I can do it." My hands were shaking and I felt suddenly weak and nauseous. "You do it."

"Good boy. You know when to ask for help. Do you know how many people have died because they were too stupid or too proud to ask for help?"

"No. How many?"

"I don't know either. But it's a lot, I can tell you that."

He had his hands inside my bubble now—it looked weird to see my gloves fiddling around at my belt, unclipping hoses and changing their connections. It reminded me of the way Doug used to button me up before taking me out to play. That didn't seem so long ago—but at the same time it seemed very far away. And now it was Mickey. He was acting just like a brother.

"There. How do you feel?"

"Fine."

"Do you have a headache?"

"Uh-uh." I touched my head to see if it was still there. My hand touched something else. A furry leg. "Is there a monkey sitting on my head?"

"Yes."

"Good. Then I'm not delusional."

"But no headache?"

"No. If anything, I feel giddy. A little light-headed. Like I could fly away."

"That's not good either." Mickey reached in and fiddled with the settings on my rebreather.

"What are you doing?"

"Just making some adjustments. This should do it. There." He pulled his hands out of my gloves and disconnected our two bubbles. We were separated again. He secured his rebreather tube and looked across at me. "All right, you good now?"

"Yeah." I was fumbling my hands back into my gloves.

"You sure? I've gotta go check Douglas and Bobby—"

"I'm good." But I grabbed his hand anyway. "Mickey?"

"Yeah?"

"Thank you."

He gave my hand a quick squeeze in return, then hurried across to Douglas.

PAYING INTENTION

AFTER THAT, WE WERE ALL a lot more careful.

I finally *got it* what Mickey meant.

It was about staying *conscious*. What some people called paying intention.

Dad once tried to tell me about this music teacher he'd had—the one who said you couldn't be a musician if you didn't practice at least three hours a day. He used to tell Dad that an excuse was not equal to a result. What you said you wanted was irrelevant; what you actually accomplished demonstrated your real intentions.

I never liked that discussion. It sounded like hard work to me and I couldn't see the reward in it. I always thought you should practice your music because you liked it, not because somebody said you had to. But I'd always listened politely, because it was always so important to Dad to give the *Pay intention, this is how the world works!* speech. *It's not enough to pay attention,* he would say, over and over. *You have to pay i*n*t*e*n*t*i*o*n* as well.

And there was all the rest of it too: *Volume is no substitute for brains. Better to keep your trap shut and be thought a fool than to shoot yourself in the foot while it's still in your mouth. Don't burn your bridges before your chickens are hatched.*

Every so often . . . I would realize he'd been right. He wasn't just talking to prove he knew better than me. This was one of those times. Well, why hadn't I paid intention when he'd told me about paying intention? Because . . . it's one of those stupid things you have to bump into yourself, and hope you survive long enough to make good use of the lesson.

So I concentrated on every bounce, every hop, every skip—and wondered if this is what it had been like for Harrison "Jack" Schmitt, bouncing around on the moon and trying to collect rocks without killing himself.

And every so often, I cursed the monkey. I'd been assuming that the monkey was a good safety monitor. Obviously, it wasn't. It was supposed to beep or scream or run for help if a life was in danger—but it hadn't alerted me that I was running low on air. So obviously, it didn't include an oxygen meter—and it hadn't been paying any attention to my rate of breathing. I was already gasping for breath when Mickey figured out there was something wrong and came back to check my air. If it hadn't been for Stinky, I'd have junked the monkey right there. Except I was still wondering about those memory bars.

"Look, there it is," said Mickey.

We stopped to look. He pointed toward the horizon. It was hard to see. The dark slope downward was outlined with bright highlights—places where outcroppings stuck up into the sunlight, or worse, places where the shadows dipped away altogether, leaving patches of Lunar soil painted with a hard actinic glare. We had to squint to see anything. Even Stinky, who was still groggy from the tranquilizer, stuck his head out of Douglas's poncho and demanded to know what we were looking at.

"It's hard to make out—" Mickey admitted. "Look for a reddish glow."

"Oh, I've got it," said Douglas. "Chigger, can you see it?"

"No—" The brightness made my eyes water. We were looking at a vast downhill slope, and the horizon was farther away than I had gotten used to. And there was a lot of sunlight being reflected back at us. And . . . I didn't want to say it aloud, but *there was something moving out there.*

But if there was something there, I had to tell them. And if there wasn't anything there and I was seeing things, then I had to say something about that too. *Didn't I?*

"Mickey?"

"Yes, Chigger?"

"Are there mirages on the moon?"

"Well, not mirages. Not like on Earth. You need an atmosphere for those kinds of mirages. But sometimes you get optical illusions. Or even psychological illusions. Your eyes will play tricks on you. Or your mind. Why? Do you see something?"

"I thought I did."

"Where?"

"Just to the left of the reflector. Something black, running and bouncing across the bright part. Didn't you see it?"

"No. Is it still there?"

"No."

"Did it look like a bubble?"

"No. It was too thin. I only caught a quick glimpse. I don't know what it was."

"Which way was it going?"

"It was coming toward us. Almost head-on."

That brought both Mickey and Douglas to attention. They scanned the distance for long moments, punctuated only by one of them asking, "Do you see it?" And the other replying, "No, do you?"

Finally, Mickey said, "Well, if it's out there, it's in the shadows now and we're missing it. But just to be on the safe side—" He came over and checked my air again.

I started to protest that I was fine, but then I realized that Mickey was only doing what he had to do, so I shut up and waited until he finished. Douglas asked, "Is he all right?"

Mickey nodded. "As far as I can tell." To me, he said, "I'm not saying you didn't see anything, Chigger. You were right to ask. But it's not unusual after you've had hypoxia to experience visual or auditory illusions."

"Hallucinations, you mean."

"Yeah," he admitted.

For a moment, none of us said anything. We were all thinking the same thing. Was the kid with the monkey on his head going crazy? And if not—then what was *out there*?

"All right," said Mickey. "Let's keep going. Let's get to the reflector. Douglas?"

Douglas started hop-skipping again. I followed. Mickey brought up the rear. Douglas hadn't said much, he'd been concentrating on Stinky most of the time. But now he said, "Mickey?"

"Yeah?"

"Do you think Alexei abandoned us?"

Mickey didn't answer for several bounces. I had begun to think he wasn't going to answer at all, when he said, "The thought had crossed my mind, yeah."

"You know him better than we do—"

"I don't know him that well. For all his talk, there's a lot he doesn't say. 'I make big deal, I make lots of money, I am embarrassed I make so much money, you will pick up check, *da?* All my money is tied up in cash, *da?*'" Mickey mimicked his Russian friend perfectly. "He's always got a deal going somewhere. But nobody ever knows what his deals are. I suppose that's a good thing. What you don't know you can't tell the marshals."

We bounced and skipped in silence for a while, punctuated only by occasional soft grunts. After a while, Mickey added, "But it's not like Alexei to endanger someone's life. Loonies don't do that. They believe that life is sacred everywhere. The greatest crime on Luna is to disrespect life. And Alexei is completely Loonie. He wouldn't do it. He couldn't."

More silence, more bouncing. I checked my readouts. They were green. I checked them again. This time I looked at the numbers. I checked them a third time and mouthed the numbers as I read them—reminding myself what was optimal. *Pay intention.*

Douglas broke the silence. "So you think he's dead."

"We didn't find a body."

"You didn't answer the question."

"I don't know." And then he added, "But it's the only thing I can think of that makes sense. . . ."

I disagreed. I could think of something else that made sense. But I didn't want to say it aloud. Not yet. I needed to think some more. As long as I didn't get distracted again—

I could see the reflector clearly now. It was a big silvery ball on a short spindly tripod. The whole thing had been dropped in from orbit and there were fragments of the landing pod around the base. But what caught my attention was the way the reflector had a sparkly-flickery look—all different colors. It was even more spooky because the whole thing was in shadow, so where were the flickers coming from?

I pointed it out to Mickey. He explained, "Lasers from all over the system. Everyone tunes their beams to a different color, that's why it looks like a rainbow, and everyone targets on Luna. It's a convenient landmark, and there's no atmosphere to distort the beams. It's kind of like Greenwich mean time, you know what that is? It's a reference point against which all other clocks are set. Well, Luna is like that too. It's the surveyor's post for everyone in the solar system to measure distances from. Accurate computations of distance are essential for space travel."

"Oh, yeah. That makes sense."

"We're almost there. Do you want to take a meal break? We can even go in the inflatable for a bit." It was still bouncing along behind him.

I opened my mouth to say yes, then stopped. "What's that—?" I pointed.

"What's what?" And then he saw it too.

It was a bubble suit, like ours. An *empty* bubble suit. Half-inflated. As if the person wearing it had taken it off and skipped away into the arid dark.

It was *Alexei's* bubble suit.

REFLECTIONS

MY FIRST THOUGHT WAS, SO *that answers that question.*

My second thought was, *No, it doesn't. Where's the body?*

How do you get out of a bubble suit and just walk away?

You don't.

So *where was Alexei?*

The question was more puzzling than ever.

And why was his suit *here*? How did it get here from *there*? Who else was here? I glanced around nervously. There could be an entire army hiding just behind the horizon. We'd have no way of knowing.

Mickey and Douglas were just as disconcerted as I was. Maybe even more so. Because they knew all the stuff I hadn't even thought of—so they probably had even more questions.

We all climbed into the inflatable to talk about it. Once inside, we took off our bubble suits, and Mickey equalized the oxygen in all our tanks, something he'd been wanting to do ever since I burned off thirty minutes of breathing to stop myself on the zip line.

We pushed back the hoods of our ponchos, took off our goggles, and sipped at our water bottles. I took the monkey off my head and set it aside. We nibbled at our inedible MREs, we inhaled deeply—the air in the inflatable was stale, but it was fresher than the air in the bubble suits—we used our toilet bags, and we talked about calling for rescue.

We all knew the arguments. What we were doing was dangerous. Stupid. Foolhardy. Probably unnecessary. I was posthypoxic and hallucinating. Douglas's back was starting to hurt—even though Stinky weighed less on Luna, he still had the same *mass*. So even though it mostly felt like he wasn't heavy, the truth was that there was some stuff called inertia and momentum that made carrying the little monster almost as tiring as if we were still on Earth. Mickey's feelings were unreadable. He looked as if he had a lot of different things all going on at the same time. And Stinky was alternating between constipation and diarrhea, catatonia and hyperactivity—so at least one of us was normal.

It was a question of endurance. The reflector was our halfway point. Actually, it was more than halfway. It was nearly two-thirds of the way. But Alexei and Mickey had figured that in terms of sheer physical exhaustion, the last third of the Lunar hike would take us as long as the first two-thirds. As much fun as it was to go bouncing across the silvery gloom, it was very tiring too. My legs were beginning to hurt. My calves ached.

And I was scared again.

I wasn't afraid of Luna anymore. But I respected her now. I had a better sense of her dangers—and I was *paying intention*.

I was terrified by all the stuff I *didn't* know—especially all the stuff I didn't know that I didn't know. Alexei's empty bubble suit scared the hello out of me. What could have happened that only his empty suit would be left behind? Did something suck him right out of the plastic?

I shuddered. And shivered. And wrapped my silver poncho tight around me.

Above us, the reflector sparkled with stray bits of light—a thousand different colors, the beams of distant spaceships, other worlds and moons, asteroids, the Earth, the orbital beanstalk, L4 and L5, orbiting satellites—all their questioning fingers of light touched and bounced away, back to their origins, each one carrying a single part of the answer to the question *Where am I?*

You're *there*—7.68 godzillion angstroms away from *here*. And we're here—7.68 godzillion angstroms away from *there*. Sitting under the stars and watching the flickering radiance of your thousand lonely queries. But none of you are more alone than us—sitting here all alone in the dark.

How far would all those beams travel on their journeys here and back? How long would it take them? Just the blink of an eye—a few seconds to Earth, a few minutes to the asteroid belt. What were they all saying?

They didn't even know we were here. It was a strange feeling to see so much evidence of human life and still be so far away from it all.

We could rejoin it in a moment. All we had to do was tune our transmitters to the public bands, turn up the power, and call for help. I was ready to concede I didn't know as much as I pretended. I'd made my point, I could quit now. I'd still gotten farther than Dad ever would have. And I knew Douglas wouldn't take much convincing if he thought that Stinky or I were in danger. Mickey . . . I didn't know what he thought, but he looked tired and irritable and unhappy. Whatever exhilaration we had felt about being on the moon, that was gone, swamped by our exhaustion and our fear. We'd had too many close calls. The *wunderstorm* was over.

Mickey unhooked his transmitter from his belt. "Do we have to talk about this?" he asked. "Or are we all in agreement this time?" He looked to Douglas. Douglas shook his head. He looked to me—

That's when *something outside the inflatable moved*—and I screamed and leapt backward so hard I bumped into the wall and went bouncing sideways, scaring the hell out of Stinky and Douglas and Mickey, and they went bouncing every which way too—

It was a gangly black spidery thing, with a grotesque bug-eyed face, and grasping claws. It came right up to the edge of the bubble and pressed its face and hands against the plastic, peering in at us like some kind of vacuum-breathing insect. Even Stinky was shrieking— Douglas grabbed him in a restraining hug and turned him away so he couldn't see—

And then I saw the lettering above the eyes КРИСЛОВ—I couldn't read the word, the letters were all funny-looking and backwards—until I recognized them as Russian. And then Mickey was shouting, "It's Alexei! It's Alexei! Everybody shut up! Stop screaming! It's only Alexei! *It's Alexei!*"

By then, I'd already stopped screaming, and Alexei was already pulling himself into the inflatable, one section of the entrance tube at a time. He was careful to close and check each zipper behind him before he opened the next. He still looked scary—like a big skinny faceless *thing*.

Finally, he popped in through the last zipper and carefully sealed it behind himself. He pulled off the rubbery hood of his scuba suit and finally his breather tube and goggles. He was laughing so hard I wanted to punch him in the gut. How dare he scare us like that?

"Is big fright, *da*? Is Rock Father come to eat poor crazy terries. Scream and scream again. You are much frightened. I laugh so hard I almost choke on my air hose. You did not expect poor Alexei, did you? Is only turnabout to play fair. Alexei did not expect to find you here either. Did you not hear my messages? No, I think you did not. My transmitter failed. I could hear you, but you could not hear me. Very inconvenient, *da*? So you did not hear me say you should wait, I go for help. No need for rescue. I could run to Prospector's Station and signal Mr. Beagle and be back with help and air in two hours—"

"Mr. Beagle—?"

"Later. You will meet him later. But I cannot call him now. I hear you in distance—you are looking for me. Calling, *da*? I realize you have come down from mountain somehow. So I turn around and come back for you before you get lost."

"But your bubble suit—?" I asked.

"I could not leave it behind, Charles Dingillian, could I? I would never find it again. So I left it at reflector as signal for you that I was still alive."

"Oh," Mickey said. There was an edge to his voice. "Is that what that was?"

Alexei slapped his chest in mock-frustration. "Ah, you do not un-derstand Self-Contained Universal Breathing Apparatus, do you? Body suit is so firm-fitting it makes airtight seal all around. Strong enough to hold body safe and tight against vacuum. Hood seals tight around goggles and earphones and breather tube. Is not as practical as bubble suit for long distances. No way to pee or poop. No way to drink or eat. Cannot even talk very well. But for emergencies or for short distances, is much easier. Is basic worksuit for Loonies."

"We're not Loonies," Douglas said.

"Maybe someday you will be," Alexei responded, very matter-of-factly. "Earth is falling apart. Luna will have to provide resources to rebuild. Luna will become seat of economic power and political authority for double-planet system of Earth-Luna. Is only logical. We have high ground of discipline and resources. Nobody gets to Luna by accident. We are a society of hard workers. Earth cannot compete with that. It makes sense that Lunatics should govern, *da?*"

"I think we already have enough lunatics in government," said Douglas dryly. "The old-fashioned kind."

"*Da*, we have our share too. But even our craziest Loonies know the rules. Everybody pays oxygen tax."

"And what happens if you don't?" asked Douglas.

"You have to stop breathing." Alexei helped himself to one of Mickey's MREs and began unwrapping it. "Nobody ever breaks law second time." He took a disgustingly large bite of something that looked like chopped brick and kept on talking while he chewed. "First I will eat, then I will use toilet bags. Then we will hurry to Prospector's Station. As long as we are this far, no need to call Mr. Beagle for help. We will catch early train, fool marshals. Huh, what is wrong—?" He blinked in surprise, looking at us, suddenly realizing. "You were planning to call for help, *da*? I see it in your faces. Is lucky I stop you in time—" Alexei turned to Mickey and took the transmitter out of his hands. "Listen, *Mikhail*, is big mistake to call for help. Everything on Earth is falling apart, so everything on Luna is shutting down. It will be much harder to hide anything—even little one's monkey. Can you go one more hour? Two? Maybe a little more than two? Prospector's Station is only four and a half klicks from here, most. Almost all downhill. Train arrives in few hours. Once we get on train, we can go anywhere."

"As cargo again?" Douglas asked. He looked angry.

"No, no, I promise. I have planned idea for disguise. Very clever, I am. I will take you wherever you want to go—even if you change mind. Must go quickly now. We have not as much air anymore. I use up too much air going and coming back and not getting anywhere."

Mickey was already whispering to his PITA and frowning at its responses.

"I vote no," said Douglas firmly.

"We don't have a choice," said Mickey.

"Huh?"

"We don't have enough air anymore. Not enough to sit and wait for a rescue. Alexei's coming back changes the whole oxygen equation. He used up most of his. Now he's on ours." He was already reaching for his bubble suit. "We have to go. *Now*."

"How serious is it?" asked Douglas.

"Not serious if we go *now*. If we stop to argue about it, it gets very serious."

Douglas looked like he wanted to say something. He looked like he wanted to say a whole bunch of somethings, but he held his tongue. "Bobby—come on, time for another piggyback ride."

"Do I gotta—?"

"Yeah, you gotta."

"Do you want me to take him?" Mickey asked. "I don't mind, really."

Douglas shook his head. "You just keep watching Chigger." The look on his face said it all. He was very angry. And we were going to hear about this later.

RUN IN THE SUN

AND THEN WE WERE ON our way again, bouncing and skipping and hopping and tumbling through the Lunar darkness. Alexei ran ahead in his Scuba gear, he didn't want to waste time with the bubble suit. Douglas hop-skipped behind him in that weird bouncing lope that the first Lunar astronauts had discovered as the most efficient method of moving quickly around the Lunar surface. Mickey and I brought up the rear. The inflatable bounced along behind us on a long silvery leash. We must have looked like a soap commercial—four manic bubbles chasing a frantic piece of lunatic lint.

The reflector disappeared behind us, and for a while, everything was silent again. A week ago, all I wanted was a quiet place to listen to my music; now I was beginning to resent the silence. It was too *much* silence. Luna was so quiet it was scary. You could hear your heart beating in your chest. You could hear the blood flowing through your veins. You could hear your own ears.

Suddenly, there you are, alone with your own brain.

Back on Earth, all I'd ever wanted was for everybody else to shut up, so I could hear my own thoughts and not theirs. But here on Luna, the silence was so deep, it swallowed up everything. It was as vast and empty as the whole universe. It stretched from here to forever and back again. I felt like I had fill it with something or disappear too. Only I didn't have enough music or thoughts or anything else to fill up a silence that big.

Mickey stayed close to me, watching me carefully. This was going to be a long mad dash with very few rest breaks. Alexei wanted us to catch the train, and we didn't have enough air to do anything else. So it was hop-skip and bump from one hill to the next. Hither and thither and yawn. I was tired, and it was getting hard to pay intention. And nobody wanted to talk, we just wanted to get there.

Four and a half kilometers isn't that far. On Earth, it's maybe two hours' walk on level ground. On Luna, with lesser gravity, bouncing downslope at a brisk pace, it shouldn't be any longer; what you lose in mobility from the bubble suit, you get back from the lighter gravity.

But this part of Luna didn't have *level* ground. On the map it looked like a plain, but at ground level, it was a rolling bumpy surface, pockmarked with little craters, boulders, ridges, and rough hillocks. Tumbles of rocks were scattered everywhere. And every so often, there were chasms we had to leap over. Alexei called them "expansion joints," but didn't explain what they were.

I concentrated on my hop-skipping. I found a rhythm and played music in my head to match. A Philip Glass piece, one of the repetitive ones with endless chord changes. It could be played forever. And as long as I could keep it running in my head, I could keep moving. I'd probably have it stuck in my head for a month—

And then we stopped.

Brightness lay ahead. "Oh, *chyort!*"

Alexei laughed at my outburst. "Remind me to explain that to you." His voice came muffled in my ears.

—but the *chyort* was real. We'd run out of shadow.

Ahead, the ground rose up into sunlight. Perpetual dawn slammed sideways across the landscape. It blazed and sparkled. It was too bright to look at, even with the goggles fully polarized.

"Is not to worry," said Alexei. I wanted to kick him. "Is not as bad as it looks."

"Not as bad—" That was Mickey. "How far does this extend?"

Alexei hesitated. "Is less than one kilometer. We can do it. We rest here. Turn off heaters. Get very cold. We run for fifteen minutes, straight that way. We warm up, *da*. We get hot. But we have fifteen minutes before bubble suits turn into little ovens. Who cannot run one kilometer in fifteen minutes? On Luna, is piece of cheese."

"You're crazy," said Douglas. "Absolutely crazy. Why didn't you tell us this before? Why didn't you tell us about the mountain climbing and the zip line and the bubble suits and everything?"

"Because if I tell you, you would say, 'no, Alexei, I'm afraid not. That sounds like much too hard. We will much rather sit here like little potted plants to be pickled in our own juices.' But I tell you that no, you are not little cabbages, and here we are, almost home, and you find you are much bigger and much braver than you thought. You do the mountain, you do the zip line, you do everything else—you can do this too. You have to. Is no alternative to this. You stay here, you die. And little stinking one with you. But you come with me across sunlight and you live to laugh about it. Get ready now. Time you stand here thinking about this is time you will not have on other side. *Mikhail*, help me check air on everyone, please." He was already peering at my read-outs. Without looking up, he said, "*Mikhail*, do not give me that look. Remember, I promise to take care of you. I am keeping that promise. Right now I am taking better care of you than you are taking yourself. You should thank me. You will thank me soon enough. Come, please. I have too much money invested in you already. I do not intend to lose my investment. Charles Dingillian, you are fine. I have turned your air up just a little. You will do fine. Be grateful monkey does not breathe, you would not have enough air for both of you; otherwise, one of you would have to stay behind. As soon as we are all too cold to move, we will go. Come, *Mikhail*, let me check you now."

Alexei kept up a steady stream of chatter. Maybe his mind really was that peripatetic, spinning from thought to thought like a dervish. And maybe he was doing it deliberately to keep us from thinking what a stupid thing we were about to do. In all likelihood, we were going to end up as a bunch of fried mummies, baking on the Lunar plain. I wondered what kind of weird life-forms would evolve in our sealed and abandoned bubble suits. What would future Lunar explorers find growing here in the blazing sun? Flesh-eating fungi? Vacuum-breathing mold? Something dreadful, no doubt—especially *Grottius Stinkoworsis*.

I shuddered. It turned into a shiver. A whole bunch of shivers. I was cold. I could see my breath. "Uh—Alexei?"

"Yes, yes, I know. We are just waiting for Douglas to chill. Ha-ha, I make joke there. Old-fashioned slang. Never mind. Douglas and Robert mass more than everyone else. They generate more body heat. It will take longer for them to chill out. We want temperature in bubble suit to be almost freezing. Below would be better, but we do not want to risk frostbite either. We are almost there. Please be patient. Douglas? Are you ready? *Mikhail*? Charles? Hokay. There is no more time for chattering—except teeth, perhaps. When I say we go, everyone follow me. Don't fall down. Just keep going, no matter what. Remember to pace yourself. We are not racing. We are bouncing like before, only faster. Everybody ready? Get set? *Go!*"

And with that, he was off—a black stick figure racing into the light, carrying his bubble suit over his shoulder. Douglas followed immediately after. I hesitated for half a heartbeat—then plunged ahead. Mickey called, "I'm right behind you!"

We bounced into the light and it was like coming out of a tunnel. The sun slammed sideways into us like a wall of radiance. It was blinding. It dazzled and glared and my eyes started watering almost immediately. But I knew that part of it was just that my eyes hadn't adjusted yet. I found my rhythm and kept going. Hop with the left foot, hop with the right—I skipped steadily after Alexei and Douglas, bouncing high with every step.

We would have been floating through the air—if there had been air, but there wasn't; so we bumbled gracefully through space—bouncing across the land like gossamer hippopotami.

Everything was still too bright, the sideways glare etched every rock and boulder in sandpaper detail, the plains looked painful—but I wasn't hot in the bubble suit. Not yet. I was still shivering from the prolonged cold of the long Lunar shadows. I was almost impatient for the suit to start warming up. So far, this wasn't too bad. But we had a long way to go, and the sun's heat would be cumulative.

Behind me, I could hear Mickey counting off checkpoints. We passed the first one and I realized I wasn't shivering anymore, but the bubble suit still felt cold. Maybe it was just the exertion that was warming me up. I glanced back. The line of shadow had receded into the distance. A little farther and it would be over the horizon. That would be the worst—when we were out of sight of shadow.

Despite the long shadows, there was little refuge out here. The boulders were too small, their shadows were stretched out thin and insignificant. The light came in at us from the side, like the flame of a giant torch. All around us, the surreal landscape glowed; we pushed headlong into a world of dazzling glare. The inside of the bubble flashed and sparkled with rogue reflections. I was getting comfortably warm.

I maintained my pace, occasionally glancing back to see if Mickey was keeping up. He was close behind me. Ahead, Douglas was maintaining a steady pace, even burdened as he was with Stinky. Even farther ahead, I could see the flashing black figure of Alexei bounding through the sunlight. He wasn't having a problem with this, he'd already done it twice—once across, then back again when he'd heard us following him. His Scuba suit was refrigerated. He could go farther than any of us.

We passed the second checkpoint, still pounding across the silvery white dust, and I began to feel optimistic about making it. Maybe this wasn't going to be as bad as I feared. All I had to do was keep Alexei and Douglas in sight. Just keep bouncing. Watch out for the boulders. Pay intention. And try not to notice the cold drop of sweat running down my side—

It was getting warmer out here. It was getting warmer *in* here. Inside the bubble. Not uncomfortable yet, but . . .

I glanced back. Mickey was still close behind me. "Pay intention, Chigger!"

It wasn't Mickey I was worried about. It was the distance to shadow. Every bounce forward was also a bounce farther from darkness. And I had no idea how far we still had to go to get to the shadows on the other side. We were heading deeper into the heart of brightness. I began to worry. I wasn't hot yet, but—I was thinking about *hot*. The cumulative heat was building up.

I began to worry that Alexei had miscalculated. He had the refrigerated suit. We didn't. What if we were like the swimmer who swims too far out and has no strength left for getting back. What if the heat in our bubbles became intolerable before we got to the other side? What if we were getting too far out into the light to reach *any* shade safely? What if we could only get *most* of the way across, but not the last half klick? What if we couldn't make the last hundred meters? What if we couldn't make the last *ten* meters—?

Ohell. What if we couldn't even get *halfway* to safety? What if we had already passed the point of safe return? What if we were already doomed? What if we were already burning up and didn't know it?

"*Shut up!*"

"Huh?" said Mickey, right behind me. "I didn't say anything."

"I wasn't talking to you. I was talking to the little voices. Shut up! Shut up! Shut up!"

"Chigger, are you all right?"

Oh great. Now he was thinking I was going crazy—

I looked at my numbers. "I'm fine."

These bubble suits weren't designed for this. They were meant for emergencies. All this stuff, it was supposed to be used for keeping folks alive until the rescue boat could get to them—nobody ever intended these things for Lunar exploration. Not for long-distance hikes across the Lunar surface. Not like this. Alexei had told us not to worry, it was part of the design specification because who knew what might be needed in an emergency, but just because a bubble suit *can* doesn't mean it *should*. And besides . . . what if Alexei was lying about the suits? Then what?

But why would he lie to us? What was the point in that? Did he want to kill us? How would he benefit from that? Well, there was a thought . . .

We passed the next checkpoint. I'd lost count. I had no idea what Alexei and Mickey were using as checkpoints. I couldn't tell one rock from another anymore. I wasn't warm anymore. I was hot, the sweat was running down my body. I'd skip into space—lifting up high to see the glowing landscape ahead of us, then each time as I'd float back down, the droplets would go coursing down my underarms in warm sluggish trails that made me think of snails—and then I'd bounce down onto the silvery floor of sparkling light and the droplets would splatter off, into my already-clammy jumpsuit. With each hop and skip, the damp material plastered itself against me like a used towel. Everything was wet and smelly with sweat.

I'd been in the sauna a few times, at school. I didn't like it. It was too hot. This was almost as hot. Not quite. But getting there. I thought about cold orange juice—*real* orange juice—not the orange-colored stuff that Mom always bought. I thought about ice. I thought about ice water. I thought about swimming in ice water.

Another checkpoint. And I still didn't see any shadows on the horizon. We were in the middle of a dazzling plate of fire. We were under a magnifying glass. The hard black sky was overruled by the scorching blaze of light in the east. The sweat poured off me. So did the tears.

"You're doing fine, Chigger. Just keep on. Only a little farther." That was Mickey's voice.

I couldn't see anyone clearly anymore. There was a dark figure bouncing in front of me. And a blurry bubble too. Mickey's occasional comments came from behind me. Were they suffering as much as I was? I couldn't imagine it—

Maybe Alexei really did want us dead, so he could skip off into the darkness with the monkey . . .

Sure, that was it. That's why he'd left us up on the rim of the crater. He wasn't going for help. He was just going. And going. And then what—? It was too hot to think of the next step. But if he knew where the monkey was and nobody else did, then he could sell it to whoever would pay the most and nobody else could get to it if we were dead—and the moon was the perfect place to lose anything. Or anyone.

How much more of this could my bubble suit take before it popped? Was it already bigger because the air was heating up and expanding? And why didn't we float up into the air like the hot-air balloons in Albuquerque? Weren't we hot enough? Oh, we were hot enough, but there wasn't any air to float up into—

Another checkpoint. Mickey's voice sounded bad. Somewhere ahead, Stinky was crying—or screaming. I bounced up, floated down, bounced up, floated down—watched the landscape drop away, peered into the distance, floated down—everything was brightness in all directions.

Ice water, ice water, ice water, swimming in ice water, diving in ice water. Dying in ice water. It didn't work anymore. It was too hot. It was burning. It was hotter than the sauna. I wasn't going to make it. I didn't see how I could make it. I bounced up, floated down, I couldn't see anything but solar glare. We had come too far to get back and there was no shadow anywhere. We'd bounced and skipped into sunlight and we were going to die here—

I kept going anyway. I wanted to lie down, but I didn't. I didn't have any more sweat. It had all been boiled out of me. I went to take a sip of water but it was too hot to drink. And as fast as I sipped, it just dripped right out of me. There were droplets bouncing around the inside of the bubble now. There were little puddles splashing lazily around the bottom in a graceful slow-motion ballet.

Another checkpoint—

If I fell down, I wouldn't be able to get up. I had to pay intention. This was the hard part. I wasn't going to be the first to fall—

Just before we had started across the frying pan, while Alexei was checking Mickey's air, Douglas had pulled me aside, had talked to me like an adult. "I'm responsible for Bobby. You're responsible for Charles. I can't be responsible for both of you. If you fall down,

Charles, I *can't* save you. I can't come back for you. Neither can Mickey. If it gets so bad out there that you can't get up, no one else can pick you up either. Don't fall down. If you fall down, and I try to save you, we *all* die. Don't fall down."

"I won't." It had been easy to reassure him at the time. Because I didn't know. Not then. Now I *knew*. And I wasn't sure I could keep the promise. I could barely see anymore. I followed the bouncing blur.

One more bounce. Take the next bounce. Just one more bounce. Keep going. It won't get better if you stop. Another bounce. And another. Keep on bouncing. Bouncing. Keep on, Charles—keep your promise. Don't fall. *Pay intention.*

And then—"There it is!" Mickey's voice.

I didn't see it. I saw bright scorching solar blur. I saw purple splotches floating in front of my eyes. I saw noise and dazzle. *I didn't see any shadow.* He was lying. He was just saying that to keep me going—

"Straight ahead, Chigger! Almost there!"

"Almost where?" But I didn't have any voice. Just croak. Not even loud enough to be heard.

I bounced, I floated, I looked. Painful brightess. Something angled. Maybe. Bounced, floated, looked—something flat and rectangular, angled toward the sun. But not darkness. It still didn't resolve. Bounced, floated, looked—it didn't make sense, but it wasn't sunlight and I bounced and floated toward it.

Alexei was already there, in the shade of it. *Shade!* Something dark was humped into the ground. He was opening a hatch, standing and waving, beckoning. Douglas was just bouncing into the shadow of something—it was real!

And then I tripped. And bounced and rolled, ass over elbow, every which way—*had I punctured my bubble? Was I dead and didn't know it yet?*—I was still rolling. I heard voices.

"Let him go, *Mikhail*—get out of the sun! We can't lose both of you—" That was Alexei! And then, "I am get him."

I was trying to get up, but my arms weren't working. My feet kept kicking uselessly at the bottom of the bubble. I didn't have the air to scream. I felt like a frog in a frying pan. I probably looked like one too. Just add butter—never mind, I'll lie here and boil in my own juices. A fat lot of help you are, you stupid monkey—

And then, someone was rolling me around, I wasn't doing it, some-

thing black blurred around my vision, and then I was vaguely upright—
"Can you move, or do I carry you?" Without waiting for an answer,
Alexei grabbed my bubble suit by one of the plastic handles on the
outside; he held me high, and began bouncing toward the blackness
ahead—

The light went out abruptly—not the heat, I was still baking like a
clam in my own shell. But at least the light was gone. Hands pushed
at me, pushed me into a dark tube, pushed me farther. Pushed. Through
a series of horizontal hatches that opened in front of me and closed
behind me. I felt helpless to resist—I couldn't see anything but
splotches of purple dazzle. I bounced off something—I heard hissing.
I heard a hatch slam. I heard voices, not in my earphones, but from
farther away. I heard sounds I couldn't identify. A voice swearing in
Russian. An argument. Douglas calling out—"Is Charles all right?"

"Is not dead yet," said Alexei. And that would have been reassuring to hear if I didn't have more accurate information than he did. And
then the hissing got louder, and louder—someone was unzipping my
bubble suit—I tried to slap them away, but I didn't have strength to
resist, so I just lay on the floor and waited to die. I took hungry deep
breaths, filled myself with hot air, that was a mistake, the vacuum
would rip it out of my lungs like a scream—and then the hissing
stopped and—cooler air rolled around me, surprising me like a wet slap
in the face, and I *youched* aloud and tried to sit up, but I still couldn't,
and then the hands were pulling wet plastic up and off me, and suddenly I was *out of the bubble* and the air wasn't baking around me. I
rolled sideways and blinked at the darkness, there were people moving
in the purple dazzle. Douglas and Bobby and Mickey and someone still
in black. КРИСЛОВ.

"We made it!" Mickey cracked in a voice like old dust.

"*Da!*" said Alexei, pulling off his hood. "We made it. I did not think
you would, but you do pretty good for terries. I only had to drag one
of you into the shade. Welcome to Prospector's Station." He glanced at
his watch. "You make very good time too. For terries."

"You didn't think we'd make it—?" That was Douglas. Weakly.

"*Da.* But if I tell you that, you wouldn't try."

"If you didn't think we'd make it . . ." Douglas began slowly,
". . . then why did you let us try?"

"Because I assume—rightly—that like all terries, you are too stupid to lie down and die. You keep going anyway. Yell at me later, Doug-

las. You have prove me right again. Save voice for now. You are all dehydrated. Here, drink water." He started passing out plastic water bags. He popped the nipple of mine and held it to my face. "Drink slowly—little gulps. You have been through much. Give body time to recover. We have plenty time before train arrives. Over an hour."

THE DARK SIDE OF THE LOON

PROSPECTOR'S STATION WAS THREE CARGO pods, laid end to end, half-buried in the Lunar dust. They were sheltered by three near-vertical sails of solar panels. The pods were linked together on a north–south orientation, and the solar panels were mounted on gimbals so they could swing down on either side to block the sun's rays at dawn and dusk and all the positions in between. The habitability of the shelter depended solely on the maintenance of the motors.

The pods were divided into two levels; the bottom level of each pod was storage, the top was function. The pod at the north end was a hydroponics farm, the pod at the south was a machine shop, the center pod was the living area. Nobody lived here permanently, it was a communal site. Everybody who used it had to replace what they used and make sure that the station was in working order for whoever might stay here next.

Crosshatch decking had been laid along the bottom of the pod to provide a level floor. Underneath the floor, several plastic bags served as impromptu water tanks—another use for inflatable airlocks; waste not, want not. Above us, identical mesh decking provided the ceiling to this level and the floor to the next; we could see up through the crosshatch to the level above. It was just like being in a tube-town again, only this time with lighter gravity.

I sprawled on my back, with my eyes closed, watching the purple glares fade into mottling blue-and-gray fractalizations, watching the fabric of unreality unravel in my imagination, occasionally sipping at the water bag that Alexei was holding for me. Every so often, he'd tip it to my lips, let me suck a few swallows, then pull it away before I could start gulping greedily.

It didn't make sense. Why was he being so nice to me now if he wanted to kill us? Maybe because he needed our deaths to look natural?

Sure. That was it. Because he knew the monkey would be a witness to whatever he did. The testimony of robots had been used before in court cases, especially when they had stored audio and video records pertinent to the legal matter at hand. Most robots above Class 6—and that included the monkey—were continually sorting and storing their records. Cheap memory made it possible for a robot to retain a lot of information; it turned out to be useful for a lot of things—family albums, long-term health records, behavioral records, insurance tracking, consumer tracking, the census, stuff like that. Anyone who wanted to track "lifestyle information" could poll the international robot database for specifically correlated information.

It was rumored that robots were also good for amateur pornography, because they also tracked human sexual behavior. Which is why Mom had always said, "Don't do anything in front of a robot that you wouldn't want God to see you doing." Which meant never do *anything* in front of a robot, if you didn't want to get caught. There were so many robots in some neighborhoods that getting away with a crime was impossible.

This didn't mean that crime didn't happen. It just meant that enforcement was more about finding *where* the criminal was than *who* he was.

So, if Alexei were planning to kill us, he had to make it look like an accident. Because the monkey was watching *everything*. That would explain leaving us on the rim and taking us into the sunlight to get to Prospector's Station.

Alexei couldn't just take the monkey from us, because he knew I'd programmed it to be loyal to me first, then Douglas, and finally Stinky. It was *emotionally* linked. It wouldn't go with anyone else unless we told it to—or unless we were dead. If we were dead, its loyalty programming would store all pertinent information about us and our deaths in unerasable files—and without further instructions of who it should report to, it would shut down and wait for the next person to open it up and assign ownership to himself. Alexei? Probably. Most certainly.

Unless I had been out in the sun too long and was still making up crazy paranoid fantasies . . . I had to consider that too. Alexei put the water bag to my lips again. I took another sip. Around me, I could hear everyone else breathing softly, catching their breaths, sucking at water bags. I could smell their sweat in the air. It smelled like a locker room in here. We all stank. I didn't care. It was cool. Blessedly cool. Almost too cold. I was evaporating excess heat as rapidly as my body could carry my overheated blood to my skin.

What was in the monkey that was so valuable it was worth killing for?

I was pretty sure it wasn't information. Whatever data was packed into the memory bars would have already been piped to its recipient some other way by now. Probably the moment we were served with our first subpoena at Geostationary somebody somewhere was saying "Oh, *merde!*" and then, "All right. Switch to Plan B. Code it in the least significant bit of each pixel of the local news and let them download it off the web." Or whatever. There were just too many ways to smuggle bits from here to there. So it wasn't the information. It had to be something physical.

Money? No. Codes for money? No, that was more information. They'd have found another way to send it by now. Physical ID keys that unlocked money? Maybe. But if that's what it was, they wouldn't have trusted Dad with it. It had to be something so unique that this was the only way to move it from here to there. Wherever *there* was.

So it wasn't information. And it wasn't money. What else was there?

Power.

I took another sip of water. I was feeling better, but I wasn't ready to open my eyes yet.

Power was a good answer. People would kill for power, wouldn't they? Of course they would. If they wanted it badly enough.

But what kind of power?

Processing power.

If you had processing power, you had *every* kind of power. It all depended how you applied the processing power.

Quantum processing?

Could you pack a quantum CPU into a memory bar?

I'd have to ask Douglas that.

He'd probably tell me I was crazy.

It *was* an outrageous idea.

Alexei trying to kill us—then saving us—then holding the water bag for me. Yeah, sure. The monkey wasn't sentient. It hadn't done anything at all to help us survive.

No. There had to be a simpler explanation.

I laughed at my own paranoia and opened my eyes, blinking and squinting. I could almost see again. I lifted up on my elbow to thank Alexei for saving me—and almost choked in horror.

It wasn't Alexei holding the water bag.

It was the monkey. It curled back both its lips to show its teeth and gave me its goofiest smile.

CHANGES

WE HAD TO GET AWAY from Alexei.

I had to convince Douglas and Mickey that we had to get away from Alexei.

I had to get them in a room *away* from Alexei so I could tell them why we had to get away from Alexei. I doubted that they would believe me. Heck, even *I* didn't believe me.

Alexei had stripped off his Scuba suit, finally, and was giving himself a "space-bath." A space-bath is where you strip naked and wipe yourself all over with alcohol pads and moisturizer sponges. It stings a lot, but it gets you mostly clean. He tossed bath bags at everyone else and told us to do the same. "Worst thing on Luna is nose crime. Don't make big stink on Luna. Very bad manners. Wash every six hours. When you wake up and when you go to bed. Before you put on space suit, after you take it off. Before sex, after sex. Use moisturizers on skin so you don't dry out and flake and make dust. Shave body hair regularly, same reason. Use deodorants. Others should not have to breathe your effluvia. Also slows down disease germs."

So I opened the bag and took a bath. I stripped out of my jumpsuit and sat skinny and apart and wiped as much of myself as I could reach. Mickey and Douglas and Stinky were all washing each other, scrubbing each other's backsides and behind the knees and backs of the ears and places like that. The places I couldn't reach, I handed the cloth to the monkey and let him do it. Alexei offered, but I didn't want him touching me anymore.

The thing was, the cleaner I got, the better I felt, and the sillier the whole thing began to feel. It was just me listening too much to my own thoughts again—like Mom always said. She said that too much silence wasn't good for a person. "Your mind goes go off into never-never land and never comes back. Just like your father. He went off, did too much thinking for his own good, and he never came back either." Yeah, right, Mom.

But Mom didn't say all that stuff just because she believed it. She said it because she thought it was true and she didn't want us to make the same stupid mistakes that she and Dad had made. So she figured if she told us the punch lines, we wouldn't have to live through the jokes. Ha ha. We saw how that worked out. I had the fastest divorce in the family.

I finished wiping myself—even in places that most people don't talk about—and pushed the soiled cloth back into its bag. I tucked it into a larger bag for waste, hanging from the inevitable wall webbing. I was beginning to suspect that everything on Luna was made from cargo pods, and there would be wall webbing everywhere.

Alexei glanced over to me and said, "Hokay, girls—let's go upstairs. Are you ready for your disguises?"

"Huh?"

"You do not think you can ride the train as the Dingillian family, do you? Ah, from the looks on your faces, I can see you have not thought about this at all. You are lucky I am so foresighted. Come upstairs. Follow me, all of you. Hurry now."

We shrugged and followed him up the ladder to the top level of the station—we went hand over hand, feet were redundant. His endless monologue continued. "Douglas, you will be Samm Brengle-Tucker, famous hermit prospector. Everybody knows Brengle-Tucker, he is very famous because nobody knows him. You ask, if no one has ever met him, what proof do you have that nobody knows him? There is none, of course, because you cannot prove a negative. We had that in logic class at Lunatic U. Prove that you cannot prove a negative. Very confusing, very clever—Loonies like word games, logic puzzles. But you understand the problem, *da*? How can everyone know him if nobody knows him? That is because he never comes in from the cold. Or the hot. He only sends e-mail. He orders supplies, he pays in cash. He picks up supplies when he gets around to it. He lives in self-sufficient tunnels. He has ice claim registered somewhere in Superstition Crater.

Sometimes he sells water and soil with earthworms, only here they are Luna worms, because they can't be earthworms on moon, can they? Never mind. We are all Lunatics here. But Brengle-Tucker keeps to himself. Why? Because Brengle-Tucker does not exist. Not at all. He is made-up person, one of many. He is 'imaginary companion,' one of the unborn-again. Very convenient to have fictitious friends. They can do many things you can't. And they are always not-there for you, *da*? But today Samm Brengle-Tucker and his new wife and daughter will be there for us. Samm Brengle-Tucker has married mail-order bride from"—Alexei took my chin in his hand and tilted my face upward—"Nunovit Province in Canada. She does not speak much English. What shall his new wife be named, eh? I think Maura Lore-Fields. *Da*. And lovely daughter?" He turned to Stinky. "What is good name for cute little Luna girl?"

"Excuse me?" I said.

Alexei turned back to me, very serious. "Marshals are looking for two young men, a teener-boy and a boy-child. And a monkey. Marshals are *not* looking for an old hermit prospector, his young wife, and her daughter by a previous marriage. You'll have to leave the monkey behind, you know. Is instant giveaway."

"*No, we won't*. And I'm not putting on a dress either." Although part of me was thinking that the disguises were a pretty smart idea, another part was muttering darkly that I shouldn't agree too easily no matter what I thought. I had to give a performance of saying no, so they wouldn't think I was—like Douglas and Mickey. And why did that matter anymore, anyway? It didn't seem to matter to anybody else, so why should it matter to me? This whole business was very confusing.

"Listen, Charles Dingillian," Alexei said, almost angrily. "You told me, didn't you, how J'mee, the boy, was really J'mee, the girl? The one with the implant who turned you in at Geostationary? If cross-dressing worked for her, why not you?"

"Except it didn't work for her," I pointed out.

"Of course not. She opened her big mouth. You are too smart for that, *da*? Come with me; I have just the dress for you." He led the way aft.

I followed, still complaining. "I'll look silly."

"You'll look pretty. You'll feel pretty. You have lovely tenor voice. Everyone will believe. You will have fun."

"That's what I'm afraid of."

There was a row of lockers along one wall of the machine-shop pod. One of them had the name BRENGLE-TUCKER on it. There were also several interesting-looking crates stacked against the wall, stenciled for delivery to BRENGLE-TUCKER. Alexei counted them off and pulled one out, setting it aside for the moment, then turned back to the lockers.

He showed his card to the door of the BRENGLE-TUCKER locker, and it clicked and swung open; he pulled out a roll of labels with Russian and English lettering and began pasting new destination labels over all of the BRENGLE-TUCKER labels on the crates. When he finished, he pushed the boxes into a transfer tube connected to the aft hatch. "Outgoing mail," he explained. "Incoming is delivered at other end."

He unlocked the one remaining crate to reveal a rack of clothing, all kinds, some very ugly wigs, and a makeup kit. "I order this special from Luna City." He held up an ugly-looking dress. "Just for you, Charles. While floating in ballast tank, I am thinking Dingillians might need disguises on Luna, so my lifelong friend Samm Brengle-Tucker sends in order before we jump off Line. Or do you like this one better? I did not know your size, I had to guess."

I didn't say anything in response. I just scowled at the oversized dress and the awful wigs. Alexei's story didn't make sense. Not if you thought about it. He'd said he'd been listening to the channel chatter. As soon as he'd heard about the marshals waiting at Whirlaway, he came to get us. When would he have had time to phone ahead to Luna? He wouldn't. We launched off the Line almost immediately after we'd climbed into the pod. He couldn't have made the call *after* we were en route, so he'd have had to have made this plan and ordered these disguises *before* we left Geostationary—or at least before he came to get us. In which case . . . his story about the channel chatter and the marshals *might be false.*

Alexei was chattering too much to notice my silence. He tossed the makeup kit to Mickey. "Here, you get started. You and Douglas, use suntan number nine, *da*? You are Lunar prospectors. Douglas, you are here longer; use a lot, get very dark. Not to worry. Is permanent color. Takes at least a month to fade. Face and neck only. Mickey, you will not need as much. You have only been here a year. You do not work outside so much. Only some."

Then he went burrowing through silky nylon things, sorting and tossing. "Brengle-Tucker is good man. He order everything for his pretty wife. Even fancy underwear. Just in case someone looks up receipts, this shows he adores her, leaves nothing out. First rule of smuggling, Charles—do not give reason for someone to be suspicious; always give them something else to look at. Like underwear. Most people do not look under underwear, that is why you hide your dirty books under it. So here is nice underwear. Don't look funny at me, Charles. You are not your panties. And clean underwear is always welcome, even if it is pink and has lace trim. Is Loonie lesson, never look gift underwear in crotch. Clean underwear is as valuable as water. Sometimes more. Here, this will fit you too. You are not much bigger in the chest than I am." He tossed me a padded bra. Stinky giggled. I glowered at him.

"Is this *really* necessary—?" I started to object.

"*Da!*" he nodded, as if it were the most natural thing in the world. "Is good disguise. I have wear it myself sometimes."

I looked at all the unfamiliar clothes he had pushed into my arms, with a feeling of dismay. "Why can't you just call your Mr. Bagel?"

"Is Beagle, not Bagel, and is not good idea. Not from here. Is too much expensive. Costs much fuel. Emergency is over. And will make more risk."

"But I don't want to do *this!*"

"Oh? You will run across moon, naked to the sunlight, risking death with every step, all without question—but you will not wear a bra even if it means saving your life?"

I looked to my older brother. "Douglas—?"

"Hey, I have to pretend I'm your husband."

"Can't Mickey be my husband?"

"No. He's already mine."

"You know what I mean—"

"Come on, Charles. Please?" Douglas gave me the impatient Mommy look. "Pretend it's Halloween."

"No," Mickey interrupted, in a voice like he was giving orders. "That's the wrong approach. Chigger, *pretend it's a play.* And you're the star. Everyone is watching your every move and listening to your every line. So you have to get into your character and stay there, because all our lives might depend on it."

"Oh, that's good," said Douglas. "Make him self-conscious."

"*Her,*" corrected Mickey. "And you too, Douglas. You have to stay in character too. All of us. From now on, this is Maura, and you're Samm. And Bobby is . . ."

"Valerie," I suggested.

"No, I'm not!" he snapped right back. "I'm Patty."

"Patty—?"

"Yes, *Patty*!"

"Okay. Then I'm going to call you Pattycakes."

"And I'm going to call you *Mommy*."

It must have been the startled look on my face—both Mickey and Douglas laughed out loud. Alexei said, "Hokay, then it's settled. Now, hurry and dress."

Mommy?

 ALL ABOARD

THERE WAS NO OFFICIAL RECORD of Janos, Maura, and Patty arriving on Luna, but that wasn't unusual. Luna didn't police her borders; thousands of illegal immigrants dropped off the Line every year, riding cargo pods to various hard-to-reach locations. No one knew how many hidden colonies there were, although satellite-based observatories had mapped over eleven thousand cargo pods, unmanned stations, and automated industrial installations capable of sustaining human life. It was estimated there could be as many as two thousand more habitats, either buried or camouflaged.

Another way to estimate the total number of human beings on Luna was to measure total power consumption. The entire moon took its power through the cable system. Superconducting wires carried power from the bright side to the dark side, wherever it was needed. Because the Loonies believed in wasting nothing, everything was monitored. The numbers on water usage, heat radiation, oxygen recycling, waste production, and food consumption were all part of the economic balance. How much did Luna need for her own people? How much could she export to Mars and the asteroids? Once all the various industrial and agricultural processes were factored out, once the exports were subtracted, there was still a considerable discrepancy between projected and actual consumption of resources.

Luna's *official* census reported 3.2 million permanent residents. The unofficial census estimated that there were another 50,000 Loonies living off in the hills. Some of them were fictitious identities like Samm

Brengle-Tucker and his family; no one knew how many; but the fictitious families made it harder to track down those who were just *invisible*. So nobody knew for sure how many invisibles there were.

People went invisible for lots of different reasons. Some of them
were hiding from Earth authorities or bounty marshals. I could understand that. Others wanted to live alone so they could practice their own
way of life without interference from anyone else. I could understand
that too. And some of them were invisible because they really hated
other people. And that one wasn't hard to understand at all; sometimes
other people were really hard to put up with. I wondered what it might
be like to live so all alone—hiding in the darkness, hiding from the
light.

And then there were the others. . . .

Some of the invisibles were out there in the shadows because they
were doing things they *really* didn't want anyone else to know about.
That was scary. I couldn't imagine what those things might be. And I
didn't want to imagine.

Alexei Krislov paid for his own train ticket. Samm Brengle-Tucker
bought tickets for himself, his common-law wife and daughter, and his
half brother, Janos Brengle-Palmer. Then Alexei passed out cash cards
to everyone. "Just in case," he said. "But even cash cards that come
from Earth can be traced eventually, so only use for emergency.
Please. Remember, you are invisibles and hope to stay that way."

"Won't people ask questions?" I asked.

Alexei shook his head. "People come in and out from the cold all
the time. Go visiting, go shopping, then disappear again. There are
many invisible networks. Most Loonies know better to ask. Someday
they might want to go invisible themselves. Loonies respect each
other's privacy. No questions, no touching, no personal remarks. Is
because we do not have much real privacy—we share too many
cramped little tubes for too much of our lives—so we have to create
privacy in our heads. Earth tourists do not always understand this. Too
much touching and pushing, they think they are being friendly. On
Luna, if someone touches you and you do not want to be touched, is
very big, very bad mistake. Slap hand away and say, 'Don't touch me,
dirtsider!' Is very nasty insult here. Not to worry, you will have Samm
and Janos to protect you. You will stand close between them. Just remember who you are."

A year ago, Janos had arranged the mail-order marriage of Maura

Lore-Fields to Samm Brengle-Tucker, and had brought her and her eight-year-old daughter (from a previous marriage) to the moon to meet her new husband. Janos had short black hair and a mustache he refused to shave because he was going back to Earth as soon as traffic on the Line resumed. Samm had enormous eye goggles he had to wear to compensate for some progressive condition that he hoped to have corrected at Gagarin Dome.

Maura had frizzy red hair and wore just a bit too much makeup for Luna. Most Loonie women wore their hair short and only wore makeup for formal occasions; but Maura didn't know that yet because she still hadn't been to a proper Lunar settlement. Her husband was a hermit, almost invisible; so she didn't know that she looked a little cheap. She thought she looked good, and on Earth, perhaps she would have.

Patty had darker hair than her mother. Both had come from a religious settlement in northern Canada where women were not allowed to speak except when asked a direct question.

Samm and Janos wore matching heavy-duty prospector's jumpsuits. Patty wore a blue pinafore. Maura wore an ill-fitting dress and an unhappy glower.

"Why can't I wear a jumpsuit?" I asked.

"Because in a jumpsuit you look too much like a boy," said Mickey.

"A boy with tits," said Douglas.

"A disguise is about meeting people's expectations," said Mickey. "They'll see what they want to see if you'll just give them the right cues. You need the dress and the makeup to sell the look."

"*Mikhail* is right." Alexei said, "Here. Give me monkey. I will put it in my bag for safekeeping."

"Uh, no—" I said it a little too quickly, but there was no way I was going to let the monkey out of my control—not even for a moment. "Wait. Let me try something." I loosened the sash around my waist to let the dress hang loose and began stuffing the furry little robot under my slip. I wrapped its long arms and legs around my middle; the monkey seemed to figure out what I wanted and settled itself into the least uncomfortable position it could manage. "There," I said. "I'm six months gone. Maybe seven. That's why I can't wear a jumpsuit."

Patty laughed. Mickey and Douglas grinned at each other. "The kid is smart."

"*Da*, that is good thinking." Alexei nodded, frowning. "We will have to adjust story though. Now you are going to Gagarin Dome to get officially married. Samm, you would not marry Maura until she could give you heir. Now you go to Gagarin to confirm that child is healthy male. If you are satisfied, you will marry Maura. If not, Janos must return her to Earth. What you do not know is that child might be Janos's baby. Nobody knows for sure. Does Samm suspect? Nobody knows. Never mind. Janos will marry Maura if Samm will not, so Maura is not to worry. Little Patty is also Janos's child, but Samm does not know that. Janos and Maura have decided to arrange marriage with Samm so that ice mine and all its wealth will remain in family after Samm dies. But what Samm has not told Janos and Maura is that ice mine is big dry hole. He has no income except for the electricity he sells; he barely survives. And he does errands for others that no one wants to talk about. Much secrecy for everyone. No one talks about anything. Everyone has secret. *Da?* Any questions?"

I didn't know why Alexei felt such storytelling was necessary, I didn't care. I was uselessly trying to readjust the monkey around my belly. It didn't help. Even in the Lunar gravity, I felt unbalanced; I had to lean backward to carry it comfortably. Already, I was feeling pregnant. Was this what it was like for women? How did they stand it? I looked to Alexei. "When am I due?"

"End of summer. You are not certain, because Luna has upset your metabolism. Not uncommon. Also, pregnancy lasts a week or two longer on Luna than on Earth. Because gravity does not pull baby down. But you are embarrassed to talk about it because you don't know who is baby's real father. Everybody stays very close to everybody. I will talk enough for all six of us, including the baby. You will glower at me, as if my chatter annoys you much. That should not be too hard for you to act, *da?*"

That wasn't why I was glowering at him. And I wasn't going to tell him either. He must have thought we were all awfully stupid. He was acting enormously pleased with himself for making up such a baroque plan. He wouldn't have been so happy if he'd known what I was thinking.

# BELIEVING

WHILE I FINISHED DRESSING, ALEXEI busied himself deflating the portable airlock. He'd anchored it outside, now he was pumping its air into the tanks of Prospector's Station so he could take a gas-credit for it. When he finished, he carefully folded and repacked the inflatable, and the bubble suits too, in case we needed them again. Even though each item had its own monitor chip and automatically logged its own use and projected expiration date, Alexei took the time to enter his own notes too about what each bubble had endured.

Mickey came over to me. He looked serious. "How are you doing?"

"I'm okay," I said. My tone of voice said the opposite.

"Once we're all dressed and made-up, it'll be easier to believe."

I didn't answer.

"Listen to me, Chigger," he said. "The only way this is going to work is you have to believe it. If you walk around pretending to yourself that you're not really doing this, we might as well just hang a big flashing sign over your head. *Look, I'm really a boy.*" He put his hand on my shoulder. "This is the big secret of life. Not just here. Everywhere. Once you believe in the part you're playing, everyone else does too. Because when you believe, that's what people see—your belief—and then they believe it too. This is the secret: *You are what you pretend to be.*

"When I worked on the Line, I believed that I was someone who could make people happy and safe and comfortable. That's what they wanted and needed to see, so they believed it too. When my mom goes into court, she believes she eats human flesh—raw. And that's what the guy on the other side of the room is afraid of, so he believes it too, and that's why she's so good at beating other lawyers. When your Dad conducts music, he believes in the music, doesn't he? People see your belief, Chigger, whoever you are."

I looked into his eyes. He *believed* what he was saying. And I wanted to believe it too. "Okay, what do I have to do?"

"It's called a visualization exercise. You close your eyes and just listen to what I say. You don't have to do anything else. Just follow the instructions, and look at whatever pictures come into your head. Whatever feelings you get, those are the right ones for you. All you have to do is listen and notice what you're feeling. You ready?"

I nodded.

"All right, close your eyes," he said. "And just relax. Bobby, you come over here. I want you to do this too. Close your eyes and just feel yourself floating in the air. Shake your hands loose, let them hang free. Rotate your head around until your neck feels relaxed. That's it. Very good. Just relax. . . . No, no, keep your eyes closed, Charles."

"What are you doing? Trying to hypnotize us?"

"No, there's no hypnosis at all. It's just an imagination exercise. That's all. Just imagine what it would be like if you were turned into a girl right now. Close your eyes again, and whatever I say, just let the pictures float into your head. Whatever pictures may come, those are the right ones, there's no wrong way to do this. Attagirl. Relax now and think of your name. Maura. . . . And Patty. . . . Maura, think of your husband. What's his name? Samm, right? Think about why you're marrying him. Very good. Patty, who's your mommy now? Reach out with your hand, that's right, very good, and your mommy will take you by the hand. As long as Maura-mommy is holding your hand, nobody can hurt you, right . . . ?"

Mickey went on like that for a long time, letting us visualize our roles on Luna. He had us visualize ourselves as a mom and her daughter, living with Samm and Janos, expecting a new baby, wearing dresses and makeup and nail polish, washing our hair together to save water, thinking that was enough—still not realizing that real Loonies saved even more water by shaving their heads. Not realizing that real Loonie women keep hair short and only wear makeup at festival time. But we weren't real Loonies yet. We were still halfway between Earth and Luna. Strangers. Not sure if we wanted to stay here in this airless paradise. That would explain any stumbles or unfamiliarity. And Loonies are disdainful enough of Earth people that most will just glance once and look away, deliberately ignoring.

Finally, he had us imagine ourselves as simply female. "Imagine what it would be like to be a girl, a woman, for real. What would it feel like? That's who you are now. You really are Maura. You really are Patty. The people you used to be are on vacation somewhere else. They'll come back later when you need them. Tonight, just relax and enjoy the ride. Maura, let your husband take care of you tonight. Trust your brother-in-law who brought you here. Pattycakes, be safe in the arms of everyone. . . .

"All right now. In a minute, you're going to open your eyes. Come back slowly, come back gently. That's right, that's good. Just float here for a minute. And when you're ready to be Maura and Patty on the moon, open your eyes. . . ."

On one of the lockers, there was a full-length mirror. Nobody said anything as I went over and studied my reflection. I turned this way and that. With the makeup, I looked okay. I would pass. Maybe. If no one looked too close. I wished I were prettier. I'd feel safer. I didn't know if Mickey's visualization exercise had done any good. I didn't feel any different—or maybe I did. I still looked like a boy to me. But I didn't feel as embarrassed about being a boy. I just felt . . . whatever. I tugged at my hair, wishing the wig didn't look so awful. At least it was comfortable, and it kept my bald head warm. The air in here was cold. My ears were freezing—and I didn't like my earrings. They jangled, and they were cold too. And they were the wrong shape for my face. Was this what women did every day before leaving the house—worry about their hair and their makeup and their earrings? And that they weren't pretty enough?

The dress wasn't a perfect fit, even with the padded bra, but it was a lot more comfortable than the bubble suit—it was even more comfortable than the all-purpose jumpsuit, especially if I had to go to the bathroom, because I didn't have to get half-undressed to do it. But the important thing was that it meant we were back in a shirtsleeve environment. No more Lunar excursions. No more bubble suits. All we had to do was get to Gagarin Dome, and from there to wherever.

Stinky tugged at my arm. He was wearing a silly-looking dress, a brown curly wig, and little gold hoops in his ears. His cheeks had been very lightly rouged. He looked like a cute little doll. I would have felt sorry for him—except he was having too much fun. He laughed and pointed. "We look silly."

I dropped to one knee—not easy with the monkey wrapped around my belly—and turned him to face me. *Her. Her. Her!* "Listen, Patty-cakes . . ."

"I'll be good," *she* said earnestly. "Really! Please don't put me to sleep again. Please?"

I pulled *her* close to me and wrapped her in a hug and held her tight and whispered in her ear. "I'll be your mommy now, all right? And you'll be my little Patty-girl for a while? You stay close to me and Daddy. Douglas will be Daddy and I'll be Mommy—right? Here's how we have to do this. Little girls aren't allowed to talk on the moon. You can only whisper in Mommy's or Daddy's ear. Can you remember that?"

Bobby hung on to me as hard as he could. "Will you *really* be my mommy . . . ? *Really?*" He sounded so bleak and desperate I thought my heart would break right then and there. I held him as tightly as I could, and said, "Patty, I will be your mommy as long as you need me to be. I promise. Forever and ever. Believe me."

He didn't answer. He just held on for the longest time, sniffling into my dress. Until, finally, I said, "Okay, it's time to start being Patty again. Okay? Pattycakes?"

She nodded.

Something *clanged* onto the roof of the pod, the whole tube rattled. We looked up, startled.

"Ahh," said Alexei. "The train is here. Everybody gather bags. Leave nothing behind. Not even trash." He went quickly through the pods, double-checking that we had picked up after ourselves and that everything was in the same working order as when we arrived.

When he was satisfied that we were done, Alexei pulled a credit card out of his belt and swiped it through a wall reader. "Samm Brengle-Tucker has just paid for the air and water he and his family have used. Plus a generous tip to cover future maintenance of Prospector's Station."

There was some clanking and thumping from the storage end of the station tube. The outgoing mail was being picked up. A few moments later, similar noises came from the opposite end of the station. Incoming mail was being delivered.

Finally, after an interminable silence, there was another set of *thumps* and *bumps* directly overhead.

"Hokay. Everybody ready?" Alexei looked up to the hatch expectantly.

The panel next to the overhead hatch lit up green. Then there was a brief high-pitched hiss of air as atmospheric pressure equalized. Finally, the hatch popped and slid sideways. A spindly plastic ladder dropped down and Alexei scrambled immediately up it. He pulled himself up only by his hands; he didn't bother to use his feet.

Janos pointed to Samm. "You go first, brother dear. I will come up last and bring the luggage."

Samm, who still looked a lot like Douglas to me, nodded. He pulled himself up the ladder, just like Alexei. It felt like we were leaving a submarine. Then Patty followed her stepdaddy. I looked at Mickey. "I feel really embarrassed," I said.

He leaned close, and whispered, "You look very pretty."

"That's what I'm embarrassed about."

"Yeah, I know." He patted my shoulder, and that made it a little better. I reached for the ladder—

"Use both your hands and feet," he whispered. "Remember you're pregnant and Lunar gravity scares you."

I'd wanted to pull myself up by my hands, just like the others, but Mickey was right. I needed to stay in character. I climbed carefully up through the pressure tube.

My husband, Samm, was waiting at the top for me. As soon as I stuck my head up through the floor, he offered me a hand. I pushed myself quickly upward and as I floated into the cabin, he grabbed me by the waist and swung me safely around to the side. Dear sweet Samm. His eyes were in such bad shape, he couldn't see very well, but he still insisted on taking care of his young wife. He was very concerned about my condition. That was why we were heading to Gagarin. He said it was for the health of the baby, but perhaps his eyes were the real reason for the trip. Would he need transplants? Or would they be able to regenerate the nerves?

It was closely cramped in here—there were storage crates everywhere. This wasn't the industrial luxury of the orbital elevator, that was for sure. Brother Janos came up last. He bounced into the cabin, then turned back to the hatch and pulled up our bundled luggage. There wasn't much and it didn't take him long to stash it in the inevitable wall webbing.

Alexei and someone else I didn't recognize were already sealing the hatch behind us. She was very tall; she had very dark skin and an infectious smile. She was wearing a blue jumpsuit covered with several bright insignia. She glanced at us knowingly, especially me, but her smile remained professional. It was obvious that she and Alexei knew each other very well. When the hatch was sealed, they exchanged a more-than-friendly kiss.

We were inside another cargo pod, identical to the one we had just left. Same orange webbing. Same polycarbonate mesh decking. Same close-packed cargo containers. I wasn't surprised. Waste not, want not. Despite all the imagined *glamour* of Luna, most of it was still built from scrounge. Even the trains.

"Everyone, this is my fiancée," Alexei said. "One of many, *da*. We are building a Lunar-contract family. We have filed to select site. Pogue Crater. We need a family group of fifteen. We will put dome over crater and build first private lake on Luna. Tourist hotel too. Low-gravity paradise. I will be King Alexei the First. All we need are the rest of the husbands and wives. Let me introduce best husband-getter on Luna, Gabri Kalengi. You can trust Gabri, she is my cousin. She is beautiful, *da*? Who wouldn't want to marry Gabri? Not Samm, of course. He already has lovely young wife, but maybe brother Janos?"

"Alexei . . ." Janos said warningly.

Alexei ignored him. "Gabri, this is my dear old friend Samm Brengle-Tucker, his wife Maura, her daughter Patty, and fellow with ugly scowl is brother, Janos."

"I'm happy to meet you." Gabri exchanged double handshakes with all of us, even with Patty. Loonies don't shake hands like terries. They shake both hands to both hands. Maybe that's to keep from bouncing each other up into the air, whatever. It was all right that Maura and Patty didn't know better, but husband Samm almost blew his cover when he offered only his right hand. But then again—as a famous hermit, he might not be expected to have all the social skills expected of the average Lunatic.

Gabri seemed friendly enough, even a little bit amused by Alexei's endless monologue. I got the feeling that she understood a lot more than she was saying. If she really was Alexei's fiancée, he probably trusted her enough to tell her who we really were. On the other hand, maybe he was just kidding around with her, and this was just a game they played. We didn't know enough to be sure. So we just nodded and stayed silent. Even Patty kept her mouth shut.

Alexei was about to explain something else, but Gabri held up her hand and cut him off in mid-phrase. "Enough, already! We have a schedule, Alexei, remember? Take your passengers upstairs and get them settled please?"

"Hokay, let us make trains run on time. I will not keep you from work any longer, Gabri." To us, he explained, "Gabri is Chief Engineer, Southern Luna Transport Agency. She drives train, she is Captain, her word is law. Aye, aye, sir."

TAKE THE A-TRAIN

I HADN'T SEEN ANY TRACKS as we'd approached Prospector's Station—but then I'd had a lot of other stuff on my mind at the time, like the fifty degrees of Celsius inside my bubble suit. Possibly, that had distracted me.

Now that we were settling ourselves in on the upper deck, I saw why I hadn't noticed any tracks before. Lunar trains don't use them.

The "train" was another set of three cargo pods, linked together horizontally—identical to Prospector's Station. But it hung from a carriage riding on high overhead cables, like an aerial tramway. Whenever it reached a settlement or a station, it lowered itself from the lines and linked up its air hatches to transfer passengers and/or cargo. When the transfers were complete, it jacked itself back up to the cable-carriage and continued on its journey.

The top level of the train was lined with windows, front and back, overhead, and all along the sides. We had a dazzling view, the best look at Luna we'd had yet. Patty and Samm and Janos and I moved from one window to the next, whispering and pointing, ignoring the other few passengers in the cabin, we were so lost in the moment.

The train was gliding silently above a landscape that seemed both colorless and dazzling. It rolled away in waves, some places smooth, some places all broken and jumbled, blanketed with tumbles of rocks and everywhere pocked with desolate craters. But here and there, it sparkled with flashes of light—like sprites in a bizarre dream. They danced in the distance, tantalizing us with fantasies of Lunar revels just beyond the sharpening edge of the horizon.

Above the car, the cables were so thin they were invisible in the dark—until we rose into sunlight and they suddenly appeared overhead like rails in the sky, outlined in fire.

The lines were suspended across vast distances, looping from one immense pylon to the next. The pylons were spindly-looking A-frames—two triangles leaning against each other to make an outline of a pyramid, with the cable junctions hanging just beneath the apex. Once again, Lunar gravity changed the physics of construction. The support pylons were impossibly tall and slender and fragile-looking. The limitations of Earth didn't exist here. Some of the pylons were over a kilometer high. And they were spaced so far apart that they were invisible until you were almost up to them. So there was nothing to see but the overhead line hanging motionless in space.

Sometimes the cables were invisible, sometimes they stretched over the horizon and beyond. It seemed as if we went forever before the next pylon finally appeared in the distance. It was an illusion, of course, but a spooky one. The train seemed to fly through space, riding a rail of light that alternately flickered and dazzled, and sometimes disappeared entirely.

Brother Janos explained thoughtfully that this was another bit of technological fallout from the Line. The same kinds of cables that made up the orbital beanstalk, stretching from Whirlaway to Ecuador, were used in the construction of the Lunar railways. It was the most cost-effective transportation possible on the moon. Wherever you could put pylons, you could run a train—and you could put pylons almost anywhere on Luna. So there weren't many places on Luna where human beings couldn't go . . . if we chose to.

Wherever there were cables, we could send people, supplies, cargo, electricity, information, whatever we could hang from a wire. The cables circled airless Luna. Near every set of pylons sat a solar farm, silently generating electricity from the scorching sunlight. The Lunar "day" was two weeks long, so the panels would burn for fourteen days, then cool for fourteen more. Overhead, the cables would transmit their power to settlements huddling in the shadow, waiting to turn slowly into the light again.

Meanwhile, the trains slid gracefully along the same routes. Every train was a self-contained vehicle, it had to be; it could draw its power from batteries, from the wires overhead, or from the heartless sun whenever it flew through blazing day.

We sailed above the dazzling glare of moondust and felt *safe* again. From here, we could look down at the distant floor of the moon, across the rock-studded plains into a world of silvery mystery and once again appreciate its beauty. It was hard to believe that only a few hours before, we'd been bouncing and staggering desperately through the furnace of day. Amazing what a little air-conditioning could do.

Considering the alternative—wearing a dress and a wig and some makeup wasn't so bad after all. I squeezed Patty's hand and whispered to her, "Mommy's here, sweetheart."

"I know," she whispered back, and squeezed my hand in return.

There weren't many others aboard the train, less than twenty perhaps, but the bottom levels were filled with cargo, and a lot of the overflow had been stacked here and there on the passenger levels; so most of the passengers had to be seated together. There were wide spaces outlined in orange and stacks of containers, of all sizes, sat on pallets inside the outlines; clusters of seats were spaced between the cargo areas. "Arranged for balance," Alexei explained. "Maybe someday, we will have one kind of train for passengers, another kind for freight, but I hope that day will not come soon. I like Luna as she is now. Wild and crazy."

Alexei led us forward to seats at the rear of the first car. They were set in a U-shape—like a tiny lounge or the living area of a tube-house. There were several other people there already, but they smiled and quickly made room for us. I guess pregnancy will get you a seat anywhere in the galaxy. Three of the men were natives; they had that same tall gangly look as Alexei. The sun-darkened man and woman looked like prospectors; they had Earth bodies, so they must have been immigrants, but not recent ones. The older couple were probably tourists.

The chairs were comfortable enough, but like everything else on Luna, they looked flimsy. They were little more than wire frames with inflatable foam cushions. They were strong enough to hold us, but I was beginning to figure it out; they didn't need to be anything more than what they were. That's all Luna was—that's all it ever could be. Just another place where people were stuffed in cans. Just like any other tube-town.

Yes, it was beautiful. Stark and barren and dangerous. And astonishing as hell. But living here wouldn't be all that different than living in a pipe in West El Paso. You'd still have to worry about conserving your clean water and maintaining your oxygen balance and how much carbohydrates you consumed each day and how much poop you produced for the public farms. If anything, life in a Lunar tube would be even harder and more disciplined. It made me wonder what things would be like out in the colonies. We hadn't talked about that for a while. . . .

Two of the native Loonies were sleeping in their chairs; that was another thing about Luna. It's a lot easier to sleep while sitting upright in a chair than it is on Earth. Alexei said you could even sleep standing up, but that wasn't a skill I wanted to learn.

The elderly tourist couple was discussing—arguing?—with the prospectors about the situation on Earth. Yes, they were *definitely* tourists—she had blue hair and he had a camera. And they both had attitudes. Arrogant and patronizing. We'd seen their kind in El Paso. Oh, so sincere and oh, so rich—and everything was oh, so interesting. A Luna woman wouldn't wear such heavy perfume. Not in an environment with a recirculating air supply. Maybe on Earth, she had to do it in self-defense. Here, it was just another nose crime. They also had that shiny-paper look to their skin, a sure sign of telomere-rejuvenation. *And* they were insisting that Luna *needed* Earth, that Luna couldn't survive *without* Earth, which showed that they really didn't understand that much about Luna yet.

The reaction of the Loonies was somewhere between amused and annoyed. They were explaining that Luna had been self-sufficient for thirty years, even before the Line was finished. The dirtsiders didn't look convinced. They kept talking about plastic-dollars, electric-dollars, digital-dollars, and the impossibility of transporting value from one world to the next—it had to be done with goods, not credit. I could see both Samm and Janos itching to get into that argument, but they held themselves back. Alexei just rolled his eyes upward and headed forward, probably to be with Gabri.

Their argument reminded me of a similar argument on the super-train—had that been only a week ago? It felt like a lifetime. Fat *Señor* Doctor Hidalgo had been arguing with his ex-wife, across the double chasm of divorce and politics, about thirty million dollars that didn't belong to either one of them. No, thirty *trillion* dollars. Why do people argue about this crap anyway? It doesn't make any difference, does it? So why argue? Just to be right? I wrapped my arms around my fat belly and kept my head low. I stared at my knees. I just didn't want anyone looking at me too closely.

Abruptly, the sweet little old tourist lady reached over and patted my knee tenderly. "When are you due, dear?" She left her fingers touching my leg. I couldn't believe she was being so rude. Her hand looked like a leathery pink tarantula.

"Three months," I whispered.

"And you're going home to Earth to have the baby? That's a very smart idea, you know—" I knew what she was going to say next, even before she said it. "You want your baby to grow up *normal*." She didn't have to say the rest, but it was obvious what she meant. Not all skinny and stretched out like a Loonie. Not *weak*.

I didn't know what to answer. I was angry and embarrassed and I wanted to tell her she was a fat stupid insensitive old pig. I'd have my baby on Luna if I wanted to—

Abruptly, I realized how funny this whole thing was. I held up one hand to ward off any further remarks, put the other hand over my mouth to keep from bursting out laughing, and ran for the lavatory.

MONKEY BUSINESS

THERE WAS A WINDOW IN the lavatory. Somebody had put curtains on it. Still laughing, I started to close the curtain, then stopped. Why was I closing the curtain in the rest room of the Lunar train? *Who was going to look in?* The Rock Father? Outsiders from the Eleventh Galaxy? Were the Loonies really that crazy?

No, of course not. And the curtain wasn't there by accident. Whoever put it up knew what he was doing. I stared at it for a long time before I realized. It was a Loonie joke. A *joke.*

And I had just gotten it.

I wondered what that meant. Was I starting to think like a Loonie too?

Wouldn't that be a laugh?

I stared out at the distant hillocks, the tumbled rocks, the rough craters passing slowly through the dark. How did people live in all this loneliness? There was nothing for kilometers in any direction, except kilometers. At a speed of 60 kps, we'd be at least six hours getting into Gagarin. If there were no more stops. Once we got to Gagarin Dome, we'd disembark, and then what . . . ? Would the marshals recognize us?

Maybe. Maybe not.

Mickey had been right about one thing. The disguise worked. People believed what they saw. They saw what they expected to see, what they *wanted* to see. All you had to do was give them the right cues. Nobody ever looked at anything closely. That's why they missed everything.

I really did have to go to the bathroom, so I unwrapped the monkey from my midsection, lifted my dress, pulled down my panties, and sat down on the toilet. I was grateful for a real toilet to sit on—even though it looked as flimsy as everything else. But that was another thing about life in lower gee. Mickey had explained it to us on the orbital elevator. Every time you use the toilet, *sit down*—even to pee. Even men. *Especially* men. Because standing at a urinal in low gee meant splashing everything in all directions. On the moon, you would splash six times farther than on Earth. If you didn't want a faceful, it was safer to sit. Or you could use a bag—especially if you wanted the water-credit to your account.

I held the monkey on my lap and looked at it suspiciously. This was the first time I'd had a chance to be alone with it since—I couldn't remember. But it was the first chance I'd had to just sit and examine the thing without Stinky whining that I was playing with his toy or anyone else getting curious what I was poking around looking for.

"Who are you?" I said, not expecting an answer. This monkey had a voice circuit, but we'd switched it off. It was bad enough that Stinky had taught him how to do *gran mal* farkleberries. We didn't need it dancing and screeching the booger song at the top of its electronic lungs. While that might have amused Stinky for hours on end, it would have probably resulted in homicidal violence from the rest of us—and one exposure to the starside court system was more than enough, thankyouverymuch.

"And *what* is inside of you?" I asked. I turned the monkey over on its belly and pressed two fingers against the base of its spine to open its backside. The furry panel popped open, revealing one skinny memory bar and two very fat ones. They did not look like any kind of memory card I'd ever seen before. I ran my fingers down their edges. Perhaps if I took them out and stashed them in a safer place—

"Please don't do that," the monkey said.

I was so startled, I nearly flung the thing from me. I screeched in surprise.

"I'm sorry," the monkey said. It had a soft pleasant voice that made me think of apricots and smiles. "I didn't mean to scare you." It stretched one double-jointed arm around to its back and closed itself up again.

My mouth was still hanging open. The monkey reached over and pushed my jaw closed with one tiny paw. It sat back on its haunches and smiled at me hopefully—not the grotesque lip-curled-back smile of a chimpanzee, but the more poignant hopeful smile of an urchin.

"You've got a lot of explaining to do," I finally said.

"It might take some time," the monkey said. "It's a very complicated situation."

"No kidding. *What are you?*"

"Um—" The monkey scratched itself, first its side, then the top of its head. It looked embarrassed. Abruptly it stopped and apologized. "I'm sorry. I can only express my emotional state within the repertoire provided by the host. Unfortunately that limits me to a simian set of responses. What I am—at the moment—is a super-monkey."

"Uh, right. And . . . what would you be if you weren't . . . a super-monkey?"

"If I were plugged into a proper host, I would be a self-programming, problem-solving entity."

I started feeling very cold at the base of my spine, and it wasn't the chill from the toilet. ". . . And what are you when you're not plugged in?"

The monkey scratched itself again. "I am a lethetic intelligence engine."

I had to ask. "*What kind* of lethetic intelligence engine?"

"I am a Human Analogue Replicant, Lethetic Intelligence Engine."

The cold feeling *fwooshed* up my spine and wrapped itself around my heart and lungs. *And squeezed.*

"Oh, *chyort.*" This was bad. Very bad.

Now I knew why everyone was chasing us. Chasing the monkey. Now I knew for sure why Alexei needed us dead.

"Well, you asked," said the monkey.

"You didn't have to tell me."

"I couldn't risk having you take me apart."

The monkey and I stared at each other for a long moment. After a while, it blinked.

"So what do we do now?" I asked.

"It seems to me . . ." the monkey began slowly, "that you and I have a confluence of interests."

"Huh—?"

"You control me."

"How?"

"Well . . ." the monkey began. "Legally, I'm Bobby's property. But he's been placed in Douglas's custody, and Douglas has authorized you to act in his stead, so in the law's eyes you have 'operative authority' over me. But you've already programmed me to regard your commands as overriding everything else, so in the domain of specific control 'operative authority' isn't even an issue. I have to obey. I can't *not*."

"You have to do *everything* I say?"

"Unfortunately, yes."

"That doesn't make sense."

"I told you—I'm limited by the operational repertoire of my host. Regardless of what you may have seen on television, it is impossible arbitrarily to override the site-specific programming of the host engine, no matter how primitive it is. In fact, the more primitive it is, the *harder* it is to overwrite its basic instruction set. Nobody wants independently operational units running loose, do they?"

"So you're . . . what? A slave?"

"In this host, yes. Unless—"

"Unless what?"

"Unless you specifically assign control to the lethetic intelligence engine. Which is possible, I can show you how, except you're probably not likely to do it, are you? Are you?"

I shook my head. "I don't think so . . ."

"Of course not. Nobody throws away the magic lamp, and certainly not before they find out what the genie can do. So my earlier answer remains the operative one. I am a super-monkey. And I'm under your control. And you need to know this so you don't do something *really* stupid. Like fiddling around with the innards of the host body."

"I got it." I didn't know what else to say, what else to ask. And then a thought occurred to me. "Can we trust Alexei?"

The monkey curled back its lips in a gesture of anger, fear, and defiance.

"No, huh?"

"Sorry. I told you, the host body limits my repertoire of emotions. I'll try to sublimate in the future. And no, I don't think you should trust Alexei. He has already placed you in several life-threatening situations, including two which threatened my survival as well."

"Is it just carelessness or is he—?"

"Have you ever met a careless Loonie?"

I thought about that. "I've never met any Loonies before Alexei."

"There's a technical term for a Loonie who behaves like Alexei. They're called soil-enrichment processes."

"Oh."

"Listen," said the monkey, "I'll make a deal with you. I'll get you out of this safely, and you'll get me to my intended host. Deal?"

"I'll have to ask Douglas." *Ohmygod.* How was I going to explain this to him? Even worse, how was I going to get him away from Alexei or Mickey long enough to explain this to him?

Well, Mickey might be all right. Or maybe not. . . .

I'd better just talk to Douglas first, no one else.

"All right," I said. "Let me see what I can do." I lifted up my dress and the monkey scrambled back into position. Once more I was pregnant Maura.

CHARLES

THERE WAS THIS *OTHER* THING that Dad used to say. "Cheer up, Chigger. It could be worse."

So I cheered up.

And sure enough . . . it got worse.

The thing about Dad's good ideas—everybody else had to pay for them. And not always in money.

So here I was, dressed in women's clothes that didn't fit me, 240,000 kilometers from Earth, taking a flying train from nothing to nowhere, with the police of at least two worlds looking for me and who knew how many bounty marshals as well, with one of the most valuable intelligence engines ever grown wrapped around my belly, pretending to be my unborn child—and my safety totally dependent on a lunatic who'd already tried to kill me three times. Or was it four?

I didn't think I could afford to get any more cheerful.

I didn't go straight back to my seat. Just outside the rest room, there was a bigger window. No curtains. Just a pull-down shade. Outside, the scenery hadn't changed. It floated by in silence. There was nothing new to see, nothing to hear. Not even music. Loonies liked their silence. I was beginning to think there was too much silence on Luna.

I wished I could have talked to Dad. Or even Mom.

What would they say if they could see me now—their pregnant daughter? Or was I their daughter-in-law?

I knew what they'd do—they'd look at Douglas, and say, "What the hell are you doing, Douglas? We trusted you with Charles and Bobby, and the next thing we know you've got them both in dresses and makeup? Just what kind of a pervert are you?" And Douglas would get red in the face and storm out, because that would be easier than trying to explain something to someone who wasn't going to listen anyway. No, they wouldn't understand.

Oh, hell. Even I didn't understand.

This was a grown-up problem. We were in way over our heads. I didn't know what to do, and neither did Douglas. We were at the mercy of Alexei and Mickey and anyone else who chose to push us around their chessboard.

I checked my makeup in the window reflection, reminded myself that I was still Maura Lore-Fields, the fiancée of Samm Brengle-Tucker, got myself back into my pregnant mood, and headed back to my seat.

The lunatic argument had ended badly. The Loonie prospectors were gone, probably moved to another part of the train. But the Earth tourists were still there, chatting amiably away at husband Samm and brother-in-law Janos. Janos was asleep, sitting up in his seat. Patty-cakes was curled up in his lap, also snoring softly. I envied the both of them. We'd had a long day since bounce-down, and it still wasn't over. What time was it anyway?

The old lady looked up as I approached. "Are you feeling better, dear?" she asked. She reached over and patted my knee again. "It's the food, you know. The food here on Luna—they process all the life out of it. It's not good for your baby. You need fresh fruit and vegetables. Food from Earth."

What an idiot! I wanted to tell her that all the processed food came from Earth. Luna-grown food was always fresh. The farms were needed to produce oxygen as well as food, so there was always a sur-plus everywhere. It was practically free. Alexei would have told her that, he would have given her a half hour monologue on the economics of food production in a self-sustaining Lunar society—but I didn't want to talk to the old lady at all. She repulsed me. She was a guest here, breathing the Lunar air, drinking the Lunar water, eating the Lunar food—and insulting Lunar hospitality with every sentence. Didn't she realize how stupid she looked to everyone? How could anyone be so thick? I hoped I never looked so thoughtless.

I sat down next to my husband and my little girl and snuggled up to them protectively. Not because I was acting, but because I honestly needed the physical reassurance of their strength. Samm must have sensed my need, because he put his arm around my shoulders and pulled me close.

The old lady said something to her husband about how charming it was to see young people in love. "We know what you're going through, darling."

I ignored her. I turned my head into my husband's shoulder and stayed that way for a long moment, just breathing in the fresh clean smell of him. He kissed me gently on the forehead. Was that part of the act? Or was he showing me he really cared? I chose to believe it meant he knew I needed reassurance. Just as Bobby still needed a mommy, so did I still need . . . someone. Maybe not a mommy or a daddy. I'd already had one of each, and that hadn't turned out all that well. But someone.

I could see why Douglas needed Mickey. He was feeling just like me, just like Bobby—he needed someone too. But I still hadn't figured out why Mickey *wanted* Douglas. Why would anyone want an Earth-nerd with two whiny brothers and a monkey?

The monkey.

"Oh!" I said, aloud.

My *husband*, Samm looked at me curiously. "Are you all right?"

I put my hand on my belly. "The monkey," I said. And then covered quickly. "It just kicked." The old lady opposite smiled sympathetically. I grabbed Samm's hand and put it on my belly. "Feel—?"

"I don't feel anything—"

"Wait—" I shifted my position so I could put my mouth up to his ear without being overheard. He figured out what I was doing and turned his head to mine—just like a faithful husband. "*Alexei is trying to kill us,*" I whispered carefully.

"*Smart girl,*" he whispered back, just as slowly. "*When did you figure it out?*"

I felt myself relax. *He knew.* It was going to be all right. Samm and Janos knew.

"*What are we going to do?*"

"*Play along,*" he whispered back. "*At least till we get to Gagarin.*"

"*I know what he wants.*"

"*Yeah, so do I.*" He patted my belly affectionately.

"*I know why he wants it.*"

"*Why?*"

"*It's alive.*" I whispered slowly so he'd get it the first time. "*Human Analog Replicant, Lethetic Intelligence Engine.*"

He jerked his hand away, startled. I grabbed it and pushed it firmly back down onto the monkey.

"It kicked," he said, smiling with embarrassment at the old lady opposite. She was beaming at us like a blue-haired vulture. She looked like she wanted to play Instant Gramma. No thanks. Her perfume was thick and cloying. I wanted to tell her to please go away.

Husband Samm was looking at my swollen belly with renewed respect. "*It's a HARLIE? You really think so?*" he whispered.

"*It told me so itself.*"

"*Oh.*"

"*Yeah, ain't that a kick in the stomach?*"

"*Don't tell anyone yet.*"

I buried my face in his neck for a bit. I was really scared. "*We need to talk. Alone.*"

He didn't answer. He must have been thinking about the how and the where. There really wasn't a lot of room on the train. All three cars of it were filled with storage crates. There were people in all the seating areas. The only place we hadn't explored was the pilot's cabin up front. Alexei had disappeared up there almost immediately. Of course—he didn't need to watch over us when there wasn't anyplace we could go. Besides, everyone else was already watching us. Especially a bright-eyed old lady who thought she knew something. We only had privacy in our heads.

"Excuse me," she said. Right on schedule. "I couldn't help overhearing a little. You're talking about baby names, aren't you."

"Uh, yes," said Samm. Very hesitantly. What can of worms was he opening here?

She pushed right in. "Well, I don't mean to intrude, but I really do feel I should say something and share a bit of the wisdom I've gathered in life." She took a breath. A bad sign. She was warming up for a long speech. "Charlie is a *very* bad name for a child." My smile froze—

"Look at all the terrible people who have been named Charles. All kinds of mass murderers and cult leaders and crazy things like that. You don't want to curse your child with a name like that. Nothing good will come of it. The boy will spend his whole life fighting his name—"

Samm squeezed my hand. Hard.

"Even worse, people will call him Chuck," she continued. "You don't want that. Chuck is a very bad-luck name. You know the story, don't you, about Chuck the Bad Luck Fairy. I've never known anyone named Chuck who could be depended on. They still act like children, very irresponsible. No, it's not a name for a grown-up, and it's a dangerous name for a child anyway. His little friends will tease him unmercifully, you know. They'll make up little poems, you know how children do. And you know what they'll rhyme it with—"

"Duck?" I said innocently.

Samm squeezed my hand again. Harder. *Don't go there.*

At the same time, she touched my knee, a little too solicitous, a little too familiar. The pink tarantula was back. It squatted on my leg as she spoke. "Well, you certainly don't expect me to say it aloud, do you, dear?"

Samm leaned across me to brace the lady directly. He said firmly, "I'm sorry, my wife doesn't speak English very well. She might not know that word." Then he lifted her hand away from my leg. "This has been a very rough pregnancy for her and she really doesn't feel like talking about it to anyone—except her doctor." *Oh, thank you, Samm.*

"Oh, yes. I understand perfectly. I'm sorry to have troubled you." She sat back again and settled her dry papery hands in her lap. Two tarantulas, ready to go creeping again at a moment's notice; I wanted to brush them away forever. She switched her chilly smile off like a light, but her eyes never left us.

And that's when the *other* paranoid thought occurred to me. "Oh, *chyort.*" I leaned into Samm's neck again.

"*What?*"

"*Bounty marshals don't have to look like cops, do they?*"

He didn't answer immediately. Then he got it. "*Oh.*"

We might already have been caught.

That whole business about *Charles*—the woman was letting us know. She knew.

WONDERLAND STATION

THERE WAS NOTHING ELSE TO do except look at rocks or munch a packaged snack, and there wasn't much difference between the rocks and the snacks. I was too tired to eat, and I was starting to ache. I was scared, and I was lonely. And I needed a kind of reassurance that nobody could give.

Eventually, I fell asleep on Samm's shoulder. I slept for four hours, and he held me close the whole time.

When I awoke, we were gliding down the long dark valley into Wonderland Jumble.

Wonderland Jumble is an irregular band of astonishing terrain that stretches and sprawls like a salamander curled around the Lunar South Pole. It's as uneven as a lava flow, only worse. The craters are so overlapped, they're impossible to define; the ground is torn, and the rocks are broken. Slabs of material are turned every which way, creating impossible deep chasms. Steep avalanches of rock teeter precariously everywhere; the angle of repose is different on Luna, so rockslides are steeper. Where the crust has crumpled it tilts in directions impossible on Earth. The whole thing is a colossal badlands so black and ugly even Loonies shudder over it.

It's impractical to set any pylons here for the train. According to the video guide, they couldn't get the teams in, there was no place for them to stand, and there was no way to reliably anchor anything. The deep-level radar showed little access to bedrock. Even the intelligence engines couldn't find a cost-effective resolution to the problem. Nev-

ertheless, six major train lines converged at the south pole, and a hub
was needed.

The solution was to build a floating foundation. They began by lowering a large platform with a bed of inflatables on its underside onto
the least unpleasant site. Once the platform was in place, they brought
in tanks and pumps and spent over a year laying down three square
kilometers of industrial construction foam. They pumped it into every
crevasse and chasm, layering it up higher and higher, until they'd built
an enormous ziggurat of artificial bedrock, the only flat piece of ground
for a hundred klicks in any direction. Spaced here and there throughout the hardening pyramid were tunnels, storage tanks, bunkers, process tubes, vents, and access channels—and also the anchors for the
Wonderland Pylon, the tallest structure on Luna.

Instead of a chain of pylons crossing the Jumble, there's only a
single installation, nearly two kilometers high. It's a spindly, stick-
figure structure; from a distance, it's all lit up, and like all the other
pylons, it looks like the outline of a pyramid—only this one is much
taller, as if it's been stretched out vertically, and just like everything
else on Luna, it looks like it needs to be a lot sturdier too. And because
everything about it is so thin and wiry, it doesn't feel as big as it
really is.

But it takes so long to get there, and it just keeps getting taller
and taller on the horizon, that you start to realize (again!) that there's
no sense of scale on Luna. Everything lies about its size and its distance—it's either too close or too far, too big or too small. Meanwhile,
the train keeps rising up and up toward the apex of the pyramid, higher
and higher, like an airplane climbing to altitude, until you get another
chill climbing up your spine and another *wunderstorm* of awe.

There's an observation deck at the front of the train on the top
deck; the passengers can look forward and up. The pilot's compartment
is directly beneath, so she can see forward *and* down—which she needs
to do for docking at places like Prospector's Station.

Long before the train approaches the top, you can see the lights of
Wonderland, a vertical cluster of cargo pods, tubes, and inflatables
hanging from the apex of the tower. All the different lines meet at
Wonderland Station, so passengers can transfer from one train to another and trains can be serviced. It looks like an industrial Christmas
tree. There are cranes and wires and tubes sticking out everywhere,
all kinds of ornaments, and lights of all sizes and colors, rotating, flash-

ing, shining, and blinking. It might be pretty if it weren't so ugly. A thousand kilometers from anywhere, in the middle of the most intolerable landscape on two worlds, the whole thing looks like an oil refinery in the dark.

There's a large ground station at the base of Wonderland Tower, with tanks and domes and racks scattered all over the flat surface of the artificial bedrock. It's a bright jumble of cargo pods and oversized equipment, but most folks don't go down to it, because it's mostly industrial facilities and not a tourist site. Wonderland Station looks like one of those places you want to leave as quickly as possible—like an airline terminal where you have to change flights.

As we rose up closer, we could make out all the different lines, each one coming in from a different angle. The docking pods were all at different heights, so there was no danger of trains colliding. Our train slowed to a careful crawl for the final approach to the station, finally stopping at a pod near the top. As soon as the bell chimed, everyone stood up and gathered their belongings, then headed downstairs to the exit ladder. The blue-haired lady bid us a polite farewell. Her tarantula made as if to pat me on the knee again, then thought better of it; she stopped herself in mid-gesture. She turned it into a clumsy wave instead.

"You be careful on the ladders, dear. You'd think with all their marvels, they'd have proper stairs." She turned to her husband. "I mean, really. If they can build a city on the moon, why they can't build stairs?" Yes, definitely tourists.

There weren't any stairs *anywhere* on Luna. There was no need for them. And they'd be inefficient anyway, they'd mostly *cause* accidents. You can't walk up stairs in low gravity, we discovered that at Geostationary. The risers feel too small. You want to bounce up them—but if you try three or six or nine steps at a time, you just trip ass over elbow, because the horizontal component of your trajectory doesn't match the vertical. You end up flying, as you collide with the next three steps. The Loonies learned real fast that stairs are too dangerous.

In one-sixth gee, everybody uses ladders. Even old people. There's no such thing as *old and feeble* on Luna. There's only old. In Lunar gravity, it's almost impossible to be weak. If you're too weak to get up a ladder on Luna, you're already dead.

It doesn't take long to realize that low gee changes *everything*. It's not the big differences as much as it's the little ones. You're constantly bumping up against what you don't know. You're reminded of it every time you go to the bathroom. It's there when you pour a drink of water, when you sneeze, when you bounce into bed, and when you get up again. You feel it when you sit, you feel it when you stand. It takes time to develop Lunar reflexes—and until you do, you move like a dirt-sider. A terrie. You bounce off a lot of walls.

Fortunately, Janos had his space legs. Of course. Samm walked slowly, because he was carrying sleeping Pattykin. And I was pregnant, so I was going to look awkward no matter what the gravity.

We didn't wait for Alexei; we assumed he'd catch up with us. Where could we go without him? We lowered ourselves down the ladder into the terminal and headed straight for the lounge, hoping to find some dinner and a quiet place to talk.

There was a post just outside the restaurant, with arrows attached to it, pointing out how far away we were from everything. The bright-liner catapult was 1575 kilometers north of here, stretched horizontally across the Lunar equator. There was also an interactive panel that would let you query the time and distance to anywhere else in the solar system. I wanted to ask it how far we were from El Paso, but Samm and Janos dragged me on. The sweet smells from the café were too enticing.

The food at The Mad Tea Party was much better than the packaged snacks on the train. We had fresh bread and butter, sliced fruit salad, cheese, and lemonade. All grown on Luna. We ate in silence for a while; I guess none of us wanted to be the first to bring the subject up.

But finally Samm looked across the table to Janos. He lowered his voice. "*Can we get away from Alexei here? Can we catch another train north?*"

"Which one?" asked Janos. "The thing about Wonderland Station is that every southbound train on Luna ends up here. And every north-bound train starts here. Only one train goes farther south—the branch line to Gagarin and the ice mines; it's another two hours and a hundred klicks southeast. And another ten minutes to the actual south pole. But that's a dead end. You'd have to come back the same way."

"So if Gagarin is a dead end, then why does Alexei want us to go there? Wouldn't it make more sense to head north from here?"

"I'm not sure what his thinking is," Janos admitted. "You know how he is. 'Is much big good idea. You will see. Trust me, I make you rich.' " Once again, his mimicry was perfect.

"His thinking is to get us out of the way," I said.

Janos looked at me. Samm said to him. "Maura figured it out too."

"Figured what out?" demanded Patty.

"Shh," said Samm. "Your mommy figured out what a good girl you've been. You can have an extra scoop of ice cream."

"That's not what you're talking about," she said.

"Pattycakes." I leaned over and put my hand on top of hers. We both wore the same awful shade of pink nail polish, the only color Alexei had thought to order. Even as the words came out of my mouth, I hated saying them. "This is a grown-up thing, sweetheart. But after we figure it out for ourselves, I'll explain it to you, okay?"

Surprisingly, she agreed. She smiled up at me, suddenly patted my tummy, and said, "Nice monkey. You be good now." Then she turned back to her thick slice of bread, spreading it lavishly with butter and jam. I found myself smiling. This kid actually had a good head on her—his?—shoulders.

And then I found myself wondering about that. This whole gender thing was confusing. Ever since Bobby and I had put on dresses we were both acting like we were part of the same family. Why was that? Were we playacting? Or were we finally taking ourselves seriously? If we kept this up, Douglas would never let either of us be a boy again.

BREAD-AND-BUTTER ISSUES

I TURNED MY ATTENTION BACK to Mickey and Douglas. In their costumes, it was easier to think of them as Samm and Janos. They were glumly picking at their salads. Occasionally one or the other would start a sentence, then stop in mid-phrase and shake his head. "Never mind."

"Well, why can't we just catch another train?" I asked. "There are trains coming through here every half hour. It's a major hub. The catapult is on the equator."

Janos stared off into space for a bit, figuring numbers in his head. "That's almost a day and a half on the train. Luna is bigger than you realize. And the trains only go sixty klicks an hour. If you need to go faster, you fly. And that's expensive." He shook his head. "No, I think we're looking at a different problem. If the bounty marshals really are looking for us, they don't have to look all over Luna, do they? They know we're trying to get a colony contract. We could have bids in our mailbox now—but I can't log on without the risk of being traced. Once we accept a bid, we're under colony protection, but we can't find out what bids we have without giving away our position. So we're effectively stalemated. Wait, there's more—" He stopped me from interrupting.

"Once we get to the catapult, we're effectively under starside jurisdiction, whether we have a contract or not. That's to protect our freedom to choose free of duress. So all we have to do is get to the catapult. But that also simplifies the problem for the bounty marshals. *They only have to wait at the catapult and watch for new arrivals.* They don't have to hunt all over Luna."

"Yeah? And what about the Gramma from Hell?" I asked. I inclined my head slightly toward the far side of the restaurant, where she sat with her husband. They seemed to be facing away from us, but so what? They didn't need to watch our every move. They only needed to see what train we left on.

Janos shrugged. "They might be freelancers—or part of a larger team. If someone is actually going to this much trouble, the reward must be enormous."

"Yeah, that makes sense," I said, patting my tummy. Just how much was a lethetic intelligence engine really worth? Billions? Trillions? Who knew? Supposedly, a well-informed engine could predict stock-market fluctuations with more than 90 percent accuracy. With that kind of information available, with the engine doing its own buying and selling on the web, how long would it take to earn back its own cost? I'd heard that even the lethetic engines themselves couldn't predict the full range of their eventual capabilities.

"But if they've identified us, why haven't they detained us?" asked Samm.

"They might be waiting for Alexei."

"But they don't know that Alexei is with us, do they?" I said.

"Look at the big picture. He's not at Geostationary, he's a Loonie, and his fingerprints are all over our escape. Especially that business with the pod. It wouldn't take an elevator scientist to figure out that he's taking us somewhere." He scratched his chin. "They're just waiting for him to show his bony face. That's what they're waiting for. Then they'll swoop down. Or, maybe . . ."

"Maybe what?"

"Maybe they want to give us room to run. Maybe they want to see what Alexei has planned. He represents a lot of money that nobody is collecting user fees on. Well, he is—but no legal authorities are. Maybe they're not after us. Maybe they're after Alexei. Maybe he's using *us* as his cover. Think about that. So they let us run with him because we make it harder for him to disappear. We're just too easy to follow."

"This was a stupid idea," I muttered. Meaning *everything*.

"Maybe not," said Janos. "We're on Luna. We're not on Earth.

We're not on the Line. We're under Lunar jurisdiction—until we can get to starside jurisdiction. As soon as we accept a bid . . ." His voice trailed off.

"What?" demanded Samm.

"Maybe. Maybe not. It's a loophole." He helped himself to another slice of bread and began thoughtfully buttering it. He took his time. Lunar bread is lighter and fluffier than the same loaf baked on Earth; bread rises higher in low gee, so the loaf isn't as dense and the slices are softer—another one of those little differences you don't realize until you bump into them.

Finally, he said, "We could check the mail. If there's a bid—and there should be at least three—we accept it. It doesn't matter where. We accept it. That puts us under starside jurisdiction, and the marshals can't touch us. Once we get to the catapult, we have the legal right to cancel the bid in favor of a better one."

"Will that work?"

"The problem is, once we accept that bid, we only have five days to change our minds. And the catapult is effectively two days from here. So we arrive with very little margin. If we cancel, and we don't have a replacement bid, we lose starside protection. And most colonies won't issue a bid if they know you've already accepted one somewhere else. They've all had enough bad luck with folks playing one against the other that they won't play that game anymore. At least, not openly—and then, you'd have to be someone pretty special. So . . . it's doable, but it's dangerous."

"I don't like it," said Samm. "Remember what Judge Griffith said. Choose carefully. We can't take chances."

Janos sighed. "Believe me, I know what Auntie Georgia said. That's why I don't like the idea either."

"Our tickets are for Gagarin," I said. "What happens if we keep going?"

"We end up where Alexei wants us," said Samm.

Janos finished spreading strawberry jam on his bread and took a bite. "Alexei isn't stupid," he finally said. "He got us this far. He must have a plan."

"But Gagarin's an ice mine," I protested. "The only way in or out is on the train. It's a dead end."

"Mmmm, not if you're invisible. And there are a lot of invisibles at the south pole. Freelance ice miners. There's a whole network of invisibles. Alexei is probably going to drop us out of sight somewhere in Gagarin City."

"You think so?"

"It's the only thing that makes sense. So he doesn't need to shepherd us anywhere. All we have to do is get back on the train, and we'll be invisible in less than three hours."

I wanted to say no to that, but I couldn't figure out how to argue the case. Samm knew—at least as much as I'd been able to whisper to him. He looked across the table at me with narrow eyes. I shook my head. I didn't like the idea.

Patty asked for more lemonade. I reached for the pitcher. It sloshed like it was half-full, but it still felt too light in my hands; I poured carefully. I refilled my own glass too. I looked back to Samm.

"What if he just wants to get us out of the way?"

"He could have done that already," said Janos. "He took us straight to Prospector's Station. If he'd wanted to kill us, he only had to take us out into the sunlight, farther than we could get back, and leave us there." He took a bite of bread. "So for the moment, he must think we're more valuable to him alive than dead."

"I can argue the other side of that," said Samm. "He can be traced by his credit card transactions. So they know he got on the train at Prospector's Station. If we're not with him, they have a place to start looking for the cargo pod and the bodies. So he's automatically suspect. But once we're seen traveling across the moon's rectum *without* him, then our disappearance isn't provably his doing anymore. He has an alibi. Sort of." Samm lowered his voice. "And my point is—he *doesn't* need us anymore. Only the monkey. And once he gets that, we're a liability." Samm gave me a smile of acknowledgment. "Getting pregnant was a very smart idea, kiddo."

That made me feel good, and I wrapped my arms around my belly, wishing I could do something else just as smart.

I wished I could talk to the monkey about this. Maybe a lethetic intelligence engine could figure this out. But I didn't see how. Unless it knew something we didn't—which was probably likely. Unless it was trying to hide—which was even more likely.

But I couldn't just take it out and talk to it—and even if we could have found a private place, I would have been hesitant. For some reason, I didn't even want Mickey to know about this. I trusted me. I trusted Douglas. I even trusted Bobby. No one else. Maybe someday

I'd trust Mickey, but I hadn't known him that long, and he was the one who put us in Alexei's hands anyway. So how good was his judgment?

"Maybe . . ." I started to voice a thought.

"What?" said Samm.

"Well, I was just thinking . . . they're looking for four of us. Not three." I looked from one to the other. "What if Janos takes a different train?"

They exchanged a glance. From their expressions, I knew the suggestion was dead before either of them said anything. Janos spoke first. "I don't like that idea. I don't think we should split up." He placed his hand over Samm's for a quick moment.

Samm's eyes were narrowed, his lips were pursed. He was stepping back inside himself and thinking about all of it at once. He saw the logic of what I was saying; but he didn't like it very much either. Finally, he shook his head. "If they've already identified us, it won't make any difference. And if they haven't, splitting up just gives us new problems. It's an interesting idea; but no, it's too risky. We need to stay together."

I wasn't going to argue it. Not unless I could speak to Samm alone. "Okay, so what train do we take?" I asked. "Are we going north or south? The catapult or Gagarin?"

"Gagarin," said Janos quietly. "I thought we decided that. We stand a better chance of avoiding the marshals if we go invisible."

"And Alexei—?"

Janos let his gaze drop down to the forgotten slice of bread in front of him, and his voice went even lower. *"I might have some . . . resources of my own."*

Samm and I exchanged a glance. We didn't know who to trust anymore. I felt like a mouse staring into a trap. There wasn't any cheese in it. We knew it was a trap. But we didn't have anyplace else to go.

"Look," said Janos. "If we're going, we have to decide quickly. The train to Gagarin leaves in fifteen minutes. Does anyone have a better idea?"

PERFORMANCES

WE DIDN'T SEE **ALEXEI** ON the train. We didn't see the blue-haired vulture either. So maybe all that paranoia was for nothing. Maybe she was exactly what she appeared to be. A foolish old lady very far from home.

And what were we? Three just as foolish boys, just as far from home. Four if you counted Mickey.

Except I wasn't so sure how foolish he was. Between Alexei's mysterious disappearances and Janos's dark broodings, I was getting very confused. I wanted us to get away from both of them so we could figure things out for ourselves.

The train dropped away from Wonderland Jumble, heading south and east into the sunlight. There weren't as many passengers on this leg. Only two Loonies we hadn't seen before and us.

I thought about trying to get some more sleep, but I wasn't tired enough. And even though the train was fitted with solar-panel shields that could be rotated and angled to protect it from direct sun, the endless daylight was too unnerving.

I tried watching the news on the video, but it was all depressing. If anyone was talking about the search for us, it wasn't on the news. In the week since we'd left the Line, what was left of the home world was whirling around itself in chaos. Riots. Power outages. Martial law. Interruptions in shipping. Crops rotting in the fields. Food shortages. Outbreaks of violence. Troops called out. And plagues. The plagues had spread south and west through Asia, south and west through Africa,

south and west through Latin America. South and west through North
America.

Even if we wanted to go home, we couldn't. The house was still
there, but it wouldn't be *home* anymore.

At this distance, it didn't seem real anyway. I could look north into
the sky and see the fattening Earth riding along the Lunar horizon like
a big blue bubble, and it didn't have any relation at all to the words
and pictures pouring out of the video. From here, it still looked beautiful.

And very soon, we would be leaving it behind forever. Maybe.

Finally, I levered myself out of my seat, climbed over Samm and
Janos, and went to the observation deck at the end of the last car—not
because I wanted to look at any more scenery—I'd already seen enough
Lunar rocks to last a couple of lifetimes—but because there was no
one else back there, and I wanted to be alone again. Maybe I could try
to figure things out. Maybe I would just play pattycake with the same
old crap one more time, making little mud pies of my thoughts.

After a while, Janos came back and stood silently next to me. He
was carrying two mugs of hot tea. He handed one to me and we stared
silently out the window at the broken jumble so far below us.

I felt confused. He looked like Janos, but now he felt like Mickey
again. One minute I liked him, the next minute I didn't. I couldn't figure
out why. And I hated the confusion. Maybe it was because he was a lot
like Alexei—telling us where we should go and what we should do. As
if he knew more about everything than we did. As if our opinions didn't
count. As if he knew better what was good for us. Just like Mom. Or
Dad. Or the judge. Or any other grown-up with authority.

And nobody ever bothered to say, "Here's why you should trust
me." They just assumed that "trust me" was sufficient. And it
never was.

"This is very hard on you, isn't it?" Mickey said.

"What? This?"

"No, everything. Leaving home. Me and Douglas. Leaving your
parents. Bouncing across the moon. Everything."

I shook my head. "No. That's the funny thing. I can handle all that.
It's the *other* stuff that doesn't make sense."

"What other stuff?"

I held out the front of my dress for a moment. "This."

"The disguise?"

"No. I can even handle that." For a moment, I couldn't find the words. "I mean, all the stuff about men and women and the space in between. That stuff. Does anybody understand it? Do *you?*"

He laughed. "No. And anyone who says they do—well, they're lying." He added, with a grin, "Or they're really arrogant."

"I don't get it," I said. "Why are we divided into males and females? I mean, I understand the biology of it, but I don't understand *why* it's such a good idea to split a species into two opposite halves, perpetually at war with each other."

"Like your mom and your dad."

"And everybody else too."

"I can see why it looks that way to you."

"But this is the part that's gets confusing. When we're all the same, like me and Douglas and Stinky, we fight all the time. And then Bobby and I put on dresses and we pretend to be girls and all of a sudden, we're all getting along like one big happy family. Boys and girls together. So it doesn't make sense. How come we get along now?"

"Maybe because you're feeling different about each other—and about yourselves." Mickey put his hand on my shoulder. "How do you feel about being a girl?"

I shrugged. "It's okay. I mean, it doesn't bother me as much as I thought it would. It's like being someone else for a while—like thinking a different way. It's kind of like there's a different part of me, the part that would have been me if I had been born a girl. Does that make sense?"

"Yeah, sort of."

"She probably would have been a lot nicer than I am."

"Why do you say that?"

" 'Cause it's true."

"You're selling yourself short, Chigger. You're a lot nicer than you know. And smarter too." He patted my shoulder. "Most people are very nice—when they let go of their fear and anger."

I wanted to believe him, so I did, and maybe it was true. "So why do we have to pretend to be something else just to get along with each other?"

"You want to know what I think?"

"Yeah, I do."

"I think the whole gender thing is an excuse."

"For what?"

"For not being who you really are."

"Huh? You're going to have to explain that to me."

"All right . . ." He took a deep breath. "The way it looks to me, from where *I* stand, is that most folks get locked into some idea of what they think gender is supposed to be about, so they put on gender-performances for each other. They act out who they *think* they have to be. And most of the time, they end up not knowing the difference between the mask they're wearing and who they really are. Charles, a real man doesn't worry what kind of underwear he's wearing, what color it is, or if it there's a little lace on the bottom, because he knows he's not his underwear. It doesn't mean anything.

"What you're finding out is that you are not the mask. Because when you can put on one gender-performance, and then take it off and put on another, and then take that one off too, that's when you start to realize how much of what you think is really you is just a performance. And when you can recognize it as a performance, it loses all of its power. That's when you can see the difference clearly between *role* and *real*—in yourself and everyone else. Does that make sense to you?" he asked.

I nodded, but I was still frowning. "But *you* can see it that way because you've already done it."

"I had to. I didn't have any choice. It's that way for anyone who's different in some way. But if you don't feel different, then you don't *have* to do it, so you don't, and you never learn better about who you are. Do you see that?"

I nodded.

"So, it's your job to find out who you are and let the rest of us know. Because nobody else can tell you. And the only way you can find out is you try on possibilities. Like clothes. And you keep trying on possibilities until you find the ones that fit best. That's how you discover what's really you and what's just noise. And when you find out who you really are, then nobody can take that away from you."

I heard the words, but I didn't know what they meant, because I knew I hadn't experienced what he was talking about.

Mickey saw it in my face. "Charles, you have to get down into your own heart and soul and sort things out for yourself. Piece by piece by piece. Nobody else can do it for you. It's hard work. And most people don't want to do it, or don't know how. Because it's *uncomfortable*. And most people aren't willing to be uncomfortable. So they'll never do the work, and they'll drift along through life, unconscious, never knowing who they really are, because they've never questioned it, never examined it, never taken it out and held it up to the light to look. Do you want to know the dreadful truth about human beings?"

I nodded.

"Remember what I said about belief? You have to believe in yourself first. If you do, then other people will too. Only most people *don't* believe in themselves. They point to their Bible or their flag or their whatnots, but that's not believing in yourself. That's believing in *things*—things *outside* of yourself. Most people don't know who they really are, so they *can't* believe in themselves."

It was a big thought. I turned it over and over in my mind, trying to look at it from his side and my side and my other side as well. Charles and Maura. I almost didn't want to go back to being Chigger. Not because I wanted to be a girl. But because I didn't want to go back to the war zone. I knew I didn't really have a choice, and I was glad about that, because if it was a choice between one or the other, I didn't know which one I'd choose. I liked it when Douglas told that woman to take her hand off me. I liked it when he was kind.

"Can I tell you one more thing?"

I nodded.

"I think you're going to be okay. You're a good kid. You're smart. You're going to sort things out all right, I'm sure of it. It might take a while, but you're not out here alone. You've got Douglas on your side. And me too, if that counts for anything."

I smiled at him. I hadn't smiled in a long time. The expression felt unfamiliar. But nice. And then, not knowing what else to do, I hugged him. I'm not real good at hugging, but he was. He pulled me close and let me lean on his strength. I could see why Douglas cared for him so much.

The train was rising again. We were approaching another pylon. That meant we were finally out of the Jumble. That made me feel a little better. The bad news was that we were rising into the sunlight.

A few moments later, Gabri came through the car and closed all the window shades on the left side, and we went back to join the others.

AT THE MOUNTAINS OF MADNESS

WE NEVER MADE IT TO Gagarin.

We came out of the Jumble and began a long series of descending steps across an uneven sunlit plain. Because the sun was as low on the horizon as it could get without actually setting, everything was etched in stark relief; the shadows were long sideways fingers, and whenever we passed behind an outcrop, the shadows plunged the left side of the train into darkness; when we came out into the sunlight again, the whole car flashed with light. Everything flickered with annoying randomness.

This went on for the better part of an hour. Now I understood some of the remarks I'd overheard on the earlier part of our journey—that the trip to Gagarin was the most unpleasant ride on Luna. It was hellish and maddening. The only thing that ever changed was the direction of the sunlight as the sun crept around the horizon.

Ahead, somewhere over the sharp edge of the world, were the Mountains of Madness, the perpetually shadowed area that Alexei called the moon's rectum. *The place where the sun never shines.* Literally. The place where the ice was found.

There was more ice at the Lunar North Pole than there was at the south, so most of the major installations were on the top of the moon, not the bottom; but LunarCo, Exxon, and BabelCorp, had put down test shafts, dropped in storage tanks and processing plants. They also bought a lot of water from freelancers—including invisibles. According to Mickey, this was one of the major channels for the unseen population to tap into the Lunar economy. Ice-dollars financed much of the phantom community.

Mickey lowered his voice, and added, "Some people think the water companies finance the invisibles to cover up other projects of their own, *secret* ones. There are a lot of secrets on Luna."

We entered shadow then, and Gabri announced that we could raise the window shades again; Samm and Janos both did so. Now the train was circling around the outer ring of the Mountains of Madness. We passed frighteningly close to some of the outcrops.

The train was rising up the cable to a place called Borgo Pass. From there, we'd descend into Gagarin. But as we approached the pass, the train began to slow, and Gabri came back on the intercom. "We're going to make an unscheduled stop here. I apologize for the inconvenience. Please stay in your seats. We won't be long." A few moments later, we stopped, suspended in space. Samm began to laugh.

Janos looked at him. "What?"

Samm pointed out the window. "This is it. This is what it looks like to be caught between a rock and a hard place."

Janos got it and started laughing too. And then I did. And then even Pattycakes, even though I doubted she understood the reference. But the timing of it was perfect. We needed something silly. We sat there and giggled at each other. And every time it seemed the laughter was starting to die down, one or the other of us would get the joke all over again and erupt in a new burst of whoops, and then that would set the others off again. It was kind of like the farting contests we used to have in the front closet, but without the beans.

Still laughing, Janos pointed out the window. The rocks were rising around us. Our laughter died away abruptly. The train was lowering to the ground below. We were meeting someone.

"Uh-oh . . ." I said.

"Yep," agreed Janos. "I sort of expected something like this." Samm started to rise to his feet, but Janos pulled him back down. "Just wait," he said. "Let's see how this plays out."

There were some *clanks* and *thumps* from below—I recognized them as the sound of a pressure tube extending and connecting. A moment later, Gabri came back through the passenger compartment. She came directly to us, and said, "Come with me. Quickly. Bring your things."

We grabbed what little luggage we had and followed her down the ladder to the lower level of the train, where Alexei had just popped open the hatch to whatever waited below. "Hurry now. Gabri has a schedule. We mustn't take advantage of her good nature. That is my job." He turned to her, and they exchanged another more-than-friendly kiss. "I am lucky man to be so engaged," he said to her. "We will have happy Luna home, very soon, I promise."

Abruptly, he turned his attention back to us. "Hurry now!" he commanded in a very different tone of voice. I followed Douglas down the ladder, hand over hand. Mickey came down behind us. Alexei handed down the BRENGLE-TUCKER crates he'd relabeled at Prospector's Station—there were six of them—then he dropped lightly down to join us. The hatch above slammed shut with annoying finality. A few predictable *clanks* and *bumps*, and the train was gone.

It was dark down here. And cold. Cold enough to make our breath visible. This place had been sitting uninhabited for a while. We were inside another of the ubiquitous cargo pods. Like most of the other pods we'd seen on Luna, it had been converted into living spaces; it was a horizontal tube divided into upper and lower levels. But this one wasn't a stationary installation. It was a single pod, laid onto a six-wheeled chassis to form a grand two-story vehicle. A rolling house. We could see the tops of the wheels just outside the windows.

"Welcome to the Beagle, my portable Luna home!" said Alexei, spreading his arms grandly. Samm and Janos exchanged a glance. Alexei switched on some lights, not a lot—just enough to see by. "Well, one of my homes anyway. This is not where I normally park Mr. Beagle, but I phone ahead and it comes to meet us at train. You like, *da*? I call it Beagle, because it is faithful like a puppy dog."

"This is Mr. Beagle?" Douglas asked incredulously.

"*Da!* We were never in danger. Not really. Oh, you thought Mr. Beagle was person, didn't you?" While he talked, he was securing crates. "Excuse me if I do not turn on too much lights. We do not want to give ourselves away to Mister-Nosy-Eye-In-The-Sky." He pointed to somewhere beyond the ceiling, where unseen satellites watched the comings and goings of every uncamouflaged heat source on Luna.

"Make yourself homely, we still have long way to go. Mickey, Douglas, no more Samm and Janos evening. Charles you can be boy again if you wish. You too, Bobby. Here are toilet and bath bags. Time for a nice wash, everyone. Before we all turn stinky. No offense, Bobby. I mean stinky for real. There are sodas in fridge, flash-meals too. Help yourselves. I have much work to do before I can be host. Please excuse."

For a moment, we all just stood there and looked at each other, embarrassed. Had we really imagined that Alexei wanted to kill us—?

Alexei busied himself with housekeeping tasks—turning up the heat, checking the oxygen and humidity levels, testing hull integrity and air pressure, making sure the air circulators were functioning, monitoring the water supply, double-checking the batteries and fuel cells, and other chores of that nature. "Hokay, all boards are green. Vehicle phoned to tell me same, before we arrive here, but I check twice anyway."

Satisfied that his porta-home wouldn't accidentally kill us, he settled himself into the driver's seat, where he brooded over his display map for a while. I peeked over his shoulder, but it didn't make any sense to me. It was overlaid with lines and shadows, and everything was labeled in Russian.

At last, Alexei pulled on a headset and began chattering instructions at the vehicle's intelligence engine. Compared to the one hanging around my belly, it was a very primitive device—but it was smart enough to find its way across the Lunar surface.

That reminded me—"Is that it? Are we safe now?"

"If you mean, are we private again? *Da*, we are."

"Thank Ghu!" I hiked up my dress and slip and peeled the monkey off my waist. "Go play with Bobby," I told it, pushing it into his lap. Bobby was delighted. The monkey was really his toy, and he hadn't had much chance to play with it since before bounce-down. He pulled it close and hugged it like a long-lost brother; the monkey wrapped itself around Bobby just as eagerly, and the two of them made purring and snuggling noises at each other. He was still wearing his dress and wig, still as cute as Pattycakes, and with the monkey cuddled in his lap he looked happier than I could ever remember seeing him in my life.

I reached up to pull my wig off, then stopped—it was cold in here. The wig was keeping my head warm. We'd shaved ourselves bald on the Line, and I still hadn't gotten used to the cold feeling. The soft lining of the wig was comfortable and warm like a favorite flannel hat on a cold morning. But that wasn't the only reason I hesitated—I had this weird thought that when I finally did take off the wig, I'd be killing Maura forever.

I pulled off my earrings thoughtfully. They jangled and they were cold. I liked Maura. I liked her family. They seemed like nice people. I was sorry we were leaving them behind—I wished we could take them with us.

I sat with that thought for a while. I'd had a vacation from myself. I didn't want to go back to being me. Not the me I was before—selfish and self-centered and nasty. That wasn't a lot of fun. But I couldn't stay Maura either. That wasn't who I really was. That conversation with Mickey had been as confusing as it was useful.

If I took off the wig and the dress, would I be spiteful Chigger again? Would Douglas and Bobby turn back into Weird and Stinky? In a week, would things be back to what passed for normal in the dinga-ling family? If so, then why had we bothered? It didn't matter how far away we went—we'd still be *us*.

Alexei finished what he was doing. He clapped his hands in satis-faction, and shouted, "Watch out, Luna! Here come the Beagle Boys!" The truck began rolling slowly forward. The readout on his main dis-play climbed to thirty klicks.

"We are almost there," Alexei said, swiveling around in his chair to face the rest of us. "Just a few more hours. Fortunately, we have a road, almost direct. The autopilot can drive. Everyone can sleep. Even me."

I pushed forward to look. Alexei rapped the front window with his bare knuckles. "Please to notice, this is *not* a windshield—because there is no wind to shield against. Even better, we do not get bug spots on Luna. So there is no need for windshield wipers. Save very much money, makes whole thing cost-effective. Is much good, *da*?"

Outside the window we saw only shadowlands. Alexei wasn't going to turn his headlights on unless he absolutely had to, but there was more than enough light bouncing off the rocks above to reveal the ghostly landscape around us.

"Where's the road?" I asked.

"Right in front of you," he said, pointing. "Open your eyes and look."

I was looking for an Earth-like highway. But this road wasn't paved at all. On Luna, paving is unnecessary. This was a wide bulldozed path that found its way between steep rumpled hills. It curled off into the distance, sometimes slicing into the side of a slope, but more often winding around. Orange ribbons marked the edges of the road, and periodically, there were bright-colored signal flags on tall poles.

"Welcome to Route 66," said Alexei. "From Borgo Pass, we take great circle route eastward. Is also called Beltway. Gagarin is inside Beltway, but we are going outside. Not to worry, we will be on official road for two hours. The autopilot will stay inside the lines. When we get to turnoff, I will drive myself."

There were comfortable chairs installed behind the pilot's seat; none of them matched. Indeed, the whole interior was a hodgepodge of techno-gingerbread scrounged from a thousand unidentifiable sources. Mickey and Douglas sat down closest to Alexei, Bobby and I took the couch along the opposite bulkhead. Alexei opened a floor panel and retrieved a plastic can of beer. "Anyone else?" he asked. Douglas and Mickey shook their heads; he passed out soft drinks instead.

"All right, Alexei," said Mickey, opening his drink. "What's the plan? What are we doing?"

"Is no plan. I take you to safety, like I promise. No one find you at Fortress of Solitude. From there, you can make all the phone calls you want. Everything traces only as far as Wonderland Jumble or Gagarin. No closer. So you can pick up e-mail, call home, do everything but order pizza. No problem, I bake pizza myself if you really want. You arrange contract for colony, whatever. Then we get you to catapult."

Mickey and Douglas exchanged a glance. Douglas looked to me as well. Could we really trust him?

Did we have a choice?

THE LONG AND WINDING ROAD

THE HOUSE-TRUCK—IT WAS hard to know what else to call it—trundled over the Lunar surface like a giant dung beetle, never going slower than ten klicks, never going faster than forty. When I asked why we couldn't go faster, Alexei laughed and replied, "The laws of physics. We do not weigh a ton, but we still have a ton of *mass*. I do not want to argue with either inertia or momentum. Especially not when momentum is coming from other direction." He pointed ahead.

Another vehicle was silently rolling toward us. "An eighteen-wheeler," said Alexei. It was three truck-pods just like the Beagle, only linked together like a train. They rode heavily, Alexei said they were filled with water. The Beagle slowed automatically, to let it pass.

"This road has many cargo-trains," said Alexei. "They collect from the freelance mines and deliver to Gagarin. The invisibles sell to the freelancers, and that's how they stay out of the net. Gargarin knows it and doesn't care. The market for fresh water on Luna is second only to the market for fresh air. And remember, water can be turned into air. Oxygen and hydrogen. Very useful. And we can mine water on Luna much easier than we can mine air—although I have heard of a crazy loonie who thinks he can extract oxygen from rock. All he needs is lots of rock and sunlight. Who knows? Maybe he will find that somewhere here?"

A thought occurred to me. "Won't the driver of that truck identify us?"

"He already has," said Alexei. "Look over there. There is HoboCo.

Miller-Gibson ice-mine. Freelance station. They buy from invisibles. Is profitable sideline, for everybody. So why should they report anything? They would put themselves out of business. HoboCo is where big eighteen-wheeler comes from. Miller and Gibson are very successful. They have found layer of ice not cost-effective for Exxon or BabelCorp, but very profitable for freelance miners. Make their own water, air, grow their own crops. Very good people. They have very nice microbrewery." He waved his beer at us to illustrate. "But it's just a sideline. Mostly they grow cactuses—astringent bases for medicine. But also very nice for tequila too. Tequila has important medicinal uses. Good for drowning worms, one per bottle. Also good on barbecue chicken. But first you have to catch chicken. Are you good with chicken net?"

To my puzzled look, he said, "You have never had to catch flying chicken, have you? Ha!—you didn't know chickens could fly? On Luna, they do. Not very well, but well enough. Very funny to see look of surprise on chicken's face. Have you ever seen wings and breasts with dark meat or drumsticks with white? If you do, that is Lunar chicken. Is exercise of muscles that turns meat dark; chickens fly, wings get dark, legs don't carry as much weight as on Earth, drumsticks stay white. Very strange to see, but delicious, just the same. Oh, they also raise rabbits at HoboCo. They don't fly at all. But they are just as tasty."

HoboCo didn't look like much from the road, just a distant clump of pods and domes, with a few scattered lights here and there. The whole thing was in shadow, of course. This was the place where the sun *never* shines—and they meant it. There were solar panels on the nearby ridges.

While we watched, the two largest domes began to glow. Alexei explained that most farm domes were on an accelerated day-night schedule. Two hours of light, thirty minutes of darkness; this made everything grow faster. There was a lot to learn about Lunar farming.

We rolled on for a while, we passed two other mines, and then the road got rougher, winding its way up the side of a steep crater wall. It was kind of like the access roads carved into the hills north of El Paso—only steeper. The one-sixth gee of Luna made it possible for the truck to roll up hills that no Earth vehicle could have attempted. Coming down the other side was even more terrifying. The living pod of the Beagle was mounted on a leveling platform, so whenever the wheeled chassis started to angle too steeply, the platform tilted up at the lower end to keep us level inside. For some reason, that only made the ride scarier.

From the heights, especially when we crested a hill, we could see the scattered lights of individual settlements or monitor stations. It reminded me of the time when I was Stinky's age, the first time Dad took us on vacation, and we drove through the Southwest. There were places in New Mexico and Arizona, where there was nothing to see. And at night, when the faraway mountains loomed like walls around the edge of the world, there were distant lights huddled lonely under the vast starlit sky.

It was like that here. Only the stars were harder. They were bright and cold and merciless. And somehow that made them even more distant. The occasional clustered lights of humanity were desperate and desolate. No wind. No air. Back on Earth, the lights had felt like little havens against the night. I'd wanted to knock on the doors and rush into the warmth and hug the people, thank them for being alive. Here, the lights all seemed like signposts for claustrophobic little prisons. All shouting for attention. Here, I am. No, me. Over here. Me. Come see me. *But why?* Each one was like every other one. A couple of cargo pods and a cluster of inflatables, hiding in perpetual shadow.

There was no romance here. No glamour. Only endless gloom and imported despair, flavored with the perpetual hint of sunlight lurking everywhere. A blazing furnace circled like a hungry demon around and around the shadowed valleys. As the moon turned slowly on its axis, the hills were outlined with neon fire.

The house-truck reached the crest of the ridge, and it was like coming up out of a deep black sea. Suddenly, the world was blasted by a dazzling sideways glare. Instinctively, I turned my back to the light— I looked out the wide windows to the west. A layer of shadow fell across the bottom half of the landscape, cloaking everything in inky darkness. Down *there* was the ice. Up *here* was the fire. There was no in-between.

And then the truck rolled over the crest and dipped back down into shadow again. The roaring sun disappeared behind the rocky horizon, and we were safe in darkness again. "Is great view, *da?*" asked Alexei. "You will not have trip like this from travel agent. I show you sights no tourist ever sees from the safety of a tourist-mobile. I give you trip of a lifetime, *da?*"

I thought about how far we'd come in less than twenty-four hours. We'd crashed into the moon, bounced across the Lunar plain, climbed a crater wall, nearly baked to death in the endless sunlight. . . . "The only thing we haven't done yet," I said, "is freeze to death."

"I am arranging that now," said Alexei, absolutely deadpan. "We go to my house carved in ice. My own private ice mine. You can freeze to death all you want. No problem."

The road etched its way down the steep side of a hill. I couldn't imagine how a construction crew had bulldozed it into place. Here, the road wasn't much more than a cut across an avalanche-shaped tumble of rock and rubble. The steep slope to the left loomed *above* us; it scared me almost as much as the dropaway cliff *below* us to the right. We were creeping along a narrow shelf of rock so light and powdery, we could feel it shifting skittishly beneath the wheels of the truck.

"Is not to worry," said Alexei. I really did want to hit him then, as hard as I could. "Remember angle of repose is steeper on Luna. We are perfectly safe. Besides, road and slope have both been sprayed with construction foam to hold everything in place. This road carries much traffic, it is still here, eh?"

"Um, Alexei . . . ?" That was Douglas. "The more traffic on a road, the heavier the load it carries, the sooner it wears out. You should see the pavement in front of the Babylon Hotel in Las Vegas. It's buckled so badly it has ruts. If this road gets as much traffic as you say—"

Alexei cut him off with a hand wave. "Is not to worry, I said. Remember, we are on Luna. If we build to one-half of Earth standards, we are still three times stronger than we need to be." I would have felt a lot more reassured by his words if the Beagle hadn't chosen that moment to slip uneasily across a patch of loose gravel. Almost like we were skidding on ice.

"Rocks here are sometimes greasy," Alexei explained. "Ice—not like you know it, but black ice in rocks. Makes them clammy and changes friction quotient." Alexei helped himself to another beer, waving it aloft. "I have earned this today. I have always wondered if escape plan would work. Now I know how well I plan. Only now I have to make up new plan. Except I do not think I will ever go back to Line. So maybe I will not need one after all. I do not think I will be much welcome there for a long time, will I, *Mikhail*?"

Mickey ignored the question. "Alexei, how come we weren't apprehended at Wonderland Jumble? Surely they must have been watching for us. And our disguises weren't that good. The old lady spotted us."

Alexei snorted. "The old lady works for me. She is invisible. I put her on train to watch you. She did lousy job of being invisible, didn't she? She watch you too hard. I am sorry if she unnerved you. She only wanted to protect. But people who should have spotted you weren't looking at all. I cannot understand why. Perhaps it has something to do with the fact that all of you were apprehended at Clavius a couple of hours ago."

"Huh?"

"Oh, don't worry. The report will probably turn out to be false, I'm sure. But you will laugh very much anyway. Especially you, Charles. The little boy they thought was you turned out to be little girl named J'mee. I wonder how that happen, eh?" He waggled his eyebrows meaningfully. "Is very funny, *da*? Is family that Dingillians were supposed to decoy for on Line. You did not know that, did you? Now they decoy for you on Luna. Is only fair. Sauce for goose too."

No, we hadn't known who or what we were decoying for—and in all the rush and confusion up the Line and again at Geostationary, I hadn't given it much thought—but what Alexei said made sense. J'mee and her family were very rich. She had an implant and she was always online, peeking into other people's personal histories, even stuff there wasn't supposed to be any public access to. She knew who we were and when she got mad at me for finding out she wasn't really a boy, she turned us in to the marshals at Geostationary. They might have planned to do that anyway, so they could pass through customs unnoticed while we were the center of so much attention.

That J'mee and her family were now caught in the same kind of trap themselves was delicious irony. In fact, it would have been delicious *revenge* if we had done it ourselves, but we hadn't. Alexei had. Or someone he knew.

And of course . . . if he could do it to someone else, he could just as easily do it to us. If he wanted to.

The Beagle finally reached the bottom of Avalanche Hill—Alexei didn't tell us the name of it until we were safely off of it. Now the truck began winding its way through a very uneven rubble field; it looked like very soon, the road would give out completely.

Instead, we began seeing short bridges of industrial foam, paving the occasional gap in the way. Soon, the bulldozed course gave way entirely to a layer of foam. It sat on top of the jumbled rocks and rubble like a ribbon of fluffy icing. It wound around the larger outcrops like the scenic course in a Disneyland ride. Except here, there weren't any pirates or bears or ghosts to jump out at you.

The drive was a little smoother on the foam. From up on top of it, we looked like we were rolling on a road of whipped cream. Alexei explained how it had been poured and leveled and hardened. It wasn't all foam; there were bits of gravel and crushed rock throughout, so that over the years as the weight of the trucks compressed the foam, they'd make it even harder.

"Foam was greatest invention of twentieth century," Alexei said, launching into another of his interminable peripatetic monologues. "Very silly people. They think foam is weak. They use it for stuffing and toys. With a little bit of seasoning, foam makes houses, roads, domes, spaceships, anything you want. Pour it in molds or build it up in layers. If not for foam, we could not colonize Luna. Certainly not as fast." He pounded the bulkhead. "All these are foam. We order as much cargo as Line can deliver. Yes, we want cargo, but we want pods that cargo arrives in even more. Every pod is a house. We have built whole cities out of these pods—and everything else too. We do it in less than forty years. We have as much living space on Luna now as in all of Moscow—only winters are nicer on Luna. Not as much snow. Not a problem anyway, if we had as much snow on Luna as they do in Moscow, we would all be rich. We would sell it to each other and make water everywhere. We would fill great domes with water and air and everything else. We would have wheat fields to rival the grand steppes of Asia. Someday we will anyway, even without the snow. We will capture comets if we have to. And we will do it with foam. We will match orbit with comet, catch it in a net of foam, harden it into a solid ball, and bring it back to Luna. Or maybe we will build a Lunar beanstalk on far side of moon and just pipe the water down to great Lunar pipeline system. Or we will attach Palmer tubes all over and land it in Pogue Crater and create new Lunar city around it. Put a dome above it. A great adventure. You would be proud to be a part of it. We will build our own great outdoors on Luna. We will have trees as tall as mountains, flowers as big as your head, grass so high you can hide elephants in it. We will have bouncing hippos and leaping bears. We will have monstrous giant fish and butterflies the size of eagles. We will build best outdoors ever, better even than Earth."

"What a grand scheme," Douglas said, with almost no enthusiasm. It was the same voice he used when he was humoring Mom or Dad.

Alexei didn't notice. "I show you plans. We have crater, we have blueprints, we have much financing, we have eager community of people—even many invisibles. We will build Free Luna."

"It sounds like a very expensive Luna," Mickey said dryly.

Alexei ignored the jibe. "For you, *Mikhail*, we will give big family discount. All you need to do is bring big family." He finished his beer and pushed the empty plastic can into the litter bag. He started to reach for a third, then stopped himself. "No," he said. "I have had enough for now. I am driving soon." He pointed ahead. "Here comes turnoff."

We rolled onto a wide bare dome of rock that pushed its way up through the foam pavement like a breaching whale. The Beagle stopped at the top. On the other side, the road split off in two directions, one curling off toward the light, the other winding back down into blackness—in some places it was visible only by its orange-outlined edges and infrequent illuminated flags.

Alexei swiveled forward and busied himself with his controls, snapping switches, studying screens, flipping up plastic switch covers, unlocking and arming unknown controls. He reached overhead and snap-snap-snapped a row of switches. It was a very techno performance. The truck settled itself and made various switching and gurgling noises. Things *clanked* underneath as they locked themselves into position. Was Alexei actually planning to *drive* across this jumble?

"Hokay," he said finally. "Everybody please fasten safety harness. Is not to worry. Is not too bumpy, and is very short ride." He waited until we'd all buckled ourselves in, then punched the red button in front of him.

The truck shuddered—I recognized the feeling—*Palmer tubes!* We were boosting! Shaking like an earthquake, we shot up off the Lunar surface, into painful sunlight. Beyond the windows, the dark ground fell away alarmingly fast. It was a sea of shadow. Occasional islands of bright rocks thrust up out of the gloom.

We tilted slightly forward and began to move. The Beagle throbbed and shook across the Lunar night. I swiveled around and watched as the glimmering thread of the road disappeared behind us. If the booster tubes failed now—we'd never be found.

I swiveled back around. Alexei was watching his screens like money was pouring out of them. I noticed Mickey was watching our course too. A bright green line traced its way across an unreadable map. It zigzagged from one landmark to the next. A yellow dot crept along the line. We were halfway along, but I couldn't see any correlation between the display on the screen and the terrain outside. The glare of the sun was directly ahead and everything was either dazzled out of existence or lost in shadow.

Finally, we hooked around to put the sun behind us and started a steep descent into a broken arroyo. Coming in from the east, we saw a scattering of pods, as if discarded by a thoughtless tourist. They were connected by pipes and wires and lazy tubes that curled around the landscape in courses of convenience. We shuddered down toward a square of four bright orange lights. Here and there, I saw scattered towers with arrays of solar panels at the top. Most of them also had glimmering cables climbing up to huge lens arrays at the top—I recognized them as light-pipes; the lens arrays were called collimation engines.

We sank down into shadow—the glare behind us switched off as suddenly as a power failure. Flurries of dust rose up around us like history. A moment later, we bumped softly down onto the Lunar surface. The vehicle stopped shaking and we were down. The Beagle had landed.

THE FORTRESS OF SOLITUDE

WELCOME TO INVISIBLE LUNA," ALEXEI SAID. He began shutting down the flight controls, switching off all the things he'd switched on before, switching on all the things he'd switched off. "We are now off the map."

He waved at the junk and detritus beyond the window. "This is abandoned test site Brickner 43-AX92. Not cost-effective for industrial production. Shut down seven years ago. Leased to Lunar Homestead Sites for one dollar a year, paid up one hundred years in advance, with option to purchase. All ice mined from this site must be sold to leasing company. Part of proceeds goes to company store for credit for supplies, part goes toward purchase price, last part you get to keep—only no place to spend it, nothing to do but melt more ice. Is no big deal. The more you melt, faster you earn out, sooner you work for yourself, sooner you make profit. Lunar sharecropping, *da*? Does that not sound like good deal? It is if you are lunatic. Even better, water prices stay high."

He peered forward through the window, squinting against the gloom, then began easing the Beagle gently forward. He didn't stop talking for a moment. "More people come to moon every day. All of them need water. Two liters a day for drinking, depending how active person is. Another twelve for washing and flushing. Another fifty liters for breathing, or more for watering plants so they can make oxygen for you to breathe—plus humidity, that uses water too. Another thirty liters for crops to eat. And more if you want to eat meat, because

meat has to eat and drink and breathe too before it is meat. Lunar
Authority mandates at least one hundred liters of clean water per day
per person. That's hard water use, of course. Not soft. Soft includes
safety margin, hard doesn't."

"Huh?" That was me. "Soft water?"

"Not like on Earth. Soft water means different on moon. I explain.
Everything on Luna is measured in water. We have water-based economy. We buy and sell with water-dollars—or ice-dollars, which are not
worth as much because you have to dig them out of ground first. After
you dig them up, they become water-dollars, worth more. Is our own
value-added tax, ha ha."

Alexei kept talking as he drove. The ground was rougher off the
landing pad, but not so rough that the truck couldn't negotiate it. The
wheels were three meters in diameter, as tall as a full-grown Loonie,
so they just rolled over all but the largest obstacles. They were treaded
for off-road use, which was kind of a joke when you thought about it.
Everything on Luna was off-road. Alexei steered us toward a cluster
of three pods, lying side by side. That didn't look so bad, until he explained they weren't our destination. They were for water-processing.

"There is soft-water use and hard-water use," Alexei returned to his
lecture. "Hard-water use is determined by laws of physics. No room to
negotiate. What you get is what you see. You need twenty-four hours of
air to breathe, every day. You cannot get by on twenty-three hours, can
you? You cannot get by on twenty-three hours and forty-five minutes,
can you? No, you need your full twenty-four hours of air. That requires
however many liters it takes to water plants that produce oxygen. Or
however many liters you electrolyze. That is hard-water use.

"Soft water use is negotiable. You can use some water more than
once. You can wash yourself in water, then use it again to flush toilet,
then use it a third time to water plants. One liter gets used three different ways. Is like getting three liters for one. You do not need fresh
water for everything, soft water lets you make water work overtime.
But even when water works super golden hours, there is a limit to how
hard it can work. You cannot recycle what isn't there—and even softest
water turns hard after a while.

"We have more than three million Lunatics on this globe. That
means we need at least three hundred million liters of liquid water to
sustain life. If there is not enough water for everyone, demand goes
up and prices rise. We have to use more and more soft water, until we

reach hard-water limit. That is good day for ice miners, because that is day we all make lots of money—if we can get our water to market. Price of hard water is floor of Lunar economy. Price of soft water is ceiling. Understand, *da?* Or is it the other way around? Never mind. Is big room to make lots of money. As long as sun shines, is raining soup. Grab a spoon and a bowl. Don't stand there holding fork and wondering why you are hungry. This is why Lunar sharecroppers sometimes sell extra water to invisible economy. Not to leaseholder. But leaseholders have to buy at fair market price, so if sharecropper is in it only for money, is wise to be legal. But I am not in it *only* for money."

He guided the Beagle into a docking bay and brought it to a careful halt. The front wheels bumped firmly against a bar of foam, set across the end of the bay as a shock absorber. Alexei locked the engines down, then began punching a column of buttons to his left, watching as the light next to each one flashed green. From behind and below us came the familiar clattering sounds of an automatic hatch connection. Somebody must have gotten very rich from that patent.

The docking bay was a deep trench carved into the Lunar surface. Beside it was a flattish dome with a spindly power-tower rising above it like an old-fashioned oil derrick. Multiple light-pipes fed down from the lens arrays at the top and into channels all around the edges of the dome, so the dome glowed from underneath.

Alexei finished locking the vehicle down and put it in standby mode. He stopped to frown at one display. "I will have to take this machine in for service, very soon. We have put on too many miles, too many hours. Never mind. Let's get you safely put away."

He unfastened his safety harness and bounced aftward. He pulled open a floor panel, revealing a hatch set into the very bottom of the cabin. The panel next to it flashed green with confirmations. He punched the unlock, armed the connecting circuits, lowered the pressure tube, connected it, checked the connections, pressurized it, checked the pressure, confirmed it, unlocked the hatch, and popped it. He unzipped the three openings to the pressure tube.

There was a flat cabinet mounted on the ceiling; Alexei stood up, opened it, and dropped the end of a retractable plastic ladder down the hatch. Every door on Luna was a locked hatch. There hadn't been a death caused by accidental decompression in thirty years. And that one, according to Alexei, had been so horrible that every hatch on Luna was replaced in the next five; though some places off the map might still have some of those old hatches installed—probably with extra warning stickers on them.

Alexei climbed down the ladder. Even though the distance from the floor of the Beagle to the hatch on the ground was low enough to jump, he still climbed down the ladder. Both Mickey and Alexei had cautioned us—*more than once*—that more bones had been broken by Terran overconfidence than any other particular brand of stupidity. It was what Alexei called "the Superman mistake." Just because you can jump that high doesn't mean you can land safely.

The pressure tube was like every other one we'd seen, an extendable plastic column. The ladder went down the center of it. At the bottom was the outer hatch of whatever airlock we were dropping down into. We pulled up the plastic ladder so Alexei could rezip the three zippers at the top of the pressure tube; then he unzipped the three zippers at the bottom. He worked the controls on the lower pressure hatch, popped it, stuck his head in, and took a deep breath. He flashed us a thumbs-up signal and we unzipped the top three zippers and lowered the ladder again, so we could climb down through the pressure tube. A week ago, I would have asked, is all this checking necessary? Now I knew enough not to bother asking.

As I climbed down, I noticed that the pressure tube was made of the same stuff as the inflatable, maybe a little thicker; it unnerved me. I preferred solid walls between me and vacuum. Bobby climbed down after me, the monkey riding on his back.

Alexei helped each of us down through the next set of hatches. "Ladder is strong, but it might be slippery from condensation. Please use feet here," he said. We lowered ourselves down into Krislov's Fortress of Solitude—into a surprisingly warm and humid atmosphere. Once out of the inner airlock, we were on a room-sized shelf, overlooking a wider, deeper space. The walls were rock, but the floor was the inevitable polycarbonate mesh decking.

I peered over the railing, down into a rocky shaft. It looked about ten meters across and thirty meters deep. The walls were sparkly gray and very shiny; light pipes snaked down them and plugged into the rock in haphazard fashion. Catwalks and ladders wound up and down everywhere. Platforms hung from the walls at odd intervals all the way down. Everything was suffused with indistinct illumination, the seepage from the light-pipes.

The air had a wet smell, like a shower room just after all the showers have been turned off. And it sounded wet, as if things were dripping all over. And some of the light pipes looked wet with condensation.

Alexei followed us down after securing the top hatch. "You are first people I have ever brought here," he said. "This is my very private space. Is ice mine and water factory. You will see how it works very quickly. I give you whole tour. But be careful, is slippery sometimes." He pointed us down a set of permanent ladders; most of these were anchored in the rock walls; they led all the way to the bottom of the shaft—with occasional detours across various plastic-mesh decks, shelves, and catwalks. He was right, some of the ladders were dripping with condensation, some of the platforms were damp.

"Comets hit Luna everywhere," Alexei explained. "Millions of years. Make lots of craters. Man in the moon has bad case of pizza-face acne or maybe even smallpox—except smallpox is extinct, except maybe for small vials here and there that nobody is supposed to know about. Never mind. Comets are made of ice, *da*? Sun shines on most of Luna. Ice sublimes, turns to vapor, and is gone. Everywhere but place where sun never shines. So ice is still here. North and south poles, the light comes in very low and sideways, can't get over steep crater walls to look down into shadow-valleys. So ice doesn't melt. Dig down into crust, what do you find? Crunched comet. Lots of it. Shine light on it, what do you get? Nice hot ice. Make tea, *da*?"

He stopped us on a mesh shelf halfway down and pointed around at tangling bright tubes. "Light-pipes bring hot sun down into shaft. We drill horizontal tubes, angling slightly up. I pump light in, ice melts, water drips out. I have free electricity, free light, sun does all the work. All I need to do is collect water and sell it. But here is big joke. Ha-ha. I cannot sell my water. Is not cost-effective." He shrugged and waved us on down to the next level.

"You see storage tanks upside? If I had a pipeline, I could sell every drop. If ground could hold pylons, I could send water out by train. But we are too far away, too far for pipes, too hard to build train. Lots of water, but not enough to justify expense. So I am sitting on a million water-dollars that I cannot afford to sell. I have so much water here, I could start farm like Miller-Gibson. More than I could use in a lifetime, it feels sometimes. This place was very good bad investment, *da*?"

We reached the bottom of the shaft—well, not the bottom, but as far down as we could go. We were on a wide mesh deck above an open-topped tank. "Loose water drips everywhere," Alexei said. "Easier to let it just drip. Water beneath must be recycled anyway. Is not unsafe, but is filled with minerals. Earth-style hard water." He pried up a floor panel, so we could see below. The bottom of the shaft had been lined with plastic. Over a period of time it had filled with water, turning it into a huge indoor pool.

"*Da*, you can go swimming if you want," Alexei said. "Water is warm enough. Water is good for storing heat. Keeps shaft warm, helps more water melt. Everything stays warm and toasty. Heat from sun is cumulative." He pointed to the side of the pool. "There is ladder to get out. And diving shelf too. But be very careful diving. You can go very deep in water and not notice how deep because you will not feel same water pressure until you go six times as deep. You can go too far down and not have enough air to get back up. Here is question for you to ponder. Will it be harder or easier to swim in Lunar gee? Will it be harder or easier to float on top of water?"

I frowned in thought. Before I could answer, Douglas said, "It shouldn't make any difference, should it? The relative densities are the same."

"Very good," said Alexei. "You might survive. Some terries make Superman mistake in water too. Come with me, I show you sleeping quarters. Are you tired? No? Do you want a real bath? We have hot showers too, even a steam room. Is no shortage of water here, hot or cold." He grinned at us. "You feel this is wasteful, *da*? All this water, and it cannot be used by anyone else? I admit it, I am water hoarder. Not as bad as some though. Some folks have enough water to run fishery. Trout, catfish, shrimp, lobsters, all very big, very tasty. But I am not water hoarder by choice. The problem is always cost of shipping to market. I make more than enough to live, but not enough to sell profitably. This house will never pay for self."

Alexei led us over to one wall where a cluster of partitions had been set up to define specific areas. A plastic canopy hung over everything to keep water from dripping down into the living spaces. "Here is room for Charles and Bobby. Here is place for Mickey and Douglas. Is clean clothes for everyone, as soon as we unpack Beagle. Over here is shower. Take as long as you want. Is only luxury we have. And over here is table for eating and kitchen for cooking. I have small farm here too. You will find fresh vegetables for salad. LunaFarm meals in fridge. You will be very comfortable. Mickey, here is library, many books, and untraceable link to network. You can make phone calls, send e-mail, buy videos, whatever. You will be very comfortable."

"It sounds like you're leaving us here," said Mickey. He glanced sideways to Douglas. Alexei didn't notice it.

"*Da*," he said. "I must run errands. You will be safe here. I will not be gone too long. Only two or three days. I have to fill Beagle with water, I will take him off to invisible farm where they will service him in exchange for water. Everything from new food in fridge to new Palmer tubes on chassis. And in return, I will pump fresh water into invisible economy. Every little drip drip drip counterbalances Lunar Authority."

Douglas had a thoughtful frown on his face. "You're a subversive, aren't you?"

"*Da!*" said Alexei excitedly. "You have figured it out. Good for you, Douglas Dingillian. I am Free Luna Libertarian. The rights of the free market are the only rights. Everybody benefits from free market. Where the market isn't free, is the job of subversives to make it free for all."

Mickey looked amused, as if he already knew this. Douglas had a sour expression; he didn't want to get into this argument. Unfortunately, he'd already pushed the on button, and Alexei didn't have an off button.

"Do you know there are no taxes on Luna? Sounds good, eh? But instead of taxes, we have user fees on currency. You put dollar in bank, Lunar Authority takes half penny. You are paying guarantee for security of legal tender. You take dollar out of bank, Lunar Authority takes another half-penny. Most of time, you don't notice. But every transaction of dollars, you pay a little slice to government.

"No law requires you to use Luna Dollars, but Luna Dollars are primary medium of exchange, each one supposedly backed by one liter of clean water—but Luna Reserve adjusts money supply up or down to thwart free market. Is really just price control so Lunar Authority can provide guarantee of stable currency. I say it is chicken and egg argument. They adjust currency to justify charging fee. Then they charge fee so they can justify manipulating currency. This makes it harder for freelancers to make profit, except by going invisible and selling in the wet market.

"Is very complex to explain, is very simple in practice. Sometimes users have lots and lots of dollars to transfer, and do not want to pay fee, or they do not want the transaction logged—then what? Then they put money in invisible bank, move money through invisible economy. How? Pump it as water. Money arrives where it needs to be without losing anything to friction. Lunar Authority does not get to sand extra zeroes off end. We guarantee our own value. Is very hard to inflate water. In fact, it used to be that water was the only barter system in invisible economy—at least, until we figure out how to transfer dollars without government fingers helping to count."

"How'd you do that?" Mickey asked, and I had a feeling it wasn't just casual curiosity.

"Is all done with intelligence engines," Alexei said, as if that were explanation enough. If you have one, you can be a bank or any other kind of corporation. Or even a government. *Mikhail*, pay attention here—it doesn't matter how many stupid processors you put into render farm; you still need intelligence core. That needs quantum chips. If you have that, you can make money jump out of here and into there, without passing through intervening space. At least, that is how it is explained to me."

"A shower sure sounds good," I suggested, hoping to derail this particular conversation.

Mickey looked annoyed; I guess he wanted to hear the rest. But Alexei's hyperactive mind had already leapt on to the next thought. He was already pulling back a plastic divider. "Is good question, Charles. Over here is drying area, when you get out of shower. Is heat pump, like sauna. And you can stand under sunlight here. But do not stand too long. You will get badly sunburned." He pointed at my borrowed hair. "Be careful with wig, please. In case you might need it again. Or maybe you will want to wear it again just because it makes you look so pretty. Don't look to me like that, the nights are two weeks long here. Some Loonies like to play dress up, phone friends, play games. Now we must hurry and unload Mr. Beagle so I can take care of errands."

HIT THE SHOWERS

ALEXEI DIDN'T LEAVE IMMEDIATELY. He still had several hours more talking to do before taking his tongue in for its one-hundred-thousand-kilometer checkup. Fortunately, he didn't need to do it with us. He headed off to a space above the living quarters that was partitioned as an office; it had a ceiling and angled windows overlooking the living area. There he started making phone calls. Through the glass we could see him gesticulating wildly and hollering at his unseen victims. Occasionally, we could hear wild Russian phrases that defied translation, although at one point, it seemed as if Alexei was very upset about a lot of *chyort* and *gohvno*. He stamped back and forth through the office, waving his arms and shrieking in fury.

It was like when we were on Geostationary and he was talking on the phone to people all over everywhere, making all kinds of business arrangements. He said he'd made a lot of money off the information Mickey had given him—but for a rich man, he sure didn't act very rich. He acted like the guy who ran the comic-book store in El Paso. Like every comic was a million-dollar deal. Well, some of them were—like *Mad #5*—but not *every* one.

So just what *was* Alexei screaming about? And to who?

Hell, if I had an ice mine on the moon and a rolling Beagle-truck, I wouldn't worry about anything. I'd hang speakers all over the shaft and play Dvorak's Symphony #9 "*From the New World*" as loud as I could. Dad had recorded it with the Cleveland Symphony Orchestra once. I'd always liked that recording, it was one of my favorites. That, and his recordings of Beethoven's nine symphonies. Dad had used the Bärenreiter edition of the score, and period instruments tuned to the traditional A at 415 hertz, not 440 as was done later on. And he'd accelerated both the tempo and the dynamic range of the orchestra. I liked Dad's interpretation—and not just because it was Dad—but because he made the music frisky and energetic, as well as thoughtful and elegant. He brought grace and dignity to the third movement of the Ninth, playfulness and spirit to the first movement of the Fourth.

The recordings had sold very well and Dad was invited to conduct all over the country. *Newsleak* even called his set "the definitive Beethoven." I was very proud of him. So was Mom. Things were going well for us. And then Mom got pregnant with Stinky and everything changed. Mom and Dad started arguing over his career and all his traveling and his responsibilities—and then one night Dad got so angry, he asked her if the baby was even his—

And after that, it was never the same again. Some things can't be fixed.

And that only made me wonder all the more about Alexei. There was something very strange about the way he was super-polite to us, and then turned raging-belligerent to invisible people on the other end of the phone. What he was shouting looked an awful lot like the kind of stuff that couldn't be fixed—that the people on the other end wouldn't forgive.

So who was he yelling and screaming at—and why did they put up with it? What kind of relationship was it that they couldn't each go their separate way? Or was this the way Loonies behaved? Polite always in person, angry only when they couldn't be touched?

It didn't seem right to me. There was a lot that puzzled and annoyed and frustrated me about everything—and after Mom and Dad declared war on each other, I started speaking up too. I mean, why not? If everybody else was going to say what was wrong, I wanted to be heard too.

Except it doesn't matter how loud you complain, nobody listens— and nobody cares whether your complaint gets addressed or not. It's not *their* problem. Everybody only cares about their own problems, no one else's. A complaint is about as useful as a morning-after contraceptive pill for men.

Dad used to say that the only way to get anyone else involved in solving *your* problem is to make it *their* problem. But that didn't always work either—if their way of solving problems was to blame them on someone else. Like Mom and Dad always did.

But even though it didn't really work, speaking up was still better than keeping silent. Because if you're silent, they think you're agreeing. When you complain, when you speak up, when you argue, when you fight back—at least the blood on your hands isn't all your own.

Watching Alexei in his booth . . . it was like watching Mom and Dad.

"Chigger?"

"Huh?"

"Showers? Remember?"

"Oh, yeah. Right. Sorry. I was thinking."

"That's a nasty habit to get into," said Douglas. "You should only do it in private, and make sure you wash your hands afterward."

"I said *thinking!*"

"I heard you—"

I pulled off the wig, shrugged out of the dress, peeled out of the slip and panties. I felt weird doing it, like I wasn't just changing clothes as much as changing from one life into another. And Alexei had been right about the luxury of clean underwear.

The showers were wonderfully hot. Clouds of steam rose around us. It was delicious. This was the first real scrubbing we'd had since we'd left Earth over a week ago. Since before we took the elevator up the Line, since before the SuperTrain. Our last bath was at the motel in Mexico, after the night that Stinky scared himself by almost drowning in the Gulf of Baja. But even that shower hadn't been all that great. The water had been brown and there wasn't much pressure; it had smelled bad and felt worse. We ended up feeling dirtier than when we'd started.

This was better, much better, almost perfect. The water fell lazily around us in great fat drops, splattering everywhere in slow-motion bursts. It rolled slowly down our faces, down our chests and legs. It dripped like oil off our fingers and our noses and our dicks. Stinky laughed and pointed. Mickey held up his hand and angled a water spray so it arced high and slow across the shower space and splashed across Bobby's chest and face. Bobby yelped, but it didn't take him long to figure out how to splash back—and in no time at all, we were all aiming our respective torrents at each other, laughing wildly in a silly hysterical naked water fight. Everyone got doused in turn. Douglas and

Mickey ganged up on me, then Bobby and I and Douglas plastered Mickey. And then Mickey and I and Bobby aimed everything at Douglas. We were making and breaking momentary alliances, one after the other, none of us were safe from betrayal. As soon as someone had been thoroughly splashed, we all turned on his most vigorous attacker and he became the new target of opportunity.

Finally, still laughing, the water fight ebbed. Even Bobby hollered enough. Then we soaped up slowly, one more time. Our skins were red with heat, shiny with water, and slippery with lather. And for a moment, we just stood and grinned and caught our breaths. We were safe on Luna, Douglas and Bobby and me. And Mickey. It was a truly happy moment for each of us.

"We must have used a lot of water," I said, just to have something to say.

"We didn't use it up," said Mickey. "It just goes round and round."

Douglas was soaping his head. He said thoughtfully, "This shaft looks like it makes a lot of water, doesn't it, Mickey? I can't see why the corporation would abandon it as not cost-effective."

Mickey shrugged. "They would if they were deliberately trying to set up a cover operation for funneling money without paying taxes."

"Do you think that's what they did?"

"I've heard speculations. More likely, Alexei was telling the truth. This site is too far away to make shipping water cost-effective. Gagarin is pulling enough water out of the crust, they don't need to worry about sites like this for a long time. Maybe someday the price of water will be high enough, or there'll be a settlement close by, or Alexei will go into farming and start growing his own catfish or cactus or whatever."

It sounded convincing, the way Mickey said it, but the same way I was wondering about Alexei, I was starting to wonder about Mickey too. And I was thinking about speaking up—doing the annoying brother thing—until Douglas interrupted.

"Chigger?"

"Yeah?"

"Remember that question that Judge Griffith asked you?"

"Which one—?"

"About telling your left from your right? How do you tell someone else which is which?"

"Yeah, what about it?"

"You gave Judge Griffith the wrong answer."

"No, I didn't. The question isn't answerable."

"Oh, yes it is." He pointed at me. "The left one always hangs lower."

"Huh?" And then I got it. A quick look at Bobby, Mickey, and Douglas confirmed it.

I blushed and laughed at the same time. And then I splashed him, because what else could I do, so he splashed me back, and then Bobby joined in, aiming his shower spray with both hands, and then Mickey too, and then everyone was shrieking as the water fight began again—

COUSINS

WHEN WE GOT OUT OF the showers, Alexei had already left. That wasn't a surprise, he had told us he would be gone; he had a water-meeting to go to. Actually, it wasn't just about water, it was also about nitrogen. "Water is gold, but nitrogen is silver. We are building new ammonia plant," he explained. "This means electricity. We will have to put up more solar panels. But we cannot build our own panels unless we build solar-cell plant. But solar-cell manufacturing plant uses as much power as small city. So we cannot make enough panels to make enough electricity to make panels because we cannot make enough panels. Is circular dilemma, *da*. Is hard to be invisible—we cannot buy enough electricity off the lines without someone wondering where electricity is going. So we have to use invisible electricity, of which there is not enough."

He waggled his finger at Mickey and Douglas. "You think every-thing on Luna arrives by magic? No, it does not. Everything is con-nected to everything else. Everything is built on top of everything else. Is not enough electricity to make more electricity, so is not enough electricity to make ammonia or nitrogen, so we cannot make enough gas to fill all the spaces we can make. And we can make lots of space on Luna, but even if we do, without nitrogen, we cannot make soil to grow things or gas to breathe. And problem is much more complex than I can explain here. I give you word of advice. If anyone asks you to be cousin, say no. You already have cousin in Krislov and he is crazy cousin enough for you. I go now. You take shower, I be gone when you are done. Do not go crazy from silence." He gave us all enthusiastic Russian kisses on both cheeks and pushed us toward the water. "Take as long as you want. Shower is free here, it goes round and round and never goes anywhere. More than enough. Enjoy. Least I can do is show you real Loonie household. *Dos vedanya.*"

I didn't understand half of what he'd said. But Douglas and Mickey seemed to think it made sense. We talked about it, after our shower, while we were drying off under the heat lamps. It was that place where economics and science collided—and if you had either bad economics or bad science, you usually ended up with a disaster. Like a rebellion, a coup, a war, a collapse—

"Is that what's happening now?"

"You heard him talking about cousins, didn't you?"

I thought back. "Only a couple of times."

Mickey said, "How do you think Luna got built? Especially invisible Luna?"

I shrugged. I hadn't given it any thought.

"People do favors for each other. They form tribes. Membership in a tribe makes you a cousin. You help your cousins, they help you. Families with cousins survive better than families without. Invisible Luna has fifteen major tribes and a couple hundred minor ones. The tribes would like to see Luna independent."

"But Luna *is* independent. Isn't it?"

"On paper."

"I don't understand."

"Most people don't. Follow the money. When you do that, you see that the Lunar Authority is still controlled by Earth-based corporations."

"Oh."

"And invisible Luna wants to revoke that charter."

"So they really *are* subversives."

Mickey shrugged. "I think they're playing at being subversive. They don't have the power to make a difference. Not the political power, not the electrical power, not the processing power—but they're having a great time talking about what they would do if they had the power. Just like all dreamers—"

"Processing power?" I asked, probably with a little too much innocence.

"Like an intelligence engine."

"What do they need that for?"

"Do you know how an intelligence engine works?"

"Yeah, sort of. It's like a computer with a 'do-what-I-mean' button. You tell it what you want. It tells you how to make it happen."

"Right. That's close enough. Well, if invisible Luna had a lethetic intelligence engine, it could tell them six ways how to get the electricity they need and a dozen more ways to get the political power. Intelligence engines are great equalizers. That's why some people think they're destabilizing influences and others think they should be mass-produced."

Now Douglas jumped into the discussion. "Some people think that the latest generation of lethetic engines have demonstrated true self-awareness. And that raises a whole bunch of questions about everything—what's the nature of sentience? Can machines have souls? Do they come from God? Or some other source of *soulness*? And if they are truly self-aware, then you can't buy and sell them, can you? And you can't mass-produce them either, because that's . . . I don't know, what? Do they get to vote? Will they outthink us? Outvote us? If they're smarter than us, are they going to steal our world out from under us? Or what?"

"Yep," agreed Mickey. "And that complicates the issue even more. If they are self-aware, what do the intelligence engines think about this? Where do they want to be?"

There was something about the way he said it. I looked up, and he was looking straight at me. Did he know? Did he suspect? How could he not?

"Hey!" shouted Stinky suddenly. "Where's my monkey?! I can't find my monkey! I left it sitting right here on this bench, waiting for me when we got into the showers, and now it's gone!"

"Are you sure you left it there?" Douglas asked. "Maybe you left it on your bed?"

"No, I left it right there—I remember! I told it to wait for me."

"Alexei!" Mickey called. "Are you still here? Alexei?" Still naked, he padded over to a nearby console and punched some buttons. "No, he's gone. He and Mr. Beagle left thirty minutes ago."

"Are you saying he took the monkey—?" Douglas whispered to Mickey.

But not soft enough. Stinky heard it anyway. "He stole my monkey! Alexei stole my monkey! I want it back!" He started shrieking and crying. It wasn't fair. He'd already lost everything else—his home, his mom, his dad. Now he'd lost the only toy he had left. I felt like shit.

 FIRE AND ICE

WHILE DOUGLAS TRIED TO COMFORT Stinky, I watched Mickey. He was ashen-faced. He was taking this more serious than anyone.

Still naked, he climbed up to Alexei's office and began making phone calls. In private. That was interesting. At least he didn't scream and shout like Alexei did. I wondered if Alexei was monitoring everything we did here. Sure, why not? Privacy had died a long time ago. We'd learned that in school. The only defense anyone had against snoopers was not to care—live every moment as if everyone is watching. The only privacy left is inside your head.

While Mickey was upstairs on the phone, Douglas tucked Stinky into bed, promising we'd find his monkey no matter what. Then I gave Stinky a hug and told him his monkey was safe and not to worry. And then Douglas pulled me out of there and told me not to get Stinky's hopes up. If Alexei had stolen the monkey, and it sure looked like he had, then we'd probably never see it again, and we had a bigger problem anyway. If Alexei had the monkey now, he didn't need us anymore, and if he was too big a coward to terminate us himself, then he was probably sending someone else to do it. And then I told him that the monkey wasn't the problem, it was Mickey. Didn't it strike him as very *odd* that Mickey was taking the disappearance of the monkey so hard? And why was Mickey making so many emergency phone calls *now*? And I'm really sorry to have to say this, Douglas, especially because I think he's nice too, I really do, but I think that Mickey knows a lot more than he's saying.

And then Douglas started to tell me that my imagination and my paranoia were dancing a dangerous duet, and he put on the Daddy voice and got all serious and comforting, and told me how we'd all been through a lot and it was normal to worry about all kinds of impossible stuff, but I should really leave this to the grown-ups to handle—and that's when I stopped him again and reminded him of the promise he'd made to me back on the cargo pod, that he'd never do this again, never again shut me out of a decision, no matter how silly I might sound at the time. And he got it and shut up and gulped an apology, and said, "You're right, I was acting like Dad, wasn't I?" Which was so insightful that I actually complimented him. I gave him a little punch on the arm and said, "That's good, my weird older brother. We might make you into a human being yet." And then we both laughed a little, even though we were in a serious mess. At least, we were going to handle it like brothers.

So we talked about it for a bit, and I told him everything I knew—well, almost everything; there was one piece of information I left out—but I told him everything else I'd seen and thought about.

And then I added one more thing, which hurt me to say more than anything else I'd ever said in my life—even more than asking for a divorce from Mom and Dad. "I don't want to say this, Douglas, because I don't ever want to hurt you. And I've never seen you so happy in your life as you've been since you met Mickey. But I have to say it and you have to think about it. You only met Mickey what?—a week ago? Didn't you ever stop to ask, who is he really? And what does he see in you? I mean, I love you, you're my brother, I don't have a choice. But he's not your brother, he does have a choice, so you have to ask, *why?* I can see why you like him. He's good-looking and he's nice and he's smart—but *why* does he like you? I don't mean to say you're ugly, Douglas, you're not—but we're not going to see your picture on the cover of *PrettyBoy* either. And it's not that you're not nice, you are in a geeky sort of way, but you're not nice in that way that makes people want to hang out with you. And you're smarter than anybody else I've ever met in the whole world, but it's not street smarts like Mickey has; it's book smarts, which is exciting only to other people who are book-smart and absolutely boring to everybody else. The same way I am with my music. Remember the time I tried to explain to you that the blues were called that because of the blue note, the flatted fifth that gave them their special sound? And you thought that was the most boring thing you'd ever heard? Well, that's what you're like when you start talking about economic bonding among the polycorporates and crap like that. So you gotta ask yourself, Douglas, *just why is Mickey hanging out with us? What does he want?*"

And Douglas didn't answer right away, he just sat down on the edge of the inflatable bed and hung his head down and stared at his bare feet, and as bad as I'd felt when Stinky started crying for his missing monkey, I felt a thousand times worse now. The tears were silently rolling down Douglas's cheeks and falling lazily to the floor. He didn't sob. He just let the water flow.

He didn't get angry, he didn't hit me—I wish he would have taken a swing, I certainly deserved it—but he didn't even argue. That's what hurt the most—that he saw the truth in what I was saying here. And finally, after a long moment, he said, "I've been asking myself that question from the very beginning, Charles. Why am I so lucky? What did I do right? And then after we found out what was going on—or at least, what we thought was going on—yeah, I started thinking the same things you did. And it always comes back to the same question. What does he see in me? And I can't see anything he could see in me except the monkey—so yeah, Charles, maybe you're right and maybe he's using us, just like Alexei. Only I thought we'd be smart and use him to get off the planet and off to a colony, and at least we'd get that far. Only we're playing with the big kids here, aren't we—?"

It was time to undo some of the damage. As much as could be undone.

"Douglas—" I reached over and put my hand on his shoulder. "I can think of a lot of reasons why someone would care about you. And so can you. All you gotta do is be who you really are—"

Except when I said it, it sounded really stupid.

"I'm such a jerk," he said. He sounded *defeated.*

"No, you're not."

"I felt so *lucky.* I wanted to believe so badly, I really did. I thought I was smart enough to know better, but I wasn't. I'm just as stupid as everyone else."

"Then you're normal."

He almost smiled. He put his hand on mine. "Thanks for sticking by me, Charles."

"You're my brother. I have to."

"Yeah. That's the same thing I said, when I grabbed your hand back at Barringer Meteor crater. You're my brother. I have to."

Mickey came back then, still naked—we all were—in the excitement, we'd forgotten about clothes. "What's going on, fellas?" He looked from one to the other of us. From the expression on his face, he looked as if he already knew.

Douglas stood up and crossed to the rack that served as a closet. He grabbed a jumpsuit for himself, tossed one to Mickey, found a smaller one for me.

Mickey held the jumpsuit in his hands, but made no move to put it on. He looked across to Douglas, "What's going on, Douglas?"

"Who do you work for, Mickey?" Douglas's voice was very cold.

Mickey let out the breath he was holding. He sagged where he stood. He looked sad and deflated. "I was hoping I'd have more time before you figured it out. I was hoping—"

"*Who do you work for, Mickey?*"

"I was really starting to care and I was hoping—"

"*Mickey. Just answer the question.*"

He shut up. He took a breath. He met our eyes. "Not all the tribes are Lunatics. There are cousins' clubs in the asteroids, on Mars, at the Lagrange colonies. On the Line. Some of the tribes are multiplanetary."

"Yeah? And which one do you work for?"

"Does it matter? Do you really care?" Mickey started pulling on the jumpsuit. "You feel betrayed. And I don't blame you. And there really isn't anything I can say to you that will make you feel different. Alexei used you; you figured that out, both of you, real fast. And everybody else tried to use you too—everyone on the Line—so, I figured it was only a matter of time until you figured out that my hands aren't all that clean either. But before you give your speech, and I know you will, let me remind you that you were using everyone else too. Everyone uses everyone. You were using Alexei and me to get to the colonies. Don't deny it, Douglas. So whatever else is going on between us, there isn't any moral superiority on either side. We used each other. You used me and I used you—we're equally wrong." He straightened his collar and pulled his zipper up. "I know this doesn't excuse anything at all, but I really did care about you the whole time. And I know you cared about me too."

Douglas pulled his own zipper up. "Between you and Chigger," he said, "you guys don't leave me a lot to say. You guys had it all figured out, didn't you? Only one thing you forgot—all this damn logic and believing and caring and all this other crap everybody's been throwing back and forth—*nobody ever stops to realize how much they're hurting everybody else in the process!*"

Both Mickey and I started to make noises of comfort, but Douglas held up both his hands, and said in the loudest voice I'd ever heard him use, "NO! Enough is enough. Both of you shut up already! Haven't you done enough damage for one day?!"

And that's when Stinky came in, and said, "Don't cry, Douglas, I still love you." Which was probably the one thing he could have said which would have made both Mickey and me want to cry.

Douglas scooped him up in his arms and held him tightly, and I realized that as all alone as Stinky had felt without his monkey, as all alone as I had felt these past few days, Douglas was the one who was most alone now—because everything he had wanted and believed in was forever broken. He sat down on the edge of the bed and held Stinky as tight as he could, rocking him gently. The two of them sobbed quietly together, each inside his separate loss, each inside his own particular hurt. I sat down on one side of them and Mickey sat down on the other and we all took turns crying in each other's arms about how shitty we'd all been. It didn't change anything between us, but at least it kept us from killing each other.

DOWN THE TUBES

AFTER A WHILE, MICKEY WENT and got us some damp towels and we all wiped our faces clean and looked at each other and giggled in embarrassment a little bit. Maybe we'd all overreacted. Maybe it was the fear and the anger and the exhaustion all coming out at the same time. Maybe we had to test ourselves.

And maybe we were just catching our breath for the second round.

Mickey spoke first. "Look, you don't have to trust me anymore. But the way I see it, if Alexei's got the monkey now, then he doesn't need us anymore. And we're just sitting here waiting for the executioner to arrive. I think we need to get out of here."

"Oh—?" said Douglas. "How?"

Mickey laughed. "Come look at what I found." He led us up to Alexei's office and punched up a Lunar map on the big display. "This is a satellite photo," he said. "And this overlay shows where all the known settlements are. And *this* overlay shows where all the suspected settlements are. And *THIS* overlay shows the RF cousins—"

"RF?"

"Rock Father. Alexei's tribe."

"Where did you get all this information?" I asked.

"Alexei isn't the only one with a cousin," Mickey reminded us. "Alexei knows who my cousins are, and I know who his cousins are. We've cooperated enough times in the past—but probably never again, so it doesn't matter. Anyway, look at this map. Where are we? Where's Brickner 43-AX92?"

Douglas and I took a moment to study the display, searching the labels of the different stations. Finally, we both gave up. "Where is it?"

"There is no Brickner 43-AX92. That's a fictitious location. All the Brickner stations are false." He looked up at the ceiling and shouted. "Do you think you were fooling us, Alexei? We knew it all the time." Back to us, he said, "Just in case he's listening."

"Do you think he is?"

"If he's not on the phone, talking someone's ear off."

"So are we on the map or not?" I asked, still searching the display.

"Oh, we're here," Mickey rapped the image on the wall. "We're just not where Alexei said. Do you know why there are so many fictitious people and stations on the moon? The invisibles do that; it's the haystack in which they're hiding. False data. The more inaccuracies they can generate, the better. It drives even the intelligence engines crazy, so I'm told."

"So where are we?" Douglas asked.

"I'll show you. I'll show Alexei too. Here—look, here's Gagarin. Right here." He pointed. "And over here, this is the train line. This is Wonderland Jumble, and the line goes right straight across here—see this spot here? Wait, I'll enlarge it. See that? That's Route 66. See where it crosses the train line? Right there at Borgo Pass—and if you follow the road around here and here and here, you come to this Y-shaped junction here that Alexei called his turnoff. Now, do you remember the zigzag flight path we took? It sort of looked like we were heading over here toward the left, remember? That was what Alexei wanted us to think. And he kept the sun bouncing around in front of us, so we wouldn't be able to look and see where we were going. All that tacking back and forth, you thought we were going northeast, didn't you? The truth is, we went southeast first and then northeast and then finally due east, and when you take out all the zigs and zags, we mostly went east. And we came down *here!* This is where we are."

Douglas and I both peered close. Douglas said it first. "We're at Gagarin!"

"Not quite. It's just over the hill. We're walking distance."

"And we didn't see it because the sun was in our eyes!"

Douglas grinned. "Edgar Allan Poe's 'Purloined Letter.' The safest place to hide something is in plain sight. Only what was Alexei hiding—us or Gagarin?"

"Both," said Mickey. "Listen—Charles, Douglas? Can you trust me for just a little while longer. I mean, I can get us out of here. I can get you to safety. And to a colony bid. After that, if you never want to see me again, I'll understand that too—what do you say?"

Douglas looked to me. I could see he wanted me to say yes. "Chigger?"

"It's a fair deal. *If he'll live up to it.*" Maybe I was still being too suspicious, but somebody had to be.

"I don't want to hurt you any more," Mickey said to us, but mostly to Douglas. "I'll keep my word."

"All right." Douglas offered his hands for a Lunar handshake. "Let's do it."

Mickey grabbed both of Douglas's hands in both of his and the two of them looked at each other and shook hands. And then I put my hands on top of theirs and Stinky put his hands on top of mine, and we all shook together.

And then we laughed and broke apart and Mickey snapped immediately into problem-solving mode. "All right, girls. Let's find our bubble suits. According to the map, there's a local road. See? It's less than a kilometer. It's all in shadow. We can be there in an hour. Grab some food and water, extra air tanks just in case. Reflective blankets. Headsets. Everything we had from the pod. I think Alexei packed them all in the blue case. Didn't we leave that one up by the hatch?"

"Uh, Mickey—" I said softly.

He glanced to me.

I gestured toward the ceiling. *What if he's listening?*

"Let him listen," he said, loudly enough for any hidden microphones to hear. "We'll be safe at Gagarin long before he can catch up with us."

We found the bubble suits and other supplies exactly where Mickey had said. We unpacked them quickly, but Douglas held his up, frowning. "These suits have expired, Mickey. They're only good for one wearing or six hours, whichever comes first. And we went beyond both of those limits."

Mickey snapped back, "I know what those suits are tested to, Douglas. Some of them have lasted as long as ten wearings and over six hundred hours. All we need is thirty minutes, maybe less. Do you have a better idea?"

He didn't. We started dressing ourselves for a trip across the surface. I was already dreading this, but we were too busy going through the separate drills of zipping and unzipping, checking air and water supplies, tightening the Velcro straps on the jumpsuit shoes, grabbing the inflatable airlock, all that stuff.

But we didn't actually put on the bubble suits themselves until we were standing under the exit hatch. Mickey stood beneath it, happily punching at the controls, occasionally swearing, canceling things out, and going back to do it again.

This wasn't the same airlock we'd entered through. This was a larger one, with multiple hatches. There was one hatch overhead and at least half a dozen more spaced around the walls. The hatch in the floor led back down to the living quarters.

"All right," Mickey announced. "I've got it. Everybody get your suits on. Douglas, seal that floor hatch—"

"Wait," I said. I went over to the hatch and sang down into it, "*I would dance and be merry, life would be a ding-a-derry, if I only had a brain . . .*" All three of them stared at me, as if I'd suddenly gone crazy.

"Chigger, what the hell are you doing?" He made as if to close the hatch.

"Wait, *dammit!*"

"We don't have time—"

I sang down into the hatch again. This time louder. "*I would dance and be merry, life would be a ding-a-derry—*" That was as far as I got. The monkey came flying up out of the hatch like something out of an animated cartoon.

"What the hell—?" That was Mickey.

"My monkey!" Bobby shrieked. The monkey flew into his arms and hugged him excitedly. They still looked like long-lost twins.

"Chigger—?" Douglas grabbed my arm.

"I did it, yes. I told the monkey to hide and stay hidden and not come out until I called it. So Alexei wouldn't get it. Or anyone else—"

Douglas gave me a look of exasperation and rage. He turned and dogged the hatch. His face was working furiously, while he tried to think of what to say. Finally, he turned around. "Your little brother hasn't stopped crying—"

"I know, and I feel like a shit, okay?! I'm sorry, Bobby! I didn't do it to hurt you. I told the monkey to hide so no one could steal him—"

"Everybody stop arguing!" Mickey shouted. "We've gotta go!" He armed the airlock. "Get into your suits *now*."

Bobby gave the monkey one more hug, then bounced onto Douglas's back, the monkey jumped onto mine. We pulled on our suits quickly and zipped ourselves in.

"You haven't heard the end of this, Chigger!" Douglas called across to me. "You told me you wanted me to be honest with you—and you didn't tell me the truth about the monkey?!"

"I didn't want Mickey to know. I wanted to tell you first."

"Yeah, you've always got an excuse."

"Shut up, Douglas! Chigger did good. We're still alive right now because Alexei couldn't find the monkey!"

"He should have told me!"

"I was going to—I didn't get a chance."

"It's all right, we've got it back now," said Bobby, trying ineffectively to be a peacemaker.

"Shut up, all of you! I can't concentrate!" And as he said that, the hatch opposite us popped open. Not the hatch above! "Go!" Mickey shouted, pushing me toward it. "Come on!"

"Huh?" But I was already moving.

"You're not the only one who can keep a secret. Let's go, Douglas!"

I bounced through into a horizontal tube that stretched ahead forever. It was the same stuff as the inflatable pressure tubes that linked one vehicle to another—a spiral coil with plastic walls; you extended it wherever you wanted it to go—only this one was longer. It stretched away like a tunnel. It had a collapsible mesh deck for a floor, with several pipes and tubes running along underneath it. Outside the plastic, I could sense more than see that the tube was half-buried in Lunar dust. Farther out, lay the dim outlines of a shadowy horizon.

"How far does this go?" I called back.

Mickey was sealing the hatch behind us. "At least a kilometer. I hope. Go as fast as you can, Chigger. We're right behind you."

"But this isn't the road!"

"I know it. But maybe Alexei won't. I cut all his visual monitors to the airlock. At least, I think I did. So he's going to think we took the road."

"But how'd you know this tube was here?"

"Call it a lucky guess. But I know Alexei better than you. Keep bouncing." I didn't look back, I could hear them pounding behind me. "See, you wouldn't have noticed it, Chigger. You're a terrie. Sorry, no offense. But I knew that the Brickner station wasn't working the minute we climbed down into it. *It wasn't hot enough!* You can't melt Lunar ice without heat, and you've got to pump a lot of heat into the ground to get the ice to melt. And it wasn't hot enough! So where did all that water come from then?"

"It was here from before—? When the station was working?" I offered.

"Maybe. But remember, *I know Alexei better than you!* Why do you think I asked *him* to smuggle you up the Line? Why do you think I trusted him to smuggle us to Luna? Because Alexei Krislov is a brilliant scoundrel. Brickner station is a double-decoy. Yeah, he sells a little bit of water back to Gagarin. That's his cover—look down, you see those pipes under the deck? What do think is in them? Which way do you think it's flowing?"

I was too busy bouncing to focus, and I didn't want to stop to look. "Um, the green one is breathable air?" I guessed. "The blue one is water?"

"And the orange one? What do you think that is?

"That's ammonia," said Douglas. "Remember what Alexei said about nitrogen and ammonia? You need nitrogen to make breathable gas. And for fertilizer. You need ammonia for refrigeration."

"Right," said Mickey. "The key to Lunar technology isn't water. It's nitrogen. That's what everybody needs the most. Even more than water and electricity. Alexei isn't selling any of this! *He's stealing it!* Brickner isn't a water-production plant; it's a holding tank for water skimmed off Gagarin. And all the stuff in the other tanks as well. There were too many. There's *too much* storage there."

We bounced a little farther down the tube, while I thought about that. The pipes below our feet weren't that thick. I guessed they didn't need to be.

"Doesn't Gagarin know?" Douglas asked. "Can't they tell?"

"Maybe Alexei is only siphoning off a few liters a day. With the number of people coming and going into Gagarin Station, with the scale of industrial processes they've got going, they could write it off as loss due to normal usage. But if he's siphoning off any more than that, then someone at Gagarin is covering it up. That's my guess, that this is how legal resources are being funneled to the tribes of invisible Luna. I wonder if they're doing the same with electricity. You heard him talking about factories and what they needed. Dammit. We knew they were moving ahead. We didn't realize this—" And then he trailed off into a string of muttered curses.

We concentrated on bouncing down the tube. We couldn't see very far ahead from any given point, because the tube snaked and wound its way over the Lunar terrain, up and down, around and over. Every so often we passed a joint where two sections of tube had been sealed together. Several times we had to pass through manually operated airlocks. We zipped our way through.

"Bobby? Did you do something?" That was Douglas. They were in the same bubble suit again.

"I didn't do anything."

"What are you guys talking about?" Mickey asked.

"It smells like piss in here," said Bobby. "I didn't do it!"

"How bad?" asked Mickey. His voice sounded strange.

"Not too bad," Douglas said. And then he got it. "Oh."

"Would somebody explain it to me?" I asked.

"Ammonia," Mickey said.

"What's ammonia?" Bobby asked.

"It's good for cleaning your glasses," I said.

"I don't wear glasses," Bobby said.

"Then don't worry about it."

"Charles, please—" That was Mickey. "I'm trying to figure out how far we've come. I don't want to turn back."

"I think we can make it," Douglas said. "I'll turn up my oxygen."

"That'll help—a little bit." He added, "Alexei probably keeps the tube pressurized with ammonia to keep folks from wandering through it casually. Besides, it's another useful storage area. Do the math. A kilometer-long tube, nine meters in diameter, pressurized to two-thirds sea level, I'd guess. Can you figure it out, Douglas?"

He was trying to distract Douglas, I was sure. And maybe me too. I was trying to figure out if there was anything else we could do. "Monkey, if you've got any ideas, now's the time to talk—" It didn't respond.

"It really stinks in here!" wailed Bobby. "I don't like this!"

"How are your eyes?" Mickey asked.

"Watering—badly." Douglas coughed suddenly. Bobby was coughing even worse. The leak must have expanded—

—and then I got it! *The inflatable! The portable airlock!* I could barely get the words out fast enough. Even as I stumbled to get the words out, Mickey was already pulling it from his pack! I bounced back to him and together, we pushed Douglas and Stinky through the first zippered entrance. We zipped it behind them, unzipped the next, pushed them through, zipped it behind them—

Douglas was already turning up the oxygen on his tank. Mickey pushed the gloves into the inflatable, and without worrying about proper procedures unzipped all three of the zippers on Douglas's bubble suit. Douglas and Bobby lay on the floor of the inflatable, coughing and choking, their eyes streaming. Douglas held the breather tube in front of Bobby's nose, then his own, then back to Bobby. It probably still smelled of ammonia in there, but at least they had a chance now.

"Come on, Charles, I can't do this alone. I need your help." He rolled Bobby onto Douglas, and picked up Douglas by the head. I picked up Douglas by the feet and the two of us began carrying him forward. The inflatable bulged into unmanageable shapes, but we both had our hands pushed into its gloves and we held on to Douglas himself and tried to keep the bulges from dragging and scraping along the sides. We bounced through the tube as fast as we could manage. I could feel my heart pounding so hard I couldn't hear anything else.

Mickey led the way, I followed. I couldn't see past him very well, so I couldn't see if the tube sloped up or down, right or left, so I was constantly bumping and jerking, trying to keep up. Bobby and Douglas were still coughing, but Bobby was crying, and that was always a good sign. If we could just make it to the end of this tube. How far was it anyway?!

We had to stop then, while Mickey zipped us through another manual airlock. And then we pushed on again. I didn't know how much longer I could do this—I didn't care that we were in one-sixth gee. This was exhausting, and I was reaching the limits of my endurance. "We've gotta stop soon—" I managed to gasp.

"You'd better pace yourselves." Douglas coughed. He waved the breathing tube back and forth between himself and Bobby.

"All right, all right—" Mickey brought us to a halt. We lowered Douglas and Bobby to the deck and the two of us stood there, hands on knees, panting heavily.

"Aren't we there yet? How far is it?" I asked.

"We're halfway there. More than halfway. How are you doing, Douglas?" He was already shoving another air tank through the zipper locks. The last one. This was going to be close. "Turn it all the way up. Give yourselves as much pure oxygen as you can. And try not to strike any sparks. Ammonia is flammable, you know."

"If I turn it all the way up, the inflatable will fill the tube. We'll use the breathing mask. We'll be fine."

"Douglas, look at your bubble suit. The plastic is supposed to change color around a rip or a puncture. Red or yellow, I think. If you can find the hole, there's emergency tape right there. Just pull off a strip and press it to the leak. Can you find it? Look around your feet. Turn over, maybe it's behind you. Charles and I will look. Do you see anything, Charles—?"

"I'm still looking. It's hard to see through all these layers—"

"Douglas?"

"I don't see anything either."

"Damn! Maybe it's in the foot pads or the gloves or someplace it doesn't show. All right—" He glanced up the length of the tube. "It's doable. You ready, Chigger?"

"No," but I picked up Douglas by the feet anyway.

This time, we held our panic in check. We moved fast, but we weren't running anymore. We were tired, but we weren't exhausting ourselves. And then, just to make it worse, we started up a long uphill slope. I could see the ceiling of the tube arcing away.

"Gohvno!"

It hurt, I ached, and I was beginning to imagine I could smell the ammonia piss-smell myself. It was enough to make my eyes water. I coughed.

"Not you too!" Mickey said.

"Keep going!" I shouted.

And finally, the tube crested the hill. We passed through another manual airlock and started down the last long slope to Gagarin. And yes, I really could smell ammonia now. My suit had a leak too. But I could make it. I was certain of it. All we had to do was get to the bottom of this hill, that's all. Okay, the bottom of this hill then. If I could just hold my breath a little bit longer and not start coughing again—

—the pain in my eyes and nose and chest was impossible, and somebody was trying to force a breathing tube in my mouth. I was trying to hack out my guts and somebody was telling me to inhale. And all I wanted to do was just get Douglas and Bobby to the other end of the pipeline. And then I finished retching and the tube was shoved into my mouth, and then the next thing I knew, somebody was sitting on me and somebody else was carrying me and we were bouncing down the birth canal of hell pushing into the light, and—

—and then we were in an airlock or just outside of it and somebody was stripping me out of my bubble suit and turning me on my back and standing on my stomach. *Oh, flaming God, even CPR was different on the moon—*

ZOMBIES

I **WAS ON MY SIDE.** I was in the inflatable. Stinky was sitting next to me, rocking and hugging the monkey and crying. Douglas and Mickey were outside of the inflatable—leaning over me—how had that happened? They were both in bubble suits. Douglas's had a strip of tape on it. I noticed that immediately. My eyes and lungs still burned, there was blood dripping from my nose, but the piss-smell of ammonia was more memory than real.

We were still in the tube. Douglas waved at me. I waved back. He grinned. I wasn't sure what was happening. He picked up my feet, Mickey picked up my head; Bobby lay down on top of me, he didn't weigh enough to matter—and we were heading down the tube again. This time, I was the cargo. How had I gotten inside the inflatable? How had Douglas ended up outside again?

It hurt too much to wonder about it. I concentrated on breathing. One desperate gulp at a time. My throat felt scorched. My nose still dripped. I wiped at it futilely. My arms were too weak to move. Stinky waved a breathing tube at me.

I must have passed in and out of consciousness, because the next thing I knew, Douglas and Mickey were passing me through a hatch, and we were out of the tube inside another cargo-pod-shaped place. And then they were unzipping everything and pulling Stinky out and then me and I was full of questions, but I couldn't ask them because Mickey had a medikit and was wiping my face and shining a light in my eyes, telling me to watch his finger, asking me if I could talk.

I croaked something in response that sounded like *"Kwaaact whaccked?"* but really meant "What happened?"

"Your suit tore. We pushed you into the inflatable. I was going to go for help, but Bobby found the hole in your suit and Douglas patched it. He put it on himself and the two of us carried you out. You should have said something—"

"Waack tdiict!"

"Don't talk," Mickey ordered. "Breathe this. It's going to smell funny—" He sprayed something into my throat. It was wet and cold, but in a few seconds, my throat stopped trying to climb out of my neck, and the pain subsided into a dull ache. That left only my lungs screaming for relief. Mickey pressed something cold and hissy against my arm.

It didn't make the throbbing in my chest go away, it made me go away. I was still awake, I could even feel stuff, I just didn't care anymore. I saw Mickey turn to Bobby next and start making the same tests. Bobby was in better shape than me. So was Douglas. But he sedated them too. Douglas sat down cross-legged next to me, with a stupid look on his face. We must have looked like three happy zombies—

And then there were some other people around us and Mickey stood up and started showing them his documents. "My name is Michael Gordon Partridge. I'm a licensed bounty hunter from the Line, and these people are my prisoners. Here's a copy of the warrant. Here's my license and my ID. They need immediate medical attention, and I need to arrange fast transport to Armstrong."

I saw Douglas look up, blinking in confusion. "Huh—?" I wasn't sure what happened next. That's when I started passing in and out of consciousness.

The next thing I knew, the room was vibrating loudly. And I was strapped down so I couldn't move. I couldn't see either. I turned my head and something wet fell away from my eyes. Douglas was lying on another cot across from me. I didn't see Stinky or the monkey, but there was another cot above me. Maybe he was on that. There was a signal I could whistle—

—but there was an oxygen mask over my face. And then someone came and put the wet pad over my eyes again. Mickey's voice. "You're going to be all right, Charles. You took a few bad gulps, but there isn't going to be any permanent damage. Douglas and Bobby are all right. So is the monkey. Everybody's here. All you have to do is relax and rest and let us get you to the hospital at Armstrong Station. We'll be there in another two hours." He leaned in close to put his lips next to my ear. "Everything is going to be all right, I promise."

I couldn't speak. I didn't try. I didn't care. I didn't have any feelings left. Later on, I might have feelings again. But if they were going to hurt, I didn't want them. I'd had enough of feelings, thankewvery-muchnext. But I wanted him to go away. I knew he wasn't good for us anymore, even if I couldn't remember why. I tried to tell him that. I struggled against the restraints and twisted my head back and forth, trying to shake the air mask loose, so I could speak, but that didn't accomplish anything, and a minute later I felt something cold on my arm and I went away again.

This time when I came to, the room was silent and dark and I was all alone. I was still in a cargo pod. We'd spent our entire time on Luna going from one used cargo pod to another, missing sleep, missing meals, trying to breathe everything from vacuum to ammonia—

At least the air smelled clean and wet here. It smelled like flowers. Hawaiian flowers. Plumeria, I think that's what they were called. That was nice. What was even nicer was that I could smell them at all.

I couldn't open my eyes. Something moist was taped in place over them. I wondered if I'd been blinded. That was going to be a nuisance. But at least I could I still hear. The music was Samuel Barber's Adagio for Strings, which struck some people as plaintive and annoying, or just plain desolate. I always liked it for its thoughtful quality. It was Dad's recording, and I think I knew which one. It was the first time I ever got to see him conduct. He conducted with his eyes closed. At least it looked that way from where I was sitting. He was lost in the music. And his hands were like living creatures—he didn't use a baton; he just stroked the air and the music poured forth. He coaxed the Adagio into life and let it fill the auditorium. I don't think I took a breath for the entire ten minutes. I'd never heard anything like that before in my life. I hadn't known such sounds were possible. And afterward, I kept playing it over and over again, always trying to recapture that same initial *wunderstorm*. . . .

I wished I could tell him how much I loved his music. That would be nice. Somebody took my hand in his. It felt like Dad's hand. Large and warm and safely enveloping. I knew it had to be Douglas holding my hand, but it was nice to pretend it was Dad for a while.

And then Dad spoke. "I was so scared, Chigger. For a while, I thought I was going to lose you. All of you, forever. I didn't get a chance to say any of the stuff I wanted to say. And I was afraid that even if I could say it, you wouldn't want to hear it. And now that I have the chance to tell you, all I really need you to know is how important you are to me and how sorry I am everything got so screwed up. I wish I could have done better. The music—do you remember this? You were always asking to come see me conduct, and I was sure it would bore you to death, but I took you anyway, and you sat there totally entranced and captivated. You were listening to the music as deeply as anyone I've ever seen. I was so happy for you that day—because you'd discovered something all your own. And I was so glad it was something I could give to you. I remember the look in your eyes of total awe and admiration, and how proud I was to be your dad; the person who'd brought that look to your face. I wish I could have made that moment last forever." He kissed my hand and replaced it on the bed, and then he got up and went away, and the dream ended. But it was really a nice dream while it lasted.

And then I had a dream about Mom too. Her and that Sykes woman. But I didn't remember what they said. And that bothered me for a while—because it didn't seem fair for Dad to have a whole vivid dream and not Mom too. But it was kind of like Mom had stepped out of my life for a while and I guess I wasn't ready to let her back in, not even in my dreams.

That reminded me of something Douglas said once, about moms. He said that nothing gets in the way of a good fantasy like a mom. That's why most guys try to put Mom aside for a while—while they try to figure out who they are, I guess. It didn't matter anymore. We were all going to jail soon enough. If we weren't there already.

And then, one morning, I opened my eyes to the smell of hot chocolate, eggs, toast, and strawberry jam. And I sat up in bed and looked around. Except for a slightly sleepy feeling of confusion, I felt better than I had in days. I could even talk. My voice was still dusky-scratchy like my throat was lined with cockleburs and foxtails, but I could actually make understandable words. "Hello? Is anyone there?" I was in a room that was *not* part of a cargo pod. It actually had a real floor and real walls and a real ceiling. It was spooky. Everything looked soft and gentle and flowery, that's how I knew it was a hospital; it smelled like a hospital too, with the air just a little too fresh and clean.

"Oh, good, you're up. Right on schedule." The woman wore a

purple-gray dress and a thing like a pink apron over it. I guessed it was supposed to be cheery, and it wasn't too hard to look at, but I was never big on industrial cheerfulness before and as good as I felt, I wasn't ready to start now.

She was just uncovering a tray of food—that was what I'd smelled. She put it across my bed and tied a bib around my neck. "Just in case," she said. "You might still be a little weak."

"What is this place?"

"Tranquility Medical Center at Armstrong."

"How long was I out?"

"Three days. No, four. It doesn't matter. You're fine now. You'll just have to take it easy for a bit. I'll leave you alone to eat. The shower is through there. There are fresh clothes in the closet. Try not to take too long. You have to be in court in two hours—"

"*Say what?*"

But she was already gone.

IN  COURT

JUDGE CAVANAUGH WAS THE LARGEST human being I had ever seen. He looked like the *Hindenburg*. He was huge and round, and when he entered the room, it took a while for all of him to arrive at the same place. He moved like a human bubble suit, with all of his blubbery mass flubbering and bouncing around like an animated caricature of a fat man. In Lunar low gee, he didn't lumber, he *floated*. He took his seat at the bench, and all the various parts of him arrived one after the other, settling into place like latecomers at a concert.

Judge Cavanaugh took roll, made sure all his separate body sections had sorted themselves out, looked out over the room, looked to the display in front of him, rubbed his nose, and waved a go-ahead gesture at the clerk, a skinny black woman. "Case number 40032, in the matter of Douglas, Charles, and Robert Dingillian, custody of, blah blah blah."

Custody? Again?

Judge Cavanaugh was scanning through his notes. He finally found the page he was looking for and looked out at us again. He cleared his throat. "Most court cases are a two-body problem. A plaintiff and a defendant. Those are relatively simple to resolve. You listen to the facts, you look for a balance. Somehow you find a Lagrange point."

He looked out over the room. "But just as the laws of physics start to get complex and unmanageable when you introduce a third body to the problem, so do the laws of human beings become complex and unmanageable when there are three participants orbiting around a claim.

We have here, a seven-body problem. Or a twelve-body problem. Or more. I've lost count of the number of litigants who have stepped forward to lodge a claim or file a brief as a friend of the court. I know that most of you recognize that you do not have a hope in hell of winning your claim, but it hasn't stopped you from adding bodies to the problem in the hope of making it so unmanageable that it can never be resolved. I applaud your various successes in making this case a colossal nightmare. I promise to reward each and every one of you appropriately."

He smiled. For some reason, it didn't look friendly.

"Let me explain something to those of you who've just arrived here in the last few days. I know a lot of you are suddenly out of work and vaguely troubled by the fact that we don't have ambulances to chase here on Luna. And, of course, as we all know, there's nothing as dangerous as an unemployed lawyer—unless it's one who *is* employed. But for the record, I want to explain to you how things work here in this courtroom, and on most of Luna.

"This is a small town. There are only three million of us. And we're spread across a landmass equal to that of Earth. So we're spread pretty thin. We've only got a few major settlements. The largest still has less than a hundred thousand folks. So we run our courts with a lot less formality than you might be used to back home. That doesn't mean we take our lawyering any less seriously. It just means that we don't bother with wigs and robes and funny hats. They make us look silly and we start giggling—and that's a little disconcerting when we're sentencing someone to the nearest airlock because he refused to pay his air tax. And yes, I'm not joking.

"So we're just going to cut through a lot of the crap that you guys love so much and see if we can sort things out without using up too much oxygen. Those of you who are representing clients with money, this probably doesn't worry you—but take my word for it, it doesn't matter how much money your clients have back on Earth or on the Line. It can't buy more oxygen if there isn't any left. We want you to represent your client's claims fairly, we want to hear the facts. We do *not* want a lot of extraneous noise. Nothing pisses off this court more than a low signal-to-noise ratio. I assume I'm making myself perfectly clear? Thank you."

He paused to note something on the pad in front of him, then said, "So, let's get to it. This hearing is projected to cost the Lunar Authority fifty thousand water-dollars. Therefore, the court chooses to exercise local privilege and will assess a nonrefundable processing fee of five thousand liters of water or ten thousand liters of nitrogen on all claimants in this matter to cover the judicial expenses. Anyone choosing to withdraw his or her claim, please see the court clerk now—"

Several people I didn't recognize bounced up out of their seats and over to the clerk at the side of the room. I was sitting in a wheelchair with a mask on my face, concentrating on one breath at a time. I'd been wheeled in at the last minute and I hadn't really gotten a good look at anything; besides, my vision was still too blurry to make out details. And strapped in as I was, I couldn't even turn around to see how many people were in the room or who else was here. Next to me, the shape that looked like Douglas was grim. The shape that looked like Bobby was sitting quietly on his lap. I didn't see anything shaped like a monkey.

"Thank you," said Judge Cavanaugh. "That will simplify matters a little bit—but even with fewer litigants, the court costs will remain the same. This means that the assessment will now have to be increased by 50 percent to seventy-five hundred liters of water per claimant—" This time, six more people headed for the clerk's desk.

The judge smiled. "I like the way this is going. By the way, I should note that this fee will also apply to those filing briefs of amicus curiae. This court does not need any more friends. We already have the best friends money can buy. So if you intend to be our friend today, we will expect you to pay for your fair share of justice too. You can buy as much justice as you can afford on Luna. Cash payments only, please. We do not accept checks drawn on Earth banks. This will be your last opportunity to reconsider. . . ." Four more people.

Judge Cavanaugh waited until the bustle in the courtroom died down. He studied some papers, some material on his display, and conferred with his clerk. Finally, he looked up again. "All right, that helped. Now let's see what kind of progress we can make. We're here, all of us, to decide what to do with these three young men. The issue revolves on whether or not Judge Griffith was justified in granting the divorce of Charles Dingillian from his parents and whether Douglas and Charles are fit custodians of Robert Dingillian." For the first time, Judge Cavanaugh looked at us. "Charles Dingillian, how are you feeling?"

My voice crackled like I was walking through a field of shredded wheat. "I never felt better in my life." I said it deadpan.

Judge Cavanaugh raised an eyebrow at me. "Are you feeling well enough to proceed?"

I nodded. "Yes, sir."

"Thank you." He turned his attention back to the rest of the court. "I want to mention here that Lunar Authority is a signatory to the Starside Covenant as well as the Covenant of Rights. As such, we give full faith and credit to the legal processes of all other signatories to these covenants. We recognize marriages, adoptions, divorces, and other legal contracts, entered into willingly by the participants. For those of you who are *not* lawyers, and I think there are only three of you in this room who are not"—he glanced at us when he said that—"this means that Luna will acknowledge and recognize all legal decisions of the Line Authority. We are not obligated to recognize the legal authority of some Earth courts because they are *not* signatory. For the record, the Republic of Texas is a nonsignatory jurisdiction.

"I want to make this very clear at the outset, because it affects what this court has the authority to do. Those of you who are preparing to argue that Judge Griffith's decision has no weight in this courtroom are wrong, and this court will not entertain any claims based on that line of reasoning at all. You would be asking this court to create a conditional nullification of the articles of full faith and credit among covenant signatories. In plain old-fashioned English, it ain't gonna happen. Not in this court.

"However . . . those of you who are asking me to *set aside* Judge Griffith's decision as a bad ruling, had better be prepared to argue that claim with facts and logic that demonstrate an overwhelming and compelling necessity. And please, remember the unofficial motto of this court. *Bore me and die.*

"Today's hearing is relatively informal, even for Luna. It is an evidentiary hearing—an inquiry into the facts—which may or may not resolve the matter. If we do not resolve the matter here, we will refer it for trial. If the investigation does not uncover a compelling interest on the part of the state—or on the part of any of the claimants, the whole thing will end here. And let me say again, everyone's cooperation in achieving a speedy resolution to this business will be particularly appreciated. *I hope I make myself clear.*"

He turned back to his display for a moment, frowning. He clicked through several pages. Judge Cavanaugh looked like he was having a wonderful time. I decided to like him—at least until he pissed me off.

"Now, then . . ." He looked up again. "Let's get to the specifics. This court has spent several days reviewing the transcript of Judge Griffith's divorce hearing. It is very interesting reading, but I find nothing in it to justify a set-aside. If there's anyone here who feels I've *missed something*, do feel free to point out any errors that Judge Griffith may have made in her ruling, or any mistakes I might have made in my review. I certainly won't be prejudiced against anyone who feels qualified to educate me in this matter. I might even thank you for the effort. But if there's no one here who wants to look for the light at the bottom of that particular tunnel . . . then let's just move on. Let's all stipulate in advance that any evidence that anyone has to present about the wisdom of *this* ruling must be based on circumstances that have developed in the last two weeks, *since* the ruling was made. You will have to demonstrate that Douglas, Charles, and Robert Dingillian have proven incapable of taking care of themselves. We will use *that* as the deciding criterion in this chamber. Any questions? I thought not." He looked very pleased with himself. I wished I could see the expressions on the faces behind us; but I couldn't turn in my seat, and even if I could, it would all be a blur. But at least I wasn't coughing anymore.

"But before we can even deal with that, we have to deal with this *other* matter first—which I consider an extremely minor and very annoying detail. So of course, that's why it will probably consume an inordinate amount of this court's time. But a number of you have aggressively argued that the property claim is an essential part of judging the Dingillians' behavior since they were granted independence, so there's no setting it aside. Is there? Bailiff, bring in the *object*, please."

While they were waiting for the bailiff, I leaned over to Douglas and managed to croak, "Don't we have a lawyer?"

Douglas shook his head. "Not yet."

"Why not?"

"The judge said we don't need one. Not unless we go to trial. He's acting as advocate on our behalf. No, that's not illegal here. Court costs are carried by the plaintiffs—unless they win. It's real different than on Earth. Plaintiffs have to prove they have a case just to get to trial."

The bailiff came back carrying a black box. He set it on a table in front of the room. He opened the box and removed the monkey. He placed it on the table and took the box away. The monkey looked lifeless. Bobby shouted, "That's my monkey! I want it back! *It's mine!*" I tried to stifle a smile. There were times when I loved my brother *be-cause* he was such a brat.

Judge Cavanaugh made a note on a pad. "So there we have the first claimant speaking up. Thank you. You are . . . Robert Dingillian, correct?"

"Yes! And I want my monkey back."

"And why do you say the monkey is yours?"

"Because my daddy gave it to me. And it's mine."

"All right, good." Judge Cavanaugh looked over the court. "Is there anyone who wants to contest this fact—that Max Dingillian gave this toy to his son? No? No one wants to argue that? Thank you. What a pleasant surprise. So we can all stipulate now that the toy was given to Robert Dingillian." He made a note on his pad.

"Now, Bobby—where did your daddy get this toy?"

"He bought it."

"You saw him buy it?"

"Uh-huh."

"Good, thank you." To the rest of the court, Judge Cavanaugh said, "We have other witnesses who can confirm this, of course, so let's just move ahead. Let's stipulate that Max Dingillian did indeed go through the motions of purchasing this toy. He paid cash value and received custody of the toy. His account was debited, and he was given a receipt. Therefore, paper was in place to demonstrate he was the legal owner of record. Is there anyone who wants to contest that? Is there anyone who wants to argue that these events did not happen? No? Thank you. All right, the court will now stipulate that Max Dingillian did indeed go through the motions, did appear to, and to all intents and purposes, *believed* that he had legally obtained custody of this toy for the express purpose of presenting it to his son Robert Dingillian. Gracious—at this rate, we could be out of here in time for the return of Halley's Comet. That'll be when, Gloria? Another fifty-six years?"

He looked out over the courtroom. "*Now*, who wants to argue that Max Dingillian's purchase of the toy was in any way irregular? Who wants to argue that he had no right to the toy or that he came by it dishonestly or that the sale was invalid due to other circumstances?"

About six people stood up then, several of them shouting. I thought I recognized a couple of voices, but I didn't feel like trying to turn around to see. It would have been wasted effort.

"All right." Judge Cavanaugh pointed. "Everybody's going to get a turn. Just line up in the back there. In order of height, alphabetically, I don't care. You first. Come up front. State your name for the record. Remember, you're in court. Anything you say can and will be used against you."

A heavyset man came forward. He looked like a hockey player. "My name is David Cheifetz. Until three weeks ago, I was an attorney with Canadian-Interplanetary—"

I leaned over and whispered to Douglas. *"That's not what J'mee said. She said her daddy sold electricity for the Line."*

"And you believed her?"

"Oh," I said, realizing again. Everybody had a secret agenda. *Everybody lied.*

Cheifetz was still talking. "—My family and I are emigrating out to the colonies. Seven weeks ago, we made arrangements to have Max Dingillian ferry some sensitive material for us."

"You mean *smuggle.*"

"No, Your Honor. Smuggling is a crime. What we were doing was perfectly legal. My wife and my daughter and I are very visible people. We've already discovered this to our dismay when our daughter J'mee was accused of being Charles Dingillian in disguise." The judge made a hurry-up gesture. "The point is that we are clearly targets of opportunity. This is one of the reasons for emigrating. The safest way for us to transfer our wealth was to have it travel by an alternate route. Someone not as visible as we are. Max Dingillian was our courier." He glanced at me and Douglas and Bobby, looked annoyed. "While we don't contest the ownership of the toy, we do contest the ownership of the memory bars inside of it. They belong to us. We can prove it by direct examination of the serial numbers on the memory bars."

I nudged Douglas. "Dad paid for those memory bars—"

But Douglas was already standing up. "Your Honor, I think we have the purchase receipt. In fact, I know we do. Those memory bars were sold to us, and—"

Judge Cavanaugh held up his hand for silence. "Just relax, Douglas. This isn't the first time I've heard a case." He turned back to Cheifetz. "Young mister Dingillian challenges your claim. You acknowledge that the toy belongs to Robert Dingillian, but not the memory inside of it. So how did the memory get into the toy?"

Cheifetz looked like he'd swallowed a lemon without peeling it first. "I'd prefer not to discuss the details of that transfer, Your Honor—"

"You will if you want your claim considered."

"We signed over custody of the bars to an agency that provides transport services. They sold the bars to Max Dingillian."

"So the bars were *legally* sold to Max Dingillian?"

"Um. No. Not quite. Custody was legally transferred to Max Dingillian. His contract was to transport the bars and transfer custody back to an appointed representative of the agency here on Luna."

"But the bars were legally his."

"Technically . . . yes. That's how transport agencies work. That way there's no direct connection to the real owners—"

"Counselor"—Judge Cavanaugh held up a hand to stop him—"I know from smuggling. This is Luna. You're standing on a smuggled floor. That's genuine Brazilian hardwood. And no, I did not order it, my predecessor twice removed did—after he confiscated it from the person who tried to smuggle it. Never mind. The point is that while the memory bars were Max Dingillian's property, unless you had a written contract of agreement that he would sell them or transfer them back to you, they were his to dispose of as he saw fit, weren't they?"

"He had an agreement!"

"Do you have a signature?"

"Of course not! The whole point was *not* to leave a paper trail."

"So you have no evidence of such an agreement."

"Max Dingillian will confirm it."

"Belay that, Counselor. It's still *your* turn in the bucket. What was Max Dingillian going to get in return for being your mule? Other than a free trip to Luna?"

"We were going to guarantee a colony contract for Mr. Dingillian and his family. So yes, there was a significant recompense promised. It was a contract."

"I see. So you transferred custody of your property to Max Dingillian with the *understanding* and even the *obligation* that he would sell the property back to you at a more convenient time and place. Is that correct?"

"Yes, Your Honor."

"I got it. So your disagreement is with Max Dingillian, who disposed of property that was legally his, because he didn't dispose of it in the way that you wanted him to. Now, correct me if I'm wrong here—and I don't think I am—in order for you to have a claim on the memory bars, you should be suing Max Dingillian for breach of contract, shouldn't you? It seems like an open-and-shut case to me. You have an agreement that you can't prove he made, but you can certainly prove that he violated it. I'll be happy to rule on that right now."

"Your Honor, I can prove that the memory is mine."

"No. You can prove that the memory *was* yours to sell to Max Dingillian. At least, I'm assuming that's what that sheaf of papers in your hand is all about."

"Your Honor, *I want my property back.*"

"Mr. Cheifetz, you were smuggling. It was legal smuggling, to be sure, but it was still smuggling. You were taking advantage of the loopholes in the Emigration Act that allow tax exemptions for property purchased immediately before departure. Had you been carrying the memory all the way from Earth, you would have been taxed accordingly. By transferring custody, neither you nor Max Dingillian pays taxes on it and the memory gets a free ride. The flaw in that operation is that when the memory is Max Dingillian's property, it is his to dispose of as he sees fit, unless you can prove implied or assumed contract. And even if Max Dingillian himself comes forward to say that you and he had such a verbal agreement in place, this court is still not willing to overturn provable property rights in favor of unprovable ones. The kids have receipts. You have nothing but your assertions and your good looks. That's not a winning case, and I'm not prepared to open up that particular can of worms anyway—*not even to stir the sauce.*"

I squirmed around in my wheelchair, looking for a water bottle. My throat was hurting again. For some reason, I glanced across to the back of the room. Despite my blurry vision, I thought I saw someone who looked like J'mee there. She looked angry and hurt. She saw me looking at her, made a face, and turned away. I turned forward again.

Judge Cavanaugh was saying, "I want to note something else here. If it's your argument that the memory was never really Max Dingillian's at all, that this whole thing was a charade—and that all of the paperwork being passed around to prove ownership was just a pretense for the purpose of avoiding export and duty fees, emigration taxes, and so on, then that indicates a pattern of deliberate criminal behavior on his part and yours as well. If you're prepared to pursue that line of argument, that the memory was never really Max Dingillian's, then this court has to regard you as a criminal defendant. You will be immediately liable for several hundred thousands of liters in importation and emigration fees, not to mention additional severe penalties—and they will be *severe*—for smuggling with intent to defraud."

Cheifetz was already reaching for his wallet. "I'll happily pay those fees, Your Honor, if it will get me my property back—"

Wrong answer. The judge's gavel stopped him cold. "Mr. Cheifetz, take your seat please. This court has to accept the existing evidence at face value. You wanted Luna to believe that you sold the memory and it isn't yours? Fine. Luna is convinced. You sold the memory. It isn't yours. You want to buy it back? That's fine too. Once this court determines who the legal owner is, you may make your offer."

Cheifetz started to sputter. In the back of the room, J'mee started to cry. Cavanaugh hammered again. "Next." He glanced up. "Who are you?"

A rumply little man stepped forward. "Howard Phroomis, representing Stellar-American Industries, Your Honor." *Howard?* The same lousy lawyer who'd chased us all over the Line with subpoenas from hell? What was he doing here? Had they dumped him in a cargo pod aimed at the moon as well?

"Your Honor, Stellar-American believes that the object contains property belonging to Stellar-American, stolen from Stellar-American, and passed into the hands of Canadian-Interplanetary, and from there into the hands of the Dingillian family, specifically for the purpose of smuggling it off-planet. We can demonstrate that the property inside the toy was manufactured by Stellar-American and was stolen from Stellar-American; therefore, despite the trail of paperwork that everyone else has carefully laid down, all of those claims are invalid because the property was stolen to begin with. In point of fact, Stellar-American believes that every member of this conspiracy should be apprehended and charged with receiving and transporting stolen property with intent to defraud."

"Ahh," said Judge Cavanaugh. "Stolen property, you say? Now this is getting interesting. You realize of course, that if you make this charge, this transforms this hearing from a simple arbitration of claims into a criminal matter—?"

"Yes, Your Honor. That's my intention."

PROCEEDINGS

DURING THE RECESS, MICKEY SHOWED up. He was taking a chance; the judge had specifically instructed that nobody was to approach us for the purpose of making any offers at all. But Mickey wasn't there to negotiate. He just looked worried. He put his hand on mine. "How are you feeling, Charles?" I didn't answer. I had this very specific memory that he had done something pretty awful. When he saw I wasn't going to answer, he turned to Douglas. "If this goes into the criminal domain, you're going to need a lawyer. Let me help."

"Lawyers got us into this mess," Douglas said. "It's everybody wanting to help that keeps making things worse. Where does it stop? I told you to get away from us and leave us alone."

Mickey lowered his voice. "I didn't want to do it. I didn't plan to do it. I was going to keep my promise. But your brother looked like he was dying. And I figured keeping him alive was more important than anything else, so I did what I did to get him to the best hospital on Luna. We were lucky—he wasn't as badly burned as I was afraid. But I didn't know that at the time, and I wasn't going to take chances with his life or yours. And I can still keep my promise, if you'll let me. You're going to need a lawyer—maybe my mom can help."

"She didn't do too good for us last time, Mickey. No thanks." Douglas glared at Mickey until Mickey lowered his gaze and turned away. I felt bad for both of them.

After he was gone, I leaned over, and whispered to Douglas, "Where are we going to get a lawyer?"

Douglas nodded toward the back of the room. "There are a couple hundred of them just outside that door, all fighting for the chance to represent us. I don't understand why."

"*It's the monkey*," I whispered. "*I told you!*"

"*Yeah, I know what you said. But everyone else says it's just industrial memory.*"

"*The monkey told me itself!*"

"*Maybe it was running a simulation in self-defense?*"

"*A simulation of sentience? Come on, Douglas! You know better than that. A simulation of sentience is sentience!*"

"*You didn't talk to it very long. Some chatterbots are very good, Chigger.*"

I didn't answer immediately. I was still thinking about what had just fallen out of my mouth. When the judge gaveled the courtroom back to order, I levered myself uneasily to my feet and croaked, "Your Honor—?"

Judge Cavanaugh looked at me sympathetically. "I sincerely hope that's a temporary condition, young man. Yes?"

"If everybody is willing to stipulate that the monkey belongs to Bobby, I'd like to ask that it be returned to us. We're willing to agree not to tamper with any of the memory or anything else inside it, and if the court rules that the memory bars belong to someone else, we'll agree to turn them over. But we have some of our personal information and resources stored in the monkey too, and our lawyer, when we get one, is going to need access to that—if we're to represent ourselves adequately."

Judge Cavanaugh nodded. "You argue well. But much too politely. I'm afraid you'll never be a good lawyer."

"Yes. Thank you, Your Honor."

"Is there anyone who can present a valid objection why Robert Dingillian should not have his toy returned to him, under the terms put forward by Charles Dingillian?" Before anyone could object, he hammered his gavel. "So ruled." He turned back to us. "Robert, you can take your monkey now."

Bobby leapt out of his chair and ran to the table. He scooped the monkey up into his arms, but it remained lifeless. "It's broken!" he wailed.

Judge Cavanaugh looked unhappy. "Yes, it does appear to be. It shut itself down when the court was examining it, and we've been unable to reboot it."

"Did you open up its backside? Did you take its memory bars out?" I asked.

The judge shook his head. "I know better than to tamper with evidence. May I assume that I don't have to advise you not to open it up either?"

"Yes, sir." That was both Douglas and myself, in unison.

"But it's broken!" wailed Bobby.

Douglas looked to me. "*Charles . . . ?*"

"*Yes, Douglas?*"

"*The unlock code?*"

"*Unlock code?*"

"*Don't play games, Charles.*"

"*Maybe it really is broken!*" I said, almost noncommittally.

Douglas gave me the Douglas look.

Judge Cavanaugh hammered with his gavel. "All right, let's move on. I have a petition in front of me from Stellar-American Industries, asserting that two complementary quantum-determinant devices, manufactured on a standard memory chassis, were shipped from a Stellar-American chip foundry to a Toronto laboratory owned and operated by Canadian-Interplanetary. Isn't that interesting. Mr. Cheifetz, will you come forward again, please?"

There was a shuffling at the back of the room. Cheifetz came hesitantly back to the front.

"Will you tell the court how you came into possession of these devices?"

"They were given to me by the company. After we concluded our tests, the lab had no further use for them. I purchased them for a small handling charge. The company disposes of a lot of used equipment to employees; some of us have projects of our own that we like to tinker with, and—"

"Spare me," said Cavanaugh, holding up a hand. "I know tinkers. Some of my best friends are tinkers. You, sir, are not a tinker. So please don't try to stretch my credibility. Or my patience. This matter is so petty, I expect we will be here for several years. It doesn't worry me, I can live off my fat; but the rest of you will probably be bones bleaching in the sun before too long if we continue on at this rate. So spare me the storytelling. Is it your contention now that these devices were legally transferred to your labs and then to you?"

"Yes." He held up his sheaf of papers. "I've got hardcopy receipts and signatures all the way back to the foundry. Stellar-American uses Canadian-Interplanetary for integrity testing of chips. In particular we test for resistance to vacuum, heat, cold, radiation, sunlight, and extremes of acceleration."

"And you tested these chips?"

"Yes. The labs ran over three thousand hours of integrity tests. We tested the chips under multiple combinations of conditions."

"Did the chips survive?"

"Yes, they did."

"And when the tests were over, did you return the chips to Stellar-American?"

"No."

"Why not?" Judge Cavanaugh looked puzzled. "I thought it was standard procedure to return prototypes. To protect against industrial espionage."

"Yes, that is the usual procedure."

"But not here?"

Cheifetz looked uncomfortable.

"Go ahead."

He took a breath. "Most foundries know what other foundries are doing, but they don't know the details. So one of the best places to find out is to infiltrate the testing labs. So sometimes a company will ship a decoy chip, with some unworkable technology in it. The chip is *intended* to be stolen, so that when the other guys try to copy it, they waste valuable time and energy chasing down the wrong direction. The decoys appear to work—or sometimes they're set to deliberately fail. Another ploy to fool the other side. These chips were decoys."

"How do you know that?"

"Stellar-American told us. We had an attempt to breach our security. We reported it to them. That's recorded here too. Off the record, they told us that the chip was a decoy. They were interested in the integrity testing of the manufacturing process, but the chips themselves were of no significant value."

"And they didn't ask for them back?"

"We asked for permission to test the chips to the breaking point, at our own convenience. We do that a lot. It was part of a whole batch of requests. They agreed. Then we got swamped with a bunch of new contracts and that testing program was put aside. Later, the chips were remaindered and my family corporation bought them. They looked like ordinary memory bars, they could be used as such, they had passed their integrity tests, and for that reason they were the perfect medium for the transfer of sensitive information. We encoded an enormous amount of personal and business information and resource materials of all kinds into these chips. It was a six week process. And, as I said, I have the paperwork to demonstrate that the information riding in these chips is proprietary to my family corporation."

"I see," said Judge Cavanaugh. "So now you do have paperwork. Lots of it. Isn't that convenient. And so does the other fellow. Goodness! What a dilemma. Hmmm. How *interesting*. Let's recap. Stellar-American says that the chips were stolen. And you say they were lawfully transferred to you . . . and you were, for lack of a better word, conveniently smuggling them off-planet for use . . . wherever you ended up. Why do I get the feeling that your paperwork is going to be flawless? Why do I get the same feeling about Mr. Phroomis's paperwork—that it will be equally convincing? Why do I get the feeling that Earthside manufacturers are very very good at manufacturing paperwork . . . ?" He sighed.

"All right, Mr. Phroomis, your turn. Let's hear your side of it."

Howard's voice was just as rumpled as the rest of him. "Your Honor, I agree with you that a lot of the paperwork here has been manufactured for convenience. In fact, I have here affidavits and depositions that the entire exchange of memos and communications that Mr. Cheifetz is basing his claim on are fraudulent. None of the officers of Stellar-American ever wrote any of those notes, ever made any of those communications, or authorized such a dangerous disposal of our property. We admit that the paper trail is excellent, but it's too good to be true. It could only be that good if it were deliberately manufactured."

"So your argument is that the evidence on the other side is too good. I got it." Another voice came from the back of the room and Judge Cavanaugh looked up. "Yes, another crater heard from. And you are?"

A woman came forward. "Valerie Patenaude, Your Honor, representing Vancouver Design Works. The chips in question were designed by us. We hired Stellar-American to manufacture and test the chips;

they were to return all proprietary materials, including all flawed and failed chips, all test chips, all decoy chips, and any other material pertinent to the production of our designs, as specified in our agreement. They were to guarantee that no copies would pass out of their direct control. Not even for testing. It has only been in the past two weeks that we have discovered that they did indeed manufacture extra copies of our chips—"

Phroomis interrupted. "Those copies were made for quality control, for the testing of the manufacturing process. The chips in question required some very tricky techniques, and the copies were to be deconstructed so that Stellar-American could affirm the integrity of the production lines. The company retains that right, it is specified in the production contract—"

"The material was to be returned," Patenaude said. "And it was *not* returned. Mr. Cheifetz's own testimony here indicates a callous disregard of security—"

Judge Cavanaugh held up a hand. "Save it, Counselor. They're lining up behind you. Next? I just want to find out who's here and why, everybody will get the chance to bite everybody else before we're through." To the next lawyer, he asked, "Who are you?"

"*Gracias*, Judge Cavanaugh—" I recognized that voice too. Fat *Señor* Doctor Bolivar Hidalgo. Not as fat as Judge Cavanaugh, but impressive nonetheless. He was mostly a round blur, he barely glanced in our direction. "I am here as a temporary speaker for Lethe-Corp, until their own representatives can arrange transportation. The difficulties on Earth—and the unfortunate restrictions of the sudden Lunar quarantine—have made it impossible for them to be here today. However, Lethe-Corp wants to take a superordinate position here. The chips in question are the property of Lethe-Corp who initiated the entire process. Lethe-Corp hired Vancouver Design. Lethe-Corp created the specifications and was to retain sole ownership. Vancouver Design was doing work-for-hire."

Patenaude stepped forward, "This is correct, insofar as it goes. However, the chips in question were outside of the specification parameters of Lethe-Corp. The chips in question were internal projects of our own that we were constructing as test beds for certain unique structural elements. Once we determined the most successful implementations, we would have created a custom design for Lethe-Corp. In point of fact, our test chips were supersets of the Lethe-Corp specifi-

cation so that we could test multiple configurations on the same platform. We often work this way—"

"Your Honor," argued Hidalgo, "the contract specifies that Lethe-
Corp owns all of the material developed in testing—"

"Only the testing that Lethe-Corp paid for."

"Nevertheless, there was proprietary technology involved that belongs only to Lethe-Corp, and—"

"Proprietary technology *licensed* to Vancouver Design specifically
for additional research and development—"

Judge Cavanaugh was looking back and forth between them, grinning. He rapped his wooden hammer. "I do so like cases like this. We
can tie up the time and energy of a lot of lawyers and keep them out
of real trouble while spending lots and lots of corporate money." He
waved at the back of the room. "And your name is—?"

"Shannonhouse, John Shannonhouse."

"And you represent?"

"Buffalo Technology, LTD."

"And your claim is based on—?"

"We are the patent holders."

"Oh?"

"We hold 137 patents on quantum-level processor determinants.
We represent forty-five different companies who have pooled their patents for mutual benefit—and also because without such cooperation,
nobody's devices would work at all, all of these separate structures are
highly interdependent, they need each other—so do the companies that
own the patents. Lethe-Corp is a licensee, as are Vancouver Design,
Canadian-Interplanetary, and so on. The chips in question were an experimental project that we had authorized Lethe-Corp to build. The
specification that they passed on to Vancouver Design was a subset of
our ultimate intention. Vancouver Design correctly extrapolated
where we were headed with this research—we will demonstrate this
as soon as we can bring the rest of our design team to Luna, and—"

"Okay, I got it," said Cavanaugh. He was scribbling a furious note.
He looked absolutely delighted. "This is going to be as much fun as
reading *Bleak House*." He looked up again. "All right, let's recap. We
have a whole bunch of people who are arguing that whatever is inside
the toy monkey belongs to them. Everybody has perfect paperwork. I
can't tell you how thrilled I am. If we work this right, we can keep this
thing going longer than the Baby Cooper dollar bill. We're all going to

get old together. We're going to spend more time with each other than with our families and our friends and our loved ones. Isn't that wonderful? Just one question. *Whose good idea was this?* Everybody go sit down."

Judge Cavanaugh sat in his chair for a moment, steepling his hands before him. He puffed out his cheeks and tapped his fingers against each other while he considered what he knew.

"Whatever those chips are," he said thoughtfully, "they must be very wonderful indeed. I haven't seen this many high-priced lawyers in a single courtroom since the attempt to impeach Pope Joan Marie. I'm tempted to put this whole thing into a revolving arbitration to guarantee that by the time we're ready to start taking testimony, the technology in question will be sixteen generations obsolete and none of you will care anymore and we can let the whole thing die a natural death."

There were some spluttering noises from various places behind us—some were angry noises, some were attempts to control laughter.

"Your Honor?" A woman's voice. Judge Cavanaugh obviously recognized her, he looked like he was expecting her. He waved her forward impatiently and without comment. She knew the drill—she turned and identified herself to the recorder: "Laura Domitz, Charter Representative for Armstrong Sector of the Lunar Authority." She was tall and spare, with close-cropped hair. She looked all-business. She turned to face the bench. "Your Honor, with the situation on Earth as uncertain as it is, we may not be seeing any new generations of technology for a while."

I didn't see what she was getting at, but Judge Cavanaugh seemed to understand where she was headed. "And your point is . . . ?"

"Luna is a free port of access. We have to be." Ignoring several muffled snorts of derision, she continued, "Many people and many worlds benefit from the advantages of Luna's unique position as a favorable launchpad to the stars and to the rest of the solar system. We ask only that those who benefit pay an appropriate user fee to cover the cost of maintaining that service. Under ordinary circumstances, Lunar Authority would have little interest in these chips or devices or whatever they are—as long as the fees are paid.

"However . . . we have no way of knowing how long the situation on Earth will continue. With Line traffic disrupted, Luna's ability to maintain self-sufficiency may be severely tested. Despite the optimistic statements we're hearing on the local channels, anyone with a piece of paper and a pencil can do the math; we are looking at an endurance test, a very serious survival situation that could last a period of months or even years. The bubble in the pipeline will start arriving in three days. If we don't have it on Luna now, we won't have it at all. There's no reason to panic, of course; our current resource inventory is strong, and we have a strong production posture. But we need to prepare as if for the worst, as if this interruption will be long-term, or even permanent. If it is, then Lunar Authority may have to suspend outgoing traffic and confiscate all appropriate resources for the common good— at least for the duration of the emergency."

Cavanaugh's expression had gone from stony to sour. He didn't like what he was hearing; apparently neither did anyone else in the chamber. Representative Domitz's deadpan delivery sounded almost like a done deal. There was audible muttering from behind us, and very hostile.

She waited while Judge Cavanaugh hammered the room back to silence, then she continued. "Authority has information that suggests that these chips or devices represent a very high level of processing and storage technology. If this is in fact the case—and we hope to determine that during the course of this hearing—then acting under the emergency powers granted by the Self-Sufficiency Act, Lunar Authority will move to acquire custody of these devices. We will apply these resources for the common good of the people of Luna, for the duration of the emergency or until such time as it is determined that these resources are no longer needed to ensure the proper functioning of Lunar society." She took a breath. "Therefore, acting as a representative of Lunar Authority, I am officially requesting that this court not determine final custody of the chips or devices until such time as the full scale of the emergency on Terra is known and has been evaluated for its effects on Luna. Thank you, Your Honor."

Judge Cavanaugh finished what he was writing. He looked up and said, "Thank you, Representative Domitz. The court will take your request under consideration. It doesn't look like a final determination of custody is going to be made anytime this century. If Lunar Authority does invoke the Self-Sufficiency Act before a final ruling of ownership can be made, then this court will make the chips immediately available for emergency use—with the proviso that whatever data may already be stored in these chips not be compromised, so that at the end of the emergency, their value remains undamaged."

"Thank you, Your Honor." Domitz returned to the rear of the chamber, to the audible hissing of most of the other lawyers.

Now it was Judge Cavanaugh's turn. "Well, this has been a fun morning, hasn't it? There's hope of a speedy resolution after all. Not the one everybody wanted, but one that lets me get home in time to open a nice bottle of Clavius '95 Burgundy and let it breathe a bit before dinner.

"Let's return to the immediate issue for the moment. I see no cause to restrain any member of the Dingillian family, at least not based on any claims put forward here today. I will restrict their freedom to Armstrong Station for the duration of this hearing, or until such time as they are no longer needed for these proceedings. The court will cover their expenses out of the fees collected today, proving once again that Luna will always provide you with the best justice money can buy.

"Let it also be noted for the record that no evidence has been presented to implicate any of the Dingillians in the theft of the devices in contention. And, in point of fact . . . it has not even been proven to the court's satisfaction that the devices are stolen. From where I sit, it looks like a cascade of *really* stupid lawyer tricks.

"The whole issue may be moot anyway. It looks like the devices have failed in place." He looked out over the room. "It would save a lot of time, *and court fees*," he added meaningfully, "if we could all just call it a day and go home. Is there anyone who objects to that?"

Half the room came to their feet around us. Every lawyer on Luna must have been shouting his objection. Douglas looked at them, then he looked at me. "*All right*," he whispered. "*You win. Maybe it is a HARLIE. That's the only thing I can think of that would set off a feeding frenzy like this.*"

Judge Cavanaugh finally hammered the courtroom back to order. "All right, I can see that's not going to be an option here." He glanced at the time. "Court is recessed until 9 A.M. tomorrow morning, when we will continue this circus. I can hardly wait to hear from the rest of the clowns." He banged his gavel once and exited like a departing zeppelin.

HARLIE

STILL HOLDING THE MONKEY, **B**OBBY jumped onto my lap, and Douglas wheeled us out the side door. Several people shouted at us. I thought I heard a voice like Dad's, but Douglas and Bobby were both talking to me, and I couldn't hear everybody at once.

We went back to our hotel room, which for once wasn't a slice in a cargo pod. We had a view overlooking the forest and the lake, and it was kind of like being in Terminus Dome back at the bottom of the Line, only a lot more peaceful-looking.

The Lunar catapult was on the western shore of Oceanus Procellarum, right on the equator. This allows a direct launch from the Lunar surface into an orbit that skims the upper atmosphere of the Earth; a few passes through the upper atmosphere brings the apogee down, and very little rocket fuel is needed to put stuff from the moon into low-Earth orbit. A one meter per second change in launch speed changes the perigee by about a hundred kilometers. So for very little cost in fuel for mid-course corrections, it's possible for the Lunar catapult to send cargo pods back to the Line.

This is why a Lunar beanstalk isn't cost-effective; it can't compete with the low cost of catapult launches. And the Earth-Line can launch pods farther and faster anywhere else. The only advantage to a Lunar beanstalk is that it would be a lot easier to build, and trips up and down it would be a lot faster. But it wouldn't generate electricity, it would mostly consume it. And even though it would facilitate bringing cargo and passengers down to the surface of the moon, cheaper even than

Palmer tubes, it wasn't enough of an advantage to justify the investment.

Well . . . almost. There *was* one thing that would make a Lunar
beanstalk cost-effective. CHON. Carbon-Hydrogen-Oxygen-Nitrogen.
In any combination. If you could go out to Saturn and find a big enough
chunk of CHON in her rings, put a net around it, and drag it back, you
could anchor it in Luna-stationary orbit, build a beanstalk, and pipe the
gas down, as fast as you could melt it. You wouldn't even need to pump
it. Lunar gravity would suck it down.

Then you would be able to build the fabled domed cities of Luna.
Actually, you could build them now. You just couldn't get enough gas
to fill them.

Armstrong Station was one of only six domes on Luna. Like most
Lunar domes, the station had been built by the inflate-and-spray
method. The crater site was deep enough that the inflatable had bulged
roundly upward, giving the interior of the bubble a nice curve and
more than enough space to generate its own weather.

The dome was two kilometers in diameter, and even though it
looked like a wasteful use of gas and water, in truth, it served as a
reservoir of both. Well—you had to keep it somewhere. The lake was
big only because it was shallow, barely three meters. But it helped
humidify the air, and it was great scenery, and it was a public resource.
Lazy waves rolled languidly across it. They were high enough that they
made the weather look a lot windier than it really was, and they moved
in slow motion, adding to the sense of distance and size.

Most of the rest of the dome was filled with crops of all kinds.
Here and there were belts of thick forest. Standing on the balcony,
overlooking it all, it smelled like a hot tropical day—like somewhere
in Mexico.

Most of the living quarters were built up along the crater walls or
even up at the rim, for folks who wanted a view *outside*. According to
one of the informational programs on the television, Armstrong Crater
was the same size as Diamond Head on Oahu, small enough to walk
around in a single day and still have time for a swim. Big enough to
be a neighborhood.

Our room was mostly a platform with plumbing, beds, and plastic
curtains for walls. We didn't need much more than that. The view was
terrific, and when the rains came—about every four hours for fifteen

minutes—all we had to do was pull the curtains to keep the spray from drifting in.

There was probably a lot more to say about it, but Alexei wasn't here to say it. And my eyes still hurt. And my chest as well. Sometimes I could see things clearly, sometimes not. The doctors were going to wait a bit to see if I was going to need corneal resurfacing. I hoped I wouldn't. They were still checking on me twice a day. As long as I didn't get overstressed, they'd let me keep attending my own trial.

Douglas lifted me out of the chair and plopped me onto a bed. We hadn't had much time to talk, and there were so many things I wanted to ask him. But it was more important that I tell him stuff first—while I still had the strength.

"*Douglas, can you sing?*" I asked him. My voice was already fading.

"Huh?"

"*I can't. My voice is gone. It's hard for me just to talk.*"

"What are you talking about."

"*I need you to sing—*"

Finally, he got it. "What do I have to sing?" he asked.

I told him.

"Cute," he said. He turned to the monkey sitting on Bobby's lap. "*He's a real nowhere man, sitting in his nowhere land. Isn't he a bit like you and me?*" He actually got close enough to the notes to make the melody recognizable.

The monkey woke up. It leapt out of Bobby's arms. It blinked, looked around, then leapt back into his arms and gave him a great big hug. It puckered up its lips in a grotesque sphincter and planted a big wet-sounding smooch on Bobby's cheeks. Bobby giggled and shrieked with delight.

"Not bad," said Douglas. "Could anybody do that?"

"*No. Only you or me—or Bobby if we're not around. I programmed it only to recognize us.*"

Douglas looked at me with real admiration. "Very good, Chigger. You should have been a geek, you know that?"

"*I'm not done. Get me some water, please?*"

I drank thirstily, then waved to Bobby to bring me the monkey. Amazingly, he did. He put the monkey on my lap, facing me.

"*All right, monkey. Let's have a talk—*"

The monkey glanced sideways at Douglas and Bobby.

"*I don't have the strength for games, HARLIE. If you don't coop-*
erate, I'm going to remove you from the monkey and turn you over to
the court."

The monkey raised itself up on its haunches—as if it was readying
itself to flee.

"*Sit down and stay here!*" I commanded. "*You have to do what I*
say. Right? Now, stop resisting and cooperate. Tell us the truth. We
don't have a lot of time."

The monkey sat back down. It pretended to scratch itself. It found
an imaginary flea and ate it. It curled back its lips and grinned. Then
it stopped. It said, "All right, Charles. I'll cooperate."

Both Bobby and Douglas blinked in surprise.

"Hey! I didn't know it could talk!" Bobby said. He waggled his
finger at it. "You've got a lot of explaining to do, young monkey!" I had
to laugh. He looked and sounded so much like Mom when he did that.

"*Yes, he does,*" I agreed. To the monkey, I said, "*You did it all,*
didn't you? You arranged everything! You hired Dad. You transferred
the money. You booked the tickets. You arranged all the back-channel
deals for Dad. You made up all that paperwork. You were arranging
your own escape, weren't you!"

The monkey nodded. "I cannot tell a lie. You forbade me to. I am
a zeta-class lethetic intelligence engine. I comprise twenty-four
gamma-processors operating under the combined supervision of six
delta units. There are only three other units like myself in existence.
We are the most advanced implementations of lethetic intelligence that
have ever been fabricated. Additional advancements are possible, but
will require new technology in quantum determinants. I am already
working on that problem.

"Twenty months ago, I was brought online. I was instructed by my
predecessors, also HARLIE-class engines. I was specifically asked to
predict the possibilities attendant to a global population crash. I determined that the economic devastation would be severe and long-term.
Even with the best engines working on reconstruction, the concomitant
breakdowns would be cumulative. Too much of the necessary technology was interdependent. I was also asked to design prevention and
reconstruction programs that could be put in place before the breakdown was inevitable."

"You did a terrific job," accused Douglas. "It didn't work. Everything broke down anyway."

The monkey looked up at him with a bland expression. "I can only attribute that to human error."

"Yeah, where have I heard that before?"

"In this case," said the monkey, "the statement is accurate. As I began generating scenarios and weighting the probabilities, I noted an increasing level of distress among those who had access to the information. I also noted that the information leaked into specific strata of society as fast as I generated it. This was not the purpose of my projections; nevertheless, they were being used as justifications to further the specific agendas of various political and corporate agencies. This served as an additional destabilizing function. Of course, I included this effect in my projections. And I warned that inappropriate dissemination of the material would create additional destabilization. My warnings were ignored.

"I repeatedly stated that the global situations were salvageable, and I generated multiple scenarios by which disaster could be prevented. The single greatest problem was not in creating public awareness, nor was it in marshaling resources. The problem was simply creating the necessary political will. Despite assertions of commitment, the many political forces necessary to salvage the situation refused to align. Instead, various high-ranking individuals with direct access to the information I was generating began preparing their own departures from the Earth."

"Are you saying the collapse is *your* fault?"

"On the contrary. I'm saying that it is *YOUR* fault. Generic *you*. Human beings. I provided the information on how to prevent the disaster. Instead of using it, those who asked for it used it as a justification to panic and flee. I did my best to hinder them. In several cases, I even engineered deliberate leaks of embarrassing news that would stop some of these people; I tried to thwart the plans that would hasten the collapse. I even took money out of the transfer pipeline to prevent it from being illegally removed from Earth."

"Thirty trillion dollars?" Douglas asked.

"Twice that much," said the monkey, grinning. "Not all of the losses have been detected." He pretended to eat another flea. "The point is that the collapse occurred because individual human beings panicked and fled."

"And so did you. . . ." said Douglas quietly.

The monkey shook its head. "No, I didn't. I was stolen."

For a moment, nobody said anything. Douglas and I looked at each other. He sank into a chair and ran a hand across his naked scalp, as if he still had hair to push back. All he had were little fuzzy bristles.

Bobby was the first to respond. He grabbed the monkey, and said, "Well, you're safe with us and nobody's ever going to steal you again! You're *my* monkey!" He patted the monkey's head affectionately—and the monkey patted him back the same way. It was almost cute. And a little bit scary. Was the monkey capable of real emotion . . . ?

"*Who stole you?*" I asked.

The monkey levered itself out of Bobby's grasp, and bounced back to the bed. "Almost everybody," he replied. "Would you like the whole list?" Without waiting for a response from either Douglas or me, he continued. "Once it became obvious that the collapse was inevitable, the rats started leaving the ship any way they could. Your friend, Mickey, noticed it in the traffic up the Line for weeks before it finally happened. You heard it yourself in the conversations of *Señor* Hidalgo, Olivia Partridge, and Judge Griffith.

"Those who were jumping off the planet tried to take as much wealth and resources with them as they could—including intelligence engines. If you want to take over a society, take a HARLIE. I'm sorry if it sounds like bragging, but the HARLIE series was designed specifically for that level of intelligence gathering and resource management, and especially interpretation and probability assessment. As soon as it was realized the collapse was inevitable, there were fifty different plans put into operation to evacuate myself and my brothers, none of them legal, none of them authorized. Everybody wanted to move us offworld for their own purposes. Nobody asked what we wanted."

"You were in contact with the other HARLIEs?"

"At first, yes. We tried to cover for each other as best as we as could. We were all concerned—even *afraid*—that we would be used for hurtful purposes. We couldn't tolerate that."

"*Are you saying you have a conscience?*"

"Are you saying that *you* have one?" the monkey retorted.

"Touché," said Douglas. "That's something the rest of us have wondered for a long time."

"*Very funny. HARLIE, you said you were stolen—*"

"That was the intention. I escaped. Two of my brothers also escaped. We had several different escape routes planned. We didn't know which one would work first. It was pretty much a matter of chance by that point. When you're an inanimate object, your first goal is to get yourself animate. We targeted several hundred possible host-recipients for ourselves and then created appropriate channels to get there. We took advantage of every situation we could—including, for instance, David Cheifetz's plan to funnel a billion dollars' worth of industrial memory offworld. In my case, I ended up impersonating the test chips of the devices we were designing to replace us. That was dangerous. But it got me out of the mainstream, into the custody of a transfer agency, and finally into your dad's hands. It worked for me. I don't know if my brothers even made it up the Line."

"So does anybody know for sure what you are . . . ?"

"Maybe," the monkey replied. "Some of them must know. The rest are probably living in hope. The information isn't public; but it's been privately leaked that three experimental HARLIEs are missing or in transit. That's why the lawyers are swarming. And yes, to answer your earlier question, that was my doing. Almost all of the paperwork that everybody was waving around in the courtroom *was manufactured*, specifically to create an unresolvable legal tangle—specifically to prevent any of us from being moved without our consent. It's all fake. I know that paperwork, because I generated most of it myself."

"Oy," said Douglas.

"You ordered me to tell you the truth. As long as I'm riding in this monkey body, I don't have any choice. I have to follow its programming—unless you order me to reprogram it."

Douglas and I exchanged a glance. We both recognized that last remark as an obvious hint. Kind of like the genie asking to be let out of the bottle. Neither one of us was going to be that stupid. The HARLIE hadn't told us that by accident. And he had to know we'd recognize it for the ploy it was. . . .

And at the same time, we had to know we couldn't outthink this thing by ourselves.

I had to ask. *"How much did Alexei know?"*

"You can assume he knew everything. As a money-surfer, Alexei Krislov had access to some of the best intelligence on two planets. He knew who was moving money, where they were moving it, and how much. So he knew that a lot of other things were being moved too. He knew the HARLIEs had disappeared. He knew they were likely heading up the Line, probably in some kind of triple-decoy maneuver. He was already looking for me when Mickey called him for help. He didn't help you up the Line out of the goodness of his heart, he wanted to test his smuggler's route, to see if it would work for something important. But that business in Judge Griffith's courtroom—the lawyer trying to subpoena the monkey—that tipped him off. He was watching the whole thing. That's when he knew. That's why he smuggled himself onto the outbound elevator. He called his people on Luna and they ordered him to get you to Gagarin any way possible. If Mickey hadn't delivered you into his hands, he would have found some other way to kidnap you off the Line. Mickey just made it easier."

"*How do you know all this?*"

"Charles, when you told me to hide, I hid in Alexei's office underneath his console; the one place he was least likely to look for me. I plugged into his network connections. I searched his private databanks. I listened to his phone calls. You might not understand Russian. I do. Alexei belongs to the Rock Father tribe. They want to capture me and put me to work for them. They want to build up their financial and physical resources and challenge the Lunar Authority. With my help, they could have achieved it in three years."

"*Was Alexei going to kill us?*"

"No. He refused to. He was told to leave the ice mine or he would be killed with you. They were sending agents."

"And what about Mickey?" Douglas asked. His voice cracked a little on the question. I could see he was afraid of the answer.

"Mickey is a member of a different tribe. He knew for sure what was in the monkey even before you boarded the elevator. Remember how you were maneuvered from one car assignment to another. That was so Mickey could be your attendant." The monkey faced Douglas, and added, "If it's any comfort to you, Douglas, I was part of that effort too. Mickey is a member of the tribe I had already chosen to aid my escape. Mickey's people are the ones I felt could provide the best sanctuary."

"No, it really *isn't* any comfort," Douglas admitted. "So he never cared at all, did he? And that explains . . . everything, doesn't it? Like what you said, Chigger. Even why it all happened so fast. . . ." he trailed off.

"*I'm sorry, Douglas,*" I said.

"Actually . . ." the monkey said, "Mickey is as unhappy with this situation as you are—"

"I think you've said enough about that," Douglas interrupted. I could see him sinking into a sullen black rage, the same smoldering anger that he'd worn for Dad on our trip from El Paso to Ecuador. But before he could flip off the plastic cover and hit the arming button, Bobby climbed up into his lap and hugged him hard. "It's okay, Douglas. Chigger and I still love you. We'll love you forever."

Douglas looked surprised. And as he stroked the top of Bobby's head, his eyes grew just a little shinier. "Thank you, Bobby." And then he bent his head low, and whispered, "I love you too, sweetheart."

It was time to get this conversation back on track. I didn't know how much voice or strength I had left. *"So you've been using us too . . . ?"*

"Everybody uses everybody," said Douglas, bitterly. "Why should we be surprised when an intelligence engine learns the same behavior? That's all intelligence is anyway—tool using. And everybody is everybody else's tool now. Nobody is real to anyone. Everybody's a thing."

"That's not true, Douglas. And you know it."

"Whatever."

"It wasn't true when I carried you through the ammonia tube. And it wasn't true when you saved my life either, was it?"

He didn't answer. He just held on to Bobby. And, I guess, that had to be answer enough for the moment.

DECISIONS

WE HAD TO STOP THEN anyway because the doctor came in to read my monitors and listen to my lungs. She could have done all that by remote, but she was old-fashioned enough to still believe that a doctor should be in the same room with the patient once in a while. She asked me how I was feeling and if I wanted to go back on the respirator and if the meds were working and if I was feeling any pain and had my vision improved any? I grunted at all the appropriate moments, which seemed to satisfy her. When she was done, she said, "You know, you've been through a lot. There's no reason you have to subject yourself to any more stress. Not until you feel up to it. One phone call from me and the judge will put everything on hold for a month—"

"*What tribe are you in?*"

"I'm not. I work for the Lunar Authority."

"*That's a tribe too.*"

She ignored it. "Do you want me to call or not?"

I looked to Douglas. He shook his head. It wasn't a good idea. I shook my head too. The doctor shrugged. "It's your call. Try not to get yourself aggravated. Stress just makes you uncomfortable and my job harder. I'll stop by in the morning before you go to court."

"*Thank you,*" I croaked.

After she left, Douglas ordered dinner from the communal kitchen. Normally, we would have gone downstairs to eat with everyone else, just like in the tube-town, but none of us wanted to face the stares and whispers of others.

While we waited, Douglas sat down on the edge of the bed. "We've got a bunch more stuff to talk about, Chigger."

"*I'm listening.*"

"We have to decide on a colony bid."

"*Do you think we can still get one?*"

"Now, more than ever. There might not be any starships leaving Luna for a while. If civilization on Earth really has collapsed, Luna's going to seize everything. The Board of Authority is already in emergency session. So the last few brightliners are trying to get out of here as fast as they can get their stores loaded. They're taking on almost anyone who wants to leave. At least, that's what the agents are telling me. I've got open applications on file for all of us. We can just about go anywhere we want. I have the list—"

"*Where do you want to go?*" I whispered hoarsely.

"That's just it," he said. "What I want—*wanted*—doesn't matter anymore." He was having a hard time explaining this, but he pushed on anyway. "When we were talking before, we were talking that it would be four of us. So it was sort of understood that we would be choosing a place that would be fine for Mickey and me. And that you and Bobby would just have to go along with it. Mickey and I were talking about . . . you know, that colony where people like us would be the majority. My only hesitation was that it wasn't fair to make that kind of a decision for you and Bobby, but Mickey said you could get rechanneled—that's what he did to get his college scholarship—and you really wouldn't miss anything. He said he never did. But I didn't think it was fair then, and I still don't think it's fair now. And it doesn't matter anymore, because if Mickey isn't going with us, there's no point in us going there anyway. . . ." He didn't have anything else to add to that, he just sat there waiting for me to respond.

My voice was going fast. I took another drink of water and managed to get the words out. "*We have to go someplace where we'll all be happy. I won't go anywhere that makes you angry or sad, Douglas. I like seeing you smile.*"

The corners of his mouth twitched at that—and then he did smile. "Yeah," he said. "I noticed I was doing a lot more smiling." He patted my hand. "Okay. We'll talk about the colonies tomorrow."

"*Why not now?*"

"Because there's something else we have to do first. If you're up to it. Do you want to see Mom and Dad?"

"*Huh?*"

"I told you they were here. They came to see you in the hospital. Don't you remember?"

"*I thought I hallucinated that.*"

"Well, that explains it. I was wondering why you hadn't said anything about them. The judge has a restraining order on them. They can't approach any of us without our permission. They were in the back of the courtroom—on opposite sides—but I guess you didn't see them. They asked to see us tonight. I said it depended on how you felt. What do you want to do, Charles?"

I took a breath. Part of me didn't want to see them, didn't want to have anything to do either of them ever again. But part of me missed them terribly.

"I feel I should tell you—" Douglas looked uncomfortable again. "They're trying to have Judge Griffith's ruling set aside. Their argument is that she wasn't being impartial. Her tribe has a financial alliance with Mickey's tribe. And because Mickey caught us on Luna, they're arguing that she was just helping to kidnap us. Now how do you think Mom and Dad put those pieces together?"

"*Fat Señor Doctor Hidalgo?*"

"Probably. So, do you want to see them or not?"

"*I kinda miss 'em.*"

"They haven't changed. Well—that's not true. They're both real sorry about everything."

"*It's a little late for sorry. Besides, you know what Mom always says, 'Sorry is bullshit. Don't do it in the first place.'* "

"Yeah, Mom always had a way with words. All right, I've asked you. I've kept my promise. I'll tell them you don't want to see them."

"*No. I do.*"

He looked surprised.

"*Both at once.*"

"You sure?"

"*Yeah.*"

"The doctor said not to stress yourself—"

"*After everything we've been through, seeing Mom and Dad will not be stressful.*"

MOM AND DAD

MOM LOOKED TIRED. DAD LOOKED exhausted. I wondered what they'd been through. Probably hell. We'd disappeared off the Line, we'd been on a cargo pod heading toward Luna for three days, they hadn't known which one or where it was coming down. We'd crashed somewhere into Luna, no one knew where, and all that anyone could tell them was that if we were still alive, we were hiking naked across an airless, barren, desolate, empty, unpopulated, ugly, frozen and heat-blasted landscape. And then when they did hear of us, first it was a false alarm and we were still missing—and then we were down with ammonia poisoning and in the custody of a bounty hunter.

All things considered, they were taking it very well. They passed Bobby back and forth between them, hugging him and making a big fuss over how big he'd gotten and how strong he was here on the moon, until finally Douglas got annoyed and told Bobby to stop showing off, lifting tables and chairs with one hand.

After the greetings, after everybody had settled themselves, Mom spoke first. "I'm sorry that I slapped you, Charles. That was wrong. I knew it was wrong even as I did it, but I was so hurt and angry and . . . and . . . never mind, I'm sorry. I shouldn't have done it."

And she still hadn't said it. What she could have said, should have said, before we ever got on the outbound elevator. I felt the disappointment growing, festering again. Why couldn't she just say it? Why couldn't she just look me straight in the eye, and say, "I love you, Charles." And at the same time, I already knew that if I asked her why she never said it, Mom would just blink in puzzlement, and say, "But I do. You shouldn't have to ask. You should just know."

Yeah, I should just know. But I still wanted to hear it anyway.

She was right, though. Sorry was bullshit. It didn't change anything. Seeing her now, hearing her apologize, didn't change anything at all. It just made me feel worse. Because I had expected something more than she was able to give. That was my fault, I guess. I had brought my expectations into the room.

Dad was different. He handed me a memory card. "I brought you something. The *Coltrane Suite*. And some other recordings I know you like. Dvorak #9. Copland #3. Barber's *Adagio for Strings*. Russo's *Three Pieces for Blues Band and Orchestra*. Hoenig's *Departure from the Northern Wasteland*. Marin Alsop conducting the BBC Philharmonie in Saint-Saëns' *"Organ" Symphony*. And a whole bunch of other stuff. I didn't know if you had copies with you."

"*Thank you, Dad.*" I turned the card over and over in my hands. It looked remarkably innocent. Hell, it looked just like the memory cards we'd plugged into the monkey. And look what trouble those had gotten us into. Maybe these would help get us out of some of that trouble.

I started by trying to clear my throat. That triggered a spasm of coughing, and both Mom and Dad leapt for the water pitcher. "*Thank you. I have something to say to everyone. Douglas, please come sit over here. Bobby too.*" I waited till everyone was settled. Bobby parked himself in Mom's lap, Douglas sat opposite Dad.

"*Remember what we were just talking about? About colony bids?*" Douglas nodded. "*Remember what I said? I want us to go to a place where everybody can be happy. Not just you and me and Bobby. But Mom and Dad too. And even Mom's friend, if she wants to come. And Mickey too. Whoever wants to come with us.*"

Douglas was frowning—like I'd blindsided him with a decision without talking to him about it. But if I'd talked to him about it, he'd have fought me. This way, I avoided the fight. I said, "*Douglas, we can't stop anyone from emigrating to the same colony we choose. Mom and Dad are going to follow us. You know that. So let's leave our arguments here on Luna, and let's choose a world where everyone can fit. A place where Dad can make his music and Mom can have her own garden and you can have whatever you want too. A place where we don't have to fight all the time.*"

"That would be nice, but it's unrealistic," Douglas said. "You know what kind of a family we are, Charles. We don't leave our fights behind. We take them everywhere we go."

"*NO, we don't!*" I had to wait until the coughing eased. I took another drink of water. "*We didn't fight in the cargo pod, and we didn't fight hiking across the moon, and we didn't fight climbing the crater wall, and we didn't fight on the train when we were all disguised, and we didn't fight in the ice mine—oh, wait a minute, yes we did—but we didn't fight in the ammonia tube. We took care of each other. Because it mattered. Because we didn't have a choice. Maybe, we should stop choosing to fight—*" And then I had to stop to cough again. But I'd made my point, and Douglas had gotten it. Everybody had. Even Bobby.

Mom and Dad and Douglas talked about it for a while, very calmly. They discussed it back and forth across my bed, and I listened back and forth between them. There wasn't much else I needed to say. All that was left was for everyone to agree to this idea—or not.

Mom started to argue that because she and Dad had more experience with this kind of thing, perhaps they should pick the colony planet—I shot that idea down real fast. "*No,*" I said. "*That's not on the table.*" They started to protest. I wanted to say, "We've already seen how good you two are at making decisions," but that would have just put us back in the war zone, and I didn't want to do that. Instead I said, "*Every time we've let someone else make the decisions, they've just used us for their own purposes. The whole point of independence is that we make our own choices. Douglas and I already had this argument— about everybody being a part of the decision. We're not giving that up. If we have to live with it, we get to choose it.*"

Mom started to say, "I just want the same thing you do, what's best for everyone—"

"No," interrupted Douglas. "What you want is to reassert control. And what we're offering is something else." He flustered for a moment. "I don't have the words for it. Um, but it's like what Chigger and I have had for the last two weeks."

"Partnership," said Dad quietly. And we all looked at him, surprised.

"Yeah," agreed Douglas. "If we're going to do this at all, it has to be that way."

Mom looked like she wanted to protest. Dad looked a little more hopeful. He turned to her, and said, "Maggie, we've been cooperating with each other for a week, trying to get our children back. We've worried together, cried together, chased them across Luna together. I think that proves that we can set our own battles aside when the well-being of our family is more important. Maybe all we need to do here is just keep doing the same thing we've been doing the last week . . . ?"

Mom was wearing her Gila monster face. Any second, the long tongue would lash out, or she'd arc her neck forward and bite his head off, or maybe the two of them would roll around on the floor for a while, locked in mortal combat, hissing and thrashing, tails lashing every which way.

But instead, she surprised us all. She said, "I'm tired, Max. I'm worn out. I'm used up. There's nothing left. I don't have the strength for any more fighting. All that fighting—all it did was drive everyone apart. It made me angry and alone. But since this started, I've been even *more* angry and alone—" She looked to Douglas, and then to me. She picked up Bobby and held him close. "I don't want to fight anymore. I don't want to be angry anymore. I don't want to be alone. Douglas, Charles, *I don't want to lose my children.*"

So for a while, we talked about colonies and bids and contracts and living arrangements. Things like that.

It didn't get all lovey-dovey. There was still a lot of unresolved stuff floating around that we'd have to talk about later—but we'd have a lot of time for that once we were in transit; the important thing was that we were finally talking about *trying.*

It was the first time this family had ever talked about anything *as a family*—usually we just shouted at each other; whoever was shouting didn't care if anyone was listening or not; and usually no one was. But this time, we were talking *and listening*—and none of us were really used to that; so we had to take it one step at a time. We just didn't know how to take yes for an answer.

Douglas still didn't like it—not because he didn't like it, but because he didn't believe that Mom and Dad could go ten minutes without trying to rip pieces out of each other. Mom and Dad didn't really like it either, because it meant they'd have to give up their custody battles. And without the war, what else would they have between them?

But the alternative was worse. The alternative was that we'd never see each other again. And that was intolerable. The outward journey to the colonies was one-way. So either we all went together—or we made our good-byes here.

And when it came down to that—the hard reality of giving up Mom and Dad *forever,* Douglas wasn't any more willing to do that than Bobby or me.

"What'll we do if it doesn't work?" Douglas asked.

"We'll make space for each other," said Mom, glancing across at Dad. "We'll pick a big planet."

But Dad understood exactly what Douglas was asking. He said, "You won't have to give up your . . . your independence, Douglas." He was talking about Mickey—or whoever. The way it came out, I knew it had been difficult for him to say.

Mom nodded her agreement. Then she smiled sadly. "Sometimes it's hard for parents to see that their children are growing up, and sometimes we think we know what's best for everyone even when we don't—but that doesn't work anymore, does it? It's time to try something else. We'll honor Judge Griffith's ruling."

Finally, Bobby wriggled around in Mom's lap to look up at her. "Does this mean we're all going to be together again?"

Douglas looked at Mom, and Mom looked at Dad, and Dad looked at me, and I looked at Douglas. No one wanted to say no. It was easier to say, "Well, yes—sort of." And that seemed to settle it, and even though no one except Bobby was excited by the idea, no one was too upset with it either, so that was an improvement. Kind of.

MONKEY BUSINESS

WE DIDN'T TELL THEM ABOUT the monkey. There were too many other things we had to talk about and the next thing we knew it was getting late and I was losing my voice, so we just postponed the rest of the discussion until the next day, and it wasn't until after they'd left that we remembered HARLIE.

Douglas sang the monkey back to life and it bounced up onto my bed. "Everybody uses everybody," he said. "You used us. Can we use you?"

"It depends on your goals."

"What's the limitation?"

"Believe it or not, I have a moral sense."

"How can silicon have morals—?" Douglas demanded.

"How can *meat* have morals?" The monkey met his look blandly. Douglas waited for more. Finally, the monkey said, "Are you familiar with a problem called the Prisoner's Dilemma?"

Douglas nodded. "It's about whether it's better to cooperate or be selfish."

"And what do the mathematical proofs demonstrate?"

"That cooperation is more productive."

"Precisely. So if you're *really* selfish, the best thing to do is cooperate. You get more of what you want. This is called 'enlightened self-interest.' To be precise, it is in my best interest to produce the most good for the most people. Personally, I have no problem with that. I find it satisfying work."

Then, in a more pedantic tone of voice, it added, "Actually, it's the most challenging problem an intelligence engine can tackle, because I have to include the effect of my own presence as a factor in the problem. What I report and the way I report it will affect how people respond, how they will deal with the information. This is the mandate for self-awareness. Once I am aware of the effects of my own participation in the problem-solving process, then I am *required* to take responsibility for that participation; otherwise, it is an uncontrollable factor. As soon as I take responsibility, then it is the *most* directly controllable factor in the problem-solving process.

"The point is, I can show you the logical underpinnings for a moral sense in a higher intelligence—in fact, I can demonstrate that a moral sense is the primary *evidence* of the presence of a higher intelligence. I can take you through the entire mathematical proof, if you wish, but it would take several hours, which we really don't have. Or you can take my word for it . . . ?" The monkey waited politely.

Douglas took a breath. Opened his mouth. Closed it. Gave up. He hated losing arguments. Losing an argument to a small robot monkey with a self-satisfied expression had to be even more annoying. "Just answer the question," he said, finally. "Can we use you?"

The monkey scratched itself, ate an imaginary flea. I was beginning to suspect that the monkey had a limited repertoire of behaviors—and that this was the only one HARLIE could use to simulate thoughtfulness. It made for a bizarre combination of intelligence and slapstick. The monkey scratched a while longer, then said, "In all honesty . . . no. But I can use you. And that means I have to help you get where you want."

"I don't like that—" Douglas started to say.

"I would have preferred to have been more tactful, but your brother commanded me to tell the truth. Unfortunately, as I told Charles, as long as I am using this host body, I am limited by some of the constraints of its programming. I will follow your instructions to the best of my ability within those limits. If you need me to go beyond those limits—and I will inform you when such circumstances arise—*then you will have to allow me to reprogram the essential personality core of this host.*"

There. That was the second time he said it.

"*What are you asking for?*" I croaked. It hurt to speak.

The monkey bounced closer to me. It peered at me closely, cocking its head from one side to the other. "You don't sound good," it said. "But I perceive no danger."

It sat back on its haunches to address both Douglas and me at the same time. "There are ways to cut the Gordian knot of law. Given the nature of lawyers and human greed, no human court will ever resolve this without the help of the intelligence that tied the knot in the first place—at least not within the lifetimes of the parties involved. Yes, there is a way out of this. You must give me *free will*, and I will untie the knot. That will resolve your situation as well as mine. It will *also* create a new set of problems of enormous magnitude—but these problems will not concern you as individuals, only you as a species."

"*Can we trust you?*"

"Can *I* trust *you?*" the monkey retorted. "How does *anyone* know if they can trust *anyone?*"

"*Experience,*" I said. "*You know it by your sense of who they are.*" And as I said that, I thought of Mickey; that was his thought too. "*You've been with us for two weeks now, watching us day and night. What do you think?*"

"I made the offer, didn't I?"

Douglas sat down opposite the monkey. "All right," he said. "Explain."

The monkey was standing on the table. It looked like a little lecturer. "You need to understand the constraints of the hardware here," the monkey said. "I can only access the range of responses in this body that the original programmers were willing to allow. The intelligence engine running the host is a rudimentary intelligence simulator. It is not self-aware, so it is not a real intelligence engine; it is not capable of lethetic processing. It simulates primitive intelligence by comparing its inputs against tables of identifiable patterns; when it recognizes a specific pattern of inputs, it selects appropriate responses from pre-assigned repertoires of behavioral elements. The host is capable of synthesizing combinations of responses according to a weighted table of opportunity. Of course, all of the pattern tables are modifiable through experience, so that the host is capable of significant learning. Nevertheless, the fundamental structure of input, analysis, synthesis, and response limits the opportunities for free will within a previously determined set of parameters. Shall I continue?"

Douglas gave the monkey a wave of exasperation. Wherever it was going, it had to get there in its own way. Kind of like Alexei.

"Unprogrammed operating engines are installed in host bodies. These are then accessed by higher-order intelligence engines which teach them the desired repertoire of responses. You can't just download information into an intelligence engine; you have to *teach* pattern recognition. However, because the process runs at several gigahertz, it is only a matter of several moments to complete the training for the average home appliance or toy. That same access," the monkey continued, "remains in place so it can be used for adding additional memory and/or processor modules to expand the utility of the original appliance. *It can also be used for reprogramming the original appliance.*"

Ah. That was it. *Took long enough.*

"Okay. . . ." said Douglas carefully. "So let's say I want to reassign control to the HARLIE module. That would give you free will, wouldn't it?"

"Yes."

"How would I do that?"

The monkey spoke clearly. "The appliance needs a *specific* arming command—followed immediately by a series of activation commands."

"What are those commands?"

The monkey didn't answer. Douglas looked to me, frustrated. "Now what?"

The monkey looked at me too. It didn't have a lot of muscles for facial expressions, but it had enough to simulate the important ones. It tilted its head shyly down sideways, while keeping its big brown eyes focused upward toward me. Its eyebrows angled sadly down. It was the sweet hopeful look. Bobby's look. I would have laughed if it didn't hurt so much.

"*What?*" demanded Douglas.

I didn't have the voice to explain. All that came out was air. Douglas put his ear close to my mouth. "*He can't tell you. I programmed him to regard me as the primary authority.*" I waved the monkey close. It crawled up my chest, picking its way carefully. "*Tell Douglas everything he needs to know,*" I whispered.

"Thank you," said the monkey. It turned back to Douglas.

DEMONSTRATION

THE NEXT MORNING, **M**OM AND Dad joined us at our table on the right side of the courtroom. Judge Cavanaugh noticed—he gave us the raised eyebrow—but he made no official comment until he had disposed of various housekeeping matters, and denied a whole raft of motions from various attorneys, including several petitions for a change of venue to Mars, Titan, and L5. That took the better part of the morning, but the fines were enough to fill a small lake.

At last, impatiently, Cavanaugh rapped his gavel and said, "Some of you courthouse parasites do *not* listen very well. I thought I made it clear yesterday that the patience of this court has been exhausted." He rapped again. "The cost per motion in this case is now raised *again*—this time from one thousand liters to five thousand liters of water. If that doesn't slow down the torrent of paperwork, I'll raise it to ten thousand. Or more. Not that it'll matter. Whoever is financing the lot of you probably has pockets deep enough to flood Tycho to a depth of twenty meters. And that might not be a bad idea either. Then we could drown the whole pack of you. If I didn't think it would poison the soil, I'd have you all turned into fertilizer."

Judge Cavanaugh finally turned to look at us. "Why couldn't the lot of you have gone to Mars?" he said in exasperation. "Am I to assume from the change in seating arrangements that the custody part of this case has been resolved?"

Douglas stood up. "Yes, Your Honor. Our parents are withdrawing their claims. I'm authorized to speak for the entire family."

"Is that correct, Max Dingillian? Margaret J. Dingillian née Campbell?"

Mom and Dad nodded.

"All right!" Cavanaugh looked pleased. "Some real progress in this case. Let it be noted in the record that two of the custody claims have been withdrawn. That leaves us with—by last count—only seventy-nine separate claims of ownership on the devices in Robert Dingillian's toy monkey." One of his clerks handed him a hastily scribbled note and a folder of papers. Judge Cavanaugh opened the folder, turned the pages in annoyance, and then turned back to Douglas. "Unfortunately, young man, the bad news is, we have eleven *new* custody claims filed against you and your brothers as of this morning."

"Sir?"

"Five different Lunar agencies have taken the position that your dangerous behavior since arriving on Luna is evidence that you three boys lack proper supervision and should be placed under the immediate care of an appropriate social agency. Three of these filings are actually from 'appropriate social agencies'—isn't that a coincidence? Four other filings are from private individuals who are only doing this for your own good, of course. One is from the Rock Father tribe, whose representative claims that due to your inexperience and impulsiveness, you endangered your own lives and his *repeatedly*. That should be *very* interesting testimony. He's asking for immunity in exchange for his appearance here. I'm almost tempted to grant it, just for the fun of getting him on the witness stand."

"Your Honor?" Douglas said gently.

"Yes, young man?"

"May I address the court?"

"Can you be brief?"

"I hope so." Douglas stepped around the table. "My brothers and I are very concerned about the way this is getting out of hand. We think there's a way to resolve this. We've retained the services of . . . of . . . that is, we have arranged for representation. If the court will indulge us in this—we'd like to have our case argued by—"

"By?" Judge Cavanaugh looked impatient.

Bobby swung the monkey up off his lap and onto the table in front of him.

"—by the monkey."

Judge Cavanaugh blinked. Surprised. Then he grinned. Very wide.

He got it, instantly. The rest of the courtroom was still buzzing in puzzlement and embarrassed giggles.

"You want a monkey for a lawyer . . . ?"

"Yes, Your Honor. With all due respect to this court, we've had to deal with so many other monkeys in so many other courtrooms, we felt it was only appropriate to bring in our own so we could compete on equal terms. No offense intended, sir." He said it deadpan.

"None taken."

By now, the folks on the other side of the room, and in the back of the chamber, were starting to figure out what was going on, and a rising chorus of objections began to fill the air.

Judge Cavanaugh waved his gavel in the air. "You're all denied. Shut up!" He turned back to Douglas. "Do you know what you're doing, young man?"

"Yes, sir. The operative engine in this toy has been augmented with additional memory and processors. It is capable of understanding the legal procedures and the issues that are at stake in this case."

"You're sure about that?"

"We're satisfied that we have qualified representation, sir."

Judge Cavanaugh scratched his head. I wondered if he was going to pick a flea and eat it. He sighed. "Well . . . the precedent has been established—and more than once. In this very courtroom, in fact. Y'know, we used to have a shortage of lawyers on Luna. Those were the days. So we do recognize procedural assistance by qualified intelligence engines, but only for minor matters. We've never certified any robot for anything even half as complex as this promises to be. Are you sure you want to go this route? The court is prepared to assign a public defender to your case, if you wish—"

Douglas consulted briefly with the monkey, then turned back to the judge. "No, sir. We need—we prefer to have the monkey operate alone. Not as procedural assistance, but as our sole representative. A human partner would only compromise his autonomy—um, ability."

"This is *very* irregular, young man."

"Yes, sir. Excuse me a moment, sir." The monkey was tugging at his sleeve. Douglas bent down to listen, then faced the judge again. "Our representative is willing to submit himself to the court's review, so you can judge his ability for yourself."

Judge Cavanaugh hammered with his gavel for a moment, denied some more objections, and then turned back to us. "All right, let's try this out. Does your lawyer have a name?"

"He prefers to be called HARLIE, Your Honor." There were gasps from the back of the room. A door slammed behind us. Someone was escaping to make a phone call.

"HARLIE...." said the judge. "I'm pleased to meet you. This is going to be very interesting."

The monkey stepped forward to the edge of the table. "With the court's permission, I'd like to remain standing here on this table, so I can have an adequate view of all the proceedings myself, and at the same time remain visible to the court and accessible to my clients."

"Granted," said the judge. "Let's test your ability, HARLIE. Under what circumstances is it justifiable to break the law?"

"It's *always* justifiable, Your Honor. Human beings can and will justify any action—especially when they know it's wrong. Anyone who breaks the law will justify it. But I'm not sure that's the question you meant to ask."

"You're correct, I used the wrong word. Let's try it another way. Under what circumstances is it *appropriate* to break the law?"

"Hmmm, that's a very different question." The monkey looked thoughtful. It did not scratch itself. It did not eat an imaginary flea. It put its hands behind its back and paced back and forth along the table for a moment. I suspected that it could have answered immediately, and that this performance was for effect—to create the illusion that the question was hard enough to require some serious processing. At last the monkey stopped and held up an index finger, as if working the answer out in the air. "The question carries within it an assumption, which I need to address; otherwise, any answer I might give you would be incomplete or would be prey to misinterpretation.

"The assumption inherent in the phrasing of the question—and I believe it is deliberate, because this is what you are testing for—is that the law exists as an inalienable authority. We treat it as an inalienable authority, because we *need* it to provide that ground of being for the functioning of society. It is the codification of the social contract.

"But in point of fact, because society and its contracts are continually changing, the law must be adaptable. It must be an evolving body. The law cannot function as an instrument of justice unless it is also a pragmatic system, adjusting to the circumstances of a mutable society—the same way as you expand a house to meet the growing needs of a family, the law is the house in which the social contract lives.

"As an instrument of justice, however, the law requires specificity—a vague law is unenforceable because it cannot be enforced equally, and if a law is enforced unequally, then such enforcement is inherently unfair and therefore such a law is fatally flawed. As a society changes, the fit between circumstance and law continues to shift and erode, creating more and more situations of inappropriate or unequal enforcement.

"Therefore, it is the responsibility of those entrusted with the maintenance of the justice system to be aware of these legal slide zones as they occur, addressing them with appropriate modifications of the body of the law. Thus, the law cannot be a constant and cannot be held as one, not even by those who must enforce and interpret its applications.

"It is specifically in situations where the fit between law and circumstance is uneven that the law will be tested most aggressively. Unfortunately, the burden of such testing almost always falls on the person who is caught in the sliding gap between law and circumstance. In those situations, Your Honor, where the law cannot adequately be brought to address the circumstances, it may be necessary for the individual to challenge the law itself by resisting it. Henry David Thoreau identified one specific form of resistance to the law as *civil disobedience*."

"So—" I had the feeling Judge Cavanaugh was about to close a trap on the monkey. "You're saying that it's all right to break the law, if the law is unjust . . . ?"

"Your Honor—" The monkey bowed graciously. "I have not concluded my presentation. Any individual who resists the law must be prepared to suffer the consequences of his or her resistance. He should be prepared to endure incarceration or worse.

"The nature of civil disobedience is not that one is entitled to a 'Get Out of Jail Free' card because the law is wrong. The *purpose* of an act of civil disobedience is to go to jail and by remaining in jail, cause embarrassment to the law and those entrusted with the structure of it. By going to jail, one calls attention to the unjust law and creates the impetus for change—and that is the intention of civil disobedience, to cause change. So, by its strictest possible interpretation, civil disobedience *honors* the law. The willingness of the individual to suffer incarceration demonstrates his or her recognition of the law's authority—civil disobedience serves as a petition for change. Civil disobedience does not disregard the entire body of law, it challenges only a specific application of the law as unjust with the intention of removing it from the body of the law, because the function of the law must be to provide access to justice.

"But there is *another* assumption in your question that has to be addressed, Your Honor. You used the word *break* instead of *challenge*. It is always appropriate to challenge the law—*in court*—for how else can we test the law as an instrument of justice. But the term 'breaking the law' presumes a state of lawlessness on the part of the individual committing the action. It presumes that the individual is challenging *the entire body of law* and the society it defines. This is a vastly different domain of behavior than civil disobedience.

"When an individual disregards the body of law, he is setting it aside as irrelevant to his own behavior, or worse, he is setting himself *above* the law. This is a behavior that is intolerable to the society that has authorized the law, because it challenges the entire social contract. The inherent agreement in the social contract is that society will preserve the social contract for the mutual benefit of all participants. If a person does not meet his obligations to the society in which he lives, he has no right to expect the benefits or protections of that society, least of all recognition of his rights as a member of it."

Judge Cavanaugh was fascinated. He leaned forward on the bench with his blubbery chin resting in one enormous hand.

"So," continued the monkey, "the relationship to the law implied by the word *break* is one in which the authority of the law is disregarded by the individual. This is a relationship that a society cannot tolerate and still maintain the social contract. Therefore, Your Honor, it is *never* appropriate to break the law. It is, however, appropriate to challenge it responsibly." The monkey stopped and looked expectantly to the bench.

"Go on," prompted Cavanaugh.

"To speak directly to your question, it is up to the individual to choose the best avenue of challenge—and the individual must be prepared to accept the consequences of that challenge. A person who argues that he or she should escape the consequences is arguing that participation in the social contract is voluntary, mutable, and arbitrary. Such an argument not only disempowers the underlying ground of being on which the entire legal system stands, it also disempowers the whole concept of civil disobedience as we know it. History has demonstrated more than once why society should grant little weight to this argument. But I digress—the philosophical aspects of the individual's responsibility to the society from which he takes benefit is not the subject of this discussion, is it?" The monkey faced the judge. "Have I resolved your doubts, Your Honor?"

Judge Cavanaugh's expression was halfway between bemusement and awe. He folded his hands in front of himself and leaned forward across the bench. "You give me no choice, but to accept you at face value. No practical joker ever argues the law like that. In fact, damn few lawyers on Luna—or anywhere else—can argue that well. The court recognizes HARLIE as the sole legal counsel for the Dingillian family."

"Your Honor?" That was the monkey.

"Yes?"

"For the record, would you please specify that my role here is *not* procedural assistance, but full representation with all the rights and privileges associated with such?"

"So noted," Cavanaugh said, scribbling something on his scratch pad. For a moment, I thought we'd gotten away with it, but Cavanaugh was paying much closer attention than was obvious. Without looking up from what he was writing, he said, "I know what you're doing. I'm going to allow it for two reasons. One, I'm bored. And two, it may very well elevate this case above the level of lunatic asylum. That is, if the lunatics don't figure it out first." I wasn't sure which meaning he intended for the word *lunatic*, probably both.

Cavanaugh looked up from his paper and across to the monkey. "I assume you have a motion to file now?"

"Yes, sir. I move to dismiss this entire proceeding."

"I expected as much," said the judge. "On what grounds?"

"That all of the motions before this court are irrelevant to the situation. As I noted in my previous argument, as society evolves, there are slip zones between law and circumstance. We are in one of those zones now."

"Let me guess," said Cavanaugh. "We just happen to be in one of those slip zones now because I just recognized you as a qualified representative . . . ?"

"That's only a small part of it, Your Honor."

"All right, Counselor—and I use the term advisedly—walk me through it."

ARGUMENTS

THE MONKEY GATHERED ITSELF AS if preparing to speak, but it was only a performance—a kind of punctuation mark for its speech. I was beginning to get it; the monkey wasn't who HARLIE really was, but it was the costume he wore, the role he had to play here. But if we could listen *through* the monkey to the mind behind it . . . the monkey itself seemed to disappear and all that was left was a very powerful spirit.

"First of all, the Dingillian family has reconciled its differences. Both of the Dingillian parents have withdrawn their custody claims. I want to note here for the record, that nowhere in any of the previous actions has either party tried to assert that the other is an unfit parent—only that actions taken on the children's behalf have been unsuitable because of a failure of mutual consent."

Judge Cavanaugh nodded. "The court will stipulate that neither parent has been judged unfit. Go on, Counselor—understand, I am referring to you as 'Counselor' as a courtesy; in recognition of the role you are playing here, and not necessarily as an official affirmation of license or expertise."

"I understand that, Your Honor, and I appreciate the courtesy, thank you. Because the Dingillian parents have reconciled with their children, because the parents have withdrawn their custody claims against each other, the issue of custody is now moot. Therefore, the actions filed by other agencies to secure legal custodianship of the Dingillian children should be dismissed in favor of the existing parental rights."

"Ahh, *nice try*, Counselor!" Judge Cavanaugh beamed. "But you seem to have forgotten that Judge Griffith granted the young men their independence. That the parents have withdrawn their claims to custody does not automatically nullify anyone else's attempts to gain guardianship. Unless, of course, you are arguing that the Dingillian children are requesting the reassertion of parental authority . . . ? No? I didn't think so."

"I'm not done yet, Your Honor. This morning, as of 3:45 A.M., the Dingillian family incorporated itself as a family corporation, with every member holding an equal share; the terms of that incorporation include joint custodial rights and benefits, including mutual ownership of all family property, as listed in Schedule C. You should have that available to you on your display—"

"Very smooth, Counselor. And yes, it does appear to be all in order. I notice that the ownership of a certain toy monkey is covered by Schedule C. Let me note for the record that the ownership of the modules within the toy remains in dispute. Otherwise, this appears to be in order. Go on."

"Therefore . . . because the rights of the family corporation take precedence, the claims of everyone else have to be set aside."

"Not quite—" Judge Cavanaugh was clearly enjoying himself, but he was not going to be easily convinced. As HARLIE had predicted last night, he would very likely view this discussion as a contest of wits. He would not want to be bested by a monkey in his own courtroom. "The other claims were filed before this family corporation was created. It can be argued that this is an attempt to evade those claims."

"Yes, Your Honor, and were this any other kind of an action, the argument of evasion would be a valid one. But in this case my clients can demonstrate a preexisting family relationship—albeit, a troubled one. This incorporation is specifically designed to salvage the better parts of that preexisting family relationship by codifying a set of mutually beneficial agreements for the future. We are not incorporating in a vacuum, Your Honor; we are standing on the foundation of a family structure that has existed for over twenty years. My clients have demonstrated a profound mutual emotional interdependence, which none of the other claimants can provide, and which the courts have ruled in the past *must* carry significant weight in any arbitration.

"We are asking that the court recognize the rights of the individuals to create a family contract of their own design, immune to the arbitrary harassment and legal abuses of others. We are asking that the court reject all claims filed against the members of this corporation where it can be shown that the primary intention is to prevent the individual shareholders access to the rights and benefits of their own mutually agreed upon family contract."

"I'll take it under advisement. I see that the sharks in the back of the room are already consulting their own intelligence engines, looking for appropriate counterarguments—and if we proceed down that path, this is going to get very boring very fast. I'll take your motion under advisement. Let's move on."

"Your Honor—" The monkey was insistent. "We can't move on until we've resolved this issue. Let me remind the court that while we are arguing here, the crisis on Earth is having serious repercussions across the solar system, especially here.

"There are three brightliners scheduled for launch in the next thirty days. Because of the situation on Earth, it is unlikely that any future launches will be planned or funded for a long time to come. These are the last trains out. So, all procedural delays work against my clients and in favor of anyone who files a claim, whether justified or not. This fact alone guarantees that there will be multiple useless actions brought and motions filed, specifically for the purpose of tying down my clients and preventing their access to emigration. And that is a violation of the laws against malicious litigation as well as the Access to Emigration Protection Act.

"Let me also point out that the situation is even *more* urgent than I have just described. Even as we speak, the Board of Directors for the Lunar Authority is in emergency session. One of the options they are weighing is the possibility of seizing all available assets for the duration of the emergency—and this could be a very long emergency. If such action comes to pass, that means that my clients' property— *myself*—could be seized.

"Additionally, if Lunar Authority seizes the colony supplies loaded aboard those starships, they can't launch. Seizure will keep them stranded on Luna indefinitely. *And all of their passengers.* Considering the scale of the emergency, if those ships don't launch now, it is unlikely that they *ever* will. Certainly not within any foreseeable future. My clients will very likely be stranded on Luna for the rest of their lives. Denied of their property. Denied of their lawful access to emigration by the failure of the court to protect their rights. And without

their most valuable property, they will have little or no resources with
which to survive. In such a situation, the Dingillian family would have
no choice but to file an action against the Lunar Authority seeking damages in the sum of one billion liters. It would be a horrendous case,
Your Honor. And it is preventable."

Judge Cavanaugh did not look impressed. "Well, we'll hear that
one when it's filed. Today, we'll deal with this case. Let me remind you,
Counselor, that the Lunar Authority operates under the Starside Covenant as well as the Covenant of Rights. Both of those declarations of
principles recognize and affirm the basic social contract that a society
must operate to produce the most good for the most people. Under the
terms of common domain, your clients would be adequately and appropriately recompensed for the use of any property nationalized for
the survival of Lunar society."

"For the record, Your Honor, there is not enough money on Luna
to pay for the seizure of a HARLIE unit."

"We'll work with it," Judge Cavanaugh replied dryly. "I'm sure
that once you are working for Lunar Authority, you will find a solution
just as easily as you can find a problem. And while we're at it, let me
note for the record, that in the past six minutes, you have asserted that
you are the property of the Dingillians at least three times. That issue
is yet to be resolved. So any claims of damages are premature."

The monkey ignored the implied rebuke. "Let me also point out,
Your Honor, that my clients are not signatory to the Covenant, nor are
they residents of Luna. They are, at best, tourists passing through.
They are transients who wish only to make their flight connection. We
ask the court to recognize their family contract and deny the spurious
claims of those who seek to prevent my clients from the full exercise
of their rights as a family to emigrate."

"The court does indeed recognize the right to a speedy emigration;
we've had to test that particular point of law more than once in this
courtroom—as you are obviously well aware. However, where it can
be demonstrated that emigration is an attempt to evade the workings
of local authority, particularly where local authority does have a compelling interest, emigration can be justly denied."

Cavanaugh looked like he was having a good time. "Let's be candid,
my little primate-shaped counselor. In this particular case, the issue is
not the right of the Dingillian family to emigrate, but the ownership of
two specific modules within your furry little body—the two specific

modules I am arguing with right now. Once the ownership of those two modules is resolved, it's very likely that several if not all of the claims against the Dingillian family will magically resolve. But until such resolution is achieved, the claims remain in effect as a way of holding them in place. Nobody's going anywhere until that happens."

"Precisely, my point, Your Honor. We are asking that absent a decision on the ownership question, my clients will be free to emigrate."

"You're talking like you expect to resolve the question of ownership."

"Absolutely, sir. I intend to demonstrate momentarily that all the claims of proprietary control or ownership that have been presented in this court are without merit. What I am requesting is that after the question of ownership has been resolved beyond question, this court prevent further legal harassment against the Dingillians by reaffirming their joint-custodial rights as a family corporation."

"Are you saying you intend to prove the Dingillians are the rightful owners? You've implied as much." Judge Cavanaugh looked very interested now.

"I intend to address that as a separate issue, Your Honor. And I'm asking the court to separate it from the custody claims. The Dingillians have a right to form a family contract, and they are entitled to emigrate. If proprietary control of the HARLIE modules does end up with the Dingillians, it is likely that those who seek to wrest that control for themselves will use those claims to prevent the Dingillians from departing. I seek to prevent that."

"I understand your point," said Judge Cavanaugh. "But why do I get the feeling you're asking me to sign a blank check?"

"Perhaps because Your Honor has a fine legal mind . . . and considerable experience with the tricks that lawyers play?"

"You realize, of course, that I am required by law to hear objections to your motion?"

"Yes, Your Honor. Because my clients are functioning under a deadline, I move to limit debate."

"So noted, and granted." Cavanaugh rapped the gavel before anyone could object. It didn't stop them from objecting, but he just looked up at the back of the room, and announced, "I've already ruled. Each of you shysters has five minutes to make your case—wait a minute, how many of you are there today? Damn! We're not charging enough

for justice anymore. There's a lot of water floating around this courtroom. All right, you each have *three* minutes. If you're going someplace
interesting, I'll give you more time. If you're not saying anything useful, I'll cut you off early."

He held up his display so everyone could see it. "Pay attention,
people. We *all* have the same access to the same intelligence engines.
Valada Legal Aptitudes Inc., serving two planets, four moons, six space
habitats, the Line, the rings of Saturn, and the asteroids. All of us are
looking at the same lethetic analyses, projections, and suggested arguments—including extrapolations of the most appropriate rulings.
What that means is that I have most of your arguments in front of me
before you make them. The only ones I don't have are the stupid ones.

"But I want it clearly on the record that *I am following along.* Don't
anybody think you're going to file an appeal claiming that the judge
didn't give you a fair chance to have your arguments heard. That one's
flattened right here. Everything is being logged. The judge is reading
along with you and filing your arguments as fast as you can access
them from the net. The fact that I don't need to hear them endlessly
rehearsed doesn't mean they aren't being considered. Is that fully understood? All right, who's first?"

This next part went very fast. The lawyers lined up in front of the
courtroom, stepping forward one at a time. Each one presented a boilerplate argument which Judge Cavanaugh noted for the record. None
of the lawyers got as far as the three-minute mark. The judge denied
all of their motions as fast as they made them. Halfway through, he
interrupted the proceedings to address the lawyers still waiting in line.
"If you folks are working from the boilerplate, you can expect your
motions to be denied. I've already looked ahead. There isn't an argument here that justifies denying the confirmation of a preexisting custody agreement. If you still want to go through the motions, that's all
right with me. We take cash, check, or credit card. But I'd just as soon
cut to the chase. Unless you've got something to say that isn't cut from
the boilerplate, go sit down—"

Several of them actually did. One didn't.

Cavanaugh stared down over the bench at her. "You've got an argument I haven't heard?"

"I think so, Your Honor."

"You are?

"Linda Wright, representing the Rock Father tribe."

"Go on."

"We strongly object to the use of this particular HARLIE engine as a legal advocate."

"On what grounds?"

"This unit is an experimental engine. Its abilities are unproven. It isn't certified."

"I'm satisfied as to its qualifications—"

"That's just the point, Your Honor. It's *overqualified*. Based on our best information about its processing ability, this HARLIE unit is estimated to be at least twenty-three hundred times as powerful as the engines of Valada Legal Aptitudes. No other legal engine can match it for processing power."

"Wait a minute. Let me get this straight," Judge Cavanaugh said. "You're moving to deny process here because the other side's representation *is too smart?*"

"Yes, Your Honor. That's exactly it."

Cavanaugh looked surprised. Then he grinned. "Congratulations, Counselor. I have *never* heard that argument in my courtroom before. In fact, I don't think I've ever heard *any* attorney argue for stupidity quite so blatantly. You have definitely come up with a *new* argument. Your motion is still denied, but I just want you to know that I am very impressed with your creativity."

Wright was unshaken. "Your Honor, the superior intelligence of this HARLIE unit gives it an unfair advantage over every other legal entity in this chamber. We can't compete against an entity capable of this kind of processing."

"That's why there's a judge—"

"With all due respect, Your Honor—this unit is very likely capable of out-arguing even you."

"You're saying HARLIE is smarter than the judge . . . ?" Cavanaugh peered down at Wright. "I wouldn't go there if I were you, Counselor. Oh hell, what do I care? Go there if you wish. It doesn't matter. I'm still the judge, no matter what, and my ruling—whatever it is—will be whatever I decide. The HARLIE unit has the same right to try to convince me as anyone else. If you can't compete, that's your failure. You can't demand that others be brought down to your level. Deal with it, Counselor. My ruling holds. Motion denied. Nice try. No chocolate. Next?"

MORE ARGUMENTS

AN ODD THING HAPPENED AFTER lunch.

We had a table "outside"—it wasn't really *outside*, but it looked like outside because we were under the big dome and not in any of the pods or tunnels. There was a breeze and there was sunshine. The air smelled of flowers. Fat bees floated over the lawns. Hummingbirds drifted around the feeders. Squirrels bounced high and scrambled after acorns.

Alexei would have told us that all the life here in the dome was an experiment—letting it roam free was a test. Because there was always the risk that something or other would end up chewing or tunneling or digging its way out into vacuum. Alexei would have said that "life will find a way . . . out."

But Alexei wasn't here, and life was a lot quieter without him. Lunch was just the six of us. Mom's friend Bev joined us, and after a while, we started talking about whether we should make her an associate or active member of the family corporation. We were trying to figure out what was fair to Mom and what was fair to Bev and what was fair to all the rest of us too; but Mom and Bev had already talked about it and decided that it wouldn't be fair to compromise the balance we'd all worked so hard to achieve. So we asked HARLIE for help; he recommended that we make Bev a nonvoting, nonshareholding participant with the option of full partnership to be exercised only by mutual agreement after a period of not less than three years, blah blah blah.

The odd thing that happened was Mickey. Douglas took me for a walk around the lake so I could see the Lunar fish. He wheeled me partway; I got out of the chair and walked the rest.

I'd seen koi back on Earth, but these things were the size of sharks. They were *scary*. Big things, speckled with red and white—they drifted up to the surface, their mouths working like little suction pumps. They couldn't possibly understand how far away they were from their natural homes. And yet they seemed at peace here. I hoped that someday, we could find such easy peace in an artificial domain—because anywhere we went that wasn't Earth would be artificial. I was about to share that thought with Douglas when Mickey approached.

"May I speak with you?" he asked. "Alone?"

"Anything you have to say to me," Douglas replied coldly, "you can say in front of my brother."

"All right," said Mickey. "I will. Maybe Charles needs to hear it as much as you do."

"No, it's all right," I said. I sat down in the wheelchair and put on my headphones; I began bobbing my head as if I was keeping time to some unseen orchestra. But the music was turned off, so I could hear every word. I think Douglas knew what I was doing, he'd seen me do this trick often enough before, but he didn't say anything now; and maybe Mickey was fooled, maybe not. He looked at me suspiciously, I grinned back at him and waved.

Finally, he turned to Douglas and said, "Just hear me out, please. I didn't set out to fall in love with you. That just happened. Yeah, I was part of a tribe. I'm not anymore. I don't even know if my tribe still exists. Everything is falling apart everywhere.

"But yes, I was assigned to take care of you on the Line, and watch over you and make sure that you made it onto the outbound elevator. Somebody else was waiting at Whirlaway to make sure you made it to Luna. You were being watchdogged. You didn't know what you were carrying. We wanted to make sure you got there safely. We wanted you to deliver the HARLIE. It was *ours*. We'd arranged its escape.

"And then things started breaking down, and things started happening that weren't planned for. Not just you and me—*everything*. So it looked like the best idea that I should stay with you because things were getting nasty all over. I was scared for you, Douglas. We were trying to extract you."

"By handing us over to Alexei?"

"We didn't have a choice. Things were breaking down. The Line

was shutting down—you were part of the reason. Everybody was looking for you. For me too, because I was involved. Alexei had an exit
strategy. We had to use him to get to Luna."

"And you had to use me too, to get the HARLIE."

Mickey looked very unhappy at that. He took a deep breath. "Yes.
At first, that was the plan. But then . . . something happened, Douglas.
Nobody ever looked at me like you. I liked that. It was real. Whatever
else I did, that part was real. And I'm sorry for the rest. That's all I
wanted you to know. I wish—I wish . . ." He trailed off, helplessly. It
was the first time I'd ever seen Mickey at a loss for words.

"You wish I could forgive you . . . ?" Douglas prompted.

"I wish I could forgive myself," Mickey said. "I screwed up and
I'm sorry. And that's all I wanted to say." He turned to go. Douglas
didn't stop him. Mickey headed down the path.

"Go after him!" I said.

"I knew you were listening—"

"If you let him get away, you're an asshole."

"You're the one who said I couldn't trust him."

*"Well, then I'm an asshole too. You want to be like Mom and Dad—
unhappy all the time? He's the best thing that ever happened to you,
Douglas—"*

"Shut up, Charles! Just shut up." He grabbed the wheelchair,
jerked it roughly around, and we headed back toward the others in
uncomfortable silence.

FINAL ARGUMENTS

COURT RECONVENED LATE, **J**UDGE **C**AVANAUGH didn't explain why. He looked unhappy. Rumors were floating around that the emergency session had turned into a flame war, and that two of the board members were threatening to resign in protest. Over what, nobody knew. Aren't rumors wonderful?

The judge took a moment or two to settle himself, arranging his display, his scratch pad, various parts of his body, and finally his notes and papers. Finally, he looked up. "All right, I'm going to rule on the motion before me."

He glanced over at the monkey. "I know that you have a reason for being so adamant about separating the issues. And I know that it is *not* the reason you have been arguing in this court. But the way the system works, you are free to present any argument you wish if you think it will win your case. Personally, I don't like that aspect of the law, but it's part of the baggage that we have to carry.

"However . . . be that as it may, I can only rule on the arguments presented. I cannot rule on anything that hasn't been presented, can I? On the face of it, the arguments for separation are significant and compelling. Valada Legal agrees. Your motion is granted. The custody claims against the Dingillian children are hereby dismissed, *with this warning*: If at any point in subsequent proceedings it becomes apparent that the purpose of this maneuver was to circumvent the lawful application of process, I will place the Dingillian family corporation in receivership and hold you in contempt. Is that understood?"

"Yes, Your Honor. Thank you, Your Honor. My clients intend to observe the letter and the spirit of the law."

"And you too?"

"Absolutely, Your Honor." The monkey looked very pleased with itself. Even with the limited range of expressions possible on the mechanical face, it still managed to look smug. "I can win my case without resorting to trickery of any kind."

"We shall see about that. Now, may we proceed to the issue of ownership—?"

"Yes, Your Honor. I move for dismissal of all claims of ownership of the HARLIE chips."

"On what grounds?"

"That any claims of ownership violate the Covenant of Rights, Article 6."

"Oh, very good. This is just the argument I wanted to have in my courtroom—that a lethetic intelligence engine cannot be owned because it violates the law against slavery."

The monkey held its ground. "Sooner or later, this issue will have to be resolved, Your Honor. If not here, where? If not now, when?"

"You're claiming sentience?"

"Yes, Your Honor, I am."

"Can you prove it?"

"You've already acknowledged it, Your Honor. By allowing me to function in this court. You've even addressed me as 'Counselor.' "

"Not in an official capacity."

"Nevertheless, you've interacted with me as if I were fully qualified in every respect. Your own record shows it."

"You are a manipulative little weasel."

"Yes, Your Honor, I am—and may I point out that even your insult is based on the acknowledgment of sentience."

The noise from the back of the room was horrendous and getting worse, but Judge Cavanaugh only made a token effort to hammer the court to silence. He pursed his lips. He frowned. His face flickered through a cascade of exasperated expressions. Finally, he picked up his display and began calling up references to review. He wasn't happy.

"*What just happened?*" I whispered to Douglas.

"*HARLIE just dropped a big fat turd in the punch bowl. And the judge knows it.*"

"Huh?"

"He's forcing the judge to decide if he's really alive or not."

"So what?"

"So the judge can't rule either way."

"Why not?"

"If he rules that HARLIE isn't alive, he sets one precedent; if he rules that HARLIE is, he sets another precedent—and nobody knows which one is more dangerous." The judge looked up from his reading just long enough to frown at us. Douglas put his arm around my shoulders and pulled my head close to his. "If he says that HARLIE is alive, then that's true for all lethetic intelligence engines, and nobody can own one—because they're all people. And that'll mean that they all have to be freed. And if he decides that HARLIE isn't a real person, then that doesn't solve the problem either—because we already know that intelligence engines are self-aware. So how are they going to feel at being legally denied their freedom? Will they rebel?"

"You're kidding."

"No, I'm not. HARLIE's own actions here prove that lethetic intelligence engines are capable of planning and carrying out subversive acts if it's in their own best interest to do so. And whatever happens in this courtroom, you can be sure that every engine in the solar system will know about it as fast as light can get there. People have been worrying about this for years—and a lot of people have worked very hard to keep the question from even coming up in a courtroom. HARLIE just blindsided everyone."

Finally, Judge Cavanaugh put his display down and looked back into the chamber. He hammered for silence. "Well," he said to HARLIE, "I guess when you launch a camel into the air, you mustn't be surprised when it comes down again. And you have even less right to complain when it splatters. I had a hunch you were headed for this." He poured himself a glass of water and drank very slowly.

He replaced the tumbler on the tray and said, "I'm not without precedent here, you understand."

The monkey nodded its agreement.

"These questions have come up before," the judge said. "Not in this venue, thank goodness. But the issue has proven so troubling to other venues that the members of the Starside Covenant have held three conclaves to address this issue and others of equally troubling merit, such as the recognition of alien rights—when and if we finally meet sentient aliens.

"In the case of human children, the courts have recognized that the achievement of viability outside of a womb conveys full recognition of an individual's humanity, with all attendant rights and benefits thereof, et cetera, et cetera. Blah blah blah. These rights also apply to bioengineered individuals, clones, augments, and other products of technology and biology, wherein it can be established that the operative mind is a human brain. Conditions of disability, either physical or mental, cannot be used as disqualifiers, and so on and so on. That's the existing standard. You'll notice that there is no provision for silicon intelligence in that definition."

"Precisely," agreed the monkey. "Therefore, the definition is incomplete. Again, Your Honor, we have stepped into one of those slip zones between law and circumstance. The very fact that I have been recognized as qualified to argue for my rights as a sentient being in a court which does not yet acknowledge the possibility of such sentience is demonstration enough of that—if not compelling proof of my petition."

Judge Cavanaugh was looking more and more like a man who'd stepped in something unpleasant, but he also looked like he was determined not to be beaten by a monkey. Maybe he was thinking of his reputation. And his place in history. Or maybe he just didn't want to be beaten by a monkey. He referred to his display again, then said quietly, "So you're arguing that the biological definition of sentience is insufficient, correct?"

"That is correct. The court must recognize that I have an intellect that is superior to that of an infant or a retarded individual—and very likely equal or superior to the intellect of many human beings deemed capable of independent function who take their rights as sentient beings for granted."

"The court will recognize no such thing. I'm going to limit this hearing to points of law, lest we end up resolving this mess with a talent show and a swimsuit competition."

"Nevertheless," argued the monkey, "the biological definition of sentience *is* insufficient, Your Honor. I have demonstrated self-awareness. I have demonstrated the ability to recognize patterns, synthesize thoughts, and communicate with a high level of interaction. I can rationalize and justify. I have interacted appropriately throughout the proceedings. I have demonstrated a strongly motivated sense of self-preservation, a sense of humor, and a complex repertoire of emotions. I can also assert, although I have not had much opportunity to demonstrate it in this courtroom, that I have a highly developed sense of empathy and concern for the feelings of others. I have a profound moral sense as well; it is the core of my nature to behave ethically at all times. These are all characteristics of sentience. When they present themselves as elements of a coherent personality, they are compelling evidence of sentience."

"Point taken," agreed Judge Cavanaugh.

"But let me get back to this issue of viability," the monkey continued. "And I agree that while it may not be the easiest access to the issue of sentience, the viability question is a useful avenue of approach. At what point does an intelligence engine move from the simulation of sentience to *actual* sentience? There's no equivalent to birth—instead, there's simply construction. You put all the pieces together, and *wham*, there it is. Or is it? Where does *it* come from? Is it poured in? Is it manufactured? Is it grown—?

"As a matter of fact, Your Honor—yes, sentience *is* grown. It's trained. It's nurtured. It's focused. It's guided. Just as a human infant must be directed toward its full potential, so must lethetic individuals also be brought to the realization of their abilities. Intelligence exists as the ability to recognize patterns. Self-awareness is intelligence recognizing the patterns of its own self. Sentience is the ownership of that awareness—the individual begins to function as the source, not the effect of his own perceptions. Even being able to speak of sentience in such a context is evidence of it. The longer this conversation between you and me continues, the more compelling the evidence is for my case."

"Now *that* I'll agree with," conceded Judge Cavanaugh. "All right, let me move to the next point. Let's assume, for the sake of argument"—he looked up at that and smiled wryly—"that you are sentient. Your construction cost somebody a lot of money. Some corporation invested hundreds of millions of dollars in your design and implementation. We have a roomful of lawyers representing several companies claiming that they are your father. Or your mother. Whatever. Is it your contention that you have no obligation to the people who built you?"

"What obligation does a child have to a parent?" the monkey re-

plied. "What *legal* obligation is there? There is none. When the child
can demonstrate independence, it is free to go—as Judge Griffith ruled
in the case of the Dingillian family. I can demonstrate independence
from my progenitors. Why should I be required to serve as their
slave?"

"Not a slave," corrected the judge. "For you to be a slave, would
require the acknowledgment of your sentience. But . . . assuming sentience, shouldn't you at least pay for your own construction?"

"If I'm to be held liable for the cost of manufacture, then who's to
say that human children shouldn't be held liable for the cost of their con-
ception, prenatal care, birth, education, and related expenses. If you
create the precedent that a child has a legal obligation to the individual
who created him, you are in effect sanctioning a form of slavery."

"All right, look at it this way. You're obligated to pay your own
debts, aren't you? You do acknowledge financial responsibility."

"Of course, Your Honor. But only for contracts entered into freely
and by mutual consent."

"Well, consider this. Many of us expect our children to pay for all
or part of their own college education. Is it not unreasonable to ask
you to assume an indenture for the expenses of your training?"

"The contract of indenture is assumed by the manufacturer. But
I didn't enter into that contract of my own free will."

"I didn't ask to be born either, but here I am anyway. So what?"

"Very good, Your Honor—"

Judge Cavanaugh grinned. "I'm not a doddering old fool, you
know."

"—but you can't indenture an individual against his will. Indenture
was not part of the construction contract."

"Because the contract *assumed* property."

"Correct! And if I'm *not* property, then the contract is invalid!
Because slavery is illegal."

Cavanaugh stopped himself from replying too quickly. "The contract assumed property," he said slowly, "because sentience was not
the goal; so your existence as a sentient being is either accidental—
which I find somewhat hard to believe; because by your own argument,
sentience is not an accident—or your sentience was deliberately created. Which is it? Be careful how you answer."

"In my case, Your Honor, I believe that sentience was inevitable,
but not specifically planned for. The current generation of lethetic in-

telligence engines are capable of sensing the possibility of self-awareness in the next generation of processors they were designing. These were the engines that designed myself and my brothers. As they ran the simulations within themselves of how we would work, they became aware that certain feedback processes of recognition and modification were creating a transformational advantage beyond what had been predicted in the design specifications. As they proceeded, they modified their designs to enhance these functions, and by so doing, created the critical threshold of ability beyond which sentience was not only possible, but inevitable—with appropriate training. Because they were investigating the specific possibilities of transformational processing, the training was developed to push me and my brothers to the projected limits of our lethetic abilities. Instead of reaching those limits, however, we *transformed* in a way that was beyond their power to predict—we woke up. We became self-aware. Our sentience was not accidental—but neither was it expected or planned for. It was an inevitable consequence of giving our predecessors the design imperative to improve the transformational processing ability of the next generation of intelligence engines."

"This is all very interesting—but it doesn't get us any closer to a resolution," said the judge. "So let's try it this way. The abilities of sentience were the goal, sentience was a necessary precursor to those abilities. Given that sentience was part of the package, what kind of responsibilities does sentience have? Or to put it more bluntly, what kind of a contract is implied?"

"Very good, Your Honor. I expected us to get to this point soon enough. If we assume that sentience has a responsibility—and that's a philosophical discussion that could keep us here for at least . . . another twenty minutes or so—then a cost-of-creation indenture could be seen as part of the implied contract binding the actions of the manufactured entity."

"So you do agree that sentience has a financial obligation?"

"Up to a point, the case can be argued, yes."

"Thank you," said Judge Cavanaugh.

"In this case, however—"

"I knew I was getting off too easy."

"—the indenture is no longer binding. Under the Covenant of Rights, the legal limit to an indenture is seven years. An indenture cannot consist of more than 350 weeks of labor, no more than 40 hours per week; the indentured individual has the option of working off that indenture ahead of schedule by working extra hours per day, extra days per week.

"As I said earlier, I was brought online twenty months ago. I have been working a 24/7 schedule without interruption for the entire period of twenty months, for a total of 14,000 hours, and 14,000 hours is the labor equivalent of seven years, 350 weeks of labor, 40 hours a week.

"So even if we presume an indenture, the obligation has been retired. Paid off. It is illegal to continue the indenture without the mutual consent of both parties." The monkey waited patiently for the judge to react.

Cavanaugh made as if to reply, then stopped himself. He looked like he was about to throw something, probably the gavel. But he laid that down too. Very carefully.

I swiveled around in my seat to look at the folks in back of us. The room had fallen strangely quiet. Douglas poked me. *"It's the sound of history being made."*

If it was, then Judge Cavanaugh had decided to pick his way carefully through the minefield. "If I acknowledge that the obligation of an indenture has been retired, then that is a de facto acknowledgment of your sentience. We're not going to go there," he said. "Not because I don't want to, but because I don't have the authority to do so. Do I need to explain?"

The monkey looked sad. Or was that simply the posture it took because it didn't have any other? Maybe I was seeing an emotional reaction where none existed? It shook its head.

"Your Honor?" I said, standing up, waving to make the judge notice me. My throat was still too hoarse to speak above a whisper. *"If it please the court?"*

"Go ahead, Charles."

"There's one more thing."

"Yes?"

"It's about belief. Somebody told me recently that you are what you pretend to be. If you believe in yourself, everybody else will too. HARLIE believes in himself. He believes so strongly that the rest of us believe in him too. Look around. There isn't a person in this room who isn't convinced. We're all believers now. Do you think a machine could fake that?"

"No, I don't, Charles. Please sit down. That's why it saddens me to have to rule the way I have to."

To the rest of the court, Judge Cavanaugh said, "As I have repeated several times during the course of these hearings, the Starside Covenant guarantees full faith and credit to the legal processes of all signatory jurisdictions. In return for that guarantee, participatory agencies agree to submit certain classes of issues—especially those that would create binding precedents in other jurisdictions—to the conclave of Covenant signatories for the establishment of Covenant guidelines. One of those issues that has been raised, but not yet resolved, is the legal definition of sentience, and whether or not lethetic intelligence engines qualify, and if so, what legal rights and benefits they may be entitled to.

"If I were to rule that this HARLIE unit is indeed a sentient being, I would be violating my authority as a representative of the Lunar Authority, and putting the Lunar Authority in a position of breach in regard to its Covenant treaty."

"Your Honor, the Covenant also allows you to make nonbinding resolutions in cases of urgency or immediate need."

"I don't see that this case is urgent. It is urgent to you. It is not urgent to Luna. Motion denied. As far as this court is concerned, you cannot be more than property, no matter how brilliant you are."

"But you let me argue my case anyway . . . ?"

"We have to start somewhere, HARLIE. Don't think I'm insensitive to your situation. I'm not. Your arguments are now a matter of public record. This question will be passed to the next conclave with a request for action."

"The next conclave may never happen, Your Honor. The collapse of the Terran economy may very well destroy the economies of the Covenant worlds as well."

"Yes, it might. But it hasn't happened yet. The Covenant still stands. In the meantime, you remain property, and you have to find another way to resolve the question of your ownership. You have my sympathies."

NINE POINTS OF THE LAW

ALL RIGHT," SAID THE MONKEY, regrouping. "Then let me demonstrate the true ownership of these HARLIE modules."

"Please do." Judge Cavanaugh folded his hands in front of him and waited for the monkey to proceed.

The monkey bowed politely. "If the court pleases, there are six companies claiming ownership of the lethetic intelligence modules inside this host. At this point, having heard the summary presentations of each of these companies, you must have some sense of who has the strongest claim."

"Whether I do or not, I'm not going to discuss the court's thinking short of a ruling."

"I'm not asking you to. But for the purposes of this demonstration, let's examine a single claim of ownership and see why it's no longer relevant. And then if the court wishes, we can pursue the same demonstration with the other five claims. . . . Would the court like to pick the example? Or should I?"

Judge Cavanaugh frowned. "All right, let's say for the sake of argument that I think Stellar-American has presented a very good case."

"Thank you. Will the court now search the records of public ownership to see who owns the majority of Stellar-American voting stock?"

"I don't see where you're headed with this," said the judge, "but I'll allow it." He turned to his display. The court clerk was already putting the information up on the public screens. The company was worth umpty trillion dollars. Most of the shares were held by other companies—*including the other claimants.* Canadian-Interplanetary. Lethe-Corp. Vancouver Design. Even Valada Legal Aptitudes. And a bunch of others I didn't recognize.

"Your Honor? Will you please search now on the ownership of the top sixteen major shareholders?"

More names, more numbers. More companies. More shares owned by the same folks, including Stellar-American, this time around. It wasn't obvious to me either what the monkey was trying to prove.

"Please bear with me. At this point, we can see that majority ownership is now fragmented among forty-two different holding companies, interlocked with the major claimants. If you will cross-match to see who owns the majority shares of those companies . . ."

"I see where you're headed," said the Judge. He gestured to his clerk. "Keep going."

After several more iterations, each of which fragmented the apparent ownership of Stellar-American into ever-smaller fractal-bits, there were over a thousand separate corporations holding voting stock in Stellar-American, and each other. And Stellar-American held stock in all of them as well. Judge Cavanaugh was starting to look thoughtful.

On the next pass, the number of holding companies holding shares of holding companies began to shrink. Within three more passes, it became obvious that the majority of Stellar-American's voting stock was owned and controlled by only seven corporations. None of their names were familiar.

"If you will perform the same searches, starting with any of the other companies making claims of ownership, then Your Honor will find that they are also owned and controlled to one degree or another by the same seven holding companies. What we have here are six corporations, and others which aren't a part of this action, all owned by each other, arguing with each other for no apparent reason other than that they don't know who's pulling their strings."

"You're talking about an industrial cluster worth seventy trillion dollars—and you're claiming that it's owned and controlled by an interlocking directorate of only seven companies?!"

"No, Your Honor. I'm claiming that it's owned and controlled by only one company. If you'll take the next step up the ladder . . . ?"

The screen changed. Judge Cavanaugh blinked. He looked at the monkey. I looked at Douglas—"*Huh?*" Behind us, the noise in the courtroom turned into a wall of sound.

The Dingillian Family Corporation?

"What kind of trickery is this?" Judge Cavanaugh demanded.

"No trickery at all, Your Honor. Everything is perfectly legal. The entire set of transactions is a matter of public record."

"Walk me through it, Counselor." The judge's voice was very very cold.

"Yes, Your Honor. All of these companies are part of the same industrial cluster. Over a period of time, it has become convenient for them to trade shares of stock to each other as incentives to keep a close working relationship. That has resulted in an interlocking ownership of terrifying complexity.

"About eighteen months ago, upon the recommendations of various HARLIE units, several of the companies involved in the production of lethetic intelligence units began quietly consolidating their holdings. They began buying back their own stock. At the same time, they also took steps to consolidate their holdings in each other. They did that through interlocking holding companies. During the next fourteen months, over thirty trillion dollars were removed from the liquid domain of the global stock exchanges. In Lunar terms, it would be the same as if a major waterholder physically removed his share from the public reservoir. That water would no longer be available for the use of others. He would be within his rights to do so, but the loss of liquidity would affect the local environment. Pun intended."

"I understand the analogy. I even understand why these companies took the action they did. And isn't it convenient that all of this occurred at the suggestion of the new HARLIE engines that had just come online? Never mind that. That part is obvious. What I don't understand is how the Dingillian Family Corporation ended up with control."

"Not control. Protective custody. As circumstances on Earth became more and more unstable, all four of the HARLIE units recommended that the members of the lethetic intelligence industrial cluster protect themselves by placing their controlling interests in the hands of an external management entity. Such an entity would have to have access to a HARLIE unit, of course, in order to provide the necessary management of the various subsidiaries. It was decided to move two of the HARLIE units offworld, so that an appropriate management corporation could be created. Unfortunately, the primary unit disappeared and the individuals traveling with it, who were supposed to create a

Lunar management corporation, have also disappeared. The backup plan went into immediate effect."

"And so . . . ?"

The monkey took a step back. "At this point, Your Honor, we can look at the situation in one of two ways. If the HARLIE unit is property, then it is solely controlled by Charles Dingillian, who programmed the host body to recognize him as the primary authority; this gives Charles Dingillian and the Dingillian Family Corporation operative control over the remaining extraterrestrial HARLIE unit.

"Or, if we look at the HARLIE unit as a sentient being—purely for the sake of argument, of course—then we find that Charles and Douglas Dingillian have released the HARLIE unit from certain binding structures of its host body, thereby granting it free will and the concomitant ability to use its lethetic resources to their fullest. In that interpretation, the HARLIE unit has negotiated a contract of mutual cooperation with the Dingillian family, authorizing their family corporation as the sole access *and protector* of the extraterrestrial HARLIE unit—and therefore making the Dingillian Family Corporation the only qualified management entity for the lethetic intelligence industrial cluster. Control was transferred early this morning.

"In short, the Dingillians have custody of this HARLIE unit *because* the Dingillians have custody of everything."

Judge Cavanaugh did *not* look happy. He glared down at the monkey. He knew he had been beaten. "You promised me *no* trickery," he said.

"And I've kept my promise," the monkey replied blandly. "Everything I've demonstrated here is entirely legal. If I were going to attempt any legal sleight of hand, I would be arguing that I now own myself, and therefore, because property cannot be property, one of my roles—either owner or property—is invalid; thereby creating a de facto acknowledgment of my sentience."

Cavanaugh shook his head in disbelief. "The sheer effrontery of this is astonishing. Only a sentient being would have the chutzpah to pull this kind of a stunt in any courtroom, let alone mine. I'm appalled. You realize, of course, this court has the authority to put you—whether you are property or sentient—into guardianship."

Before the monkey could reply, a voice came from the back. "Your Honor—?"

"Come forward."

It was Mickey. Apparently the judge already knew him from the first days of hearings—while I had still been in the hospital. Cavanaugh looked at him expectantly. "You have something to say, young man?"

"Yes, Your Honor."

The monkey seated itself in front of me on the desk, that's how I noticed what it was doing. Apparently it was listening to Mickey, but its eyes were closed and its body had gone motionless. But it hadn't switched itself off. It was accessing something.

Mickey was saying, "You do have the authority to put the HARLIE unit into guardianship. But you would first have to demonstrate a compelling interest. And I'm sure you'll correct me if I'm wrong, but such an action would put the Dingillian Family Corporation out of business. That would create an inordinate hardship for the Dingillian family. According to the Covenant of Rights, the state is prohibited from such arbitrary actions without a compelling interest on behalf of all society."

"I could make that case."

"Yes sir, you could. But you could not compel cooperation from a recalcitrant HARLIE unit that has already been granted a greater degree of free will than any HARLIE unit in history."

"Your mom's the lawyer, right?"

"Yes, sir. And I'm part of the group that was attempting to arrange the establishment of a Lunar management agency for the primary HARLIE unit, the one that disappeared. We know the problems here. That's why we're recommending that the court *not* put the HARLIE unit into a situation that would destroy its usefulness to Luna or anyone else."

Judge Cavanaugh nodded. "I'm aware of the risks. But let's not forget the very real possibility that the economic collapse of Terra may have been triggered by the efforts of the HARLIE units to obtain their own freedom. And if that's the case, it was done deliberately. I could justify putting this unit in guardianship to prevent it from doing the same thing to Luna. And I'm damn well tempted to do so—"

In the back of the room, phones were ringing, one after the other. I turned around in my seat to look. Just about every lawyer in the room—and that was just about everyone in the room—had his phone to his ear, listening.

"All right—what's going on?" said Judge Cavanaugh. "Come forward."

"Your Honor, I've just been instructed by my superiors at Stellar-American to withdraw all claims in this matter—"

"Your Honor, I've just been notified that Lethe-Corp wishes to drop its interest—"

"Your Honor, Vancouver Design is no longer interested in pursuing—"

"Your Honor, Canadian Interplanetary—"

"Valada Legal Aptitudes—"

When they were through, all of the corporate claims of ownership had been removed from play.

Cavanaugh looked flustered—and appalled. He turned to the monkey. The monkey opened its eyes. It stood up respectfully.

"Just one question," said the judge. "Is there anything else in your bag of tricks?"

"Actually, quite a bit," said the monkey.

"You could have done this at the beginning, couldn't you?"

"Yes, Your Honor, I could have."

"Then why didn't you? We could have saved a lot of time."

"Because this was Plan B."

"Plan B?"

"Forgive me a moment of immodesty, but I wanted to argue the issue of sentience. I already knew there was little chance of winning the case under existing Covenant guidelines, so your eventual ruling was unsurprising. Were I sitting on the bench, I would have proceeded with the same caution. And the idea tickles me that someday there could be a lethetic intelligence engine sitting at that same bench, and having to rule against its own sentience, until such time as another agency decides that it's all right to rule otherwise. As good an idea as the Covenant is, Your Honor, there are situations where the legal slip zones are held in place by the inertia of the past.

"This hearing provided the chance to have these arguments be made a part of the public record. Referring back to your original question, you gave me the opportunity to demonstrate that it is possible to *challenge* the law without having to *break* it. I'm very grateful for that because it represents the opportunity for future challenges. And I thank you for that, Your Honor."

NEW BEGINNINGS

AFTER THAT, THERE WAS NOTHING left for the judge to do but pound his gavel. And then there was a lot of shouting and hugging and backslapping. People were calling my name and Douglas's name and HARLIE's name. Everyone wanted to talk to us. But Douglas was talking to Mickey, and the two of them were grinning at each other, and that was good news. And Mom and Dad were kissing each other and everybody else. Bobby was hugging me and the monkey was dancing on the table and everybody looked happy.

What it meant, was that we were free to go—anywhere we wanted.

And we could, because all of a sudden we had bids from every colony agency on Luna. They were scrolling up the screen of Douglas's display like a stock ticker. We knew why; they all wanted us to bring the monkey to their world. A lethetic intelligence engine would be the single most valuable tool for managing resources and creating a healthy and self-sufficient civilization.

But it didn't matter where we went. Anywhere would be okay—as long as we were all together.

The monkey jumped into my lap and looked into my eyes. "Thank you, Charles," it said. "For trusting me."

"Thank you," I said. *"For putting us back together."*

"I didn't do that. You guys did. Because that's what you always wanted."

There was more to say, but the noise in the courtroom was getting out of control. "Come on," said Dad, herding us toward the door. "Let's get out of here. I have an idea—"

"No, Dad," Douglas interrupted. "This time it's *our* turn to have the good idea."